ALSO BY ESTHER CHEHEBAR

I Share My Name

Sisters of Fortune

Sisters
of
Fortune

A NOVEL

Esther Chehebar

RANDOM HOUSE

NEW YORK

Random House
An imprint and division of Penguin Random House LLC
1745 Broadway, New York, NY 10019
randomhousebooks.com
penguinrandomhouse.com

LIBRARY OF CONGRESS CATALOGING-IN-PUBLICATION DATA
Names: Chehebar, Esther Levy, author.
Title: Sisters of Fortune : a novel / Esther Chehebar.
Description: First edition. | New York, NY : Random House, 2025. |
Identifiers: LCCN 2024049343 (print) | LCCN 2024049344 (ebook) |
ISBN 9780593734544 (hardcover ; acid-free paper) | ISBN 9780593734551 (ebook)
Subjects: LCGFT: Novels.
Classification: LCC PS3603.H44558 S57 2025 (print) | LCC PS3603.H44558 (ebook) |
DDC 813/.6—dc23/eng/20241125
LC record available at https://lccn.loc.gov/2024049343
LC ebook record available at https://lccn.loc.gov/2024049344

Printed in the United States of America on acid-free paper

1st Printing

First Edition

BOOK TEAM: Production editor: Jocelyn Kiker • Managing editor: Rebecca Berlant •
Production manager: Samuel Wetzler • Copy editor: Muriel Jorgensen •
Proofreaders: Debbie Anderson, Emily Cutler, Julia Henderson

Book design by Debbie Glasserman

The authorized representative in the EU for product safety and compliance is
Penguin Random House Ireland, Morrison Chambers, 32 Nassau Street,
Dublin D02 YH68, Ireland. https://eu-contact.penguin.ie

For my children
One day you'll appreciate my cooking

And if a woman have an issue, and her issue in her flesh be blood, she shall be in her impurity seven days: and whosoever toucheth her shall be unclean until the even.

LEVITICUS 15:19

Sisters of Fortune

BRIDE'S NAME: Fortune Cohen
GROOM'S NAME: Saul Dweck
WEDDING DATE: April 24th, 2009
GROOM'S FAMILY RABBI: Rabbi Tawil

Brides,

If you're reading this, then you've done it. You're engaged! The trials and tribulations of single life are behind you. But let me tell you girls, the real work is yet to begin. As you prepare for the next and most vital step in your life, it is essential that you familiarize yourself with the laws of Niddah.

Girls, I am here to be your vessel. As your Kallah teacher, I will try to the best of my ability to acquaint you with these laws, which have remained an integral part of Jewish family life for thousands of years. I should know. I've been practicing them since dinosaurs roamed the earth!

All right, that's enough joking around for one day.

The Torah discusses Niddah in great detail and its laws make up the fundamental components of a successful union. It is a wonderful thing, girls, that as a young Syrian bride, you will enter the canon of women who have practiced these laws for generations. You will be one more in a legion of Israelites who have them to thank for Shalom Bayit.

I know I do.

Throughout our meetings I will try to present this information to you in a personable and logical manner. I'm not your typical yeshiva morah, girls. It's key that you know that. Think of me as your cheerleader, your coach, but most importantly as your friend. A much older friend—but a friend, nonetheless.

Throughout our lessons you will no doubt see how our rabbis have interpreted the Torah in order to set up an effective system of laws for us to follow.

At first, some of this information may seem overwhelming or intimidating, even. But remember, "practice makes perfect!" Over the course of these lessons I will do my best to prepare you for your wedding night and your new and exciting life as a wife. Starting with the information enclosed here.

Let us begin!

Geveret Sandy Beda

SO, WHAT IS NIDDAH?

Niddah (nee-da-h)
(n.) A woman who sees blood that originated from her uterus. This refers to the blood of menstruation, postpartum bleeding, and staining from the uterus.

The Torah states that those who disobey the rules of Niddah will receive severe punishment—"Karet," the same penance owed by idol worshippers and heretics who consume hametz on Passover.

During and in the seven days after your menstrual period, you and your husband are not to engage in sexual intercourse of any kind. You are not to touch. You are not to eat from the same plate. You are to push apart your mattresses when you sleep at night.

The Rabbis have interpreted the laws of Niddah this way for a reason. Use these two weeks of separation to get to know each other again. Rest your bodies and enjoy a friendly sort of intimacy. Take frequent walks. Indulge in lengthy conversations. Humor yourselves with a bit of reality television.

So vital are these "days off," I can't even tell you. They are the bedrock of a sustainable Jewish marriage. These laws are what separate us from the goyim.

By the time you are clean again, your husband won't be able to keep his hands off of you.

FORTUNE

Chapter One

....

I'm in my future mother-in-law's Formica kitchen, raking bits of bela-hat soaked rice and eggplant heshu off of dinner plates and into the garbage bin. I hand the plates to Marta, my future mother-in-law's long-standing housekeeper, to be cleaned with Palmolive and water. The future mother-in-law doesn't believe in dishwashers and for that reason, among many others, she reminds me of my grandma Fortune, who we call "Sitto." Like Sitto, my future mother-in-law, my MIL, believes in doing everything by hand. Shortcuts are for the lazy and incapable. The MIL calls Marta into the dining room to help clean the challah crumbs and wine-stained napkins from the table. Saul and my future father-in-law are already reclined in the den, poring over the *Post* and last night's Knicks game.

The MIL is no dummy, and it's only a matter of time before she catches on to my lie. The hard truth is that I've been pawning off grocery store–bought knafeh as my own for six weeks now. What would Saul say if he found out that my "Best in the Community!" knafeh wasn't mine at all but the product of a multimillion-dollar goliath of kosher baked goods? Would he still have asked to marry me? It would cost my ring a carat, *at least,* if he found out how I unwrapped the (parve) margarine-glued kataifi square from its frozen casing, tossed it in the oven, and waited exactly seventeen minutes until it browned. He would never trust me again if he saw how I sprinkled crushed pistachios on top to create the illusion that the store-bought pastry was mine.

In the other room, I can hear Saul over the exhausted hum of the Frigidaire say, "Ma. This one's gonna fatten me up, Ma. I'm a dead man." The MIL has finished clearing the dining room table, which means she has retreated to the den and I'd better get started on dessert.

I move from the garbage bin to the kitchen island, where cookies and pastries wait in their still-warm tins. I begin to plate the mamoul in symmetrical rows of four, wiping the excess sugar from around the silver tray. I feel the saliva collect inside my cheeks as I imagine sinking my teeth into one of the date-filled pastries. This, too, the MIL made from scratch. She made them from scratch like she makes everything from scratch. Mamoul and atayef and sambusak and yebra. Her freezer is its own supermarket, packed to the gills with Costco-bought Ziploc bags full of readily defrostable "pickups." She can whip up a meal faster than you can decline her invitation. This is a fact, and it's one she takes great pride in. According to my Sitto, there are only two things in a woman's life that should never be kept empty: her womb and her freezer. And you'd do well to remember that the contents of one of those won't grow up to talk back.

I decide in this moment that I absolutely will not tell Saul about the knafeh. Ever. But she knows, the MIL. I know that she knows and she knows that I know that she knows. And do you know how I know? Because she still hasn't asked me for the recipe. Then again, why would she? Would Cher ask Gaga for voice lessons? Instead, the MIL got to work and baked the most exquisite-looking knafeh that this side of Brooklyn has ever seen. I tiptoe into the den and set the tray of mamoul down on the coffee table.

"Sit, honey, please." The MIL taps the spot on the couch next to her.

But I'm not dumb; I don't take the bait. Some women might think that a ring on their finger guarantees their security. Those women did not grow up with my Sitto, and they would be wrong. A daughter-in-law only stops kissing ass when that ass is six feet underground, and even then, it helps to continue the tradition.

"Just a couple more!" I chirp, and retreat back into the kitchen for a fruit plate and some sweet kaak. Marta follows with the rest and when every dessert is on the coffee table, I take a seat next to my fiancé, Saul. The vinyl-covered floral sofa squeaks as I shift and I pull my cardigan tighter around my body. In the center of the dessert spread is the MIL's knafeh, brimming with the iridescent pride of one thousand G-D-damn suns.

"G-D forbid your mother should measure up to your bride, Saul, but here, don't kill me for trying," my MIL says. She kneels to reach the cake knife laid beside the Pyrex and feigns heaviness, as though her knees threaten to buckle beneath her weight, all 175 pounds of her.

"Here, Ma. I got it, sit down!" Saul jumps to take the knife from his mother, as if she's decades beyond her fifty-two years. This is the way the MIL carries herself at all times, as if her undying commitment to her children might break her at any moment. She welcomes the pain. I imagine her saying:

"Throw me on the pyre!"

"Epidurals are for women who own bread machines!"

"Let my tombstone read: Marie 'I will always get the last word' Dweck, Beloved Wife, Mother, Grandmother, and MIL."

My MIL pulls the knife away from Saul and proceeds to cut into the knafeh. Rose water pools inside each sliver. This is not a cake that came frozen from a box. As she hands Saul the first slice, the MIL tells us her new diet is working—she is down to 165 pounds as of last Thursday. Which means she's no longer seeing the old doctor, a miracle worker before he was a liar and a crook and, eventually, as these things tend to go, an anti-Semite. How quickly the consensus around him had shifted over a plate of kaak and a particularly spirited game of canasta. Which brings me to the second lesson Sitto has taught me: Only two things can happen to a professional who stakes his reputation on women who play canasta; they're either broken or made over the game. There is no in-between. My mother-in-law tells us that somebody in her group got wind from somebody who was buying *mazza* from somebody, that the *real* miracle worker is two offices over in the ramshackle building in Sheepshead Bay that houses sixteen holistic dietitians and not one work-ing scale. She had her doctor of three decades fax over her medical re-cords within the hour.

The MIL hands a slice to her husband and smooths her skirt, then shifts an oblong platter of green grapes and cantaloupe two inches to the right. "The rules of the diet are simple," she says. "I can't even believe I have to pay a grown man to tell me not to make my own plate."

"Two hundred and fifty dollars a visit for a quack doctor to tell you to eat like one of my grandchildren." Saul's father spits. He motions for my MIL to put some fruit on his plate. I catch a whiff of stale cigar smoke as he points a tanned finger at the mango, and I'm immediately reminded of my grandpa Jack.

"But I swear to you, it works. You really *will* drop weight if you vow never to make your own plate," Marie says, paying him no mind.

"She just eats off mine," Saul's father says, rolling his eyes.

"Well G-D knows there's usually enough on your plate for two." The MIL spears a piece of cantaloupe and wraps it in a napkin for her hus-band. "I mean, *shoof*, it's working, isn't it?" Marie smooths her sweater over her hips and looks at Saul with wide eyes.

"You look great, Ma."

"I got no high cholesterol, blood pressure. Nothing," Saul's father says, eyeing the plate of mamoul I brought out.

"We know," the MIL says, rolling her eyes. "You're the regular pic-ture of health."

I've seen it with my own eyes. The MIL hasn't made her own plate since I said yes to Saul's proposal. She doesn't order an entrée at restau-rants. Instead, she watches her company eat, and only after they're done does she dig into whatever scraps are left over on *their* plates. If the plates have been wiped clean, the MIL does not eat. If the plates have been prematurely whisked away, the MIL does not eat. If a stray hand strikes a glass of water and the contents of the plate are drowned, the MIL does not eat. She would rather starve than settle for soggy rice and blanched string beans.

The nature of the diet has severely impacted her social life, as you might imagine. "What would people think?" I've heard her tell my future father-in-law. Of course, my FIL doesn't want to seem complicit while she scavenges for leftovers. People would label them insane, or worse, cheap. G-D forbid. He wants her to eat like a human, not a sewer rat. But to fight his wife on this would only strengthen her resolve. So like the rest of us, he stays quiet.

"Anyway, it's obvious your father likes my knafeh," she says, turning her attention to Saul. "Don't tell me you're watching your weight for the wedding, too. You're too thin as it is. *Yalla,* take a bite already, honey. Let me know if it measures up to Fortune's."

The MIL keeps her eyes trained on Saul as she backs away from the table, secure in the knowledge that she won't trip over any clutter. The hardwood floor is so clean, you could lick soup off of it. Her words, not mine.

Marta lingers outside the den, her pink apron soiled with canola oil, allspice, and tears. One hand grips a dishrag as she peers through a crack in the pocket door that separates the den from the kitchen.

The MIL's round knafeh is the size of a small pizza pie. When the MIL cut into the oven-bronzed shredded phyllo, the sweet filling beneath it didn't loosen up like mine sometimes does. It stays firmly in place, serving the perfect wedge of cake. This knafeh is baked well, one only a mother's love could birth.

"If you ask me, parve knafeh is a sin. Rich whip and cornstarch is no substitute for ricotta cheese." The MIL scoffs, handing the plate to Saul. "But you love Fortune's so much I decided to give it a try."

I take a mental note of the MIL's surrounding dessert arrangement: a banana cream pie; a decadent chocolate trifle cake; robust biscotti, bound by whole almonds, raisins, and chunks of dark chocolate. A fruit platter pieced together like a mosaic with melon, mango, and papaya sliced into perfect half-moons, whole kiwis peeled and carved out like exploding stars. Blueberries the size of eyeballs and green grapes with Botoxed skin. Pomegranate seeds sprinkled like confetti. You know, for color. Rumor has it that Marta lost her finger to a pineapple, but as the MIL would say, "A pinky is a small price to pay for the perfect fruit kabob."

"Maaaaa, *Hadid. Wow!*" Saul's teeth sink into a bite of knafeh, leaving a trail of rosewater syrup dangling by the scruff of his chin. "Delicious, Ma, there's just one—" But before he can finish, the MIL reaches over to dust the surface of the cake with crushed pistachio nuts.

I watch as they fall from a stainless-steel sieve.

"Fortune, honey, you could use a slice." She wedges a cake knife into the flaky crust, then hesitates before shifting the knife three inches to the right. "There." She slides the enlarged portion onto my plate. "Get too thin before the wedding and we'll have to get a bridal attendant just to keep pinching color into your face, *hazita!*"

Two months to go until the wedding.

Chapter Two

·············

66 ifty-seven days till you can *kish* this place. No offense to your father." Saul spears a piece of kale with a plastic fork and gingerly
dips it into the small container of balsamic vinaigrette he'd requested on
the side. "I'm *mooting* in here, Forch. Where's the control for the AC?"

"AC? It's the middle of February!"

"It could be the middle of the North Pole for all I care. There's a *ree-
hah* in here too." Saul scrunches his nose.

"If you're going to complain every time we're in here, we should
start eating lunch at your office." I smile to take the edge off, but really I
mean it. "Here." I get up to plug in the large fan that sits behind my father's desk, quickly turning my face to avoid the flurry of dust that coats
the blades. I take a seat next to Saul on the dark brown polyester couch
that my father swiped from the clearance section of his own store at
least seven years ago. *A fantastic deal!* he marveled at the time. The whir
of the fan obscures the sound of the Thirty-fourth Street traffic below us,
but only slightly. My father's office sits one story above Mr. Cheap, the

ninety-nine-cent store he's owned and operated since before I could say "discount." Every Monday, Saul and I have lunch together in his office upstairs. Monday is the only day that my father spends outside of the store, taking meetings with the wholesalers whose offices dot Seventh Avenue. Once I decided to drop out of college and help my father full-time, Saul and I made it our little tradition to have lunch here while he's out. A soup and a salad for Saul from the Hale and Hearty on the corner, and just a soup for me.

"You're joking," Saul says. He pushes aside the loose documents that litter the couch to make more space for me. "Surely Morris can afford to install an AC, *dechilak.*" He laughs, angling his face in front of the weak breeze. "Or is recycled air another thing your father doesn't believe in?"

"Again," I repeat. "It's February!"

Saul's right. My father doesn't believe in many things: instruction manuals, paying full price, diabetes . . . But nothing gets his blood boiling like the AC. For my father, it's more than dislike—it's distrust. Meanwhile, I could go on about Saul's mother and the modern luxuries she eschews for no good reason, but I know it's useless. Saul has a blind spot when it comes to her and I'm not looking to lose my head today. My grandpa Jack (*alav hashalom*) used to claim that recycled air ruined the quality of his food, and Sitto still echoes this ideology when it comes to most modern home appliances—tools you'd think would have an immigrant doing cartwheels while shouting, "America!"

Instead, Sitto uses the dishwasher for storing plastic bags because *"The hand that makes the food should scrub the dish."* Before she moved in with us, she would hang her laundry on a clothing line in her front yard, saying, *"If you don't be careful that machine will take every good panty you own. Haram."* She dutifully pounds dough out with her knuckles as the KitchenAid my mother gifted her collects dust in the cupboard beneath the sink. The microwave, though, the microwave they all love. *"A thirty-second miracle!"* My grandparents cried with glee, eyes aglow with radiation as they watched the machine heat and reheat lukewarm cups of coffee.

"It's all good," Saul says. He tips the fan toward his face, closing his eyes as the air struggles to upend the fell swoop of his gelled hair. When we first started dating, I'd tease him by running my fingers through the hardened wave, loosening the product's grip on his hair until it fell forward across his brows. Now you look your age, I'd say. But Saul didn't want to look his age; he's been in a rush to grow up ever since I'd known him. Now he taps his Cole Haan loafer–clad foot in tandem with the whoosh of the fan.

"Give it a second," I say. "It's pretty powerful."

Even in the muggy summer months, Grandpa Jack refused to turn on the AC. He died on one of the hottest days in April on record, a frail body committed to a hospital bed at Maimonides. Sitto swears his last words were, "Will somebody tell the G-D-*dumn* nurse to lower *ze* AC? They bleed money! Bleed!" It reassured us all to know that even in his last moments, Grandpa had been concerned over a bill he didn't have to pay.

Of course, Saul wasn't around for any of that. It took my grandpa Jack dying for us to meet.

"We'll eat in my office next time." Saul returns to the couch and pops a cherry tomato between his teeth.

"I told you I couldn't get away. I'm swamped. The manager's wife just had a baby so it's just Carmen working the registers downstairs."

Saul doesn't need to know that these days, it's mostly just Carmen and me regardless. The Christmas season was slow on account of the snow and the Internet, and Dad let go of the two temp cashiers right after New Year's. Plus, he had me now, and I'm basically a glorified volunteer. (Unless you count the "marriage clothing fund" that Dad claims he contributes to on my behalf, in lieu of a traditional salary.) I'm not complaining, I'm just happy to be busy. And Carmen is like family. She was my dad's first real hire, twenty years ago, when Mr. Cheap's doors first opened. We're only a year apart, the store and I, and I grew up in its aisles. I learned how to add at its registers, counting out customer change with Carmen on slow days. I discovered how to unclog a backed-up toilet with a full bucket of water in the bathroom outside my father's office. I was able to use a price gun by age four and by seven or eight I was proficient at spotting shoplifters, of which there were many. My two sisters and I spent our Sundays ransacking the clearance bins on the far end of the store, looking for anything to fill the large blue plastic bags Dad would give to us at the start of the day—restitution for him having to work Sundays, and Saturdays, and most weeknights until nine, when he'd finally lower the metal gates and shut the lights for the night. If it was a Sunday, Dad would take us to the Kosher Kingdom on Forty-second Street and we'd gorge on eggrolls and duck sauce chicken until we felt sick and Mom would tuck us neatly into the car where we'd sleep the entire ride home.

I glance over at the framed photo, which sits proudly on his desk, of my dad cutting a twine bow on the day he opened the store. In the photo, my grandpa Jack holds the shorter end in his hand, his chin proudly lifted toward the sky. Grandpa Jack had given Dad the loan he needed to open the store. Carmen still jokes that Grandpa Jack had been so frugal he'd insisted on the leftover twine instead of springing for ribbon. The twine was roughly eight inches, long enough to cover a quarter of Mr. Cheap's door. Carmen was only sixteen, and not a day goes by that she doesn't smack her gum and remind me that she saw me grow up, honey.

"I don't understand why your dad doesn't just hire a secretary," Saul says. "Or at least take Nina back, it's not like she's busy these days."

"What do you know about what Nina does with her days?" I say, surprised by the way Saul's jab at my older sister rallied my defenses. Stubborn and lazy as Nina may be, it isn't Saul's place to call her out.

He looks taken aback. "I'm just saying, this place is a mess. And you have enough to do with the wedding two months away. I'm gonna call your dad tonight. I might have a girl that could work for him."

"Don't, I think he has someone." It's a lie. I feel like I'm jumping out of my skin.

Saul doesn't understand that I like the mess. I look forward to Mondays in Dad's office, where I can be surrounded by all of his things: the countless leaves of loose paper, past due invoices, busted pens, and torn bags of expired Haribo gummy bears. I like the way his chair sinks in anticipation of his frame when I sit in it. I like the little Post-it notes Dad leaves tacked to the screen of his Dell desktop, reminding me to readjust the height of the chair before I head out. Sometimes we get lunch together at the Chinese place down the street, where he makes me swear not to tell Mom about the veggie fried rice and dumplings he's eaten for the fourth day in a row.

"All right," Saul says, tossing his salad aside. "But you told him you're not gonna work once we're married, right?"

"What?" I say, even though I heard him just fine.

"*Haje.* I want you to relax."

"Oh, yeah." Another lie, because it never seemed like a good time to discuss it. I'm not itching to work. It just seems like Saul's itching for me not to, and something about that rubs me the wrong way. Saul would say it's the Nina in me. And I knew he was less than thrilled about my older sister's influence on me. I'd say it's the part of me I keep hidden from him. Whichever it is, it's a side he either doesn't care to or would rather not see. Could I blame him? In me, Saul sees a safe choice. And why wouldn't he? I know what the rules are and I play by them. Maybe I do it for my parents, who desperately needed calm after Nina made it her life's mission to challenge them whenever possible. Mom says that even as an infant, I never cried. As if I'd known from the womb that my older sister was colic- and later tantrum-ridden and even later OCD until finally, as my mother says, she settled into the woman she was always meant to be: a bitch. Meanwhile my younger sister, Lucy, was only happy if she was being fed and then became too beautiful to rebel—why would she when her beauty gave her everything she wanted anyway—another type of problem I anticipate my parents would have to contend with sooner rather than later.

Always—

Dad: "Fortune never gave us any problems."

Mom: "If you were home you'd know that. But yes, thank G-D for Fortune."

"Where does your dad keep the chips? I know he keeps a stash some-where." I watch Saul rifle through a desk drawer but before I can guide him we hear a familiar voice travel through the landline's speaker.

"Fortuuuune," the omnipresent voice sings. "Fortune, you in there?"

Saul half smiles and then picks up the phone. "Who's asking?"

"Carmen, yes, I'm here!" I yell. I attempt to wrestle the phone away from Saul but it proves futile. "Stop," I say, laughing. I reach for the cord again. "Haj, give it to me."

Saul dangles the phone above my head.

"Come on, I'm waiting on something!"

He shimmies the cord away from me. "Oh, you're *waiting* on some-thing?" Saul mocks and then turns to the receiver. "Carmen, you're working her too hard, *hazita*. She has no time for her own fiancé." That's when I pull the cord from the receiver so the line goes dead. "Relax! I'm messing with you." Saul gently smooshes my cheeks together with his thumb and index finger.

"Sorry," I stammer. "I'm just—I'm in a weird mood. I think it's the birth control, it's messing with my hormones or something." I touch the hot space on my cheek where Saul's hand had been a second ago and start to feel the shame creep up behind it. Then I do the only thing I know how to do when things feel weird: I start to clean. A coping mech-anism borrowed from my mother.

I close drawers and wrap loose rubber bands around bundles of pens. I collect loose papers in a stack and wipe a hardened coffee ring from the desk. I wipe it again. I grab a damp paper towel from the garbage bin and ream it against the stain like I've seen my mother do so many times.

"Fortune." Saul puts his palm over my hand. "You're doing it again."

"Sorry." I cast my eyes downward and toss the paper towel back in the bin. I miss.

"You good?"

"Hormones." I sigh.

"You don't have to take those, you know. I wouldn't mind . . ."

"Me neither, but Nina . . ."

"Right. Even though I think that's crazy and Nina wouldn't give a crap if you had a baby before she got married."

"She would never admit it, obviously, but she would care."

"You're too nice." Saul kisses the top of my head. "But that's why I love you."

"That's why you love me."

"All right." Saul stands and gathers his things. "I gotta head back to the office anyway. Call me after your class tonight, all right?"

"I will." The truth is I'd almost forgotten about it. I hadn't accounted for the class when mapping out my day. I'd have to take the train home to Brooklyn at five, meet the wedding planner at six, and make it to class by eight. Thankfully, Mrs. Beda only lives a ten-minute drive away.

"Send Mrs. Beda my regards, too. She plays canasta with my mother." Saul pecks me on the cheek before leaving, his half-eaten salad forgotten on the couch. I toss the container in the bin and begin riffling through a pile of invoices collectively labeled DUE on Dad's desk. It's going to take at least two weeks to sort through all of his stuff. Dad initially hired me, two years ago, to help Carmen on the floor, but after seeing the dismal state of his office, I convinced him to let me help him on the back end of things. Dad is terrible at two things: organization and asking for help. Naturally, one feeds into the other. He prefers to do everything himself and so he is perpetually unorganized. I know from overhearing the angry phone calls and voicemails that Dad is late to pay for inventory. Whether that is because he's short the money or he just doesn't care is unclear. If you were to ask him, he'd simply say that everyone is a shmuck or a crook. But the new lines on his face tell me that he's struggling, and so I vowed to do everything I could to at least try to get his things in order, starting with the open invoices. Things wouldn't have gotten so bad if I had just started working in the office from the beginning. Of course, I'd still planned on finishing college then. When I decided to drop out after two semesters, nobody objected.

Saul always reminds me that I could go back if I wanted. I could take some nonmatriculated writing classes, or whatever. It helps that I didn't enter community college with any lofty ambitions. I didn't have an end goal in sight, something I wanted to be or do. I just expected to graduate, really. I'd gotten A's in high school. I would've gotten honor roll every semester, too, if it weren't for Mrs. Schechter, who tested us on the facts and figures of Jewish history, something we lived and breathed but rarely studied.

If Nina was disappointed by my decision to drop out, she didn't show it.

"I figured" was her immediate response.

I can't really be mad. She didn't know how badly I needed her to say more. Nina did, however, caution me against working for Dad. When I was in high school, she used to work the register twice a week at the now defunct Fulton Street store, Silk Road. They'd apparently listen to the radio on their forty-minute drive there, during rush hour. And like clockwork, every Monday and Wednesday at seven P.M., only Dad would return.

"Morris, where is she?" Mom would ask, arms folded against her stomach.

"Why don't you ask her?" Dad would say, practically a grunt, and that would be the end of it. He'd say it like, that daughter of *yours*, when we all knew the blame was equally shared.

Then Nina would pussyfoot through the back door several hours later, her effort to be silent echoing like a bullhorn throughout the house. No matter how quietly or quickly she moved, she never got to the alarm in time. And if the beeping didn't wake the rest of us up, then their voices certainly did. We were all privy to Dad and Nina's insults and accusations.

"This is why Silk Road will never get to the next *level*."

"My store's *level* paid for your private school tuition."

He was sloppy and short-tempered. She was stubborn and disrespectful. Neither of them knew how to insult on occasion, and so everything was fair game: her lack of social life, her relationship status (single, perpetually), her bad habits: loose with money and boys and, he suspected, cigarettes. His foreignness, bigotry, and the way he dismissed our mother. His ways were antiquated, bygone; this was *America*, not Syria, she stressed.

If you ask me (which nobody did), they shared a blind spot where self-reflection was concerned. Had either of them paused long enough to look inward, they might see just how remarkably similar they were.

"We're a much better match," Dad said to me on my first day. I'd initially planned on going back to school, but that prospect seemed dimmer every day. Now it's been nearly two years, and working at the store makes me feel needed in a way that school never could. I'm agreeable, dependable, organized.

Most importantly for Dad, working with me isn't like looking in the mirror.

I count fifteen invoices and begin to tally up the numbers. Even with Saul's family connection swinging us some imperfect baby clothes at a lower rate to sell at the store, we can't afford the volume we used to. I understand Dad not wanting to sully relationships with the wholesalers that Grandpa brought on in the early days, but is being behind on payments any better? I also can't understand why Dad keeps ordering mesh slippers in every color when even the shoplifters looked past the slipper-stocked clearance bin at the front door. Besides, we both know that the only ones that sell are red, purple, pink, or green. If you want a black slide you aren't looking in Mr. Cheap.

Around page fifteen the invoices transition from bath mat bills to wedding bills—my wedding bills. Bills I hadn't yet seen. Numbers and notes are sprawled across yellow legal pad paper in Dad's signature *self-taught* penmanship, which means that I should probably put these down. But I can't because, even through Dad's illegible handwriting, I can read the desperation.

"Just scrap the wedding and let Daddy give you the money he would've spent," Lucy suggested a few weeks ago. It isn't a secret that every aspect of my wedding spells misery for one of my sisters. Floral arrangements on every table mean Lucy has to forgo a "weekend wardrobe," an unthinkable sacrifice, since at age eighteen she is in the midst of her "dating Rumspringa." A violinist at the ceremony? Nina is now forced to put a pause on her bass lessons. (But really, it's her fifth attempt at a musical instrument and isn't she a little too old at twenty-six for G-D-damn music lessons? You either have it or you don't.)

I thought the buffet of lamb chops would be the first thing to go, but Dad insisted that a wedding without them would be embarrassing. Needless to say, Mom has to wait another anniversary to take that vacation to Morocco. Sitto is even starting to chime in about the sorry state of her custom orthotic inserts.

I can't take it anymore. Who is this wedding for again, anyway?

I restack the papers and make a mental note to discuss them with Dad tomorrow. I have to head out early if I'm going to make it to the final meeting with the wedding planner. Apparently there are still a few kinks we have to work out before the big day. When I asked Mom what these kinks were, she sighed and told me not to bother coming if I was going to have that attitude.

I unplug the fan and reconnect the phone, dialing downstairs for Carmen.

"Carmen, I'm going to head out, okay? I'll leave the keys behind the register. Dad will be back at nine to lock up."

Sometimes I miss working the registers with Carmen. She likes to joke that since getting engaged three months ago, I'm too good for her. *Don't forget who taught you everything you know,* she frequently reminds me. Carmen embarrassed me at first. The way she would sing my father's name over the store's loudspeaker, her *r*'s rolling like loose marbles off her tongue. She seemed to use any excuse to say his name, beginning and ending her sentences with a casual, *Senior.* Either she didn't know that this made me uncomfortable or she just didn't care. I knew that my father liked having her around almost as much as he liked complaining about her. We both knew she wasn't going anywhere.

"Isn't it hard to ring the customers up with those nails?" I asked about two weeks in. Those long, tacky nails of hers—visibly fake, all French tips and lavender icing.

Carmen clicked her tongue. *"Not as hard as it is to do all that head-scratching you do with your lil' nubs."*

I was surprised when my face cracked into a million little pieces, my *lil' nubs* wiping the tears from my eyes as we both roiled with laughter.

Soon I started to hang around the store late, waiting for Carmen to turn customers away. We were unlikely companions, to say the least. Her: bedazzled clothing, painted eyebrows, a nose ring that changed just about as frequently as the color of her hair (currently auburn). Me: a consistent yardstick against which Carmen could measure her growth.

We'd talk while she closed up and I organized the merchandise. Everything in aisle three cost ninety-nine cents and it was always chaos by the end of the day. Buckets of athletic socks needed re-sorting by size. Packages of men's underwear commingled with ladies' thongs. A thick film of dust coated the spiral notebooks, Lisa Frank folders, and glittered pencil cases, no matter how many times a day Carmen ran a rag over them.

"This dust is giving me some migraine. If he wasn't your father, I might sue, you know. My friend over on Forty-second Street banked $40K tripping over a crack in the sidewalk in front of her workplace. I'd take a sprained ankle for forty k, wouldn't you?"

I'd grab the rag from her hand. "Gimme."

I did stuff like that for Carmen all the time. I lied to Dad when he asked me how many packages of Juicy Fruit gum she ate a day.

"Not a lot? Maybe like one a week?" Meanwhile, I knew full well that she swiped nothing short of two packs a day from the display in front of the register.

"I'm doing your daddy a favor," she justified. "This gum's older than that shit *Senior* got playing on loop in this store. No wonder the customers have been staying away."

Now, I sneak through the door that connects Dad's office to the back of the store, where Carmen is energetically ringing up a customer. I mouth *Bye* and head toward the front.

"Fortune," Carmen shouts over the aisles, waving a pair of cherry embroidered underwear in the air. "What happened to you? Your ass get up and leave you in the middle of the night?"

"Yeah, but it forgot to take my thighs with it."

"Well, I know for a fact Jewish boys like a little meat."

I spun around and headed for the door. "Bye!"

Outside on Thirty-fourth Street the air smells like old milk, vermin, and cologne-masked body odor. I take a deep inhale and head down Seventh Avenue toward West Fourth Street, where I catch the F train to Brooklyn. The walk from my dad's store down on Thirty-fourth Street to West Fourth Street adds thirty-two minutes to my normal eighty-minute commute from Midtown to home in Midwood, and that doesn't account for my usual cappuccino stop. But it's worth it to pretend, for even just those thirty-two minutes, that I'm a normal twenty-one-year-old in the village, headed to class or my after-hours job as a barista.

I turn my engagement ring inward and pick up my pace like I have somewhere I actually want to be.

Chapter Three

....

I'm late but the wedding planner is apparently later, her black Volvo absent from the driveway of our house. I open and close the side door gently and tiptoe up the stairs and into my parents' bathroom before anyone else can catch me. I sit on the toilet and tap my toe until the last trickle of urine leaves my body, and then strip down to my cheeky briefs and step onto the scale.

Eleven pounds lost since the proposal. That's one-tenth of my total body weight in three months. But really, it's probably more like twelve or thirteen pounds given I usually weigh myself in my pajamas—just a cotton tank and shorts, nothing heavy, but still. Plus, if I got on the scale after I pooped it'd probably be even less.

Each of us women—my sisters, my mother, and I—walk around the house pretending like we're the only one *not* on a diet. Nina judges me, I judge our youngest sister Lucy, and my mother tells us all we look good the way we are, and then is the first one to compliment us when a quarter of a pound is lost.

Nina claims to be above dieting. *Right.* Like anyone is naturally that thin. My grandmother Sitto calls Nina skin and bones, and she is. The tallest of all of us, she stands hunched at a proud five-foot-six. Nina blames her height for her relationship status. "There isn't a guy over five eight in this community," she always huffs. "And if there is, he wants to date a *cute little petite girl.* Like Lucy or Fortune."

Next is my mother, who at four feet, eleven inches, currently clocks in at ninety-eight pounds. I know this because she forgets to slide the pointer back to zero after weighing herself, which she has clearly done, once again, right before me.

And then there is Lucy, who seems to gain weight exclusively in her chest. My mother never misses an opportunity to draw comparisons between herself and *her* Lucy. She keeps her distance from my breasts (she had no part in making them), my deflated pancakes, made with whatever drops of batter G-D managed to scrape from the bottom of the mixing bowl.

I would say I started growing into myself around the same time I discovered laxatives. The tiny pink pills I found while going through Nina's drawers looked innocent enough, and so I popped two of them. Six hours later with nil effect, I'd assumed the pills were old, tasteless candies that Nina had saved and forgotten about. Six hours after that I was sure I was dying. Cramps tore through my stomach like flies on a roadside carcass. The pain was so blinding, I hadn't realized what I needed to do.

I sat doubled over the toilet for sixty whole minutes, my left hand alternating between the flusher and a bottle of Poland Spring. When I began to see spots, I closed my eyes and allowed myself to feel dizzy. I felt that morning's breakfast and last night's dinner and then, it seemed, every meal I'd eaten since I weaned off my mother's breast exit my body. Just when I thought I was finished, I realized I wasn't. My insides churned and gargled, and for the next few hours, I lingered in close proximity to the toilet, never sure when the next exorcism would hit. For the rest of the day, everything I ate came out of me within minutes. The scale the following morning told me I'd lost four pounds. Four pounds! It was just the head start I'd needed. When two days passed without a bowel movement, I headed to Duane Reade. I found the laxatives near the pharmacy counter. The pink ones indicated that they were mild. Pink was for "sensitive" stomachs. I wondered what the green version could do.

"Forch!" My mother's voice through the phone's intercom lurches me back to reality.

I quickly throw on my clothes, grab my checklist from my bedroom, and stumble down the stairs. "I'm coming," I sing.

I steady myself before walking into the kitchen, half expecting to find the wedding planner knocked unconscious, a bouquet of pink peonies lodged between her cold, parted lips. Instead, I find Mom and Sitto at the kitchen table quietly rolling yebra, the Syrian version of stuffed grape leaves. A compact radio sings Spanish sweet nothings throughout the kitchen. The tangy smell of simmering Turkish apricots and prunes fills the air.

"Where is everyone?" I ask.

"Well, Lucy is studying at Giselle's house. And Nina is locked up in her room, where else?" My mother sighs.

"Hiya, *rohi*, come, help me with the leaves," Sitto says and pulls out the chair next to her. I turn my ring back around so that the diamond faces outward again.

"Your hands, Ma!" My mother grimaces over the oily imprints on the chair where Sitto's hands had been.

"*Oooli.* Sorry, Sally. But that's why you have the ghee. What do you pay her for?"

"Where's Nancy?" I ask and take a seat in the soiled chair. Sitto's large, solid hands are immersed in a glass bowl of chopped meat, rice, and onion. She scoops out a thumb-sized portion of the raw mix and rolls it between her two palms until it forms the shape of a perfectly smooth torpedo. She can do this with her eyes closed, but she doesn't. Although Sitto has made yebra once a month, *every* month, for G-D knows how many years, she executes each one with laser-like focus and precision. My mother takes the grape leaves out of an unmarked glass mason jar and lays them flat to dry on paper towels for Sitto to fill. As they dry, Sitto places a thumb-sized portion of raw meat and rice onto each leaf.

"*Fadal*," she tells me, and slides the paper towel of open grape leaves toward me.

"I can't do it." I roll my eyes. "Mine always come apart while they're cooking."

"It's like riding a bike, *rohi*. Do it once and you will never forget. *Humdullah*, roll up your sleeves."

I do as I'm told and slide off my ring, placing it in the pastry dish along with my mother's and Sitto's. "You start from the bottom up." Sitto begins to demonstrate on her own grape leaf. She takes its pointed bottom and folds it up toward the meat in the center until it is suffocating within the leaf. She then tucks the sides in.

"The trick is to keep tucking, tucking, tucking the sides as you roll," she says.

I begin.

"Not like that." Sitto leans over to assess my yebra. I sit calm in the knowledge that on the next one she'll grow so frustrated at my incompetence that she'll take over completely. "You have to keep it tight. If your roll is too loose, they *will* come apart in the pot." She rolls and tucks the grape leaf over the meat filling. "Like that." She picks up the completed yebra and holds it like it's a baby she's just delivered.

"You can pat the end part of the leaf a few times, to make sure it doesn't come undone," my mom chimes in.

"You can." Sitto nods. "But if you do it right, it won't come apart."

"I'm just saying—to make sure."

"So *fadal*, pat away. But if you do like I tell you . . ."

Every so often Sitto sprinkles a bit of kosher salt and allspice into the bowl of filling. Then she scoops up the condensed mix of heshu, rice and meat, and throws it back down, as if it were a safe she was trying to break open. Sitto groans as she digs her knuckles into the heshu, shifting slightly forward in her chair. Every so often she dips her fingertips into the bowl of warm water beside her. There's a box of freezer bags beside my mother. When we're done, my mother will fill the bags with at least six dozen perfectly rolled yebra, to be defrosted and used over the course of the month's Shabbat dinners.

"Let's see it," Sitto tells me.

I take a second leaf and begin to fold the outer corners inward, rolling as I tuck.

"Ma, Nancy's never late." Last time Nancy told me she wanted me to be more proactive in the planning of the wedding. We both knew it was too late for that, but I'd decided to introduce Nancy to the world of Pinterest nonetheless. Of course, she'd hate it.

"I fired Nancy," my mother says, folding and unfolding the corners of one particularly *nitty* grape leaf. "Ma, pass me the bowl of water." My mother wets the tips of her fingers before folding the corners of the grape leaf inward, trapping the meat inside.

"What do you mean you fired Nancy?" Was she having an aneurysm? Had the nervous breakdown she always threatened finally come to pass? "The wedding is in less than two months."

My mother ignores me, her gaze hardened toward her yebra, her nose so tightly scrunched her brown freckles appeared knitted together. Meanwhile, Sitto keeps her eyes trained on the table, her brows raised in anticipation of a fight, as if they'd been pinned up to her forehead.

"I know when the wedding is," she says. "Do me a favor, Fortune. Start lining a pot with those." My mother points to a Pyrex pot on the kitchen island behind us. It brims with two dozen perfectly rolled yebra, topped with whole dried apricots and sliced prunes. "I'm going to cook those now for Shabbat. Might as well." My mother does her best to downplay the fact that she just told me she fired our wedding planner. She hums along to an unnamed flamenco tune from her spot at the head of the table; there are three empty chairs separating her from Sitto and me.

"Oil the bottom of the pot before you do that," Sitto says. But I don't move.

"I'll do it," she says, and rises slowly from the table. She shuffles over to the stove and when she's just out of earshot, my mother whispers,

"She's driving me crazy. Your father promised me twenty years ago that I'd never have to share a home with her again. And lo and behold, here she reigns! I mean I don't care. It's *my pleasure.* Really. But does she have to sleep in the room next to us?"

"Ma. Focus. Ma, what happened to Nancy?"

"Would *you* want to live with *your* mother-in-law, Fortune?" My mother shakes her head. "Of course not. And Saul would never do that to you. *Hazita,* she's lonely. But the whole situation is crazy. It's been a year! It's just crazy!"

"Ma, you know she can't live alone. Since Grandpa died—"

"Don't you dare, Fortune. You're not gonna guilt me, too. I could take it from your father and Nina. That's bad enough. But I'm not going to take it from you."

"Okay, Ma. Sorry. Just tell me what happened with Nancy."

"Nothing happened with Nancy. I was getting ready for our meeting and I just thought to myself, *We don't need this woman.*" My mother looks up at me. "We don't need her, Fortune. I've been doing every-thing on my own anyway. What did she do, really? We have everything set—the flowers, the caterer, the music . . ."

"Ma, we have all of those things *because* of Nancy. She did everything! You can't just *fire* a wedding planner after she practically planned the whole wedding! And we still need her. Didn't Daddy give a deposit?"

"She had attitude."

"Attitude?"

"Uppity. I found her to be snobbish."

"Wow . . ." I trail.

"You *would* take her side. Here I am working like a dog, slaving away rolling yebra. Because I know *you* love them." She nods at the stacks of tins lining the kitchen island. "Not to mention the sebet I'm cooking for, on top of my regular orders."

My mother's job as a community caterer evolved naturally, once my sisters and I were grown and in school. Sitto is considered to be one of the best Syrian cooks in Brooklyn, and she took it upon herself to make sure her daughter-in-law upheld this reputation. My mother offered to help cook some of the *mazza* for a cousin's engagement over a decade ago and the jobs started rolling in afterward. The only complaint was that the kibbe was so good, it drew guests away from the dance floor. These past few years she's veered away from large events and more toward Shabbat dinners and *mazza,* traditional Syrian pickup food.

"I'm sorry, Ma." I don't have the energy. "What do you want me to do?"

"Nothing," my mother says and sighs. "It's already done."

I can feel my head throb. I crane my neck to see the time on the oven. Now that it seems a meeting with the wedding planner isn't happening, I have some time to kill before my marriage class tonight. I'd recently found Nina's reading syllabus for her freshman English Lit course while going through the summer bins in the basement. I planned on diving into the first book listed, *Pride and Prejudice.* I can feel that book and my bed calling me.

"Ach!" Sitto shouts. "Why do you pile your pots like this in the drawer, Sally? It's impossible to get anything out! *Haram* to treat your things this way." Sitto groans as she rummages through various stainless steel pots before settling on a weathered twelve-inch All-Clad. She measures a glass dinner plate against the pot's surface to make sure it fits. According to Sitto, a glass plate is far superior to any pot lid, allowing just the right amount of moisture to seep in.

"Breathe," my mother mutters. She takes a deep inhale and widens her eyes at me, and I back away from the table slowly. "Where are you going?" she snaps.

"I'm gonna go lie down," I say, slightly picking up my pace. "I'm exhausted."

"Oh, really? Because I just remembered, you can do something for me. Let me think."

"Let me know when you remember!" I call out, scurrying out of the kitchen for the stairs. I'm pretty sure I hear a glass shatter in the kitchen but I don't turn around.

I make it to the halfway point up the stairs when the intercom sounds with a *beep beep.*

"More apricots," my mother's voice says, echoing throughout the house. "Apricots and oot."

Beep beep.

"And bizet. For company. And Fortune," she says, louder, "run next door before Spice closes. Tell Isaac to add it to my bill. I'll pay him tomorrow."

Beep beep.

"Fortune?" my mother calls out.

I press the button and hold it. "Apricots, oot, and bizet? Is that it?"

"And phyllo dough."

"Okay, so apricots, a jar of oot, and a package of phyllo dough?"

"And the bizet."

"The bizet, right, okay."

"Oh, and you know what—a can of tomato sauce. Saul likes my string beans with the tomato sauce, right? I'll make them for him. I should really get the bulk from Costco, but who has the time. Truth, maybe I'm better off getting it all in Costco . . ."

"Okay. So, no?"

"You know what, just go. Apricots, oot, bize—"

"I got it." I bolt back down the stairs and swing the Moncler jacket that I'd left hanging on the banister over my shoulders. I grab my mother's hat and scarf from the small console table by the door and I'm outside before she can add anything else.

"And riiiiiiiiice!" I hear Sitto shout from behind our closed door. I pull the gray beanie on and over my ears.

There are no quiet days, no slow hours, no seasonal lulls, in Midwood. Even on Saturdays, when the shops on the southern tip of Ocean Parkway shutter their doors for Shabbat, the foot traffic persists. But as far as the weekday goes, Wednesdays are relatively *light*. Mondays are for grocery trips and post-weekend errands. Tuesdays spell personal care and miscellaneous to-do list items: the tailor, the Judaica store for that book you were missing about the thing *they* told you about, painter's tape.

The side streets clear on Wednesdays for indulgent trips into the city and Thursdays are about weekend prep. And you don't leave your house on a Friday unless you have a death wish. The hour before sundown was reserved for a particular type of sadist, and the pitied man who forgot to buy his wife flowers for Shabbat.

There are only two cars double-parked outside of Spice, the two-hundred-square-foot grocer famous for carrying every single culinary ingredient of the Middle East, and Fabuloso floor cleaner. The rest of the curb in front of the shop is populated by wooden crates filled with bananas, potatoes, Spanish onions, plum tomatoes, bagged sunflower seeds, and dried eggplant stacked wrapped in rubber bands. The sidewalk perpetually smells of expired yogurt and cumin, but the convenience of the store generally makes its customers look the other way. Produce is being unloaded by an assembly line of three men who transfer the goods from a large white truck to a dolly to an arm until it reaches the door, which is propped open by a blackened brick of ice left over from winter's most brutal storm. Isaac, Spice's prodigal son, stands by to accept the boxes.

We all know that Spice's owner has been grooming his only son Isaac to take over the family business since Isaac could say, "It's *best* by, not *use* by" and "No, we don't do refunds." You can hardly tell the father and son apart, between the shared gait and the way their eyebrows inch toward the center of their foreheads. Isaac usually works the floor and the back room with the stock boys while his father manages the register and the bills. Spice's youngest daughter, Gila, used to occasionally take orders over the phone but she stopped working after she got married and now comes in as a customer like the rest of us, a diamond the size of a blueberry propped up on her finger.

A woman I vaguely recognize as a customer of my mother's catering business bickers with a meter maid out in front. The uniform remains firm; everything about her stiff shoulders and averted gaze says that come hell or high water she's going to give this woman a ticket. It doesn't help that the woman clearly didn't bother to pay the meter at all. A meter in Brooklyn is kind of like a low tire pressure signal; you either drive it out of existence or ignore it until, eventually, it pops—in which case you'd curse the weather, or the potholes, and, reliably, the mayor.

I listen as the cop proceeds to write out the ticket while the woman yells into her phone, "Can you believe it? Right in front of Spice! A head of garlic is costing me fifty dollars now. They sit here all day, waiting to meet their quotas. They hate us. Nothing better to do than pick on *us.*" All roads lead back to the anti-Semite.

I flash a sympathetic smile in solidarity and enter the store.

Spice's only organizing principle seems to be: *Make it random.* Fava beans are stacked beside Downy. Vinegar-pickled cabbage is barreled beside dried Turkish apricots and stacked near paper of dismal quality and the knock-off Bic pens that write through it. A portable AC unit whirs atop a pile of Glad garbage bags, a lawsuit waiting to happen. But, of course, no one in our community would dream of taking Spice to court.

I grab a metal shopping bin and pass Sofi, a friend from high school. Her basket sways against an impressive baby bump I haven't seen yet.

"What's up, Forch?" she says casually. "Did you hear? It's bring-your-own-bag now." She rolls her eyes.

"Is it really?"

"That's what they said."

I notice Sofi doesn't have any bags. "I live next door. I can run and grab some for us."

"It's fine." Sofi waves her hand. "Isaac has a stash in the back. Charges for them, but who's noticing at $1.79 a lemon?"

"You look so cute, by the way. When are you due?"

"Thank you, *abal.*" Sofi tosses a container of dried mint leaves into her basket and I follow her as she moves down the aisles. "But no, I'm an actual cow. Isaac!" Sofi shouts over the din of chatter in the store that seems to be steadily rising. "Any shelled pistachios?"

I hear Isaac yell out that they'll be in tomorrow and I follow his voice to the very back of the store where he'd moved from outside. I find him standing on a ladder, price-tagging bags of bread and the pyramid of rice cakes they support.

For a Wednesday evening, I suddenly realize, Spice is unusually crowded. Or maybe it's just loud. And not *loud* loud, but hush loud, as if customers are spilling secrets all at once. The air in the store feels different, charged, and not only on account of the Hebrew jingles blasting from the store's only speaker.

I'm starting to get the feeling like something has happened.

Sitto swears her body knows when it's about to rain. The weather outside could be seventy-five degrees and sunny, not a cloud in the sky, but if Sitto's arthritis starts to act up, you better grab your umbrella. Midwood is like that. It has its own energy, and when it's disrupted, all of its inhabitants feel the shift. Rumors zoom down streets and zip around corners like blood rushing through veins.

When the community's beating heart quickens its pace, everyone stops to catch their breath. And then, of course, come the words: *Did you hear?*

"You must have heard about it." I snap back to reality to find Sofi's face a mere three inches from mine. Her eyes dart from side to side.

"Of course. But about which thing?" I have no idea what she is referring to. But I can't give my position away so easily.

"There's more than one thing? Oh, G-D." Sofi pinches her stomach. "Did someone die?"

"No. G-D, no. I mean, what are you talking about?"

"Wait, what are *you* talking about?" Sofi holds her secret hostage against my fabricated one.

"Nothing," I insist. "I swear. Wait—what's going on?"

"LH." Sofi shakes her head, using shorthand for *lashon hara*, gossip. She places a hand on her swollen stomach. "I shouldn't."

"You can't do that!"

"Fine," Sofi says. She smiles. "Something happened at the wedding last night, but that's all I'm saying." She holds her hands up in defeat. "Have you ever used hawaj in soups? I feel like you would know."

Whose wedding was last night? I rack my brain. I had the wedding calendar for the year memorized, mostly. Finding a date on the community's social calendar to put your wedding on is like shopping for shmura matzo on the day of Passover; you had to be ready to put your life savings down the second the opportunity presented itself. I can't recall who last night belonged to.

Well, whatever happened at whoever's wedding last night couldn't have been that scandalous, right? Otherwise, Saul would've known about it, and he definitely would've told me about it at some point during our lunch today. Right?

"Anyway." Sofi scans a box of Osem chicken consommé for an expiration date. "I'm sure your mother will have heard by the time you get home. Also, we're baking challah for my ninth month next week. *Fadal,* it's good luck for you, too, you know, for the future." Sofi places the consommé back on the shelf. "I'll text you," she says, heading away from me for the register and taking the mystery gossip with her.

"That one loves to talk, no?" Even at a modest height of five-foot-nine, Isaac seems to tower over me. He's wearing an oversize black hoodie and tapered sweatpants and he looks nothing like the young boy I've known in the seven years my family has lived next door to Spice. He's older, obviously. But he's also broader, taller, and the baby face Sitto would occasionally pinch has deepened in complexion and chiseled in scope. Even his eyes, once hidden beneath a row of bushy brows, seem greener. Despite being the same age, Isaac and I rarely acknowledged each other's existence outside of the freezer aisle. Girls must be noticing him now, I think, before pushing the thought out of my mind.

He motions for me to follow him, past the customers who wait in line for the single register in the store. Isaac leads me to the front, where he's placed a basket of all of the items I'd come in for. "Your mother called."

"Of course she did," I say.

"Next!" His father calls the next customer up to the register. I hear a disapproving *tsk* from the woman behind me and push my basket off to the side with my foot.

"I'll wait," I say. "It's fine."

Isaac's father, Eli, takes the pencil from behind his ear and scribbles something down on a torn piece of paper in front of him. "Tell your mother I'm sorry about the trucks," he says. "I tell them not to block her driveway while they unload, but you know these drivers, they don't listen."

"I'll tell her," I say, although we both know nothing will change. Isaac hums along to a clubby Arabic tune that plays over the store's speaker.

"Really," Eli says as he rings up the next customer. "I'm sorry. I threw in some malawah—extra. For your grandmother, I know how she loves them."

"She'll be happy. Thank you."

"If you think we're bad, just wait until Boreka opens." Eli nods his head begrudgingly across the street. It seems like everyone has been talking about Midwood's newest Syrian cuisine storefront. My mother, because Boreka threatened to eat into her profits as a community caterer, took umbrage over what she called *the commercialization of tradition*. Recently we heard that the store would carry dried fruits, nuts, and various grocery items, which is why Eli seems pissed about the competition. Everybody could agree that the new store would be bad for traffic.

"*Haram*," Eli continues, "this street used to be so clean and pleasant." How quickly he's forgotten that he was once new here, too.

I take note of the customer line, which snakes around the two-hundred-square-foot store and wonder why Eli doesn't just put in another register, and why we continue to put up with the wait. Ever since Spice opened its doors seven years ago, my parents have been in a silent war with Eli, its owner. The store brought more traffic to an already congested block. There are the graffitied trucks that unload goods six days a week, blocking my parents' prized driveway in the meantime. And then there are the double-parked cars that clog the street on account of the customers who call in their grocery lists for pickup and can't be bothered to legally park their cars. There are the black garbage bags piled up on the sidewalk outside and the food waste and wrappers that didn't make it inside them. Every morning, my mother curses the day that Spice opened and every afternoon, she contributes to its existence with a few dollars. What choice does she have?

I look at my watch. This quick errand was eating up more of my time than it was supposed to. Isaac lingers beside me.

"Need anything else?" he says.

"You'd know better than me. My mother has you on speed dial apparently."

"Nah," he says with a laugh. An older man pushes to the front and dangles a package of frozen puff pastry in front of Isaac. "How much?" he questions.

"Pop." Isaac turns to his father. "*Kam al sa'ed?*"

His father throws out a number, seemingly at random.

"Benny has it for $8.99 a pack." The man scoffs.

"Then go to Benny's. *Allah ma'ak.*" Eli waves and the man scurries off, back to his place in line.

Isaac has a scent that lingers, a fact I try to forget as he rearranges rows of Must gum in front of the register. Spicy and clean, the kind of smell that would enmesh itself in a bag full of oranges or a pack of dish towels. It's subtle but has legs, following you out of the store and into your car. A small black kippah hangs low over his forehead, covering his right eyebrow. Suddenly, as if remembering it was there, he feels for the kippah and stuffs it into the front pocket of his jeans.

"Eh?" His father nudges him. He puts the kippah back on and for the first time since I've known him, Isaac looks embarrassed.

"Busy today, no?" I cringe at my own attempt at small talk. We've never made small talk before. Previous conversations were limited to the questions: *Where can I find . . . How much is . . . What time is closing?*

I still have Sofi on my mind, the burning question of what happened at last night's wedding still unanswered. Isaac effortlessly lifts my basket onto the counter and Eli begins to ring me up. He throws the rice, the tomato sauce, the oot, and whatever else he can into a black plastic bag before he starts to fill a second one. When he's done, Isaac grabs the bags off the counter.

"Thanks for the bags," I say. "I wasn't aware of the new law."

"Please." Isaac waves his hand dismissively. "Liberals think a few extra bags are gonna destroy us all. Here," he says. "I'll help you home."

"No, really. It's fine," I stammer. Home is only ten yards away, but that is at least nine too many.

"Really." Isaac nods his head in his father's direction. "I could use a break."

I follow him out.

The moment we leave Spice, Isaac rounds the corner, leading me toward the store's back door. He places my bags on the ground and pulls a loose cigarette from his hoodie's pocket and lights it. I stand stiff against the wall and check to see if anyone is coming. Isaac just laughs, taking a deep pull of his cigarette.

"What are you *doing*? Your father could come out at any second."

"And bum the rest of my pack, yeah." Isaac winks and blows out a haze of smoke between us.

Isaac moved here when he was five and when he speaks, you can hear a twinge of Damascus. We had an acronym for families like Isaac's, the more recent community transplants: OTB, or *off the boat.*

OTBs play and live by different rules: stricter in their observance, looser in their lifestyle. They work twice as hard and have twice as much fun. Most live among one another ten blocks east of the parkway, cloistered in rows of two-family homes. Growing up, we didn't mix much. Different yeshivas, neighboring synagogues. You need only to open my family's pantry to see examples of our assimilation into American culture, but OTBs still shopped and cooked in the way of their homeland. Not a cereal box in sight. But in recent years, the social lines have begun to blur and I've seen Isaac at weddings and various parties. There's been more dating and marriages between the two communities, too. Some of my friends' parents even prefer it, convinced that the more recent transplants are hungrier, more determined to succeed in business. They think we got lazy, complacent, and unappreciative of our parents' and grandparents' hard-earned wealth. The OTB girls are in demand, too, lauded for their *shatra* ways in the kitchen and in motherhood.

"The wedding's soon, no?" Isaac remarks, as if he just noticed my presence.

"Uh, about two months." I shift my weight awkwardly and try not to think about what this might look like if someone walked by. Sally

Cohen's engaged daughter hanging out with Spice's son behind the store. And with a cigarette in plain view nonetheless! Sofi's gossip would become irrelevant so fast, you'd need a Ferrari to catch it.

"Nice," Isaac says. "Saul Dweck, right?" Isaac reaches for a nearby broom with his free hand and sweeps a spot on the ground where a cumin canister exploded. "I used to play ball with him. He's small but quick. Say hi for me."

I try not to think about how Isaac's name was on my original guest list until Saul ran through it with a thick black pen to narrow our friends list down to two hundred from three.

"He's my neighbor," I had countered. *"Ibe."*

"His *store* is your neighbor. You're a customer, that's it. Anyway, you'll barely see him once we move to the city, where you'll shop at Whole Foods." Saul flicked his free hand downward in a gesture Nina called sexist, homophobic, and just fucking stupid.

"By the way," I say. "The invitations already went out, but *fadal,* please come. Right after Passover, legit. I'd give you an invite but my parents are already freaking out that we don't have enough."

"Nah, it's okay." Isaac smiles. "I know the deal." He flicks the half-smoked cigarette on the ground and before he can get to it, I put it out with my foot, twisting the front of my UGG boot against it until it's black ash. Isaac looks at me, amused.

"Sorry," I say, half laughing. "Always wanted to do that."

"Dare I say you're a natural. Don't tell me golden boy Saul smokes?" He gasps dramatically in horror.

"Don't be silly," I say. "Saul's scared enough of dying as it is."

"Tell him it's the stress that kills you"—Isaac taps the side of his head—"not the cigarettes."

"I've never had one," I say.

"I'd be surprised if you did." Isaac smirks.

"Really." I stomp my foot. "And why is that?"

"Because you're you," Isaac says. He swallows and I notice the exaggerated Adam's apple in his neck. "The rule follower of your sisters."

"Hm." I quickly avert my eyes from his. "I guess I am."

"It's a good thing. You're the only one with a ring on your finger, aren't you?" It doesn't sound like a good thing, coming from Isaac's mouth. I have the impression that he'd grow bored with someone like me. Half of me wants to challenge his assumptions while the other half wants to run home. I bend down to reach for one of the bags and the diamond on my engagement ring flashes, suddenly reminding us both where we are. I feel the air deflate between us. Isaac's gaze darts toward the pavement. He grabs my bags. "Let's go. Don't want to keep your mom waiting."

Ninety seconds of silence later, we're home.

"Thanks," I say, as he gingerly hands me the bags.

"You got it." He lingers for a moment. "Oh, tell your mom we're starting to get Passover in. Next week . . . I know she was asking."

"I will."

"All right." But Isaac doesn't leave.

"Oh." I shake my head. Of course, Isaac is waiting for a tip. I rummage through my bag for a few singles. "Here you go."

"What?" A look of confusion, and then horror, flashes across Isaac's face. The tip of his nose is red from the cold. Whatever warmth the sun gave off during the day is now gone, and the streetlights look effervescent against the darkening sky. His cheeks glow beneath his stubble. "No." He pushes the roll of singles back toward me and backs away.

"I'm sorry, I . . ." I stammer, and pocket the cash back in my purse. *Fuck.* "I didn't—"

"It's cool." He smiles again and I watch him walk back to the store. "I'll see you in like twenty minutes, when your mom remembers what she forgot," he shouts over his shoulder.

"Right, ha!" I yell back. *Fuck.*

"Fortune?" My mother pops her head out the front door.

"Mom!" I jump. "You scared me."

"Was that Isaac?" She cranes her neck. "I need—"

"No." I quietly step past her and into the house.

NINA

Chapter Four

....

There's no easy way to check rice. Actually, let me rephrase that: There's no easy way to check rice while maintaining your sanity, even if your mother is paying you one hundred dollars a day to do so. I rip open another ten-pound bag of Uncle Ben's, pour an eighth of it onto a plastic cutting board, and get to work. I run my fingers through the grains, sifting the kosher pieces into the Ziploc bag I'd fastened to the edge of the kitchen counter with blue painter's tape. I'm looking for *impurities* or, in other words, *chametz*. Since I'm unlikely to find any, because like, it's 2009 and agriculture and stuff, I just discard anything that looks remotely brown. I find a few tiny rocks and allow myself to feel unbridled joy, because this process is monotonous and the victories are small.

I take a large gulp of my 7-Eleven iced coffee and try not to think about the fact that I have a bachelor's degree from NYU and I'm working for my mother, the Syrian cuisine purveyor to the community at large. It's been two-plus years of working for Sally Cohen, managing her orders, assisting in the kitchen, handling payments, and even delivering when necessary. If you had asked me what I thought I'd be doing with my BA in English, well, I honestly couldn't tell you. But it wouldn't be this. A *lifeline,* my mother called it, when she offered—nay, forced—me to take this job. It wasn't like I had other opportunities. And so for three days a week, every week, I submit to being my mother's bitch. Although lately it's been five days, because we're six weeks shy of Passover, which is our busiest time. Plus, Mom has been taking on extra work catering small events and parties, to bring in some extra cash with Fortune's impending nuptials sucking everything dry. Even if it would kill my parents to admit it. They'd rather just skulk around in obvious misery and balk at anyone who points out the obvious. But who am I to judge. (Judge, I do.)

All of the kitchen windows are open. Every so often, a breeze kicks in and the circular tins Mom had lined up skid across the kitchen counter and she scurries to grab them. I tell her we should shut the windows but she'd rather chase aluminum. I tell her to just stack the tins but she ignores that, too. She's wearing her navy blue Eberjey robe, even though we've bought her a customized apron for nearly every Mother's Day I can remember. We engraved something new every time. KITCHEN BOSS. KIBBE QUEEN. THE MAIN COURSE. And my personal favorite: OVERSALTED.

Her thick brown hair is tied up in a bun, where it will remain until there are six hours of kitchen time behind her and it's time for a shower. Not for the first time, I notice how she is annoyingly beautiful, the kind of beautiful only further emphasized by her lack of effort. It's not that she doesn't try, but not compared to the other mid-to-late-forties-pushing-fifty women she's surrounded by. She barely even wears makeup, just a brush of concealer under her eyes (a swipe of mascara across her lashes if there's a card game).

It's the freckles on her face that do all the talking, a constellation of tiny brown specks that dance over the bridge of her button nose. More often than not, she's mistaken for a fourth sister, to which she'd feign surprise before whispering, *But really, how old do you think I am?*

I try not to think about that, at just twenty years my senior, she *could* actually be my sister. *God,* I hate remembering that at my age—twenty-six—my mother was pregnant, and with two kids at home. What's more pathetic, I'm spending my days exactly how she did, barefoot and in the kitchen. The only difference is that I have nothing to show for it.

"Spice is selling bags of checked rice," I volunteer, although my mother probably has Spice's Passover inventory committed to memory.

"Sure they are," she chirps sarcastically. "For fifteen dollars a bag they'll throw in a kidney, too."

"Don't be silly." I swipe a small mountain of grains into the Ziploc and mouth a quick apology to *Hashem.* "You have to go to the butcher for that."

"It's *haram,* really. And to think there are people who actually pay for it," Mom scoffs, and proceeds to carefully submerge kibbe, one by one, into a Jacuzzi of bubbling vegetable oil. I wince every time one disappears into the FryDaddy. The dangers of frying Passover kibbe are well documented—something about the matzo meal used as a substitute in the dough being super flammable. More than once, the oil springs up and stings Mom's face. She skips back each time her slotted spoon breaks the surface of the oil. She'll smell like a McDonald's until May.

Every year, between February and April, the Cohen kitchen turns into an industrial catering hall. And for the volume we do, we probably should be cooking in an industrial kitchen. I've suggested this multiple times. But similar to how Dad was when I worked for him, my mother is stubborn and not open to suggestions. She blames it on financials. Moving to a commercial kitchen would require us to have a rabbinical *hashgacha,* for kosher reasons. And do you know the way that would eat into our profit? So we do everything by hand, at home. It's mostly *mazza,* small Syrian pick-up food. Of course, we offer a weekly Shabbat menu, too; staple dishes like eggplant mehshi, chicken and spaghetti, hamid, belahat and kibbe cherry. But this year, as if we didn't have enough on our proverbial plate, Mom decided to offer a kosher-for-

Passover menu as well. She's one of the few community cooks to do so. There's a reason for that—and it's because you have to be slightly fucking insane. Mom invested in a separate, Passover set of meat pots and cookware a few years ago, which she unearthed from the basement to great fanfare last week. *Here we go again,* she sighed, as she schlepped the plastic storage containers up the stairs. We started koshering our dairy pots and cooking utensils about a month before the holiday. Mom is always careful to set aside a few things we could use for *chametz* purposes, but it's understood that the kitchen is more or less closed off to "recreational cooking" until after Passover. The real cooking is saved for the customer. It's takeout and Morningstar Farms Chik'n Patties for us from here on out.

The process of koshering is simple, really. You fill your pots with boiling water, plop a rock inside, and dip whatever utensils you want to purify. It isn't hard, just tedious. And much like checking rice for things that no longer exist, it's a *custom,* which is an explanation—I've come to understand—used for an action that makes little sense but carries great significance. We have a lot of customs.

My mother slides off her rings and gets knuckle deep into a bowl of mashed potato, filling for some borekas. Then, as if she just recalled a conversation we'd been having earlier, she says, "We can leave it here, because G-D knows I don't want to talk about this anymore, especially with Fortune's wedding seven weeks away, but I find what happened at that wedding last week completely unacceptable. I mean, I feel so bad for the girl, *hazita.* Her reputation is in the bin. I'm just grateful that none of my daughters ever went through something like that." She smiles, indicating that I'm meant to take this as a compliment. I roll my eyes. Nothing ignites the community like new gossip. It's like barn seed; you toss out a few kernels and the chickens come running. Hands will be bit. But nothing, *nothing,* ignites a mother like gossip about *someone else's* daughter. Because how lovely it is to be able to pat yourself on the back at the behavior of your daughter, who managed not to fuck up this time, and who now positively glows in comparison to the girl who did. I do not want to discuss this anymore—this thing that apparently everyone in our community is talking about. Not with my mother, or Fortune, or Lucy, or my grandmother.

"Yet," I say, against my better judgment.

"What do you mean, *yet?*"

"I mean none of your daughters have gone through something like that, *yet.* The jury's still out on Lucy."

"Please." Mom wipes her hands on a damp dish towel. "I know my girls. And I know how I raised you."

"Seriously?"

"What? It's *somebody's* fault."

"You mean it's her mother's fault then?"

"I'm just saying, for a seventeen-year-old girl to get so *drunk* at a wedding that she—I can't even *imagine*"—my mother gulps—"passes out and is woken up by men coming in for morning prayers." Mom shudders at the thought. "Something is wrong there. The clues as to *what* can usually be found in the home."

"Aren't you always telling us to stop blaming you for our problems? And here you are. Your default is to blame this girl's mother, who you don't even know, by the way."

"I'm familiar with her," she says.

"We should all just be sympathetic to this poor girl's mistake and move on."

"If you think that the answer is to just forget and move on, then you have clearly missed the point. The girls are too fast and loose these days. If this happened in my day, forget it. We had enough sense to drink in private, at the very least. But to get this wrecked at a wedding, it's *ibe.* And for what? What kind of message are you sending to the men there? Never mind their mothers. If I had a son, I wouldn't want him bringing home someone like that, no offense. And neither would any of my friends, I can promise you that. There are just no limits these days. Where's the shame, the self-respect? Even the clothes—to wear a short dress like that to a wedding?" My mother shakes her head in disapproval. "Please, it's just inappropriate. I just hope you girls take this as a lesson. It's obvious I should hope."

"And what's the lesson? Please, enlighten me."

"If you can't figure it out, then we have bigger problems."

"The bigger problem is all of those people who were in that wedding hall. The bartenders who served her, the adults who did nothing to stop them, and the friends who didn't come to help her."

"I heard she's not so innocent. I heard she's done things. People weren't *surprised*."

"G-D!" I punch the half-full bag of Uncle Ben's with a force that startles even me. "Everyone is just so fucking *cruel*. So she made a mistake! Isn't that what seventeen-year-old girls are supposed to do? So her life is ruined now? She's condemned for eternity? Have a little compassion, for G-D's sake. Think about where you were at seventeen!"

"I know exactly where I was."

"This is exactly why I can't live *here*." I try to take a breath to steady myself but all I can feel is rage.

"Taking care of my dying mother," she says.

"Make one stupid mistake and you're Hester freaking Prynne."

"Who is that?" my mother asks. "Is she Syrian?"

"And don't even get me started if this was a guy, which—by the way—happens like every other day. But of course, nobody is talking about that. Nobody ever remembers the boy's name!"

"Do you *know* this girl?"

"No! But—"

"Because you're getting *very* defensive here."

Suddenly Fortune waltzes into the kitchen, carrying two dresses. "Know who?"

"Nobody." I clench my fist around a scoop of rice and toss it into the checked bowl. Does it matter if I know her? She's Lucy's age, for crying out loud. As if Lucy and her friends haven't been sneaking liquor from their parents' cabinets since they turned sixteen. Is my mother that naïve? Of course, the real clencher in the story is that the girl was woken up by a group of men walking into synagogue for morning prayers. That's all it took for the rumor mill to start turning. I heard that half of her dress was off. Another version of the story mentioned that there may have been a boy with her. One story added that the men coming in to pray had to splash cold water on her face to wake her up. Another said there was no water splash but they found puke in the pews. The details were constantly shifting and taking shape. Every single community rabbi is surely drafting the speech they'll give at shul on Saturday. I can just imagine it: "The lack of religion among the younger generation is to blame. Increasing wealth plays its own part—but don't stop the donations. We need to hold tight to our traditions, our morals. The answer is more tribalism, not less." Needless to say, I'm not looking forward to my father's inevitable recap afterward.

"Tell me!" Fortune presses.

"The drunk girl." Suddenly my mother is breathing over my shoulder. "You're not even checking the rice!"

"Oh." Fortune grabs a Honeycrisp apple from the loaded counter. "Yeah, that was sad. But it's been almost a week, no? *Haj.*"

"Sad for her parents, that's who. Very nice people." Mom shuffles back and forth to the fridge, her tiny padded Jacques Levine slippers gliding across the white marble floor. She is slowly morphing into Sitto, but maybe we all are. "Anyway, there will be none of this at your wedding."

"Yeah, right." I raise my eyebrows at Fortune.

"I'm twenty-one, anyway." Fortune tosses half of her uneaten apple into the trash can and holds up the two dresses for us to see.

"But all of your guests aren't."

"Let's just drop it." My mother eyes the dresses in Fortune's hand. "Are you going to try those on?"

"Yeah—I wanted to know what you thought."

"I'll be up in a minute. Nina?" Mom's eyes scan the contents of the fridge shelf as Fortune heads back out. "Nina."

"Mustard," I offer.

"I was *going* to say, grab my Rolodex from upstairs. The addresses for deliveries are all in there." She reaches for the container of Gulden's spicy brown mustard and shuts the fridge.

"You know you can store those in your phone now, right?"

"I like having them written down," she says.

"It'll make your life easier. Just saying, what if you lose your Rolodex?"

"What if I lose my phone?"

"You can back up—"

"Just get my book!"

I hurry the rest of the unchecked rice into the "clean" bag and head upstairs.

"Is this horrible?" I find Fortune in Mom's closet, wearing a daisy yellow tweed dress. There's a pile of crinkled dresses and skirts strewn across the floor. "For the swanee?"

"Why does she make me so angry?" I slump against the wall and slide downward until my butt hits the carpeted floor with a soft thud.

"Why do you let her?" Fortune smooths the front of the dress and turns to the side to examine her body's profile. She has clearly lost a ton of weight, but I'm done indulging people for the day. "Thoughts on this?"

"I feel like you could do better. What she doesn't understand is the reason behind *why* this poor girl got so drunk. I mean the pressure, the anxiety that comes with going to these weddings. It's too much. And no one talks about that—especially not Mom or her friends. If it were me, I'd be taking shots, too! If I still got invited to things."

"If you pass out at my wedding, I *will* hurt you."

"Saul will get to me first, so not to worry."

"True though." Fortune holds up a floral A-line Carolina Herrera dress I vaguely recognize. "What about this?"

"Pretty." I shrug. "By the way, shouldn't you be at the store today?"

"Dad gave me the day off." Fortune turns around. "I have so much to do. Can you unzip?"

"Mom wouldn't give me the day off if my legs were on fire." I unzip the dress and Fortune shimmies out of it. When she bends down to pick up the Herrera, I can practically see her ribs.

"You're not getting married in less than two months."

"Thank you for reminding me."

Fortune looks taken aback. "Sorry. I didn't mean—because you're always saying how you don't want to get married. Sorry."

"Shut up," I say, laughing. "I just want everyone to stop reminding me that I'm not getting married. I don't care that you, my little sister, are getting married before me. I care that everyone else does."

Fortune fastens the hook and eye at the nape of her neck. "I know that."

"Good." I grab Mom's Rolodex from the shelf. "I like this one."

"Yeah?" Fortune looks for something in the mirror.

It's still hard to believe she's going to be married soon, a wife who is responsible for keeping a home, one step closer to becoming a mother. It's not that I don't think she can do it. Fortune is surprisingly resourceful. I'm just not sure if she cares about anything enough to give it deep thought. Although what Fortune lacks in introspection she makes up for in common sense. And she's good at coexisting. God knows she lasted this long working with Dad, and in her relationship with Saul, both of whom are stubborn, needy, and prone to mood swings. She can spend long stretches with Mom, too, while I have to take frequent breaks or else risk detonation.

Fortune doesn't inspire awe or infatuation, but she's hard to dislike. That's something.

"It's perfect," I say. "Very virgin bride."

"Ugh. Just get out."

"I'd love nothing more," I whisper.

And it's true, I think, watching Fortune go through the motions of becoming a bride. I need out. I walk the halls and it's like I can hear my family mocking me. *There goes Nina, different day, same shit.* I've aged out of my room, too. No amount of vinyl art—The Strokes, Arctic Monkeys, and Grizzly Bear records—or *Flight of the Conchords* posters can obscure the ballet slipper pink walls. I have nowhere to be and that makes it all worse. I don't want to be prayed for under someone else's chuppah. At a challah bake. At the mikvah. I don't want to cook for my mother. I don't want to be told what good practice it is. I don't want to hear about another eligible divorcé. I want people to stop pitying me for different reasons than I pity myself. I don't want to become fodder for the next round of gossip. And I don't want to worry that one drink too many at a wedding will destine me for a scarlet letter. I want to fit in somewhere. I want my life to begin, like really *begin*.

Beep beep.

I take a deep breath and prepare for my mother's voice to fill up the house reminding me of why she sent me up here in the first place. Whoops. I leave Fortune in the closet and race down to the kitchen.

I drop the Rolodex next to a bowl of squash and egg. "*Ahh.*" I close my eyes and let out what I hope is a convincing wince.

"What's wrong?" My mother wipes her hands on a nearby towel and riffles through her Rolodex looking through rows and rows of phone numbers and addresses.

"I think I need to go lie down." I clutch my stomach like a for-hire actress in a Tampax commercial. I'm still in my pajamas, an old and tattered T-shirt from a prom I rejected before it had the chance to re-ject me.

"That means Fortune's getting hers soon." My mother sighs and turns a page. "I hope she stays on schedule . . . for the wedding night."

"Oof." I lurch forward slightly more than I meant to.

"*Hazita.* Go. You'll drop those when the Midol kicks in." She nods to an assembly line of labeled tins that I'll have to deliver to the Bedford area later.

I head upstairs to my room, close the door, and prop my laptop open to finally write the email I'd been planning now for weeks.

Buried under my duvet, which somehow still smells like a thirteen-year-old, I hit compose and type in Steven's email address.

To: Steven@Bananastandrecords.com
From: Tallnina007@aol.com
Subject line: HEY! (It's Nina) ((Cohen)).

Steven!
Hi! It was great running into you. I'm not sure if you're still there—although, why wouldn't you be?—but I was wondering if the music label you're at is hiring? Even if it's just an internship, or whatever. I'm not above getting people coffee! Would be good to get out of the bubble either way. I know you know what that's like—ha. Anyway . . . let me know?

Hope to hear from you soon.
Nina

When I ran into Steven last month at the Barnes and Noble in Park Slope, he'd given me his email address and made me promise to get in touch. He was one of my few guy friends in high school. I think I was one of his few friends, period. Mostly, we'd go to concerts together. It had been eight years since we both graduated and I had remembered him as being shorter than me, awkward with an acne-prone chin and spotty facial hair. But even under those awful fluorescent B&N lights it was clear he grew up since then and his acne was gone, revealing a face that was, dare I say, *attractive.* I hadn't heard any news of him marrying, and he wasn't wearing a wedding ring, either. I tried to appear nonchalant as he told me that he was working as the office manager at an experimental indie label in Bushwick.

"You should come check it out," he said. "The guys are really nice. You'd like it."

"Definitely," I promised, trying not to appear too eager and hoping he meant what he said. That kind of job sounded like a dream. A far-off, distant dream.

A little less distant now, I think. I hit Send before I can proofread my email or catch my breath. I'm done waiting for my life to start.

Chapter Five

....

$\mathcal{W}$ hat do you wear on the first day of what could jump-start the rest of your life? I realize I have no idea, as I attempt to pull together an outfit for my first day as an office manager at the label. When I emailed Steven a few weeks ago, I half expected him to not respond—instead he told me that the label he worked at actually had an opening. I look through the clothing options I've laid out over my bed and immediately hate everything I've chosen. I'm sure music people are the type to hate trends and trendy people. In fact, they seem to have built their business on bucking trends, which is a bit risky for an independent record label if you ask me.

I waited a few days to tell Dad I got the job. Of course, when I finally did tell him I'd be working at an experimental indie rock label that operated out of the owner's Bushwick apartment, he laughed. He told me that there was no way I was starting this job. "If you want to work, you'll come back and work for me," he said. To my surprise, it was my mother who ultimately convinced him to let me go by assuring him that a boy, still single, from the community works there, too. And my father, comforted by the fact that at least I'd be in the company of a potential suitor, relented on the condition that he pick me up and drop me off every day. *I don't want you on the streets there alone.* Like they were sending me off to the strip. As if I hadn't spent four years commuting to NYU for classes, and to the store.

"We'll pack you lunch," my mother said, "so you don't have to wander."

It was so pathetic, this suggestion that a twenty-six-year-old woman shouldn't take lunch outside, but I didn't care. I wanted to cry, because the other side was within my reach, and finally I could taste the thing I'd been chasing: freedom.

I decide on my black BDG skinny jeans and an Animal Collective T-shirt I got at their Bowery Ballroom show a year ago, the last time I had fun. I pull on my Doc Martens and throw a denim shirt over my shoulders. I gather my straight hair into a high bun and rub some tinted moisturizer on my face and neck. I suck my cheeks in and bite down on the flesh inside my mouth. I knew I wasn't single because of my looks, which almost made the idea that my personality was entirely to blame palpable.

Minutes later I'm in the kitchen saying goodbye to Sitto.

She looks at me simultaneously like there is zero daylight between us and as though she is the only person in this house, maybe in this world, who understands me. When my younger sister Fortune got engaged before me, Sitto sat me down and said plainly, "You know, you're going to draw the pity of many people now." She flicked her wrists as though she were shaking out a damp piece of laundry. "*Kish!* Send it away. The worst thing a woman can be in this world is a *hazita*. And not just for attracting a man," she said, "but for yourself." Sitto never was one for beating around the bush, and she wasn't about to start with me. She carries herself like a woman short on time for bullshit; wander too close to her weeds with your complaints and you'll be hit with a smack and a *lehh* so fast it'd give you whiplash.

"This is what you wear?" Sitto looks me up and down, her red polished fingers wrapped around a dwindling piece of mamoul. The sweet smell of pastry and dates fills the kitchen. "Maybe take a skirt from your mother, *yanni*, the pencil shape." Sitto says this as if it's a suggestion, not an order.

The digital clock on the stove where my mother fiddles away at a pot of fasoulya reads eight forty-five A.M. Steven, while admitting that rules at the company were "lax," suggested I get in by ten. The kitchen shows no signs of my father, who promised he'd be ready to go by nine. The address in Bushwick is forty-two minutes away; it may as well be on another planet.

"Sitto, it's not that type of place," I say, pouring myself a cup of coffee.

"It's a job, no?" Bits of powdered sugar–coated pastry flings from Sitto's mouth as she speaks. "You look like the lady who washes the color out of my hair."

"I can't believe it." My mother moves from the pot of fasoulya to the small window above the kitchen sink, where she can see our driveway outside. She rams her satin Jacques Levine slipper into the kitchen floor. "They're blocking the driveway, *again!*"

"Oh G-D." Sitto rolls her eyes at me and we both brace ourselves for the argument to come. I join my mother at the window and take a small sip of coffee. A large white produce truck is already causing a backlog of cars up the narrow street, but more importantly, it is blocking our driveway. A group of men sit atop closed cardboard boxes. They appear to be taking their breakfast from insulated thermos containers, paying no mind to the resounding chorus of honks now drumming up and down the avenue.

"Wait till your father comes down. Where's Eli?" my mother says, referring to Spice's owner. She tightens the belt of her robe around her tiny waist as though she might actually go outside and confront him. "Where is that SOB?"

I can see Isaac pouring a human-sized bag of pumpkin seeds into a white container.

"He don't care." Sitto grabs another piece of mamoul. "Forget it. No matter how many times you tell him, he's not going to listen. Business is business. *Floos is floos.*"

I take a deep breath. In an hour, I'll be in another world, one in which the rules of my current one do not apply. Where comparatively, my once strong opinions will seem subtle, timid, even. I feel the glands in my armpits expanding. My stomach twists in knots.

"Here we go," my mother chants excitedly. "Here we go!" She balls her tiny fists like she's readying for a fight. We both crane our necks to watch as a man in a dark suit leaves his car in the now trafficked street to confront the truck driver. My mother cracks open the window and the sound of honking fills our kitchen. Just then, Isaac abandons the bag of bizet to mediate. We strain our ears against the window screen in order to hear the confrontation, but it's useless. Isaac places a hand on the suit's back and leads him back toward his car in a show of diplomacy. He returns to the men taking their breakfast and motions with his finger to *wrap it up.* Just then, he makes eye contact with my mother and me. He mouths "sorry" and shrugs, as if he hadn't been the one to order the truck there in the first place.

"He's lucky he's good-looking," my mother mutters through clenched teeth.

"You know I was just thinking that." Sitto slaps her thigh. "Maybe he will take Nina out?"

"That's not for Nina." My mother waves dismissively, her eyes still trained on Isaac. She smiles at him as if she hasn't been cursing him dead for the past three minutes. The men put their breakfasts away and begin to move their dolly to the sidewalk. They close up the ramp on the truck and pull it a few yards forward, blocking our neighbor's driveway.

"This street is just not made for retail. That's the problem." Mom returns to the stove and sprinkles some cinnamon into the pot of simmering beans.

"But look how convenient for you," Sitto says, ever one to look for the silver lining in Brooklyn. "Everything around you. You never even have to get in your car."

"And just wait until Boreka opens across the street from Spice. Forget it. You won't be able to walk down the street, let alone drive." My mother sighs but it sounds more like a growl. We are all sensitive to the fact that Boreka spells danger for my mother. The shop will directly eat into Mom's profit, selling *mazza* and Shabbat dishes from one convenient location, all made in a kosher kitchen in the back and kibbe being freshly fried on the hour, every hour. Mom shakes every time someone mentions Boreka, and she has anxiously watched as the store progresses toward opening. We all dread the day.

"You have your loyals. *Hallas,* that's all you need. But you"—Sitto beckons me toward her with a meaty finger—"go up and put something respectful on."

"It's a record label, Sitto. They distribute music." I take a seat next to her at the kitchen table.

"Her friend got her the job," my mother says, intervening. "Nice boy. Nina, maybe that's a better outfit for the second day. You want to make a good first impression."

"What do you know about first-day impressions?" I scoff.

"*Haje* with the defensiveness, Nina. You're being a little *teil,* no?" My mother rolls her eyes.

"*Dechilak,*" Sitto mutters beneath her breath, regretting the fight she had a part in starting.

"I don't have time for this," I say.

"SY?" Sitto raises a brow. "This boy?"

"I think so?" My mother looks at me in silent acknowledgment; we'll drop this battle.

"Yeah," I say and roll my eyes.

"Married?" Sitto dips a piece of sweet kaak into her coffee. "With this job, he can't be, no?" She remains cautiously optimistic.

"He's not married, Sitto. He's just my friend."

"Why just a friend? When you say 'he's my friend,' he will only ever be your friend, when maybe, one day, he can be your *nassib.*" She spits, her half-eaten pastry waving erratically in front of my face. The worst thing a woman can be is a *hazit* case.

"They say friends make the best partners," my mother adds, nodding.

"Okay, bye." I scoot my chair back. "I think I hear Dad calling me."

"*Allah ma'ak,*" Sitto says.

"I don't hear anything." My mother squints her eyes to make her ears work better.

My father drives like he is being chased by Nazis and like he's fallen asleep at the wheel. I crack every knuckle in my hand as we roll through a red light, drifting from our middle lane over to the left and then to the right, before settling back in between the painted white lines, where we are safe for the time being. The windows are slightly cracked open and the smell is familiar, spring and pigeon shit.

In years past, the start of the season turned my stomach. What should've signaled excitement and possibility filled me with dread. I knew better than to expect my life to change with the arrival of leaves; I'm done allowing my imagination to get carried away with the radio's promise of a love-filled summer spent gathered around a bonfire with friends I don't have, and whatever other aspirational images that a complimentary Free People catalog wanted to sell me. I learned a little while ago that warm weather signaled little else than a fear of chafing.

"You know I could just take the train," I say. "Transfer to the M at Delancey, or my friend offered to pick me up."

"I said I would drive you." My father fiddles with the radio.

"I know sometimes you need to open the store early, so it's really not a big deal."

"I said I'll drive you." There's a tone of pity in his voice.

I settle back into my seat and close my eyes. I'm unaccustomed to sitting in long silences with my father. With my mother, it's easy. Silences are a welcome alternative to the bickering we'd otherwise be doing. The hostility between my father and me isn't as obvious. My bad attitude, while readily available to anyone who rubs me the wrong way, seems inappropriate, an overreaction to the general apathy with which my father handles me.

He settles on 1010 WINS. Despite his reluctance to engage with me on any topic that did not include logistics—How are you getting to so and so? How much does X cost? What is your email address, your computer login?—I do feel like he understands me on some basic level that seems to escape everyone else. We are both foreigners, him by nature and me by choice. Whereas my father worked hard to shed his otherness, his accent, his taste in clothes, his childhood as a young immigrant, I hold tight to mine, wielding it like a weapon. I told the story of how he escaped religious persecution as a young man in Aleppo during small seminars at NYU, where this *otherness* scored me points among my hipster classmates. And then I promptly flipped the script upon returning home, where this narrative was as banal as the pita they sold in every store. In Brooklyn, I aspire to the type of otherness I recognized in my NYU classmates, one that was undeniably American, individualistic, progressive, where otherness was touted but not always earned.

"Do you want me to answer that?" My father's phone rings nonstop between Avenues R and L. The Bluetooth option lights up the screen. Incoming call from: VENDOR, PANTY.

"*Kisa amak,*" Dad mutters under his breath, Arabic for "kiss my ass." He punches the screen with his index finger to ignore. VENDOR, PANTY is undeterred and calls again. This time Dad picks up.

"Morris!" The voice on the other end is rushed, as if anticipating that the call might end at any moment.

"I am. Going. Into the tunnel." My father lies, exaggerating the volume and tempo of his voice.

"Morris, wait! You owe me for two shipments. My guy says you haven't paid since September. I need the goods back, Morris. I'm *mooting,* too. I love ya, you know I love ya, but I need the goods or I need the money for the goods. The product's moving, Morris. My other guys all tell me the products are flying off the shelves, they love it. The *g*'s. You still in Midtown? I know it's gotta be moving over there. If it ain't moving there, it ain't moving anywhere. And I know it's moving everywhere."

The voice on the other end sounds like it belongs to someone around my age. Someone my mother would like to see me end up with. I imagine he smooths his hair back with his own spit.

"It's moving." My father drags out his words, urging patience. As he speaks, the car veers slightly into oncoming traffic before veering back. He picks up speed, ascending the ramp onto the Prospect Expressway.

"So where's my money?" VENDOR, PANTY asks. "It's not me, Morris. I love you. I know you're good for it. You know, it's my father. Between us. You know how he can be, my father. No patience, that man. No patience at all. It's just Business. Business. Business."

"*Rohi*, I knew your father back when all he was good for was quarters in abandoned alleyways. Tell him Morris will pay by the end of the month."

"You said that last month."

"I put my daughter on your account," my father says. "Fortune's good. Organized—like her mother," my father lies. We both know that neither my father nor Fortune is going to single out VENDOR, PANTY's account. There are bigger fish to fry. "You know she's marrying Marie Dweck's son next month. Good family—I guess your invitation got lost in the mail."

"Right, well, *mabrook* to your daughter, asshole. *Sabi andak.* All the well-wishes—I'm sure she's a very nice girl," VENDOR, PANTY rushes.

"Thank you, thank you. Very nice." My father ignores the insult, his hand hovering over the button that would promptly disconnect the call. He jumps on the brake to avoid rear-ending the Volvo in front of us. "So you understand when I say things are a little tight around here."

"I have four daughters, Morris. What, you don't think I need to pay for things?" VENDOR, PANTY grows impatient. "So I can expect payment this month—March?"

"Next month." The car drifts three lanes over, nearly causing a four-vehicle accident.

"March thirty-first, I should tell my father to expect the money?"

"March thirty-first," my father contemplates under his breath, looking up at the roof of the car in exasperation. "April," he thunders. "Next month is April, *dib*, use your head!" He pounds the steering wheel, letting out a loud, relieved honk.

The driver in front of us flips us off through his window.

"Dad!"

"Fuck you, Morris," VENDOR, PANTY cracks. "My father says you don't pay, I say let's give the man a chance. But fuck you! You pay by March thirty-first or—"

My father jabs a finger at the screen, effectively ending the call. *Mejnoon.*

I look at him, horrified. "Dad! You can't talk to people like that, that's horrible."

"*Tsk.*" My father laughs as he speeds through the toll booth. "Don't tell me! That's how men in this business talk, Nina. Watch, everyone will be polite at this music company, but they don't do *business.*" He rubs his index finger and thumb together, the universal sign for money. "*Shoof,*" he nods toward the BQE.

"They don't even have an office in Manhattan."

"I can't believe your dad drove you here," Steven whispers as he helps me get set up. "I thought you were a goner once he saw the Bushwick address." The two other employees at the communal table both wear oversize headphones and seem to be completely enthralled by whatever is on their screens.

"Adam and Yasmin," Steven mouths, nodding at my tablemates. "Interns. Both sophomores at The New School, I believe."

Of course. Adam and Yasmin have the distinct aura of unpaid interns working at an indie rock label. The furrowed brows, the pursed lips, the tired eyes. The Hydro Flasks (I suddenly feel self-conscious about my plastic water bottle). The mothball-scented flannels. The Merrell hiking boots. Why does everyone on this side of Brooklyn wear hiking boots? Are there secret trails I am not aware of?

Yasmin slides one of her earphones off, holding it between her head and neck like a telephone. "I'm Yasmin." She smiles and rolls her eyes playfully toward Adam, whose eyes remain glued to his screen. "Adam's not usually this rude, right, Adam?" She flicks her green eyes at him.

"Correction. Adam is always that rude," says Ethan, one of the co-founders, from across the room. I notice a Bengal cat lounging on top of a portable radio from which the sound of NPR drones.

Adam reaches his hand out toward me. I shake it and he returns to his computer.

"Welcome," Ethan shouts, clapping his hands together. He has the distinct and unremarkable bellow of a frat boy, not at all what I'd expected from the co-founder of a music label named Banana Stand Records. He wears his hair long but neat, tucked behind his ears and parted to the left, where it appears to melt into a trimmed beard flecked with gold. He pushes his chair back and walks toward me. He, too, wears a flannel, which I'm beginning to think is the unofficial uniform of this place. I suddenly feel incredibly stupid about my concert tee, which basically screams *"Love me!"*

Steven pats me on the back. "Welcome to the Banana Stand."

Before I know it, Ethan scoops me up and encloses me in a massive bear hug, his arms wrapped around my shoulders. Adam and Yasmin holler and whistle, as Steven counts down, 5, 4, 3, 2 . . . Ethan smells like spearmint, cigarettes, and a breakfast burrito. Being in his grip terrifies and thrills me all at once. Unsure of where to rest my head or when this will end, I hold it back so that my gaze is in direct alignment with his ear. Then I notice a piercing where an earring must've once been, and beside it, an almost indistinguishable Star of David tattoo. Right on his earlobe.

"All right, cut her loose, Ethan." A giant of a man, older, with graying hair, saunters into the room. The depth of his voice matches the largeness of his presence, and his mug of coffee looks tiny in the embrace of his palm. He wears jean cutoffs, open-toed Birkenstocks with tubular white socks, and a blue button-down with the Lacoste emblem label displayed ironically on the chest pocket.

Ethan puts me down. "Dad's here." He winks as he gives my shoulders a gentle squeeze. His fingers are adorned with chunky silver rings.

"They insist on calling me Dad. I promise, it's not some weird paternalistic fetish of mine. And you are Nina, correct?" Dad shoos the cat off the table that he and Ethan share. "You're from," he waves his hand in the air, "the same thing-a-ma-jig as our Steven, right?"

"Community, I guess, yeah." I cross my arms in front of my chest.

"You need to leave early on Fridays, too?"

I laugh nervously. "In the summer I can leave later. I just need to be home by sundown."

"I'm just joking. We're all Jews here. Well, not like you two. But you know, we're all part of the tribe."

"Not really," says Yasmin.

"Except her." Dad bows in prayer motion.

"She's our token goy," Ethan adds.

"That's right." Yasmin pounds the table. "And proud of it."

"Is that anti-Semitic?" Steven asks.

"What isn't these days, am I right?" Adam winks at me.

"Anyway, Steven will show you the ropes." Dad powers on his computer. "And if you have a question, just shout, so long as Pony's not on the table." Dad motions toward the cat who has relocated to between his massive feet. "When Pony's on the table, that's quiet time. And no eating by your desk. That's it, those are the two rules. Follow them, and you'll fit right in."

"And on Mondays we drink as a team," Steven adds.

"Ah, Steven always makes sure to cover all the bases," Ethan says. "Yes, Mondays are Banana Stand happy hours. And whad'ya say, it's Monday! I'm sure we'll get to know you better then." Ethan slides into his chair. "Pony!" He pats the desk. Pony leaps up on the table and the room falls silent. Dad turns up the NPR and everyone else puts on their headphones, eyes fixed on the screens in front of them. I wonder what music everyone is listening to. I'm too embarrassed to ask.

I take a seat and open the email account Steven had set up for me. He takes the seat beside me and props open his laptop. Within seconds, I see an incoming message from him.

Steven: Lunch at 1? There's a deli around the block that sells the dopest sandwiches. Random, but I'm telling you, they're sick.

I think about the salad my mother packed for me, the romaine lettuce wilted and possibly decayed by oil and salt. The rule is no going out to lunch. But Steven is circumcised and wants to have lunch with me. My parents can't argue with that. Or maybe I just won't tell them.

Nina: Sounds good.
Steven: I can give you a ride home from the bar later, btw. So don't
    worry about that.
Nina: Thanks.
Steven: Tell your dad, lol.
Nina: Shut up.
Steven: All right, check your inbox. Sharing a Google Doc to get you
    acclimated. It's lengthy but clear. Read it and we'll get
    started after lunch.
Nina: Got it, thank you!

As office manager, I'll technically be taking over Steven's responsibilities while he transitions to a more senior role, reviewing contracts and dealing more intimately with the musicians. From what I understand, the office manager wears many hats, barista being one of them. I make sure no one is looking and lower the brightness on my laptop until my screen goes dark. I smooth the flyaway hairs that popped out of my bun, brush my eyebrows upward, and blend the concealer that had congealed in the creases under my eyes. I try not to notice that Ethan is possibly the most attractive male over six feet to introduce himself to me and that Steven has grown up a lot, too. I tell myself that tomorrow I'll steal some of Lucy's bronzer. Yasmin is gorgeous, but I'm not bad, either. I make a mental note to try harder.

"Ethan's the best." Steven and I sit on a red bench outside of the deli. When he wipes a drop of hot sauce from his lips, it's hard not to notice how much he's changed since we were friends in high school. His old mushroom haircut replaced by a close shave. He's lost weight, too, and appears taller in his slim-cut jeans. The thick eyebrows that used to get him teased are now tamed and shaped, lending an attractive intensity to his face that hadn't been there before.

I wonder if he remembers how he sent me Shabbat flowers every Friday during our freshman year in high school. He was open about his feelings toward me, and that always made me cringe. I never looked twice at him, fearing that if I did he'd see me for who I really was—someone who was desperately seeking attention from the herd—and look away.

Steven kind of fell off the map, as my mother might say, after high school. He didn't have many friends, which probably explains why he gravitated so easily toward me. But now he seems to have so many. *Upstates,* as he calls them, a reference to the friends he made at Purchase, where he went to college. Still, Steven could decide to "come back" tomorrow, and he'd have girls all over him. That's just the way it is.

Steven takes another bite of his sandwich. "Dad takes some warming up to. He's kind of behind the scenes and you don't want to fuck with him, big bear that he is. Ethan's dope though. He let me crash on his couch for like three months before I got my own place. Girls love him, too, I've seen it." He nudges me in the ribs. "Admit it, you think he's cute, right?"

"Oh. I mean he's definitely not ugly." I take a bite of my sandwich, pushing the bread back with my teeth and scooping the tomatoes out with my tongue.

"Come on, the man looks like a young Matthew McConaughey."

"Is Matthew McConaughey old now?"

"Fine, a young Kurt Russell then."

"Relax." I gently shove Steven. It feels good to joke around. "It sounds like you have a crush on him."

"I fully have a crush on him. I'd swing for Ethan, yeah." We both laugh now. "Not ugly," Steven repeats, shaking his head. "That's what Yasmin said before they hooked up." Steven makes a motion with his hands that I can only assume translates to sex.

"Wait, what?" I put my sandwich down. A group of guys congregates on the sidewalk in front of us, laughing, passing a cigarette around.

"Oh yeah." Steven takes another bite. "That happened on, like, day three."

"But he's, like, *old.*" I feel my face grow hot.

"Dude, he's thirty-four. Like people we know don't marry guys three times their age, please."

"That's true." I want to know more but also don't want to seem too interested.

"Isn't your sister dating someone older than us? David something? And she's what, like, fifteen?"

"She's eighteen," I snap, surprised by my own impulse to defend my youngest sister, Lucy. I barely have any details about David so how did Steven know? Plus, wasn't he supposed to be above the gossip of his old zip code?

"Same thing. Yasmin's cool though, she knew what she was getting."

"What do you mean?"

"Meaning girls love Ethan, and Ethan likes to mess around. Ethan's not interested in marrying you."

"I don't want to marry Ethan." I scan the storefronts of the street, desperate for an iced coffee.

"I'm just saying, I wouldn't be surprised if he's got his eye on you. He'll probably give you shit about your shirt at drinks later, though."

"My shirt?" I feel my stomach clench. I hope I sound like: *What shirt am I wearing again? I'm too cool and/or preoccupied to notice.* But I probably sound like a fucking loser.

"Animal Collective. Interesting choice." He sees right through me. I swallow my embarrassment over thinking I could reinvent myself here. Steven knows exactly who I am, and he isn't going to let me forget it too easily.

"Whatever." I remove the scrunchie from my bun and let my hair fall down my back. "It was clean."

Steven grins and checks his phone. "We should get back. It's not a good look to take lunch so long when we're closing up early." He pats the place where I recall there being a belly once. "I'm ready for a drink, you?"

"Just remember you're my ride home, degenerate." I stand up, and a man walking by compliments my legs. I pretend not to notice. I pretend not to notice Steven look me up and down. Or that I feel something akin to a buzz of excitement for the first time in a long time.

"Precious cargo." Steven rolls his sandwich wrapper into a ball and tosses it into a nearby garbage can. It's a miss.

"You suck."

Chapter Six

....

Happy hour is at a bar on the ground floor of the apartment building next door. Like everything else on the block—or at least everything I've seen so far—it looks like a bodega in which someone had dropped off a wood table and forgotten to pick it up. Behind the bar, U-shaped and graffitied with local paper advertisements, a jovial man with a towel slung over his shoulder bops around to reggae music while pouring shots of something white and syrupy into tiny glasses. We're the only ones in here. Steven, Ethan, Yasmin, Adam, "Dad," and myself. I take a seat at the bar, where there are six shots lined up, presumably for us. Ethan slides onto the stool beside me. Adam and Yasmin fiddle with the music on a jukebox that looks like it hasn't worked since 1952 and Dad leaves the bar to take a call outside. I scan the room for Steven and breathe easy when I spot him lingering by the restroom.

"Cheers." Ethan raises a shot glass with one hand and slides one toward me with his other.

"Cheers," I say. The base liquor of my initiation shot is rum and some other things that should've been sweet but instead taste like flavored medicine. Ethan watches me take it and I try not to wince. It's hard to play it cool while your phone buzzes under the table with a text from your mother: Make sure that boy waits for you to get inside when he drops you home.

Ethan raises another shot and an eyebrow, daring me to go for number two. Is this some sort of test? I imagine Yasmin taking welcome shots with Ethan on her first day and quickly push the thought out of my mind.

The second shot goes down easier. I feel my jaw loosen and I smile lazily at the bartender, who places a water pitcher shaped like a hula dancer in front of us.

"Impressive," Ethan says. The bar seems to take on an iridescent glow. All of a sudden, the Christmas lights strung above us feel half charming. I see Steven join Yasmin and Adam by the jukebox, and I can't decide if I desperately want him to stay there or come over.

"Let's head to a table, yeah?" Ethan scoots off his stool and waits for me to do the same, so I do. He grabs the hula pitcher—which I now realize is full of beer, not water—and some cups. I follow him to a picnic table off to the side, and I can feel Steven's eyes on my back.

"Sorry if the hug thing caught you off guard before," Ethan says while I feel my body relax into the hard recesses of the bench. Ethan slides in next to me, leaving two-thirds of the bench empty. I'm relieved I had the foresight to reapply deodorant before coming here. He lines up six cups and fills each of them with beer. Every time his arm grazes mine, my skin peppers with goosebumps. Adam brings over the remaining shots from the bar, takes one and a beer, and returns to the bar to join our boss in conversation. Either he's an asshole or he just doesn't like me very much. I wonder if he thinks I'm just some new conquest of Ethan's. I push the thought out of my mind and Ethan takes his third shot.

"Impressive," I say, sarcastically.

"That's nothing."

"Except you have a—here." To Ethan's surprise but mainly my own,

I wipe the spot on his upper lip where the syrupy liquid from the shot remained glued to his mustache.

"Well, that's embarrassing." Ethan pouts his lower lip and hangs his head. I can feel my stomach growl loudly, and I'm thankful for the bar's loud music. I remind myself that today is real. A few weeks ago I was checking rice with my mother and today I am sitting with this person who knows nothing about me, and what a wonderful thing that is.

Ethan doesn't know that I'm the eldest of three sisters, a frequent wastebasket for pity from my younger, betrothed cousins, and the subject of my mother's prayers. He doesn't know that my younger sister, Fortune, is getting married next month and that our youngest sister is probably on her way, too.

To Ethan, whose mouth, I realize, is moving, I am twenty-six and that is young. Like, desirably young. I'm attractive, if not pretty in the obvious way. I have long legs that more or less make up for a lack of curves and olive skin that browns in the sun. And it's not weird if I smile a lot or if I'm *nice.* Because Ethan doesn't know that my mouth's default is grimace. None of these people do. I can say or do as I please and not have to worry about being "out of character" or gossiped about. Steven might have some aged perception of who I am, but he's always liked me in spite of it. I realize now that for the first time since the squandered opportunity that was college, I have the chance to be someone else.

"Nice tattoo," I say.

Ethan touches the tiny Star of David on his earlobe. "Does it offend you?"

"Why would it offend me?"

"Well, I don't want to assume . . ." Ethan says, seeming a little drunk. "You see Steven, our resident Sephardic Jew over there." Ethan raises his glass and calls out Steven's name. Upon hearing it, Steven holds his fist high in salute, which is borderline Nazi-ish, but the drinks feel too good to care. I wonder why he isn't coming over. Nobody is. And the four extra cups of beer Ethan poured remain untouched. Ethan turns back to me. "Steven tells us that the powers that be won't bury a dead dude with tattoos in you guys' cemeteries or whatever."

"Did Steven say that?"

"That's what the man said," Ethan says and smirks.

"I guess it's true. But then again, I don't know anyone with tattoos. So I'm not sure that rule's ever been tested."

"You could be the first," Ethan suggests.

"I could." I shrug, as if the mere suggestion wouldn't send my mother prematurely to her grave. "It would probably kill my mother, actually. And then I'd be a murderer so I'd probably be excommunicated for that, anyway."

Ethan leans back in his chair. "I got one of those, too."

"A mother?"

"A Jewish mother."

"So you *are* Jewish?" The question sounds like something my mother would ask—accusatory by nature. I hope Ethan doesn't feel judged by it.

"The Star of David not tip you off?"

"I'm sorry." I should've just shut my fucking mouth.

"I'm only messing with you." Ethan gives my kneecap a squeeze. "I'm a member of the tribe. Well, not your tribe." He takes a swig of beer and tips his cup toward Steven and then back at me. "Your people are another level of Jew."

"My people?" I feel whatever comfort Ethan's Judaism welled within me dissolve. I take a sip of beer, even though my head's already swimming and I probably shouldn't.

"Your *community*," Ethan says, with air quotes. "Sorry."

"What about it?" I'm surprised by my own defensiveness. I know that the community's reputation traveled beyond its physical borders in Brooklyn. But unlike the Hasidim in Borough Park or the Satmars in Williamsburg, we didn't entirely shun the outside world. We toed the line; one foot in, one foot out. We were consumers of clothing, music, travel, certain types of food; we bartered in pretty much everything, except outside ideas.

I shift on the bench, wanting Ethan to take stock of what I look like, how I dress. My fitted jeans and band T-shirt. *We're not like them,* I want to say. Although admittedly, it would be easier if we were. If we embraced a singular religious code and lived by it, instead of crafting our own rules. If G-D was the thing we feared most and not one another. But I don't have time to explain any of that to Ethan.

"The Syrians—the Sephardics, whatever," Ethan corrects himself. "According to them, I'm not Jewish. Dad's a convert. Irish Catholic originally. Throw in Judaism." Ethan puffs his lips and lets out an exasperated gust of wind. "It doesn't matter. Everyone knows that you girls don't date outside of the community."

By "you girls" he means Syrian Jewish girls.

"Jewish or not," he adds. "You stick to your own."

"And your mom?" I ask, ignoring his comment.

"Orthodox Jew from Philly." Ethan lets out a full laugh, like this was the funniest thing he's ever said or heard.

"She must've really loved him."

"She might've . . . once upon a time." He chuckles and pretends to take a long swig of beer. We both pretend like the cup isn't already empty. "Anyway, I've got no shot with you." Ethan frames this more like a question than a fact.

"I'm capable of making up my own mind," I say and shrug. "I'm here, aren't I?" For a moment, Ethan seems to believe me.

Ethan smirks. "No shot."

I shake my head and laugh. "None."

One wholly unnecessary beer later and the space between our bodies has shrunk over the course of our conversation. For the second time tonight, Ethan is close enough for me to smell him: sweat, bike grease, and antibacterial Dial soap. He places his elbow on the table and rubs the back of his neck with his palm. His body is so slouched over that he's looking up at me despite being at least six inches taller. I replay in my brain the conversation Steven and I had over lunch. Is this Ethan trying to get with me? Admittedly, I've never been in this position. But

I'm not an idiot. He's wearing a Cheshire grin and has slits for eyes. I feel a wave of panic rush over me.

How typically me, to be falling in love with and simultaneously repulsed by this stranger with the stringy hair tucked behind his ears. I cock my head to the side and allow myself to smile back. As I contemplate whether or not this is actually happening, I wonder what my mother would say. Or Steven.

Where is Steven, anyway? *Cool* and *different* as he is, he still carried the code of the place we both called home. What would he think of this little dance Ethan and I are doing—or are we? I don't even fucking know. But if we are doing it, well, then, I already had the scarlet letter attached to my clothes, right? I might as well make it count.

"Yo!"

Ethan and I snap our attention toward the voice. It's Steven. He yells from across the room and dangles his keys in the air. "Cohen, you ready to go?"

Fuck it.

"I think I'm gonna grab a bite with Ethan!" I yell back.

"Oh, really." Ethan straightens up. He's smiling for real now.

"Nice! I'm starving!" Steven yells back, inviting himself.

Like everything else recommended by the staff of Banana Stand Records, the place we go to grab a bite is a closely guarded secret. It's a ten-minute walk away and Steven offers to drive. Ethan's got his motorcycle, which is really more of an electric bike. When Ethan asks me to ride with him I do, even though his unapologetic efforts to get with me are making me queasy, and his greasy hair, sexy as of thirty minutes ago, now just looks hungry for shampoo, but mostly for attention.

I consider flagging Steven down as he pulls his car out and whirs past us. Steven, who asked me three times, "Are you sure?" before taking off. Now Ethan pops the back seat of his bike and hands me a snug white helmet. I think about Yasmin, and the dark curls that fall over to one side of her head like a tidal wave. And what a shame it is that they'd ever been dampened by this salad bowl that Ethan calls a helmet. I put it on even though what I really want to do is climb into the familiarity of Steven's Jeep Wrangler, which is probably looking for parking by now.

Ethan encourages me to hold tight as we sail through traffic lights. The breeze should feel good but instead it feels like breathing in recycled air. I want to tell him to slow down, but I don't want to sound like a loser. I also don't need to give Ethan another excuse to take his eyes off the road, which he does every sixty seconds, to validate *How awesome this is* and *Isn't there nothing like it?*

All I can think about is the fact that Ethan's had six drinks while Steven nursed one beer the entire night. I'm relieved to see Steven's taillights beside us. He could've been at the diner already. The fact that he clearly felt responsible for me is partly endearing and, if I'm being honest with myself, partly the reason I got on Ethan's bike in the first place.

Steven and I both knew that *if* something were to happen to me, my mother would be on the phone with his mother in ten seconds flat. In normal circumstances, I'd see his protectiveness over me as infantilizing and condescending, the result of a traditional hierarchy designed to keep women stationary while men orbit around them. But at the moment, I just feel thankful. And a little sorry for Steven, who has clearly convinced himself that he's evolved beyond the gendered stereotypes of our community.

"Found a spot," Steven shouts from a cracked window. The diner is run-down and fluorescently lit, like a scene from a Tarantino movie. "I'll go in and place our order," Steven says before disappearing behind the front door.

"I love that guy but damn is he clingy sometimes." Ethan unbuckles my helmet, then his own. I feel a brief pang of pity for Steven. This morning, he was an old friend who'd managed to escape the predictability of our lives for a way cooler one. But unbeknownst to him, he is just an annoying interloper who hasn't quite managed to fit in completely. I feel sorry for him, but mostly, I feel angry. As if Ethan hasn't arrived here from somewhere else. As if we all don't spend our lives trying on different hats, playing dress-up, looking for ways to feel closer to our true selves.

I hang my helmet on the bike's handlebars. "You must like him, though, to let him live with you for three months."

Ethan runs his fingers through his hair, shaking it out before flipping it to one side. "So he told you about that."

"He did."

"He had nowhere to go," Ethan says. "Doesn't seem like he has many friends."

"Right," I say, realizing that Ethan mistook my observation as a compliment for his virtuousness.

"Nah, Steven's my guy. I just didn't mean for this to become a three-way."

"What do you mean?"

"I mean I wanted to spend time with you. Jesus. Have I not made it clear? The age gap between us is not that big, is it?"

"Is it?" I smile sheepishly. My face grows hot.

"You're a cutie." Ethan kicks a stray Solo cup. "No wonder Steven's got a crush on ya."

"He doesn't?" Through the diner's big windows, I see Steven slide into a corner booth and prop open an oversize menu. Who checks the menu at diners?

"Come on." Ethan grabs my hand, interlacing his fingers in and out of mine. "You must be used to that, though."

"And you? Why are you single?" I take a step forward. Ethan is so much taller than I am. It feels nice to feel small.

"Never seemed right." Ethan angles his body toward mine. He is close enough now for my nose to graze his chest.

I pull away from him. "We should go inside. Steven's waiting."

"He'll be just fine." Ethan's smile is so lazy, it looks like it might slip off.

I pull back farther. "I'm not, you know. I don't do *that.*"

"You don't do what?"

"Don't make me say it."

"I'm not asking for anything," Ethan says, putting his arm around my shoulders. "Come on, let's get us some food." We walk toward the diner.

Ethan holds the door open for me and we step inside.

"Okay, but what's his *last* name?" My mother is as relentless as I am stubborn.

"I told you already." Her voice to my hangover—nails on a chalkboard. The only thing giving me more grief is the knowledge that I have to see both Ethan and Steven today, in two hours to be exact. I still have the taste of rum in my mouth and the smell of Steven's car in my hair. It's been a while since I had a secret to keep from my mother. Having one over her makes it easier to be nice.

"Tell me again." My mother rests her elbows on the kitchen island in front of me in a show of desperate camaraderie. She blows into her coffee, then sips it.

"I'm not doing this."

"Steven Shami," she recalls. "Okay. Do I know his mother? Does she buy from me? Are they the Shamis that used to live on Bedford . . . the father does accessories?"

"Ma, I have no idea." Yes, I don't say, they are those Shamis. "He was in my class in high school. I told you already."

"Didn't that guy fall off the deep end?" Lucy drags her feet into the kitchen, her skirt sweeping the floor. Even dressed in the de facto yeshiva girl uniform, Lucy looks incredibly sexy and disheveled and cool in a way I could never be.

"You know him?" Our mother's ears grow eight inches.

"I heard of him. He went to, like, a hippie college and got messed up on drugs and whatever, like, I feel bad for his sister. She's my age and she's so normal."

"Steven does not do and never did drugs," I say. This is true.

"Well, when a boy drops you home at one in the morning on a Monday, I like to know a little bit about him," my mother says, reasoning.

"Hold on. Let me get his Social Security number for you real quick." I pretend to text on my phone.

"Why is Steven Shami driving you home at one A.M.?" Lucy's eyes widen. My mother has found an audience.

"Where were you at one A.M.?" I snap back. "Your bed still made?"

"With my *boyfriend.*"

"Please."

"The *doctor,*" she adds.

"I can't right now." I squeeze my forehead.

"Okay, stop," my mother presses, but not hard enough that we actually stop. A fight among sisters means my mother gains more information. Being that we're all *of age,* she'd be a fool to pass up the opportunity.

"Minus the drugs, I actually feel like you guys make a good couple." Lucy draws an air heart with her index fingers.

"You're not getting in the car with someone who does drugs." My mother puts her mug down. "You're not working in an office with someone who does drugs."

I snort.

"Watch how fast you'll quit that job. You want to end up like that girl they found passed out after that wedding?"

"How are you still talking about that? And he doesn't do drugs! *Oh my G-D.*"

"I'm ready." My father appears.

"He does drugs? *Allah ma'ak.*" Sitto follows him in. Does everyone hear everything in this house? "Say your goodbyes."

"Can everyone relax!" I feel the tips of my ears grow hot, a large ball form in my throat, and I will myself not to cry. Don't you dare fucking cry.

On the other side of the kitchen, I hear my mother and Sitto conduct their own private conversation in whispers.

"Shami . . ." Sitto says, connecting the roots of Steven's family tree in her mind.

"Dad, I'm ready when you are."

"You sure you don't want to wear the pencil skirt?" Sitto clocks my outfit, a daisy-printed minidress I'd scored from the clearance rack at Urban Outfitters and my checkered Vans.

"You mean I don't scream marriage material in this?" I do a little twirl.

"Someone's chipper for being so hungover. *Thank you, Steven*," Lucy mutters under her breath.

"Who's hungover?" Mom shoots darts at me.

"Dad, I'm going to be late," I say and grab my bag from the kitchen counter.

"*Hallas*," Dad says and grabs his keys. "This boy Steven—he can take you home again?"

LUCY

Chapter Seven

....

"Hurry up, Lucy, we're going to be late again," Giselle says and picks up the pace, her black low-top Converse barely touching the pavement as she jogs toward the subway station on Sixteenth Street. Giselle and I have been riding the Q train twenty minutes to our high school together since we were freshmen.

"We're seniors now. Who cares?" I check my watch and hustle after her. We pass the Chinese butcher shops with the pigs hanging in the windows and clench our noses shut. The heat traps the smell in the air. They're just beginning to put out the skinned ducks, and the fruit stores are uncovering their bins of shiny apples.

"I care," she says. "I'm not sitting in detention again because someone can't be bothered to set an alarm."

"I despise early minyan." My Central Park West maxi skirt pools around my ankles, cutting my stride in half. I look ahead to see that Giselle is already halfway up the stairs and I can hear the Q train rumbling toward the station. "I can only walk so fast in this thing!"

"So hike it up and run," Giselle shouts and dashes through the subway turnstile as the train comes to a screeching halt.

I bunch up the hem of my skirt and hold the fabric against my knees as I sprint up the stairs after her. My hand-me-down red Kipling knapsack ricochets against my tush. I swipe my unlimited MetroCard and fly through the turnstile, making it into the subway car with two seconds to spare, sweat beading across my hairline.

Inside the car, the air is muggy and still. It's half empty but Giselle and I stand, her back up against the metal pole. I extend the sleeve of my shirt over my hand and wipe my face with it. The fabric smells like cooked onions. Every garment in our house does, thanks to my mother. We are all walking advertisements for her business, the smell of her cooking sticking to us like gum. So much so that the night before my first date with David, I left the clothes I'd wear in a plastic bag outside, changing into them only moments before he picked me up. I grab the pole as the train abruptly pulls out of the station.

"Okay." I take a breath. "Let's go over it one more time. The four *harchakot* during Niddah are, one, no physical contact."

"No physical contact," Giselle repeats. "One."

"Separate mattresses." I hold up two fingers and gather my skirt up with a hair tie so that the hem skims my knees.

"Separate sheets and bedding, too," she adds, "if you want to be legit."

"Right." I roll my eyes.

"Dress modestly in front of your husband. Three," Giselle says. She runs her hands down her own Central Park skirt, the unofficial uniform of our school. I notice that the form-fitting ankle-length skirt is pulling at her thighs, and I can see the outline of her underwear from behind. We've all been having one too many bagels at lunch, but Giselle seems more susceptible to the carbs. Her cheeks are full and round, no matter how skinny she is, and her chest ballooned in fourth grade.

"I can't." I burst out laughing. I can't help but think about Fortune and Nina, who have both taken the very same class, in the very same school, before me. I imagine Nina was contrary and disruptive and Fortune studious and mousy, her head buried in her notebook. Not that I'd ever discussed this information with either of them. Niddah wasn't something any of the women in my family openly discussed, although I can't understand why. Fortune and I are only three years apart, but sometimes it seems like there's an entire generational divide between us.

"I know. *Haj* already." Giselle rolls her eyes. "Like get with the times already."

"Do we think a turtleneck is all it would take for David to stay away from me?" I hope not.

"Legit." Giselle presses her palms together. "Now finish telling me about the date."

"Morning, Howie!" Giselle and I simultaneously greet the security guard, Howie, who is possibly the best, if not the *only*, good thing about walking through the school's doors.

"Girls." Howie tips his bald head toward us and I catch a strong whiff of the cologne he's known to smooth over the place where hair once was. He loops his two thumbs over his belt and nods toward my knees before quickly looking away. "Better fix that. I hear Stern is on one today. I seen her hand out six pink slips and the sun's still rubbing its eyes."

"Shit," I mutter, loosening the rubber band to let the navy stretch material fall sadly back to the floor, where its hem will sweep stray hairballs and safety pins until the dismissal bell rings at five-twenty. "Thanks, Howie."

"Now get in there," he says as we turn away.

As Giselle and I shuffle into the main auditorium with the rest of the senior class, I think about how funny it is that after these past three and a half years hating this building, I'm going to miss this dungeon when I graduate. The yellowing walls, the bathrooms with the pink chipped paint and loose doors. The smell of chlorine. The smell of tuna bagels and stale corn muffins. The *smell*. The narrow stairwells. The basement vending machines (always out of order). The lopsided chair desks and the mountains of chewed gum stuck underneath them. *Torah yeshiva* had its charm, in its own twisted way.

As always, boys go left, girls go right. A *mechitzah* divides us, three large white sheets that hang loosely across a plastic rod. Just a few weeks ago, a ballsy freshman cut a hole in the center of one, an obvious wink to the sex-through-a-sheet thing. As if. When David and I are married I'll buy all of my sheets from Matouk and there will be no cutting holes in the sateen, thank you very much. The kid got a week's suspension and the auditorium got a new Torah, penance from his father. Rather than replace the disgraced sheet, *Torah yeshiva* covered up the hole with an amateurly drawn stop sign that reads, HASHEM DOESN'T GOSSIP AND NEITHER SHOULD YOU.

I spot Mrs. Stern standing toward the back, examining the girls as they fill in each row. As always, her shoulder-length brown wig is slightly askew, arms crossed in front of her. The pink slips she gave out for violations, tardiness, immodesty, talking during Amidah, peek out from the breast pocket of her baby blue collared shirt.

"*Boker tov*, Mrs. Stern." I smile as I glide past her.

"*Boker tov*, Leah," Mrs. Stern says, using my Hebrew name.

"Kiss ass," Giselle whispers when we are out of earshot.

"Eh, Geulah," Mrs. Stern calls out, snapping her fingers.

"Shit," Giselle mutters. She spins around and makes her way to Stern. I follow her.

"Did I ask for the peanut gallery?" Stern looks at me, eyebrows raised.

"Moral support," I say.

"Then you can moral support your friend in detention." Mrs. Stern takes two pink slips from her front pocket and begins to scribble on them. Last year, or even last month, the threat of detention would've rattled me. But since David and I started dating seriously, everything else seems so inconsequential. Stern thrusts one pink slip in my direction and the other at Giselle. "And Geulah, help yourself to a skirt from the front desk bin. You know that color is not allowed." She motions toward Giselle's beige skirt. The light color clearly accentuates Giselle's curves, not to mention her panty lines.

Giselle's cheeks flush. "All of my dark ones were in the wash," she says.

"Go." Stern points her finger toward the door.

"Save me a seat," Giselle whispers and takes the two pink slips from Stern's cold hands. She heads out of the auditorium toward the front desk, where she'll rifle through the lost and found basket of sweatshirts that fall past the knee and navy blue pleated skirts left here for G-D knows how long.

I grab two siddurim from a bridge table and take a seat in the middle of the third row, next to Sari and Freda. I open to the first page, *Modeh Ani,* and the chazan on the boys' side announces that prayers begin in three minutes.

Giselle appears moments later, her curly brown hair gathered into a high bun and fastened with a rainbow scrunchy. She's wearing an ankle-length pleated black skirt that looks like it's been sent straight over from Borough Park. Still, it's better than the black Hefty bags Nina's grade were forced to wear for clothing violations. What I would give to see any of my friends in one of those, a circle cut out at the top for your head.

Giselle slides into the seat beside me. "Wait! Lucy. I want to hear about last night."

"Sh!" I pause for the sound of the boys' prayers to drum up, masking our conversation. Along with probably every girl here, I watch Mrs. Stern take her seat in the front row and bow her head in prayer. Freda and Sari scoot closer. With our knees all draped in the same cotton skirt, our legs look like a navy tufted sofa. We all wear Converse, except Freda, who wears her brown UGGs even though it is late March and the building hasn't switched over to AC yet, and thank G-D for the lack of natural light in here, or else we'd all be roasting like little pigs in a blanket.

"First of all, he is stunning. Like actually handsome, not just community handsome. Even my mother thinks so," Freda says.

"You told your mother!" I smack Freda's shoulder.

"I didn't have to tell her. She *knew.* Hello, everybody knows."

"Legit everybody," Giselle agrees.

"Whatever." I flip my hair over to the side and run my hand through it. It still smells like the keratin treatment I had done a few weeks ago; formaldehyde and heat. I make a mental note to shampoo it tonight before my date. "It's not like it's serious."

"Last night was your fifth—excuse the number—date?" Giselle asks, careful to avoid tempting the evil eye with the number five, which feels silly. I'd like to believe our friendship transcends any jealousy Giselle might harbor over my dating life. I'm not naïve enough to think I won't have to compete with other girls over men, but not my best friends. Still, sometimes it feels like we're sparring countries pitted against one another in a fight over limited resources: eligible bachelors.

"Okay, you guys, so it's a little bit serious." I turn a page in my siddur and my friends do the same. "He asked me to be exclusive last night. Like, we're not going to date other people."

"Ohmyg-d!"

Giselle squeals while Freda punches me. Freda is a puncher, a hand talker, a shover when she gets excited, and blissfully unaware of how forceful an impact her meaty hands can pack. I punch her back.

"Sh!" Sari lifts her chin to catch a glimpse of Stern. "I want to hear. Continue."

"Okay, so basically, we were in his car . . ."

"Doing . . ." Freda rolls her index finger forward like a pinwheel while everyone shushes her.

"So like, we're in his car, just chilling outside of my house after dinner. He took me to this Greek restaurant on the Upper East Side, Milo's. It was amazing, oh my G-D. But the whole community was there. And he knows everybody, so he's like introducing me to a million people. I'm just like, 'Hi, I'm Lucy Cohen. Yes, Sally and Morris's daughter, and no, I don't fry kibbeh, too.' We have the best night. Our waiter doesn't even ID me because he knows David. So obviously I get drunk, which is why I look like a train wreck right now."

"Some train wreck." Giselle rolls her eyes. "Go on."

"So on the way home I'm still like, tipsy. Oh, did I mention I'm an alcoholic now?"

"Love that for you," Freda deadpans.

"Yeah. So basically we're singing along to the radio . . . being cheesy, acting cute."

"Stop." Sari clasps her hands together. "I'm dead."

"Shaking." Freda shivers dramatically.

"Dead. So we pull up to my house and he lowers the music because Sally has a sixth sense for fun, you know. And he turns to me and says that he doesn't want to date anyone else."

"And what did you say?" Giselle demands.

"Obviously I said that neither do I." I put my hands against my cheeks because I'm smiling so hard, just retelling the story.

"Melt," Sari says and sighs. "*Aboose.*"

"And then you guys made out," Freda says, laughing.

"And then we made out," I say. "And I'm seeing him again tonight."

We all rise for the *Amidah*. My heart is racing just from the retelling of last night's story. I feel untouchable, like I hold the keys to some secret box that every student in this auditorium wants access to. We simultaneously take three steps back, then three steps forward, and bow. I smile, thinking about getting changed for our date tonight as soon as I get home. Then we all fall silent in prayer.

When the auditorium erupts with the sounds of *Aleinu* ten minutes later, Freda, Sari, Giselle, and I start to make our way out of the auditorium. Halacha is first period, which means we have only fifteen minutes of study time at breakfast before the quiz Geveret Mizrahi promised us is coming. Freda and Sari rush ahead.

"Save our seats," Giselle shouts as we weave around other students, making our way to the stairwell. "So are you going to invite him to Fortune's wedding? I kind of feel like you have to now, no? Are you still going to go to prom? I have so many questions."

"I definitely have to invite him to the wedding, no? But I was also kind of looking forward to being single at the wedding."

"Lucy, no. Saul's friends suck. Who are you expecting to meet? You already met your *nassib*. The search is over. Roll up the map. Done."

"You're right," I say. As we both start to skip downstairs to the gym, where breakfast is served, I can practically smell the burnt coffee waiting for us.

"Drop him an invitation this week. You're going to invite his parents, too, right?"

"Is that aggressive?" I ask. "Plus the wedding is in, like, a month. They won't be offended?"

"They'll be offended if you don't invite them."

"Yeah? I don't want to seem too eager."

"Trust me, Lucy. My parents run in that circle. This is how it works."

"Fine. And of course I'm still going to prom. I'm not married."

"Yet," Giselle says.

"Whatever."

"You're off the market. What are you so pissed about? The only person who should be mad is Jeffrey and he will be, once he hears that you and David are official."

"Please," I snort. "It's not like it was going to happen between us anyway."

"Tell that to Jeffrey."

"Someone better tell him."

"Someone will," she says, leaping off the final step. "Don't you worry."

The gym's lights cast a dim yellow glow as if they, too, are exhausted by the humdrum routine of yeshiva life. Dozens of freshmen sit on the bleachers by the far end of the gym. They chomp on bagels and blueberry muffins, unburdened by the notion of a calorie and what it might mean for them in another year. I used to eat the same way. Now almost finished with my senior year, breakfast consists of dry Raisin Bran (minus the raisins) or Special K and a black coffee with Splenda. Still, I allow myself one everything bagel with cream cheese a week, usually on

Fridays. My hangover could use a bagel right now, I think, but I hold off, knowing I'm seeing David again tonight.

The left side of the gym is for the sophomores, unofficially, but they'd never dare sit anywhere else. The left side is also closest to the boys' locker room, which smells of dirty pool water and feet but, even so, is a step up from the ass splinters the wooden bleachers will give you. Juniors occupy the right side, seated around rows of bridge tables flanked by white plastic coverings. They're closest to the bathrooms, which is a good or bad thing, depending who you ask. And we seniors get the lounge, which is more of a cordoned-off space outside the gym with a couple of bridge chairs, one deflated beanbag, and a beat-up sofa. It functions more as a way to keep us in the building and out of the nonkosher pizza place down the block. But still, it's ours.

Giselle and I make our way over to the lounge, trays in hands, and pause to watch a group of boys kick around a hacky sack made of tightly wound rubber bands. Their tzitzit dangle sloppily outside of their untucked shirts and their kippot are stuffed into their pants pockets. I try to imagine David as a high school senior but all I see is the David I know, perfectly put together in a slim sports jacket and Tod's loafers. Jeffrey stands in the middle, playing referee of sorts; always the loudest, always the center of everything.

"Oh," he wails, as another boy, Jack, makes a quick save by the grace of his pinky toe. The group erupts in cheers. Jeffrey falls to the floor like he's in a Broadway production of *Hamlet* as the other boys slap Jack on the back. Rabbi Stern, husband of Mrs. Stern, and sure to be on guard wherever fun could be had, confiscates the rubber ball just as Jack is about to take his victory lap. Four seconds later, the group disperses and Giselle and I take our seats on the sofa next to Freda and Sari.

"Idiots," Giselle snorts.

"What's that?" Jeffrey plops his tall and lanky figure onto the arm of the sofa. "Hi, girls."

"Why do you talk to us like you're a sixty-year-old camp counselor who's about to 'accidentally' sideswipe one of our breasts?" Giselle grins and pops a raisin into her mouth.

"*Giselle*," I snort. "My G-D."

"Lucy." Jeffrey ignores Giselle, leaning over her to look at me. He squints his big brown eyes. "Why is your friend so mean to me?"

"Maybe she has a crush on you," I say, only half joking.

"Yeah, right." Giselle smacks me, knowing it's true.

"Giselle, you just let me know when and where." Jeffrey stands back up and swings his backpack over his shoulder.

"And ruin your chances with Lucy?"

"You lose one hundred percent of the shots you don't take." Jeffrey mimes a jump shot.

"Never and nowhere," Giselle says, cheeks burning red. "Now leave, we have to study." She leafs through her notebook.

"Study for what?" Jeffrey says, already walking away. "We're done with this place." He picks up his pace and jumps at least a foot in the air to smack the doorway with his palm as he exits the lounge. "See you in detention?" he shouts.

"He's lucky he's so hot," Sari says.

"He's annoying *because* he's so hot," Freda adds.

Giselle skims her notes. "I bet he asks *that girl* to prom after he dumps Lucy."

I shove Giselle in the shoulder. "Who said I'm getting dumped?"

"It's nothing personal, but everyone knows that guys only ask the girls they want to get with. Now that you have a boyfriend, Jeffrey will probably ask someone else to go with him. Someone easy. That sophomore who got drugged at that wedding." Giselle snaps her fingers as if by magic they'd recall the girl's name.

"Confirmed she was drugged?" Freda's eyes widen.

"Please, she was not *drugged*." Sari rolls hers. "She drank too much. That's it."

"Wait—wasn't she supposed to get shipped off to seminary in Israel?" Giselle asks.

"Nah. The parents always say that when a girl messes up somehow. They have to say something drastic until the hype dies down," Freda explains.

"True." Giselle nods. "Have you seen her? She's cute. There's no way her parents would send her away now. She's about to enter the *market*." Giselle makes air quotes, referring to the dating scene.

"Honey, I think she's already entered the *market*," Sari says. "And I'm not sure anyone's looking to date her."

"Whatever," I say, slightly annoyed at my friends, and myself, for how annoyed I am at this conversation. I don't know if it's because I am sick of talking about this story at home, or if it's the fact that I am dating a thirty-year-old and somewhat removed from the singles scene in which these stories tend to circulate. Or maybe it was both, *and* Giselle's nonchalant certainty that I was about to be prom-dumped. "Anyway, Jeffrey wouldn't ditch me like that. We're friends."

"Yeah, tell him that." Giselle smirks. "Freda, Sari? True or false?"

"True," Sari says, nodding. "Sorry."

"Who cares?" I look through my binder.

"Maybe David will take you," Freda says.

"He could buy us the alcohol," Sari snorts.

"Okay, he's thirty, not fifty." I cross my arms over my chest. I think about David at prom, watching Jeffrey and the rest of my friends make definite fools of themselves, and I shudder. I love our age gap when we're together. I love the safe feeling he gives me, of being taken care of and prized. But every time one of my friends mentions it, David's age goes from sexy and in control to Medicaid. I remind myself that they're just jealous, that any one of them would snatch David up without so much as a batted eye if the opportunity presented itself.

"Oh, we're starting with the Dad jokes? Okay. Because it might be a good idea to have a chaperone . . ." Giselle says, teasing.

"Spend five hours of his life trapped in a sweaty basement bar on the Lower East Side with a bunch of horny high school seniors? I don't think so." I stiffen and Giselle pulls back.

Her eyes widen as she scans the lounge for Rabbi Stern. "*Sh!* The last thing we need is the school finding out where prom is. They'd shut it down faster than Jeffrey's gonna get it up for—*dammit, what's her name again?*"

"Shut up, Giselle," I say.

"Don't worry, Luce, the drunk wedding girl is a sophomore anyway," says Sari. "She can't go to prom."

"She already gave it up. No mystery," Freda says matter-of-factly. "Guys don't like that."

"It's like my mother always says," Giselle says and leans in close. "A girl here messes up, she's ruined for life. But a boy? All he has to do is take a shower."

"Too true." Freda sighs.

"*Hazita*," Sari says, shaking her head.

"Lock David up before a) you mess up somehow, or b) someone else snatches him."

Or c), I think: *I end up like Nina.*

Suddenly the bell for first period rings and the rest of the seniors in the lounge scramble to collect their things.

"Shit." I slam my binder shut. "I'm failing this test."

Giselle stands and swings her backpack over her shoulder. "It's multiple choice. You'll be fine. Just remember, when it comes to the rules of Niddah, go with the strictest answer possible. And *be'hatzlacha*."

"*Be'hatzlacha*." I curtsy, and we head up to class.

Geveret Mizrahi marches up and down each row of desks in the classroom, a hand cupped on each hip. Unlike most of the teachers at this school, Mizrahi seems to actually care what she looks like. She is tall, slim, and wears floral midi skirts that hang elegantly off her middle-aged frame. Mizrahi wears her hair uncovered, and it looks to have been quickly dried with a blow-dryer. Every so often, she gathers it into a loose braid at the nape of her neck, letting it unravel after a few paces up the aisle.

The room is quiet and still, except for when someone smacks bubble gum against their teeth. When that happens, Geveret Mizrahi claps her hands once in the direction of the chewer, and all is still again. I bury my head in the crook of my elbow and try to focus on the test in front of me, but Giselle's words ring in my ears. It was widely understood by pretty much anyone in our senior class that Jeffrey was going to ask me to prom. Would hearing about my relationship with David really change his mind? Or is this just Giselle's passive-aggressive way of getting under my skin? We all know she's harbored a crush on Jeffrey since fifth grade, even though she'd never admit it. I love Giselle, but I wouldn't be surprised if she secretly planned on stealing Jeffrey for herself. Jeffrey, who I call "a thorn in my shoe" *to his face.*

Why am I so hung up on this? I resolve to not spend another iota of mental energy thinking about it. If Jeffrey decides to dump me, so be it. It's not like I'm even remotely interested in him anyway. The nerve of him to even think that I am! What I need to do is focus on my relationship with David, a man, not a boy, who isn't wasting my time. The last thing I want is to end up like Nina, single at twenty-six and in a semipermanent state of self-imposed isolation, a chip on her shoulder the size of my would-be engagement ring. No thank you.

"*Hamesh dakot*," Mizrahi warns. "Five minutes!"

Someone groans in the back, and eighteen no. 2 pencils hurry to complete the quiz before time runs out.

Chapter Eight

....

I scoot the stool away from the small vanity Fortune and I share to get a look at the alarm clock by her bedside—7:08 P.M., twenty minutes before David rings the bell to meet my parents for the first time. Well, Mom, at least. Who knows what time Dad will be home? I can hear Saul yapping away downstairs from up here. It's no wonder Fortune chose him; the man takes up every inch of space in a conversation and Fortune was always more of a listener. Here's hoping they'll be gone by the time David gets here. Doubtful though. These days, in the final countdown to the wedding, Fortune and Saul settle for ordering in and watching movies in the den over going out. They already act like an old married couple. I don't know David *that* well yet, but it's obvious he has a taste for the finer things in life: trendy restaurants downtown, fine dining uptown—he even mentioned in passing that he'd like to take me to some jazz lounge. Giselle said that it sounded like something her grandpa would do. Well, I think it sounds classy. I also think I'll be holding back how much I divulge to Giselle, to all of the girls. It's not like they can relate anyway.

Nobody was as surprised as I was when David asked for my number at Francine's wedding two months ago and then called me the next day. Just kidding, I wasn't surprised at all. But Sitto is always saying that a lack of humility invites *ayin hara* so I'm going to pretend to be modest about the whole thing. The truth is that I looked hot that night, and David was right to take notice.

There are only two things a guy who doesn't feel the need to introduce himself can be: a nobody or a somebody. So I did what Sitto always taught us to do and snuck a glance at his wrist: a Panerai with an army green rubber band. The watch was sporty, elevated, but it didn't give him away entirely. The people around us did. All of the girls within a Cartier love bracelet arm's reach were craning their necks to see who David Bakar was talking to. That person was me.

He would've been just *okay* if he were simply an orthopedic surgeon in training. Impressive, obviously. But our kind of people aren't the "in training" type, a designation more often code for: *He's poor now but he may be rich someday.* Most families want financial assurance *now.* Whether or not your wholesale electronics business will implode in the next three years is irrelevant if you have good Christmas sales. Hey, Brooklyn houses aren't going to afford themselves. But David is the ultimate, because not only is he a soon-to-be professional, but he has the family business to back him as he pursues his very Ashkenazic ambitions. And he is handsome.

But like I said, I knew none of this. And so I was cool as a fucking Persian cucumber.

I dab a makeup brush into my NARS Summer Solstice Cheek Duo and swipe it across my cheekbones, hairline, jawline, and the bridge of my nose. I unscrew the cap on the Benetint liquid blush and paint three dots on each cheek before blotting the rosy liquid into my skin with my index finger. A hint of Maybelline Great Lash Mascara and a drop of concealer beneath my eyes and I'm done. I rifle through Fortune's side of the vanity drawer for the Dior lip oil Mom bought her when she started dating Saul and swipe a layer across my lips.

I run my fingers through my hair like a comb—"mermaid hair," Nina sometimes calls it, although it never sounds like a compliment when she says it. I allow it to hang down my back in clean shiny ripples, a small bend in my front layers to frame my face. Our shower walls stink of formaldehyde, but the smell is a small price to pay for perfectly air-dried hair.

I stand up and swing a tailored black blazer over my bare shoulders. I stole it—and the jeans, charcoal Cheap Monday skinnies—from Nina's closet. Not that she'd find out. Ever since she started this new job, she's never home. I swear, a month ago she was the freaking foyer centerpiece—Mom's right hand in the kitchen and Sitto's at the TV— and now, she's as scarce as lead paint. Honestly, good for her. Even if she is hanging around people she probably shouldn't be. I make a mental note to return the blazer and jeans to her closet when I get home.

To get downstairs, I have to pass Sitto's room. Dad had the walk-in storage closet converted into a bedroom when Grandpa Jack died, and Mom's been complaining that she has nowhere to store extra Bounty ever since. I walk past Sitto's door, which is closed, but the blue light from the TV is flashing under the doorway. The familiar theme music from *Jeopardy!* spills into the hallway. I imagine Sitto asleep in her recliner, the bowl of sesame candies on the small table beside her prepared for visitors, and feel a pang of sadness. As I tiptoe past her room I hear the squeak of her bottom heavy against the edge of the polyester seat cushion. I retreat back to her door and knock gently. "Sitto . . . you up?"

"Come in, *rohi*," Sitto says immediately. As I creak open her door I'm hit with Sitto's familiar scent: quick dry nail oil and butterscotch. Her hair, thinning and overdyed a deep shade of brown, is done up in pink rollers. There's some residual dye along the crown of her head for which her colorist will have hell to pay in the morning.

"Well, don't you look pretty. Are you going out tonight, honey?"

I take a seat at the edge of Sitto's bed and pop a sesame log in my mouth, rolling the syrupy candy around my tongue.

"A date with the doctor, maybe?" she says.

"A date with the doctor. David." I smile.

"We've never had one of those in the family." Sitto stretches her knees out in front of her and winces. "*Hazita,* it wouldn't be the worst thing."

"I'll see what I could do." I wink.

"Inshallah, honey. Just have fun. You're young and beautiful. Don't forget it."

"I won't."

"Before you know it you'll be an old bag with color on her forehead—don't think I didn't notice—just with better jewelry."

"A girl can dream."

"And what of your sister Nina, *hazita.* What are we going to do for her?"

"You're asking *me*?"

"Maybe David has a nice friend for her. She just needs a push." Sitto flings her hands out in front of her.

"I'll ask him, Sitto."

"Do her the favor before your friends ask for themselves. Your sisters come first."

"I don't think Nina wants my help, but—"

"*Fik.* Please. Your sister doesn't know her ass from her elbow. Pass me that box, *rohi.*" Sitto points to a small wood box on the dresser by her bed. She rummages through it for a moment before retrieving a silver ring, a small oval turquoise stone set within it. "Take it." She stretches her hand out toward me. "Wear it on your date tonight."

I take the ring from Sitto and slide it on my index finger. "Now they're really gonna be jealous." I admire the ring in the blue light of the TV.

"No." Sitto shakes her head and one of the rollers comes loose. "Turquoise repels the *ayin hara.*"

Sensing my discomfort, Sitto explains, "The evil eye comes with the territory. The more you have, the more you tempt it. But not to worry, go on your date. Have fun, *rohi.*"

"Thank you, Sit." I get up to give her a kiss on the cheek. "I don't want to be late."

"*Hallas.* And let me know when the doctor plans on meeting me. You know I don't like surprises."

"I will." I laugh. "I promise."

"Leave the door open, honey, *Allah ma'ak.* Bye." She turns her attention back to the TV.

I skip down the stairs, jumping over the last two steps before sticking the landing with a larger-than-expected thud.

"What are you, five!" Nina squeals and jumps back, a giant mug of what I'm certain is that Chinese ballerina laxative tea I hear everyone is using.

"Sorry," I sing. I quickly slide past her.

"Is that my blazer? And my jeans!"

I run into the kitchen, Nina's blazer flying behind me like a magician's cape. "No," I shout.

"I see you, bitch! You can't just *ask?*" Nina darts after me. I round the corner and slide into the refuge of the kitchen, where I find Saul, Fortune, and my mother congregated around the island. I run toward my mother, wrapping my arms around her waist. "Save me," I whimper.

"Oh, you look pretty." My mother strokes my hair. She cups her hands around my shoulders and gently pushes me a few feet away from her. "Let me see you."

"She took my clothes again!" Nina huffs into the kitchen and slams her mug of tea on the island.

"Hey," my mother shouts. "Take it easy."

"I didn't take your stuff." I sidle up beside her.

"Are you joking? I'm looking right at you! That's *my* blazer. Those are *my* jeans!"

My mother looks at me in surprise. "They were in my closet." I shrug.

"So just because something's in your closet, it belongs to you."

"Much better with the heels and jeans look"—my mother nods in approval—"than those tattered combat boots, Nina."

"Take them *off*." Nina grunts. "Now."

"I thought they were mine, Nina, my G-D. Relax! Drink your laxative tea," I say.

"Aren't you going to miss this?" Saul says jokingly to Fortune.

"Shut *up*," Fortune mutters back.

"So now you're a klepto *and* a liar. Mom! Make her take them off."

"What's laxative tea?" Saul asks.

"What's the big deal?" my mother says and sighs.

"I'm not changing. David's coming in five minutes," I plead with Nina.

"It's like detox tea," Fortune whispers to Saul.

"Can I try it?" Saul pats his stomach. "The boys went a little hard on the meats at backgammon last night."

"I don't care if it's midnight and David's about to turn into a pumpkin. Next time, you ask." Nina shoots Mom a look, *right*?

"Nina. Do you need the blazer and jeans *right* now? Are you going somewhere tonight?" my mother asks Nina pointedly, already knowing the answer.

"She's going to Club Nina's Room," I snort, which makes Nina's cheeks flush in turn. I watch her sneak a quick glance at Saul, who is rifling through the pantry.

"So what's the big deal if Lucy borrows some clothes?"

"The big deal is that you're always taking her side." Nina throws a finger in my direction.

"Enough," my mother says.

"And then you wonder why she's a spoiled brat."

"Enough, I said."

"Fine." Nina picks up her tea. "You look like you're going to a funeral for one of your ten cats anyway."

"Before I call your father," Mom yells and slams a hand on the kitchen counter.

"Call him, I dare you," Nina says. She then marches out of the kitchen just as the sound of the doorbell echoes throughout the house. We all stand at attention.

"Oh, I'll get it," Nina yells back into the kitchen.

"Mom," I plead. My mother runs to get the door, but it's too late.

"Hi, David," I hear Nina say as she opens the door. "Just know that Lucy isn't really that nice or smart, but you'll figure that out eventually."

Fortune and Saul look at me, wide-eyed.

"And then she wonders why people think she's troubled," I say to them.

"Sisters." I hear my mother laugh nervously as she ushers him toward the kitchen.

"That's why Fortune's gonna give me sons." Saul gently nudges Fortune as they all enter the kitchen. "Right?"

Fortune laughs timidly.

"You think I didn't want sons?" My mother fills a glass of water and places it in front of David, who thanks her and then quickly takes a sip before placing a hand firmly on my shoulder and squeezing it.

"It's whatever G-D wants." Saul throws his hands up in the air.

"That's right," Mom agrees.

"Hi." A huge grin spreads across David's face as he looks down at me. Without my heels on, he stands a full head and a half taller than me. He looks handsome in his half-zip gray sweater and black jeans, his dark hair cut close to his head.

My eyes meet his. "Hi," I say, smiling back.

David crouches down and kisses me on the cheek. The spot where his lips touch my face feels like it has its own pulse. I feel exposed and vulnerable in the kitchen of my house, where my family's dysfunction is in plain view. Suddenly, I am very afraid of losing David. I need this meet-and-greet to be as short as possible. Another minute here and he may come to the same conclusion that I'm sure half the community has: *I can get anyone, so what am I doing with her?*

"We're excited to finally meet you," my mother says, clearly trying to sound casual. It would almost be better if she didn't try to hide her excitement. "Finally," she adds with a wink.

David chuckles nervously. "I'm sorry it's taken so—"

"Saul." Saul cuts David off and slides in between him and my mother, thrusting his hand out.

"Nice to meet you, man," David says, shaking it. He peeks over Saul's shoulder. "And I'm guessing this is Fortune?"

"Hi," Fortune says, smiling sweetly.

"*Mabrook.*" David pats Saul on the back. "Lucy tells me the big day is soon, no?"

"*Fadal,*" Saul answers. "We'd love to see you."

"That's up to this one." David gently squeezes my hand.

"We'll see how tonight goes," I joke.

My mother clears her throat. "Of course you'll come!" She rifles through the *crap* drawer beneath the kitchen counter and pulls out her Rolodex. "I was just going to ask for your mother's address." Her pen is locked and loaded, pressed against a free sheet of paper. "Oh, actually, don't tell me. I definitely delivered to her a couple of times." She snaps her fingers. I admire her acting skills. She, I, and the four walls are very aware that she knows damn well where David's parents live.

"Corner of—" David starts to say.

"Ocean and S. Right." She scribbles David's parents' names and address into her Rolodex. "Who is she buying her *mazza* from now, if you don't mind me asking?"

"Mom," I say, shooting a horrified glance in her direction.

"What? I can't ask?"

"Of course you can," David says, laughing. "I honestly have no idea."

"It's good business to know who your competition is." Mom crosses her arms.

"To be honest, I haven't been home for Shabbat in a couple of weeks. But I did notice the kibbe's been slipping." David squeezes my hand behind his back.

"Just wait until Boreka opens up across the street." My mother nods toward the window. "A whole new generation will grow up on defrosted kibbe."

"Be careful, you're starting to sound like Sitto," I say.

"From what you tell me, that doesn't sound like such a bad thing." David crosses his arms over his chest and grins.

"I like this one," Mom says, wagging a finger in David's direction.

"Nothing beats your kibbe, Ma," Saul says.

Ma? The kitchen falls silent for ten seconds, as we all contemplate the fact that Saul and Fortune aren't even married yet and he's already calling Mom *"Ma."* Saul always comes off a bit desperate for affection, but this is fresh.

"I've never had a boy call me Ma." Mom places her hand against her heart.

"Was that weird?" Fortune asks.

"Why should it be weird?" Mom looks at her, aghast.

"Now, a month from now, what's the difference?" Saul watches David carefully. He seems to be ready for approval or a battle. David doesn't give him either.

"I guess." Fortune refills the glass in front of her.

"You know my mother expects you to call her Mom when *we* get married, right?" Saul raises an eyebrow at Fortune.

"Right when we get married?"

"The second my heel hits that glass," Saul says, a bit more seriously.

David looks at his watch. "Honestly, I can sit here all day but our reservation is in twenty. We should get going." He places his hands on my lower back and I feel a chill run up my spine. "It was great meeting all of you."

"It was nice to have you come inside." My mother winks and follows us toward the door.

"Where are you guys going?" Saul's close behind.

"We're going to that new place on West Broadway, Libertine?" David opens the door slightly. He's playing nice, but I can tell he wants to leave.

"Libertine, yea. Nice." Saul nods. "I heard that place is hot. How'd you get a reservation? You know a guy? I'm hoping Forch and I stop eating out once we're married. Go full kosher, less confusing for the kids in the long run."

"All right, guys," Fortune says, grabbing Saul's hand and gently pulling him back. "Let's let them go. They'll be late."

"Of course." Saul opens the front door wider and we step out into the cool air. "Don't bring her home too late!"

When we're out of earshot and in David's car, we both take a breath before he starts the car up. "Oh my G-D," I say. "He's usually a lot, but that was another *level.*"

David leans his head back and lets out a big laugh. "That guy is what we call a *dahak.*"

"You could say that." I catch my reflection in the side mirror, making sure my makeup is still intact.

"So." David runs his fingers up my arm and I feel every lasered follicle where there should've been hair stand to attention. "How'd I do?" He tilts his head to the side innocently.

"Have you been practicing?"

"Only a little," he says, tucking a strand of hair behind my ear. "You look pretty."

"So do you." I close my eyes in anticipation of his kiss but instead David asks how the quiz was. My stomach does a premature summersault. How cute of him to remember that I had that quiz today. But also, how lame to be reminded of the fact that we are over ten years apart, and I still have to deal with high school BS.

"It was fine," I say, hoping to change the subject.

"Fine? Because I expect only A's of my girlfriend."

"Right, because I'm your girlfriend." I tip my head sideways. "I forgot."

"No you didn't." David leans across the middle console and kisses me, deeply. His hand is still in my hair, and he pulls it gently, as if he needs all of me. I've only kissed one other boy before, but I know David is a good kisser. It is the kind of kiss that I wish I could swallow or bottle and save. I place my hand on his clean-shaven cheek and lean farther into him. To my surprise, I gently bite his lower lip. David twirls the bottom of my hair around his finger and pulls away slightly, his face inches from mine.

"You don't know how much I hate to say this, but we should probably stop." He gestures his eyes toward my house, which we were still parked in front of.

"Oh my G-D, you're right. Saul's probably peeking through the window."

"One thousand percent." David buckles his seatbelt and I do the same. He signals before peeling away from the curb and heading up Ocean Parkway toward the Prospect Expressway. I feel a rush of exhilaration as we head toward the Battery Tunnel and closer to the city. David places one free hand over mine and I lace my fingers through his. His hand feels solid, steady, and makes my own feel small in comparison. I could get used to this feeling.

I consider asking David to bypass dinner entirely and head straight to his apartment, which he'd casually mentioned was in Greenwich Village on our last date. But I don't want to seem like a slut. *And there's still a game to be played,* I remind myself. David is into me now, of course, but guys like him can turn on a dime. I can't give it all away, not even half. I slide my hand out from under his and fidget with the radio.

"Two hands on the wheel, mister," I say, settling on the KTU station.

We emerge from the tunnel and stop at the red light that brings us onto the West Side Highway. David turns his head and looks at me. There's a hint in his eye that says he wants to skip out on dinner, too. I try not to focus on how good he looks, the dimple on the left side of his cheek, his broad shoulders. I try to picture him in his blue scrubs instead. No luck.

"What?"

"Eyes on the road." I say, nodding toward the green light.

"Whatever you say." David steps on the gas.

FORTUNE

Chapter Nine

....

"What's this?" My father sits on a stool at the kitchen island, hunched over a bowl of Wheaties, the breakfast cereal for America's champions. My mother and I leaf through a pamphlet of rhinestone-embellished tiaras given to us by the lady who sells the head-pieces. My mother points to one and I shake my head no. *Too much.*

"What's what?" my mother asks in return. My father slides the month's Amex statement across the laminate countertop to her. He'd circled a charge for $342.79 in thick black marker.

"Oh that." My mother wipes an invisible coffee ring from the counter. "Something for the swanee," she says.

"The swanee!" A half-ingested wheat flake catapults from my father's mouth and onto the counter. My mother wipes it off just as quickly.

I contemplate leaving the kitchen. I'm in no mood to bear witness to yet another fight that revolves around my and Saul's wedding and the financials of it.

My mother pretends to busy herself at the stove. "You know, the party that our future *consuegros* are throwing tomorrow, where they will present your daughter with beautiful things for herself and her home and we're expected to do the same for their son?" Mom looks at me and widens her eyes as if to say *Back me up here, Fortune.* But I say nothing. I haven't even told her that Dad has stopped paying me a salary. Instead, he claims, he is funneling all of my would-be-earned money into the wedding. I guess I can't argue with that.

"I know what a swanee is," my father mimics. "What I don't know is what the boy needs for three hundred fifty dollars?" *The boy.* He taps angrily at the charge on the paper.

Sometimes when Dad speaks, I swear it's Sitto talking. They share a tongue, the frustration at their adopted language biting at each word.

"Three hundred fifty dollars?" Sitto shuffles into the kitchen, her Propet-pedic walking shoes sweeping the floor. Her pink cotton nightgown hangs loose around her doughy frame, laying bare an impressive network of varicose veins and liver-spotted skin, weathered but tough.

"Nothing, Ma. Don't worry about it," Dad says. He leans farther toward the bill, then back again. Then forward again, as if the problem is his range of vision and not the numbers on the statement. As he rocks forward and back, the gold rope chain around his neck dips in and out of the cereal bowl, as though it were a fishing rod that might catch some cash.

"I don't worry. And don't worry, too, you. Your wife should buy nice things. Your father, *alav hashalom,* always bought me nice things."

We all know this isn't true. But people change in death and my grandpa had become a saint after his. Sitto hobbles over to the stove and reaches for the small copper coffeepot. She boils water and pours two spoonfuls of Turkish beans inside. Waits for it to boil.

"It's not for me, Ma," Mom clarifies. "It's for Saul. A gift for the swanee tomorrow."

"Ahh, for the swanee, inshallah." Sitto clicks her teeth. "G-D always provides when you need it. But, I'm curious, what he needs for three hundred fifty dollars?" The coffee in the pot begins to bubble and she lowers the flame. She drops three spoonfuls of sugar inside and stirs slowly, until a thin layer of foam forms on top.

"It's different now, Ma. It's not like it was when Morris and I got married," Mom says. She glares at my father, waiting for his gaze to meet hers. But his eyes remain fixed on the bill. The reading glasses he bought from the drugstore near Mr. Cheap hang by the tip of his nose.

My mother lets out one of her deep, exhausted sighs. "I don't mean our swanee wasn't beautiful, but they spend a lot now. And it's worse for the boy's parents. Michelle's son—"

"Which Michelle?" Sitto interjects.

"Jijati. My fr—"

"Wife of Gabe?"

"No, the other one. Married to Nate . . . You know . . ." Dad snaps his fingers, recalling, "Lizette's son."

I toss the pamphlet aside and grab two small coffee cups from the cabinet, handing them to Sitto.

"Ahhh, son of Lizette." Sitto nods, the connection nodes firing off in her brain. "The one who gave problems, *hazita* Lizette. The wife left, no? *Ya haram* . . ."

"I don't know, Ma," my mother says, cutting her off. "I was just telling your son that Michelle was telling me . . . forget it, it's not the point. But she's paying an arm and a leg for the girl's swanee. Her son is marrying some high-up and it's Chanel this and Vuitton that. She's *mooting, hazita*, running up and down Fifth Avenue like a paperboy."

"Well, bite off more than you can chew." Sitto shrugs as if to say, *To hell with Lizette*. "The girl's family . . ." She makes a mental calculation. "They have *floos*?" Sitto rubs her thumb and middle finger together.

"Mafi *floos*," Dad confirms. "Loaded."

"Then let her parents buy her a nice layette for the honeymoon and *fik*. Leave the boy alone." Sitto fills one of the cups with Turkish coffee and places it in front of my father. "Your generation, they only want to impress each other. Why lie about what is in your pocket? Your father, *alav hashalom*, didn't have a pot to piss in. *And* he wanted my sister! *Hallas*, I still married him."

A saint.

"It's the truth," Sitto continues. "This country has spoiled you. All of us. We have everything here and still we want more. The kids are not happy, *yanni*. In Halab, we do everything by hand," she says, using the traditional name for Aleppo, where she'd raised her family. "We want sweets, we make by hand. We want milk? We go to the goat. We bake the tomatoes on the roof of the house all day in the hot sun, and afterward we make the paste. Not this"—she motions toward a can of tomato paste by the stove—"this aluminum *chada*. No. *Tsk*, we have everything we need in Halab; the fig, the pistachio, the date—you won't believe the dates . . ."

"Sit down, Ma." Dad pulls out the chair next to him but Sitto doesn't sit. The three of them continue to talk about me as if I'm not there. Which is how it feels most days lately, as the wedding draws nearer. I don't know what's worse, having to listen to their opinions or being asked what I think.

"Your friend Michelle and her husband, who disrespects his mother, by the way"—Sitto snaps her fingers—"they think money make a good *nassib*. Rolex. Cartier. Prada. A boy should work! Instead, his poor parents spoil the girl. So she has the Louis Vuitton luggage—but no money to travel!" Sitto slaps her knee as if this is the funniest thing she's ever said and fills a cup for herself. She dunks a kaak inside, allowing the semolina cracker to come up for air once it's soggy and saturated with caffeine. She takes a bite and a sip.

"Sit, Fortune," my father says, acknowledging my presence for the first time. I do as I'm told.

"You know what your Jido got me when he proposed?" Sitto asks.

"What, Sitto?" I indulge her, even though I can see what's coming next from a mile away.

"Nothing." She makes a zero with her fingers. "We got engaged seven days after meeting, because he had to go back to Damascus, and as his wife, I had to go with him. In Damascus, we have a house but no furniture, because every day Jack promises me that the next day will be the day we finally go to America. We lived in Damascus nineteen years with no sofa, *ya haram*. My back still hurts." Sitto shakes her head, remembering.

"*Haje*. Enough about me." Sitto pops another kaak into her mouth, whole. "So tell me, Sally, what did you buy him? *Adami* boy, Saul. He deserve the best, G-D bless."

Sitto wouldn't notice the line in the sand if it had been drawn in lamb's blood.

"A wallet," my mother conceded. "From the outlets at Woodbury Common. On sale!"

Dad flings the *New York Post* on the table. "Three hundred fifty for a wallet." He nearly chokes on his spoon. "Shhooor! Grab it," he says, and flings his hands upward, grabbing at the thin air above him. "The money grows on trees, Sally!" His fingers open and close around the space above his head. "Just take it!"

"*Shht*, Morris." Sitto smacks his shoulder with her free hand. "Don't be cheap!" She hands me her empty mug. "Inshallah, it should always be kept full. The wallet."

"What should always be kept full?" Nina walks into the kitchen, flicking on every light as she makes her way to the water cooler. She's dressed for work in her usual uniform of skinny jeans and a T-shirt. I feel a pang of jealousy for the life Nina is living. It seems like she's actually done it. She's managed to "get out" or whatever. It was easy to dismiss her when she was angry and not doing anything about it. When we could all regard her outbursts and contrarian opinions as compensation for the sad and lonely life she was living, spending all of her time at home in the kitchen with Mom. But ever since she started this job a couple of months ago, she's had a quiet confidence about her. Less to prove, I suppose.

"*Ca'an the money grows on trees,*" Dad mutters under his breath. "Good morning, daughter!" He clears his throat.

"*To you, too.*" Nina feigns sweetness.

"Your stomach, *rohi*. It should always be full," Sitto says. She pushes the plate of kaak toward Nina. "You look sick. Eat. She looks too thin, Sally"—and then back to Nina—"Eat."

"You know they don't listen to me," my mother says.

Nina rests her chin on Sitto's shoulder. "Can you not put so much sugar in the coffee, you know it's what kills you in the end."

"*Kisa amak!*" Sitto shoos Nina. "Leave me alone."

"It's true, Ma," Dad concurs. "They say it's the worst thing. The sugar."

"For you, maybe. All those injections make you weak."

"He has diabetes, Ma," my mother says.

"He does not have the diabetes," Sitto replies.

"He does, Ma. The doctor put him on some diet. You should check yourself—"

"Just like his father, *alav hashalom,* had, too. And my husband was an ox, B'H."

"Yes, Ma, but Morris, he has it."

"He is good. My Morris. Healthy, G-D bless him."

"They're all good, I think. They're all good until they're lying in a hospital bed and then it's, *Could you believe that shmuck missed the diagnosis?*"

"So, when's the thing starting tomorrow?" Nina stands in front of the refrigerator. "Do I *have* to go? I'm missing the entire morning of work. It's just so unnecessary. No offense." Nina shrugs at me.

"The music industry will survive, I'm sure," my mother says.

"Don't look at me," I say.

Suddenly Lucy skips into the kitchen. "Check mine!" She saddles up beside my father, who is pricking his finger with his newest toy, a blood sugar monitor he'd ordered online.

"*Hara,*" he scoffs. "Piece of shit, this thing." He tosses it aside.

"Well, you're eating frosted Wheaties, Dad!" Nina yells.

"Take!" Sitto pushes the plate of kaak farther across the kitchen island.

"Check mine, Dad," Lucy pleads. "Do it."

"Does Mr. Bakar want to make sure he's making a good investment?" Nina winks and slams the refrigerator door shut. "Now that it's *official.*" She sidles up beside Lucy.

Nina's skin looks extra fair next to Lucy's. Mom says that when Nina was a baby, people would frequently ask, *Where did this one come from?* Her eyes were light to match her skin, hazel flecked with orange and green. Her hair, well who could remember what her natural hair color was. She changes it so much. At the moment, it is so black it borders on purple. She'd been blond as a baby, and for a moment it seemed like her eyes might be blue. She was a marvel to our family. Aunts and uncles fawned over her Ashkenazi looks, each of them fighting for a stake in her genetic code. ("My mother's two brothers had blue eyes!") Lucy and I share the same olive skin and brown hair and yet we couldn't look more different. Lucy's confidence lends her an appeal that I'm not too proud to admit I'll never have.

"Can we even afford another wedding?" Nina says seriously.

"Of course we can, if it comes to that." My mother eyes Lucy adoringly. We all knew we'd sooner mortgage the house than let David slip away.

"Why would you even say that, Nina?" Lucy pinches the edge of her middle finger and blood balloons beneath the surface. "Don't be jealous." Lucy winces as Dad pricks her finger.

"Jealous of what?" Nina lifts a mug to her face. "David is old enough to be your dad. It's creepy."

"Isn't he around your age?" Lucy cocks her head to the side and grins. She holds up the machine. "Ninety-eight. That's good, Dad, no?"

"G-D gives you what you need when you need it," Dad says, to himself more than to any of us.

"Amen," Sitto nods.

"Now do hers." Lucy waves the device in Nina's face.

"Get out of my face." Nina smacks Lucy's hand away.

My father buries his head back into the *Post*, but I can tell he isn't reading. Three daughters means three weddings, but that pressure is nothing in comparison to what he'd have with sons. Daughters stay with you, but they ultimately become someone else's financial responsibility. The more sons a man has, the faster his business must grow to accommodate them and their families. The task of marrying us off mainly falls on my mother. We all know it keeps her up at night. Nina would say she was preoccupied by it. *"Obsessed,"* even.

My mother's usual response:

"I've seen what happens to girls who slip through the cracks. My own sister! Her eggs expired long before they had the chance to hatch. Now she lives alone in our mother's vacant house. I don't want that for my girls! A job can get you far, but having children makes you immortal."

I suddenly feel nauseated. I chalk it up to too much coffee on an empty stomach and nerves about the party tomorrow. But there's something I can't get out of my head, something my mother said to me off-handedly while she needlepointed the *kuracha*—the bag Saul would use for his tefillin and tallit. She said, "Love is something that grows as you build a life together." Sometimes the shape it takes doesn't fill a heart. Sometimes love looks more like a triangle, or a hexagon. Sometimes it doesn't take shape at all, and instead looks more like a scale, tipping slowly from one side to another or as mercurially as early spring weather.

Whatever your love may look like, the job of sustaining it always falls squarely on a woman's shoulders.

But it's a love all the same. "Trust me," she insisted. "I know."

"Fortune! Hello." I snap out of it to find my mother's face inches from my own, the smell of coffee and Sensodyne heavy on her breath. "What's with you today?"

"Sorry." I shake my head.

"Did you hear me? I said Betty is coming to do makeup tomorrow at eight in the morning. She'll start with you."

"Right," I manage. "Right, yeah. Okay."

"I'm not getting mine done," Nina says defiantly.

"I'll go after Fortune," Lucy says. "Wait. Am I supposed to invite David to the swanee?"

"No," Nina and I say in unison.

"I don't think that's necessary, honey," my mother says, softly. "It's just family. Plus, we don't want to seem eager. Those types of people get turned off by that."

"What types of people?" Lucy says. "Sounds terrifying coming out of your mouth."

"Oh, shut up, Lucy. You know you got one of the good ones," I say half jokingly. "And right when he came back, too."

"What do you mean, came back?" Lucy asks. "Where did he go?"

"I mean like, to the city, you know? Doing that whole thing. School, girls outside the community, whatever."

"So important for a man to do that. Better when they're young and single than to wake up married with children and feel stuck. It happens, you know." My mother opens the can of tomato paste near the stove. I feel a pang for Saul, knowing that if he decided to take a no doubt sin-ridden sabbatical from the community to sow his oats, my mother might've dissuaded me from accepting that first date. But David does it, and it's like he spent five years building houses with Habitat for Humanity.

"G-D." Nina practically yanks the refrigerator door from its hinges. "The double standard is just too much."

"Excuse me?" my mother says, baffled by Nina's reaction. Lucy and I eye each other, braced for a fight.

"First of all, if David were another guy, a guy with no name or family money, you would not feel as sunny about his little spring break." Nina's voice drips with disdain while I try to hide the part of me that likes it. "You'd say he was lost or—and I'm *sure* you've used this phrase before—off the deep end."

"Did you miss the part where David went to *medical school*?" Lucy stresses.

"Second of all," Nina continues, ignoring Lucy, "if a girl did the same exact thing, took some time to live on her own in the *city* and *outside the community* doing *G-D knows what,* she'd be marked for trash quicker than a carton of expired eggs."

"Here we go with the word-twisting and assumptions." My mother waves her hand dismissively.

"Are you really going to deny what I just said?"

"So go!" My mother shoos Nina, who bolts from the fridge like a scared cat. "Live your life! Who's stopping you?"

"Actually, I am living my life," Nina says, regaining her calm. "I'm not waiting around."

"Oh, by the way—did you hear that your old friend got engaged? Joyce. The one who sells the exercise clothes."

"Good for her!" Nina tries hard not to crack.

There aren't many single girls left in her age group as it is, and news of another pairing is a not-so-gentle reminder of one's own solitude. Kind of like visiting an old age home and being reminded of your mortality. It stings, even if Nina won't show it.

"Sally!" Nobody noticed Sitto leave the kitchen. My dad seems to have made an early exit, too. But now Sitto's voice booms through the house. It's been this way since Dad taught her to use the home intercom. A dangerous weapon for a woman who has limited mobility and a desire to be everywhere at once. "My appointment is for nine-fifteen! You can take me now, no?" It isn't a question.

"Yes, Ma," Mom shouts back. "Girls, I'm taking Sitto for her manicure. Do any of you need one? I know Fortune got one. Lucy and Nina, I can have Kim squeeze you in."

"I don't get it," Nina huffs. "The swanee is just us and them, no? Why are we going all out? You think his family is going all out for *us*?"

"They're nice people." My mother skirts the question.

"Are we not nice people?"

"Just be happy for once," Lucy chirps. "You attract the energy that you put out, Nina. Remember what the rabbi told you." Lucy is referring to a "talk" Nina recently had with the rabbi. Mom made Lucy and me swear up and down we wouldn't tell Nina she's told us. But Lucy never was one to keep promises.

"You *told* her?" Nina pushes a stool back angrily.

"She overheard. I didn't tell her anything," my mother lies.

"That's so shitty, Mom. I didn't even want to go to that stupid meeting. I did it for Dad, because he asked me, because he couldn't take *you* bothering him about me anymore."

"Enough, Nina." Mom shoots daggers at Lucy.

"Oh my G-D. Guys. Stop." I carry my empty mug to the sink and begin to wash it.

"Maybe if you spent half the energy on me as you did them"—Nina thrusts a finger toward Lucy and me—"I wouldn't have so many problems! But no, I didn't bring home a boring fiancé or a rich boyfriend, did I?"

Mom cringes at the accusation. "I just ask that you don't bring home a Reform."

"Or an Ashkenaz," Nina yells.

"They have a different way."

"Or a redhead!"

"They have skin issues."

"Or a student," says Nina.

"How will he support you?"

"Or a divorcé!"

"They come with baggage."

"Or a convert!"

"Your children will never marry!"

"A woman?"

"Fine! Bring me the redhead, then!"

"Yalla, Sally." Sitto waddles back into the kitchen, large pink curlers set in her hair. "We have to go. If we get there late, Kim will put me with someone new and you know how they get—no patience with the cuticles."

Before entering the Dwecks' living room, where the swanee is set up, I make a run for the powder room. I close the door and flick on the lights. I suck in my cheeks and bite them, creating the cheekbones I definitely don't have. I feel like a little bit of a joke, with my smokey eyes and painted-on lips, like a baby doll left alone in a room with a toddler and her mother's makeup. I feel like someone else, like a person begging to be looked at. Maybe that's how I should feel. I shut the lights and walk toward the living room to greet Saul and my future in-laws.

"I see your father isn't too familiar with Lalique." Marie, my MIL, nudges me in the ribs. We watch in horror while my father fondles an ornate vase with a devil-may-care attitude. He stands next to Saul's father, whose distressed expression tells me he definitely knows a thing or two about Lalique, or at least how much it costs. The MIL saunters over to gently take the vase from my father's grip and I follow her.

"And you know," my father says, paying no mind to me or Marie, "the rabbi made an excellent point in shul yesterday, an *excellent point.*"

"I think I heard this," Saul's father says in return, stroking his stubbled chin. "I think I heard this, but tell me."

"Of course you heard it, because everyone's talking about, because it was brilliant." My father lets his assessment of the rabbi's speech hang in the air for a moment. "What he said was this, he said: *When unfortunate things happen to a child in this community, every single parent clutches his or her pearls, so to speak. What do I mean by this? I'll tell you. When a mother hears gossip about another woman's daughter, what does she say? Hopefully nothing, right? But I'm realistic, so let's be honest. She probably says, 'I'm so happy that wasn't my daughter.' And if she doesn't say it out loud, I can tell you without a shadow of a doubt that she's thinking it.*"

"Without a shadow of a doubt," Saul's father agrees. "Was that not the first thing you said, Marie? When we heard the story about that girl?"

"I'm not too proud to admit that it was." Marie crosses her arms over her chest.

"Of course it was," my father assures her. "What? You don't think my wife said the same thing? But this is exactly what the rabbi was explaining. That our natural, *gut* response isn't necessarily the correct one." My father pounds his fist against the display table as if he is at the podium, rattling the vase and making Marie grimace. "What do I mean by this?" he continues. "Instead of saying to ourselves *Thank G-D that wasn't my kid* or *My kid would never do that,* we should be saying *If only that was my kid!*"

"Right." Saul's father strokes his chin. "Right, I definitely remember hearing this."

"So we were all confused like, Why is the rabbi saying this? You know, where's he going with this? And then he makes the brilliant point. He says that when unfortunate things befall our children, whether it be something serious, or they're the center of gossip, that is *Hashem* speaking through these children. *Hashem* chose that child as a vessel to communicate with us. To show us that we have strayed. To show us the better path."

"Right." Saul's father taps his foot. "Right. Wow. Wow."

My father goes on. "You see, it's not that He doesn't love that child, or the parent of that child. He *loves* that child!"

"Got a funny way of showing it," Marie snorts.

"He loves that child so much he decided to use her to show the rest of us how we can get better—how the kids these days have deviated from the path, and how negative the consequences can be."

"I'd still rather He 'communicate' through someone else's child." Marie holds her hands up. "That girl's reputation is ruined. *Haram.* No mother is going to want that for her son."

"I think you're missing Morris's point, honey," Saul's father says.

"Oh no, honey, I got his point. And I'll make it even more simple. I didn't have a sip of alcohol until I was married. Until that ketubah was signed, sealed, and delivered. The girls today want to be fast and loose? Well, there's a price to be paid. My mother would've given me the belt and a broom, but this girl got a first-class ticket to Jerusalem. Please." Marie snorts.

We all stand in silence. Even my father wouldn't dare contest Marie. Finally, he says, "Marie and I were brought up the old-fashioned way. There was no room for mistakes in Halab, no?" He chuckles.

"Let's get to it." Marie wraps her arm around my hip. "This day is about Fortune and Saul."

Saul's father stands at attention. "*Hallas,* come. My wife worked so hard! Morris—cigar?"

Marie leads me away from the men and toward the far end of the display table. "Look at you." She squeezes my hand "You're over-whelmed, *hazita.* I almost remember what it feels like to be your age."

The Dwecks' living room is divided in two, Saul's gifts displayed on the right, mine on the left. The swanee, a small party in which the bride and groom are showered with presents from their future in-laws, is underway. Saul crosses the room to embrace me and we walk to the center of the room.

"We have to," Saul whispers, and we both turn toward the photographer. Saul looks handsome in his navy blue sports jacket and chinos. He takes the photographer's direction and looks into my eyes, smiling. We both freeze our expressions as the photographer clicks away. I try not to pay too much attention to the cracks in Saul's lips.

"I love your makeup, by the way" Saul says through his grin. "Unlike you to go so . . . bold."

"Is it too much?"

"Hold it just three more seconds," the photographer urges.

I quickly smooth the hem of my dress, a white Missoni mini that my mother had scored from the sales rack at Saks a few months ago.

The photographer breaks to look at his footage. "I want to get the dads next. Dads!" he belts into the air. I take a deep breath. The Dwecks' living room smells like it's been bathed in artificial gardenia.

"This photographer's the best," Marie whispers to me, then gives him a thumbs-up. "But between me and you, he says your mother didn't call him for the wedding?"

"He was booked," I lie. "But we got someone just as good." And half the price, I don't add.

"I don't doubt that." Marie gestures for me to follow her.

"Go." Saul smiles. "My mother worked *very* hard."

Marie leads me to her side of the living room. The furniture has been cleared out of the space to make room for the two elongated tables on either side.

"I want my side to tell a *story.*" Marie draws an imaginary box in the air as she stands proudly in front of the showcase she set up for me. The Lalique vase my father had been admiring stands proudly in the center, housing four white orchids. To its right and left are two twin Christofle silver cake stands and, in front of them, a matching bowl filled with white lebes—sugar-glazed Jordan almonds. Sitto sidles up beside us and fills a FORTUNE AND SAUL monogrammed cocktail napkin with some. She pops a few in her mouth.

"They're part of the display, Sitto," I say, horrified.

"Nonsense," Marie says. "They're good luck. Make sure Nina and Lucy bring some home. Especially Nina."

Sitto raises her eyebrows.

Where is Nina? A momentary panic settles over me as I realize I haven't heard or seen her since we arrived. I feel bad for thinking she might be up to no good when I spot her by the dessert table, engaged in conversation with Saul's oldest sister.

"Come." Marie puts her hand on my back. "I want to show you the rest." Marie leads me down the elongated table toward the end. She'd scattered paper snowflakes across the white tablecloth and sprinkled silver glitter on top. "Butter." She picks up a pair of leather gloves, before moving on to a Moncler hat and scarf.

"It's too much to take in," I say, and I mean it. "I don't even know what to say."

"Just enjoy it," Marie says. "These things will take you far. Inshallah soon Saul will be able to afford to buy you everything you desire and more, but until then . . ." She waved a hand across the table like a game show host getting ready to do a big curtain reveal.

"Let's get a photo of Fortune with the Chanel?" The photographer motions to the centerpiece with one hand. "Marie?"

Marie picks up the pièce de résistance, a large quilted classic black Chanel bag. "Is she going to freak or is she going to freak?" She hands it to Saul, who snakes the gold chain over my head.

"Oh my G-D," I manage.

"Let's get a few shots of Fortune holding the bag," the photographer repeats.

I turn my hips toward the photographer. He places my left hand over the front of the bag and fans out my fingers. He takes a close-up of my ring and the bag. He handles both like a newborn baby. I simultaneously want to please and kill this man. Suddenly, without warning, the image of Isaac lighting a cigarette behind his father's store flashes across my mind. I imagine him making a mockery out of this whole thing. I wonder what he'd think if he saw me in my white Missoni dress, taking direction from a first-rate photographer. I hate myself for caring.

I push the thought out of my mind when I see Marie watching me out of the corner of my eye.

The swanee is a delicate dance. You're expected to admire, to ogle, to give thanks like you just jumped the list of patients awaiting a kidney transplant. You want to be gracious without seeming phony, impressed but not destitute. As the gift giver, you want it all to seem like no big deal. As if you didn't fight with your husband every day over a recent charge, as if the Loro Piana summer loafers you bought for your daughter's fiancé were par for the course and not the reason we downgraded from Charmin Ultra to Scott.

"That's enough." I feel a hand on the small of my back and breathe a sigh of relief as Marie dismisses the photographer. "Go get a few shots of the dessert. Let Fortune enjoy." Marie hands me a flute of champagne and I clink my glass with hers. I'm guessing it's her third or fourth.

"You outdid yourself, really. I don't deserve all of this." I feel my cheeks blush as I run my fingers across a white satin robe with BRIDE written across the back in glittering silver rhinestones.

"Of course you do." Marie takes a sip of her champagne. "Any girl who is going to be with my son does."

"Thank you." I scan the room for my mother but she's nowhere to be found.

"It's nothing." Marie waves. "All of this stuff is great, sure. Don't believe a woman who tells you she doesn't need things. We are all materialistic at our core, there's no shame in that. A designer pocketbook here, a piece of jewelry there. I trained my husband well. He knows better than to come home from work on a Friday without a bouquet of flowers. Saul's witnessed all of this and I know he'll do right by you.

But you need to do right by him, too. Saul will try his best to provide for you, and in return, you will make him a home."

I nod along, knowing that there are so many young women who would kill for this sort of plainspoken assurance. My mind wanders back to the young girl at the wedding, which it has been doing lately. I'm sure she, of all people, would kill to hear all of this. So why do I find myself envying her?

"And don't mistake me." Marie shakes her head. "This isn't as simple as making the beds and cleaning the toilets—although a man should never come home to a dirty house. But those things come second to what I am talking about. I am talking about the *suffeh*—the essence of the home. You, and only you, are responsible for this. It's the smell of the food on the stove and the sound of children at your door. It's the Shabbat spirit that lingers from Friday through Saturday evening. It's the small bowl of kaak you leave out on your mantel in anticipation of guests. It is a full freezer, freshly baked challah, a warmth that envelops your home, even when outside is cold. You see, anybody can build a home, but it takes the right type of woman to fill it up. It takes the right type of woman to recognize her strengths and utilize them." Marie takes another sip of champagne. She pauses, as if contemplating something and then deciding to say it against her better judgment. "You think I don't want to go to work every day? Spend my time in an office or impressing buyers at fancy restaurants? I could do what they do in a heartbeat." She motions to my father and her husband. "I could do what they do. And better, probably. You can, too. The path to making money may be bumpy, but it's a path. Having a family, making a home, now that is messy, tireless work. And it is hard. And sometimes thankless, I won't sugarcoat it. Women today, they all want to work, work, work. They're running to Manhattan. Having children and leaving them in the care of others, or worse, not having children at all! G-D forbid. Their priorities are all wrong, I'm telling you. Do you know why they're all running to work? Because it's easy. That's why. What we do—I know you work for your father now, but what you *will* do, inshallah—now that is hard. They can have their paychecks, their bonuses and commissions. But we have rewards that can't be measured in dollars and cents. And if you do things right, you will reap the benefits for generations to come."

Marie pauses. "But I don't have to tell you. Some things are better learned on our own." She waves me toward the far end of the display table, the kitchen section. I slide in beside my mother and Sitto, who are admiring a cookbook.

"All she needs is to learn how to cook now," my mother says.

"Oh please. She has you for a mother! And your mother-in-law," Marie says to Sitto, who fondles a pair of oven mitts. "There's no better cook in the community than this one." She pats Sitto gently on the shoulder.

"When Sally got married, she knew nothing. Nothing," Sitto says. "I teach her to make the mehshi, the heshu, the hamid the way Morris like—with a pinch of tomato sauce and sugar. Now *shoof*, people pay for her food!"

"That's the problem," Marie says, refolding a pair of monogrammed dish towels. "The girls got lazy. Everything is 'buy this and buy that.'"

"Exactly." A speck of almond flings from Sitto's mouth.

"They don't know how to make anything anymore."

"Nothing," Sitto agrees.

"We had to make things, you know. The stores didn't sell kibbe balls and sambusak. There was no buying knafeh in the freezer section, a store on every corner." Marie looks at me, and I wonder if she's alluding to my store-bought knafeh.

"What was I saying yesterday!" Sitto widens her eyes at me. "What store?" Sitto says. "There were no stores like we have here." Her cheeks grow so red, they practically absorb the rouge she overapplied.

"Don't get me wrong, it's great that the girls selling these things are making money." Marie looks at me. "Sally, you're an original. But you know what I mean. It can get out of hand."

"Oh, you know, but I enjoy it." My mother smiles.

"She loves it," Sitto says, shaking her head. "She could stop anytime. She doesn't need the money." We all know this isn't true, but we nod in agreement anyway.

"Oh, but the people would riot," Marie says, smiling.

"Come," my mother says, changing the topic. "I want to show you Saul's side."

We cross the room in unison. Marie, my mother, Sitto, and I. Nina passes us as we reach the table, she smiles politely at Marie, and for a moment I feel a pang of jealousy for her unmade-up face. Lucy has been chatting up Saul's sisters for twenty minutes now. I always found them standoffish and unapproachable, and I wondered if people found me and my sisters the same way. But Lucy had no problem breaching their defenses. I overheard David's name mentioned more than once.

"You did it beautifully," Sitto whispers to my mother and me as we reach Saul's side. "Above and beyond."

My father admires the *kuracha* that I had crocheted for Saul. "Where was this when I was getting married?" He laughs and takes the top off a Baccarat scotch decanter, sniffs the contents inside. "Apple juice." He winks at Saul. "Don't get any ideas now."

I feel an anger well up inside me. Just the other day, my father was badgering my mother over this item and that, picking apart the credit card bill with a fine-tooth comb. He resented this very party and all of the pressure it came with, and he made sure my mother knew it. I knew from snooping that my mother had spent her fair share on Saul's gifts and that she'd taken on extra work in order to do so. If the problem was, as Sitto had said, that everyone was living above their means, why do we all partake in this charade? Why was my father ogling the very wallet he'd nearly started World War III over? It's one thing to close your eyes to it all, it's another to pick and choose when and what you wanted to see. I guess it doesn't really matter whether or not you can afford something, only that others think you can. And my family isn't the only one to blame here. Saul was comfortable, but the things on that table went way beyond comfort.

Sitto clears her throat and we all turn to attention. "I wanted to take the opportunity," she says, "to give a gift to you, Fortune—my name-sake and the first of my granddaughters, inshallah, to be married."

"Ooh," Marie coos.

My mother looks at me adoringly, like she knows what's coming. "Lucy, Nina." My mother waves my sisters over. "Come see."

Sitto dips one hand into the pocket of her red sweater, producing a small crushed-velvet bag. Even Saul's father, who is keenly tuned to a basketball game in the den, perks up. "Come, Fortune." Sitto motions for me to get closer to her and I do. I have to kneel slightly when Sitto draws my left arm out from behind my waist. Has Sitto been shrinking? I suddenly want to hold her as tight as I can.

"These belonged to my mother," Sitto says, pouring the contents of the bag into her palm, a set of six yellow gold bangles. Each one is engraved with a design, fine welded lines that swoop from one end to another in an infinite loop.

"I had to cut them from my wrist, and one day you will, too."

I hold out my hand as Sitto slides the bangles, one by one, over my knuckles and up to my wrist.

"You see, no clasp." Sitto traces her fingernail along the edge of the bangle. "The energy has no end. It goes round and round. And"—Sitto pushes the sixth bangle up my wrist—"there we go." My knuckles, where Sitto had pushed up the bangles, are raw and red. I admire the gift, turning my wrist left and right and hearing the wonderful sound they make as they clang together.

"My mother and father, *alav hashalom,* give to me before I marry. In Halab," Sitto says proudly. "Eighteen karat each. You see, even if my husband could not provide, or something bad happened, I would always have value. Something of my own. Go on," she says. "Really shake them. The music they make is the best part."

I jiggle my wrist and instantly the bangles come alive.

"This was the custom in Syria," Marie adds. "We didn't know nothing from diamonds. It was all gold. Gold was precious."

"It is still the most precious," Sitto says matter-of-factly.

"How is this fair?" Lucy says half-heartedly.

"Oh, please," my mother says. "You'll get plenty, trust me."

"What's that supposed to mean?" Nina appears.

"That she won't need it," Sitto says plainly.

"Sitto!" Lucy, Nina, my mother, and I say, all at once. Even though she's right. Sitto is right about most things, a fact better reckoned with sooner than later. I've always felt an immense sense of pride in sharing a name with my grandma Fortune, whose reputation as a gifted cook and a wicked bridge player preceded her.

"Thank you. Sitto, I love you." I kiss Sitto on both cheeks and allow Saul to admire my new gift. He tilts my hand left and right. He *oohs* and *ahhs,* says all the right things, but I can tell he doesn't understand how much this means to me. In this moment, these bangles mean more than the diamond on my finger or the bag hanging from my elbow. For the first time since getting engaged, it feels like someone took *me* into consideration; *me* as in Fortune, and not just another bride. Is Saul capable of making me feel that way? Would I even let him if he tried?

"They don't make 'em like these anymore," he remarks.

"No, they do not," Sitto agrees. "You know the name Fortune, it translates to *Mazal* in Hebrew." Sitto has an audience now, and damn if she isn't going to take advantage of it. "My own mother give me this name because when I was born, it is what she needed the most. Luck. And look at us now. Look at where we are? G-D is always listening." She taps a manicured finger to her temple. "Even when we aren't speaking."

BLEEDING AND THE SEVEN CLEAN DAYS

Girls, *this* is the magic ingredient to a successful marriage. It's the hint of cinnamon in your nuneh's fasoulya, the sprinkle of allspice, the pinch of blood in your cheeks. *Hilchot Niddah* are the laws that sustain the Jewish union, not the occasional "I love you" or the chance diamond here or there—although those things don't hurt, either. These laws are what separate us from the goyim.

SO, HOW DO WE IMPLEMENT NIDDAH IN OUR LIVES?

A woman becomes Niddah when she sees blood that originated from her uterus. From that moment on she and her husband must separate physically until she is able to immerse herself in the purifying waters of the mikvah. According to Sephardic law, a woman must wait a minimum of four bleeding days before she can begin to count her seven "clean" days. (If your period lasts fewer than four days, consult your husband's rabbi.) In order to begin counting your seven clean days, you must demonstrate that the menstrual bleeding has stopped.

Chapter Ten

....

"Just a second, girls," Mrs. Beda cries out from the kitchen.

I take a seat at Mrs. Beda's oak dining room table, the one reserved for Shabbat dinners and holiday meals with extended family. The
table seats ten, fourteen if you pull out the padded leaf extension. There
is more than enough room for our group of three to spread out. But instead, Brigette, Nicole, and I sit in a tight cluster at the far end of the
table. Brigette sits to my right, Nicole to my left. Mrs. Beda's papers are
set up at the other end of the table. An armchair (presumably Mr. Beda's)
remains quarantined in the corner of the room, out of respect for his absence.

"What do you guys think?" Nicole leans over, her eyes directing the
question at me.

"She's definitely more *modern*," Brigette says.

Nicole agrees. "I mean that's why I chose her. My sister took lessons
with Mrs. Alwani and told me *horror* stories. Supposedly the girls had

to take double the amount of classes and she was, like, super strict about the rules and stuff."

"Well, obviously. She's black hat. What do you expect?" Brigette says. "Mrs. Beda is progressive. I even heard her husband made some sympathetic comments toward converts."

"Really?" Surely my father wouldn't want me learning with someone who accepts converts. But then again, I doubt he knows I'm taking these classes at all. Either that, or he pretends not to because he'd rather die than acknowledge his daughter is preparing for her sexual life.

"Like he believes that we should allow them to marry *in*. I don't know—I'm just telling you what I heard." Brigette crosses her arms in front of her chest. "His congregation's small, though. Can you imagine if a bigger rabbi said those things?"

I pick from the small glass bowl of trail mix on the table, rolling salty bizet over my back molars, pinning it between my tongue and the roof of my mouth before cracking it open with my two front teeth. No hands necessary, just like Grandpa Jack taught us. I spit the empty shell into a plastic cup. "People would freak."

"Yeah . . ." Brigette trails off, eyeballing a plate of chocolate-dipped apricots. "New topic. Fortune. I heard Lucy's getting serious."

Nicole leans in.

"With who again . . . ?" Brigette plucks at her eyebrows. "My mother was *just* telling me." We all knew Brigette knew with whom, for how long, and where Lucy had dinner last night.

"I mean, it's not *that* serious," I try.

"David." Brigette smacks the table. "David Bakar. That's who it is, right?"

Nicole rubs a smooth macadamia nut between her thumb and index finger. "Oh, David Bakar? Really?"

"That's what I heard."

"I guess," I say coyly. By the time this class was over, half of each of their phone contacts would receive a transcript of whatever I said. "Why?"

"Knew it." Nicole looks like she is nursing a secret.

"Nicole, why'd you say it like that?"

"No, nothing." Nicole tosses a craisin back into the bowl.

Brigette snorts. "You always do that. It's so annoying."

"The craisin?"

"The gossip, you idiot. Don't be a tease with it."

"Well, I don't want it to come out the wrong way," Nicole says.

Brigette rolls her eyes.

I don't have the kind of relationship with either Brigette or Nicole that they have with each other, having only recently gotten close with them through the marriage classes we are all required to take as brides-to-be. This is our second meeting, so while the initial awkwardness is out of the way, we aren't exactly best friends. Brigette and Nicole, however, are both twenty-two. And while I don't feel like gossiping about my sister with them, I know that whatever Brigette has to say probably represents the consensus of the community at large.

Nicole waves her hand. "It's just that my sister Jacqueline dated him, too. What is he, thirty now? It was a while ago, though, before he went to med school." Nicole tries to act casual, knowing that Brigette and I hang on her every word. "They went on, like, a bunch of dates and he was *very* into her. My sister was kind of tough with him, though, because she knew his type. You know, the kind that knows he could get anyone." Nicole pauses and takes a dramatic exhale. "So Jacqueline's, like, twenty-two and things are going well, so naturally, they start to talk more seriously and he basically promises not to waste her time, right?" Nicole picks up her phone. "Is she kidding? It's been ten minutes. I'm supposed to meet Jack for dinner at eight."

"Go on." Brigette pounds her knuckles against the table.

Nicole turns her phone over. "So, one day he just stops texting. After the *seventh* date. Like, that's a lot."

"That is a lot," I say.

"He doesn't call, and—this is the worst part—he doesn't even answer her messages. The man falls off the face of the earth."

"*No.*" Brigette exhales.

"But wait, it gets worse. They see each other at a wedding a week later . . ."

"And what does he do?" Brigette's butt is so far off the edge of her seat, she's one cliffhanger away from a face-plant.

Nicole raises her eyebrows. "Just says hi and kisses her on the cheek. Done." She shrugs. "Like she's his grandma. Like nothing ever happened between them. No apology, no explanation. *Nada.*"

"*Ha-zi-ta.*" Brigette shakes her head with each syllable.

"That makes zero sense, I'm sorry," I say, suddenly feeling defensive. In the back of my mind, I'm wondering if this is something I need to tell Lucy about. "Something must have happened. You don't just disappear like that, especially after you've *talked.*"

"Fortune," Nicole says, deadpanning. "The guy is a flake. After the fact we heard he did the same thing to, like, two other girls. My sister was devastated but, like, she obviously dodged a bullet. I really don't want to talk bad because Lucy's great. She's stunning. And young, which I'm sure he likes. But I'm only telling you because she's your sister . . ."

"They're actually boyfriend and girlfriend," I say, eager to draw a distinction between Nicole's sister's situation and Lucy's. I don't want to spill Lucy's beans, but I also want to know if this caveat makes telling Lucy more or less urgent.

Nicole holds her hands up. "Let's hope with her it's different."

"I know what happened," Brigette says, deflating. "I know David's family. His sister is married to my second cousin, remember? I'm just saying, the family is very *intense.*"

"Yeah, so?"

Brigette places her elbows on the table, resting her chin on her knuckles. "Let me ask you this: Did Jacqueline ever meet David's mother?"

"I'm sure she saw her at some event or whatever. It's hard to miss each other here."

"That's not what I'm saying. Like, did he ever introduce them?"

"I don't know . . . Maybe." Nicole shifts in her seat.

Brigette grins. "Boys like that, they need an introduction before the *introduction.* Listen, after seven dates, isn't it kind of time to meet his parents? No? I mean I'm sure he met yours when he picked Jacqueline up for dates, right? I'm just *assuming* here," Brigette stresses. "But he probably told his mother about Jacqueline and she shot it down. Probably for no good reason! She's a vegetarian. Who knows?"

"Jacqueline isn't a vegetarian," Nicole says, missing the point.

"It's nothing against you," Brigette says, apologetically. "It's just, certain families, they want certain kinds of girls." Brigette looks at me for backup, but I look down at my fingernails and pretend to pick at a cuticle, knowing that with Saul and me, there were no red flags. I was as safe a choice for Saul as he was for me. Our families occupied similar rungs on the social ladder. We had a comparable level of faith and observance. Both of our mothers complained about the escalating prices at the butcher and our fathers rode the seesaw of wholesale and retail. No surprises, no upsets. It makes people uncomfortable to watch someone jump a few steps in status. Probably because they believe it should be them, or their daughter. I chalk Nicole's warnings up to jealousy but make a mental note to keep an eye on David.

We suddenly hear Mrs. Beda's feet clap down the hall and make their way into the dining room.

Brigette leans in and whispers, "None of this is confirmed and I never heard anything. I don't need the Bakars coming after me."

Mrs. Beda claps her hands as she enters the room, startling us all into submission. "Sorry about that, but also, not sorry. Wait until you have young children of your own! *B'ezrat Hashem!*" She smiles.

I feel the tension in the room dissolve. Mrs. Beda looks as though she can't be a day over thirty. Had I not known about her three young children, I'd say at least a decade younger. Her smooth brown hair hangs in natural waves, hitting slightly above her shoulders. A Missoni turban covers the top of her head, and her skin is fair and smooth, a hint of blush swiped hurriedly across her youthful cheeks. She is taller than most, but still petite in frame. A chambray button-down dress loosely covers her, hitting just below her knees.

My mind wanders to Lucy and David as Mrs. Beda continues her introductory monologue. Where did he take her for dinner last night?

Somewhere expensive, for sure. Is he the type who takes charge? Ordering for the both of them, half a dozen small plates to share, a beer for him and some version of a beach cocktail for her? What does Lucy know about orthopedics anyway? She passed freshman biology by the skin of her perfectly aligned teeth. If Nicole is right, surely he would have ended it by now. Instead, he asked Lucy to be his girlfriend.

Saul enmeshed himself into our family almost immediately. Sitting with my mother and father over kaak for hours as we missed reservation after reservation. Bickering with Nina as if she were his own flesh and blood. He even cozied up to Sitto, who probably reminded him more of his mother than my own did. Saul's intentions were always clear and an engagement felt like the natural next step in our relationship. I'd never second-guessed any of this. My parents were happy and I was glad to be the reason for it. But Lucy's happiness seems different than mine. It's the kind of happiness that doesn't take others into account—it's for her. As if what my parents think is inconsequential. Of course, it doesn't hurt that they're thrilled. But Lucy's love for David isn't contingent upon the approval of others. Can I really say the same?

"The community," Mrs. Beda says, raising her voice about three octaves, "has Niddah to thank for our relatively low divorce rates. It's the fourteen-day abstinence that keeps the fire, or rather blech, burning." She winks. "The secular way, you know, the premarital sex, the cohabitation . . . This is why so many relationships disintegrate over the years, even the ones that seem indestructible."

I feel the room collectively inhale. Brigette, Nicole, and I are all, presumably, virgins. But you always wonder, what kind of girl, if any, crosses that line. It's a waste of time to think about it, though, as neither of them would tell each other, let alone me, if they'd done it or not. We all understand that it is too risky.

"You could say it's been a while, but believe me, girls, I still remember learning these laws for the first time myself." Mrs. Beda walks toward us and I catch a whiff of her floral scent as she floats around the table. Definitely the kind of woman who moisturizes before bed, I think. That's the kind of woman I want to be.

Mrs. Beda places a spiral-bound booklet in front of each of us before returning to her post at the head of the table. "Now, these booklets have been slightly tweaked since my time, but not by much. After all, it's this consistency, the timelessness of these laws—as you will see—that makes the act of Niddah so special." She shakes her fist. Laughing comes easily to Mrs. Beda. It definitely helps diffuse the awkwardness of the material at hand.

Mrs. Beda tells Nicole, Brigette, and me that she envies us; how she wishes she could learn these laws for the first time, over and over again. She makes me feel special. Like I'm the only virgin in the world, like maybe two very attractive men with many muscles *would* start a world war for their right to my intact hymen. I look over at Nicole and Brigette and I know that they feel the same, because I see the high-grade anxiety in their faces dissipate to low-grade anxiety, and this is good. By next month we'll all be married in Lev Aharon's grand ballroom, a hall of epic proportions situated in the beating heart of the community. Nicole has a red theme, I'll work with whites, and Brigette has a plan to transform the blank canvas into a jungle. We'll each try to eke out some semblance of individuality, but to our guests, each of our weddings will be just that, another wedding. Yet another function that they are obligated to attend.

Brigette's wedding is one week after mine, and Nicole's wedding is three days after Brigette's. Their bridal parties are practically carbon copies of each other. The bitches and moans from their friends over having to buy *two* gowns for *two* weddings three days apart have been heard all up and down the parkway. I have no doubt that they've all been subjected to some version of a warning from their mothers. Don't get too drunk (nobody is actually naïve enough to think their daughters won't drink at all). Stay classy and pay close attention to the hems and necks of your dresses. Make sure your boob tape and lipstick remain intact. Don't end up like *that* girl. That poor girl, who hasn't been granted the grace of another scandal to cover up her own. That girl who no doubt still causes a flurry of whispers and headshaking when she enters a room. That girl whose name has been crossed off countless guest lists to date. Incongruities of that night still pop up. Rumors are still being spread. There were two boys, not one—no three. Were there drugs involved? Nobody could say that there weren't. The girl and her family have remained mostly mum, and fiction has become fact in their silence. Even her younger sister, not yet old enough to attend the parties, is facing reputational repercussions. I wish she would speak up and defend herself. I know words can get you in trouble, but silence does something far worse. It lends elasticity to people's imaginations. And if there was one thing you *didn't* want when dealing with a scandal, it was imaginations running amok.

After Saul and I got engaged, his rabbi explained to us that we'd each have to take our own version of marriage classes before our wedding. I had assumed I'd take a private lesson. I chose Mrs. Beda as my Kallah teacher mainly because I left this until the last minute and she was willing to accommodate my schedule. I was relieved to hear that she was "open" and "lenient." My mother told me that Dad had wanted me to take classes with our rabbi's wife, but I convinced her to lie on my behalf, telling him that she was booked solid for the next four months.

Of course, I have my complaints regarding Mrs. Beda. Like, must she smile every time she says the word "penetration"? I do like how she refers to her own husband by his first name and encourages us all to put her number in our phones, *insisting* we call her *anytime,* for *anything.*

Nobody asks questions during the lesson. We just scribble notes into our booklets and giggle when she asks us to turn to the quick bio lesson labeled "The Menstrual Cycle."

> The menstrual cycle is the series of changes a woman's body undergoes to prepare for a pregnancy. Providing your periods are regular, your uterus will grow a new lining once a month in order to get ready for a fertilized egg. When there is no fertilized egg to start a pregnancy, the uterus sheds its lining. This is why we bleed during our periods.
>
> A woman's cycle technically lasts from Day 1 of bleed-

ing until Day 1 of her next bleeding. A typical menstrual cycle is 28 days, although it's normal for them to vary among women. Tracking your menstrual cycle will be a fundamental component of future lessons.

Like, I'm sorry, we all know what a period is. As far as I'm concerned, it is something that gives a woman license to talk shit. A period pardons nasty language and bloated bellies and weird cravings and maybe, with a doctor's note, an excused absence from the Israel Day Parade. A period = fertility, a woman's most prized possession.

Mrs. Beda continues. "A woman who does not get her period is barren, a pity, in need of a miracle. Rachel was barren, 'Give me children or I'll die!' she exclaimed to her husband, Jacob. She then allowed him to lay with her servant, Bilhah, so that he might fulfill his procreative duty." Mrs. Beda reads from the text in front of her. " 'Then God remembered about Rachel's plight and answered her prayers by giving her a child. For she became pregnant and gave birth to a son.' Rachel, of course, was thrilled. 'God has removed the dark slur against my name!' she exclaimed."

"Why would *Hashem* do that?" Nicole asks. "Why wait until *after* Jacob slept with Bilhah to give Rachel a child?"

"It is a test," Mrs. Beda answers. "A measure of Rachel's loyalty to her husband. By the way, I assume you've all been to your first OB appointments?" Mrs. Beda drops her booklet. "It's none of my business what you choose. Whether you wish to use contraception at first or if you decide to roll the dice. Of course, if you *do* plan on trying for a baby right away, we can discuss that, too. I'm here for whatever questions you may have."

Now Brigette's and Nicole's hands shoot up in the air.

One of the first things we'd done after the proposal was visit the gynecologist. Dr. Mandel was my mother's OB, too, and she assured me, as best she could, that he was nice and that he took my insurance—or rather, Dad's insurance. I knew from my friends that I could use birth control to manipulate my period, ensuring that it wouldn't come on my wedding day or honeymoon. Getting a prescription was the first order of business, even if I was still a virgin. Mom scheduled an appointment a day after the proposal and we drove into the city together.

The exam room was cold and sterile. After the nurse, Kathy, had me put on a Pepto-colored gown, Dr. Mandel walked in a minute later, his eyes cemented on my chart.

"So," he began, eyes downcast, "I see you're getting married, which brings you here. Congratulations. You must be excited?" He kept his hands busy, flipping back and forth through my form. "Twenty-one years old." He grinned and looked up. "How long have you been menstruating?"

"Um, I got my period when I was thirteen," I said, crossing and uncrossing my legs.

"Doctor," my mother added. "Her period's been semi-regular for the past six months. Should we be concerned?" When had she walked in? She sat on a bridge chair in the corner, flipping through a stale copy of *OK!* magazine. JENNIFER ANISTON PREGNANT! Again.

"It's not uncommon." Dr. Mandel sizes me up. "Fortune, are you eating normally? Exercising more than usual? Of course, stress has an effect on a woman's period. I wouldn't discount the pressure of the wedding."

"She's definitely been exercising more than usual. No, Fortune? She was also diagnosed with anemia when she was five. Can we check her levels, too?"

"We can ask one of the nurses to take some blood afterward, sure." Dr. Mandel turned to my mother. "I'm going to ask that you leave the room for a few minutes, just so I can speak to Fortune privately, Mrs. Cohen."

"Of course, Doctor. Fortune, honey, I'll be outside if you need anything."

Was my mother always so cooperative in the company of strange men? Dr. Mandel lifted his gaze. "So, Fortune, are you sexually active?"

I shifted uncomfortably in my seat. "I mean, I'm sexual, but not—"

"Are you having sex?"

"Oh, no."

Dr. Mandel scribbled something onto my chart.

"And you're a virgin?"

"Yes."

"Are you and your partner planning on using some form of contraception?"

Saul and I barely talked about it. He was always saying how he'd like to be a young father. How you can't plan these things. G-D will always provide for you what you need. His mother had given birth to all five of her children by thirty. As had mine. They'd be such spry grandmas!

"Yeah," I said. "I guess the pill. Something not so hormonal, maybe?"

Dr. Mandel smiled. I'd been so nervous the night before this visit. My Google history was an incriminating catalog of anxieties:

WHAT HAPPENS ON FIRST GYNO VISIT?

WILL MY GYNO FEEL MY BARE BREAST?

DOES IT MATTER IF MY GYNO IS A MAN?

GYNO MOLESTS PATIENT RECENT

DO YOU GET AROUSED FROM A PAP SMEAR?

WHAT IS A PAP SMEAR?

CERVICAL CANCER PERCENTAGE RATES WOMEN AGES 18–21

"Before we talk about any of that, I'm going to do a quick internal exam. It'll only take a few minutes."

Kathy, the nurse, entered the room and approached my chair. She pressed a button as she spoke. "Just lie back and try to relax, Fortune. I'm going to ask you to put both of your feet in these stirrups." The treatment chair began to recline. I grasped its arms, planting my feet firmly on the chair, my legs pressed tightly together.

Dr. Mandel took a seat on a stool in front of the stirrups and the nurse stood behind him, attentively peering over his shoulder. He slapped on a pair of latex gloves, the same kind that my mother used when she crushed garlic.

"Honey." Kathy placed her hand on my shoulder. "You're going to put your feet in the stirrups, and then you're going to slide your bottom down until it feels like it's just about to fall off the chair. I know that sounds silly."

Dr. Mandel held up an index finger. "I'm just going to insert my finger into your vagina," he said, almost as if he thought this bit of information would make me feel more comfortable. *Please! Tell me what other specials are on the menu today!* Dr. Mandel rubbed a clear jelly over his gloved finger.

"Honey." Kathy looked at me, and I could tell from her eyes that I was far from the first. "Do you want us to call your mother in? Would that put you at ease?"

"No!" I said, a little more forcefully than I'd meant to. I scooched my body down, placed my chapped heels in the stirrups, and silently prayed for an electrical blackout.

"I know this might feel a bit uncomfortable at first," Dr. Mandel said, his hand resting gently on my kneecap. "But you're going to need to spread your legs."

Spread your legs: a phrase that only gross men uttered and easy women complied with. Spreading your legs left you vulnerable, exposed. I would be visible; whatever labia and smells and fluids I had down there would show themselves, openly and unprotected and without the consolation of dim lighting or a sizable comforter. These two strangers would be the first people to bear witness to a part of me I hadn't yet seen. This sixty-something doctor with a salt-and-pepper beard was going to walk through the door before Saul had even rung the bell.

I opened my legs slightly, the space between them big enough to fit a small shoebox. I thought about telling the doctor that I'd never so much as stuck anything up there, except for a tampon. I wanted to ask him why that felt okay, but every time Saul let his finger creep too close my legs snapped shut. I wanted to know if he heard the story about the Hasidic girl and the banana; if he's ever treated someone who tried to finger themselves with a foreign object and gotten it stuck, or if this was just the stuff of urban yeshiva legend. I clenched my butt and opened my knees. The rest of me withdrew back into the chair, as if my body might disappear into the folds of its awful maroon upholstery. I braced myself against Dr. Mandel's touch, every inch of my body up in arms.

"Nurse." Dr. Mandel sighed, placing a silver weapon down on the exam table. "Mind grabbing me a Q-tip?" he asked. "There." He twirled the cotton swab between his two fingers like a baton. "We'll start with this."

Now, Mrs. Beda seems to be wrapping up. I close my eyes, allowing my mind to wander back to an equally horrifying memory. I remember the day I became a woman because it was the same day that Albert Pinhas became a man, except that nobody threw *me* a giant party. Tina and I were crouched in a photo booth box, the main attraction at Albert Pinhas's bar mitzvah party in the grand ballroom of Lev Aharon, the same ballroom where I would soon be married. Word around the southern tip of Ocean Parkway was that his parents had spent close to a quarter million on the party. As soon as the invitation hit our pavement, my mother grabbed her bag and said, "We're going to Heathers."

It's funny to think that Heathers was once *the* community shopping destination. My friends wouldn't be caught dead in there today, but it wasn't too long ago that we'd sack that place like it was the only store selling matzo on Passover, rabidly in search of the new UGG boot or Junk Food tee. It was a time in which a girl's net worth was measured in Juicy Couture velour sweatshirts. The candy-colored zip ups were the only way to differentiate ourselves from one another; a mark of individuality to top off our bottom halves, which were uniformly outfitted in charcoal, navy, or black floor-length skirts. Renee was the baron of the yeshiva because she owned a sweatshirt in every color. Her closet resembled a sorted packet of rainbow Skittles. Tina told me in confidence that her mother had put a canary yellow one on layaway for her fourteenth birthday. *Hazita,* by the time she picked it up, the school announced it would be mandating uniforms.

Nobody so much as lifted a finger when we walked into the store. I told my mother, I *begged* her, "Ma, let's just go to Loehmann's!" It was a ten-minute drive to Sheepshead Bay and if I'm being honest, the public nudity of the communal dressing rooms calmed me. Sometimes I forgot that women came in all shapes and sizes; I myself had only seen two: 0 and "*Hazita*, she must have a thyroid problem." But this was Albert Pinhas's bar mitzvah party, and it was no place for last month's second-rate goods. My mother would take me to Heathers, where the unofficial motto was, "If you're not overpaying, you're poor."

I took one look at her feet and knew she meant business. I'd never seen her in flats, let alone sneakers, let alone charcoal gray New Balances. And once she started there was no stopping her. Swiping through racks and sifting through piles! Pulling this dress and that skirt and swapping size 4's for 2's and 2's for 0's in a dizzying display of Olympic consumer talent. My mother, the gold medal athlete; the just barely five-foot tour de force, rippling through Heathers with the energy of an eight-piece Mariachi band on a crowded subway. My mother, who insisted I "hold the wheel!" on drives into the city because her arms were prone to cramping, had about forty-five pounds of silk cotton wedged in the crooks of her elbows, and she showed no signs of slowing down.

Before I knew it, the entire staff of Heathers was assisting us in our mission. After all, the sales force warmed up to us once we revealed the occasion. They shot down a pink taffeta skirt that another girl had bought for the same party. They gave us a ballpark figure of what the other girls were spending, and after careful deliberation, someone came up from the basement carrying a navy blue skirt and matching tailored jacket. I knew that my mother hated it but would pretend to like it, because everybody knew that the sales force didn't "run down to the basement" for nobody, certainly not for a customer who didn't plan on spending.

"She looks like a judge, no? I think it's a little too lesbian, maybe." My mother said, "Let me see the ruched floral dress on you," she demanded, following my gaze in the dressing room's 360-degree mirror.

But I loved the suit. I loved the way its lapels framed my collarbones.

How the tautness of the pencil skirt pushed my thighs together. I loved how my olive complexion looked so ordinary against the maturity of the navy material. It was essentially a uniform, though entirely different from the ones they made us wear at yeshiva. My mother agreed to buy it after I agreed to cut "the flower power garbage" and start eating meat again. I'm still convinced that the onset of my period came in response to all of the brick roast I'd consumed in the weeks leading up to Albert Pinhas's bar mitzvah party.

Albert's mom had the room completely transformed, bringing in ornamental centerpieces made of peonies and gumballs. There was a fondue fountain the size of a tall child. We were greeted at the ball-room's entrance by a life-size cardboard cutout of the bar mitzvah boy, dressed in a dapper suit with outstretched hands and a snaggletooth grin that seemed to say, "Which one of you beautiful ladies wants to dance the Cha Cha Slide with me? Now sign my forehead!"

There was a Skee-Ball machine and basketball hoops and a station-ary candy truck and a petting zoo consisting of only Sphynx cats because Mrs. Pinhas was "extremely allergic to animal fur still affixed to ani-mals." A Gorski fox festooned her bony shoulders. Mr. Pinhas had called in a favor from the Knicks City Dancers because his son was "a huge basketball fan. The *hugest.*"

I was squatting in the photo booth box with Tina, painfully aware of my electric blue rubber band braces, when I felt something warm and sticky pool between my thighs. I knew without knowing, like every girl does, that my life was about to change.

Of course, I had yet to attract the attention of a nice boy—a Tawil, or Levy, or if I dared to dream . . . a Mizrahi—but I still had *years* for that—five at least. Panicked, I nudged Tina in the ribs and without a word she led me into the last stall of the women's restroom. Once inside, she opened her green satin clutch to reveal three plastic-wrapped logs of cotton. Like a seasoned blackjack dealer, she fanned them out in front of me.

"Lite, Regular, or Super?"

"My mom says young girls shouldn't use those. Maybe I could just stick some tissue up there?"

Truthfully, I couldn't see how the diameter of that thing could manage its way up there anyway (wherever "there" was). I didn't know that there was not one but three separate entrances. That the tampon went through the VIP door, a contracting and expanding cavity used for *other* things.

"Calm down, Fortune. Trust me, okay? Take the Lite one. It's easier. Just put one foot on the seat and squat down reaaaaallly low and then you just, like, stick it up there. I'll legit be right outside the stall." Tina closed the door behind her.

I didn't ask how she knew all of this. They said that Tina got hers young, like very young—but she never addressed the rumors. I always suspected they were true, though. Tina was already wearing underwire bras and filled out a whole C-cup at age twelve. I didn't envy her. Boys never looked her in the eye when they spoke to her and some were even known to brush by a little too closely when they passed her in the hallways. I lined my underwear with a sheet of toilet paper and flushed the unused tampon down the toilet. Tina was waiting for me when I opened the door.

"Come on." She grabbed my hand. "Your mom's gonna want to know, no?"

I was too ashamed to tell my mother that I'd ruined my outfit, so I stashed it in a plastic bag and hid it in the back of my sock drawer. I had a feeling she wouldn't ask where it was. For two days I walked around with a Bounty-induced bulge in my crotch. And that smell! It reeked of Borough Park, like gravlax and the Industrial Revolution. I patted my nether regions with my father's Aqua Di Parma before class and changed my underwear every couple of hours. When I ran out of clean underwear, I stole my sister's. When Nina finally caught on, I told her the truth. She drove me all the way to a Walgreens in Brighton Beach to avoid seeing anyone we knew, where she bought me one box of panty liners and one box of maxi pads. Nina promised that she'd eventually teach me how to use a tampon. "Thirteen is too young," she said. "I just started last year, and I'm six years older than you."

"Done," Dr. Mandel said, holding his hands up. I opened my eyes and allowed myself to breathe an audible sigh of relief.

"Done!" Mrs. Beda claps her hands together, snapping me back to attention. "Fortune, I hope we didn't bore you with all of that baby talk," she says sweetly as she approaches me. Mrs. Beda crouches down in front of me and lowers her voice. "I understand that some girls might be more shy than others when it comes to these things. If you ever want to speak privately, I'm more than happy to do so." Mrs. Beda stands up and smooths her dress.

I feel my cheeks grow hot and red. "Thank you," I say, gathering my things. Nicole and Brigette wave goodbye.

"My cell is at the bottom of the first page." Mrs. Beda nods to the booklet I left on the table.

I grab it. "Of course, really, thank you."

I check my phone as I head out the front door. Two missed calls from Saul. A message from my mother telling me to lock up when I get in. Another one from my future mother-in-law, who'd recently learned how to text in T9: See U 2tomoro!

Mrs. Beda gently closes the door behind me and I breathe a big sigh of relief, allowing the cool April night air to fill my lungs. It's half past nine, and the streets are quiet and dark, save for the warm glow cast from the inside of her neighbors' homes. I dial Carmen's number and leave her a voicemail, saying that I'm going to get in late tomorrow. The MIL and I have a gift registry date at Wish You Well.

An incoming text from an unknown number lights up my phone.

It's Isaac (from Spice) Is this urs?

A photo of a red paisley scarf follows. The scarf is mine, or rather, my mother's. The same one I'd grabbed from the table before visiting Spice a few weeks ago. I haven't been back to the store since my dumb attempt to tip him. My stomach still does somersaults when I think about it, so I prefer not to.

Another text follows: If it is I can drop to u . . . leaving the store now.

I quickly unlock the car door and slide into the driver's seat.

It is but dw!! I frantically text.

What would my mother think if she opened the door to find Isaac standing outside, her Etro scarf scrunched up in his hand? Or worse, Nina, who was most definitely waiting for me by the front, ready to take the car keys so she could jet off to another part of Brooklyn that may as well be a world away. No, I absolutely could not risk him showing up at my front door close to ten P.M. with a piece of my clothing in his possession.

Or you can swing by the store and pick it up tomorrow. Here all day ☺ Isaac responds.

I'll come by tom! TYSM! I reply.

My fingers remain glued to the keyboard, as if they have more to say. I wonder who Isaac asked for my number. A customer whom he knew me to be friendly with? My mother? Why didn't he just text my mother? I'm probably making too much of this anyway. It isn't a big deal, even if Isaac had asked someone for my number.

Actually

I press send before I can contemplate the outcome of what I'm about to do.

I'm out right now—I can come by if you haven't locked up.

It feels like forever waiting for Isaac to text back. But finally he does:

Unfortunately for me but lucky for u, I'm still here.

I quickly turn the key in the ignition and put my foot on the brake, shifting the car into drive.

Great! C u in ten.

My mind races as I speed toward the stop sign. I'm just going to pick up my scarf. I tap my fingers against the steering wheel. Isaac won't make anything of this, right? It's just that my mother really needs that scarf. She's always complaining her neck feels cold.

· · ·

I park my mother's Jeep Grand Cherokee in a spot miraculously found in front of our house. I switch the headlights off and wait a few seconds before exiting the car. Nina could wait five more minutes for the keys. Do I text Isaac to let him know that I'm here? The mere *idea* of having even one more incriminating text on my phone is enough to make me sick. Instead, I walk the few yards to Spice, passing my house, where I can see the blue glare from the TV screens in each room shine through closed curtains. Sitto used to pine for a two-family home on Ocean Parkway, where she could spend her days reclined by the window, a spectator to the bustling outside world. Now it seems she spends most of her time alone in her room with Pat Sajak. She's even been spending less time in the kitchen. My mother often says that the day she lets another woman cook for her is the day we'll all know she's fully lost it. She complains that her kitchen's been hijacked by Sitto ever since she moved in, but even my mother would agree that her presence has been missed lately. Sometimes I worry we've all been too caught up in our own lives, acting as if we're not on borrowed time. My mother has been stressing about Sitto's dress for the wedding, knowing that the responsibility of finding one falls on her. It might be nice to take Sitto to the store, her and me. I'm sure my mother wouldn't mind unloading the errand.

The wooden crates in front of Spice have been emptied. The sidewalk in front of it is quiet and still, and in the absence of the cardboard boxes and the workers who unpack them, you can actually see how dirty the sidewalk is. The lights in the store are off, except for one up front by the register, where Isaac sits with his slipper-clad feet propped up on the counter. He nibbles on the gold rope chain that usually hangs from his neck, the same one my father wears and my grandfather wore before him. I watch him for a moment, as he texts on his phone, ashamed to admit I wonder who he's talking to and if he has somewhere to be. He registers my presence and waves me in. When I get to the front door, Isaac jumps up to unlock it and crumbs fall from the creases of his black sweatpants and oversize T-shirt.

"You should've told me you were on your way," he says as he leads me inside. "I would've brought it out for you."

My insides feel like they're doing gymnastics. "It's fine!" I say, shrugging off my embarrassment. "I didn't want to bother you."

"You saved me, actually," Isaac says as he walks toward the back of the store and I follow him. "My father put me on inventory duty, mind-numbing stuff. I'll take the distraction."

"Didn't look like you were working."

"Were you watching me?" Isaac turns around suddenly and I stop short in my tracks, my head nearly bumping into his chest. I take an unsteady step backward.

"No." I stumble. "I mean I *saw* you. As I was walking to the store."

"Uh-huh." Isaac smirks and opens the door to the stockroom, flicking on the light. "It's in here."

"Are you going to murder me?"

"You're the one who was stalking *me*, remember?"

My cheeks glow red. "Shut up."

He grabs my mother's scarf off a broom hook, a score from our recent jaunt to the Woodbury Common outlets. "Thanks," I say, reaching for it.

"You're lucky I found it." Isaac loosens his grip. "One more day in the store and one of the stock boys' wives was getting a really nice present."

"Funny." I wrap the scarf around my neck, which is starting to feel sticky and wet despite the coolness of the room. A single bulb illuminates the space, and an array of dust particles hang in its balance, casting a hazy glow around us. Isaac leans confidently against a wire shelving unit and crosses his tanned arms over his chest. "What are you doing out so late anyway—Saul just drop you home?"

"No—I was out, at class."

"School? You take night classes?"

"No. No, not those kind of classes. It's dumb, really . . ."

"It doesn't sound shady at all."

"They're these marriage classes we take with a Kallah teacher. All of the girls are required to take them before they get married."

"Uh-huh." Isaac spins a loop of keys between his fingers. "The classes that teach you how to bang as husband and wife."

I nearly choke on my own spit.

"The rules around your period," Isaac continues, amusing himself. I can feel the blood rush to my cheeks.

"They aren't all about that."

"About what?"

"You're annoying."

"Come on. How are you going to do it if you can't even say it? Look, *sex.*" Isaac taunts. "Say it with me: S-E-X."

"Are you having fun?"

"Very much, actually." He stands up straight and begins to organize some stray aerosol cans: Foaming Bubbles and Lysol. "I mean if you're going to do the deed soon, you should know how to talk about it."

"What makes you so sure I haven't done it already?"

Isaac stops what he is doing and looks me dead in the eye, daring me to break. He cracks first. His laugh is contagious, and with every emission he inches a little closer, until all that separates us is a mop that leans against a wall in the space between us.

"I've never been so sure about anything in my whole life. I bet it's about to be Saul's first time, too. *How romantic.*"

"You say that like it's a bad thing."

"Hey." Isaac holds his hands up in surrender. "I was just guessing. It's up to you how you want to interpret what I say."

"And you?" The question comes out before I can think to stop it. "Like you're so experienced?"

Isaac shrugs. "Again, you'll make your own interpretations, no matter what I do or don't say."

"You know, you're actually pretty rude." I cross my arms over my chest.

"Oh sure. When I'm not ringing up Muenster cheese or picking the ripest cantaloupe, I'm rude."

"That's not what I meant! But of course there you go flipping the whole thing around! Because this is what you do. Like it's all some kind of game to you, right?"

"Fortune." Isaac says my name slowly, that mischievous grin creep-

143

ing once more across his face. I hate how mad I am and, at the same time, how little I want to leave. "Why are you here?" he says finally, his green eyes set intently on my face.

"I'm here to pick up my scarf."

"No, I mean why are you *here*, talking to me."

"I—"

Before I can think of something to say, Isaac continues: "You never looked at me in high school. You've lived next door to Spice for as long as we've been in business and you've never spoken to me outside of the frozen food aisle. I didn't care. It is what it is. I know what I am to you."

"Whoa," I say, a little more sternly than I mean to. "That's not fair."

"Fortune, I mean no disrespect. I swear, it's all good. I just prefer to say it like it is. We can cut through the bullshit. I'm just curious . . ." Isaac says, with a twinkle in his eye, "why now?"

The answer is I don't know. I don't know if it's Isaac as a person, or a pull toward the unexpected. I can't say why I'm here, at ten P.M. in a stockroom with a boy who isn't my fiancé, or that I would necessarily mind getting caught. Maybe I just want to know how it feels to be in a place that is equal parts dangerous and desirable. It's an intoxicating cocktail. I just wanted a sip.

My hands are clammy. I twist my ring around my finger with one hand and try to breathe. I know I should leave, but my feet remain planted firmly on the ground. It's true that I never looked at Isaac twice. Even now, as he begins to show the slightest interest in me, the slightest vulnerability, I feel myself pulling away.

"I don't know—I don't know anything." I clasp my hands behind my back.

"None of us do."

"You seem pretty content with yourself."

"Me?" Isaac raises both eyebrows in surprise. "You think I'm content? *Here?*" Isaac lifts his arms up as if he's trying to encapsulate the entire store in a single, bitter embrace. "I'm grateful for our customers, don't get me wrong, but I'd rather be in college than ringing up bags of pita bread." He shakes his head. "My parents didn't come here with four young children so that I could be lectured by some trust fund kid whose only rebellion was becoming a philosophy professor."

"You're interested in philosophy?" I say, intrigued.

"That's not the point." Isaac waves my question away. "The point is that we all have a role to play. You coming in here, maybe you want to try on a different costume. Maybe you're a little bit bored of your lines. You know how your movie ends and that scares you. Well, this is my advice to you: Stick to your script. Stick to your script. And"—Isaac takes a step toward me—"if you still insist on deviating, if you're still not convinced that that's what you want . . . then I'll take another step."

My heart is beating so fast, I feel like it might burst in my chest. We're a foot apart now, and I can sense something new in Isaac's eyes, something that wasn't there before—a sadness, a desire to be accepted, to please. We're not so different, are we? Deep down, we all want the same things. Isaac's hands are burrowed deep in his pockets but still, I can tell they're balled into tight fists. I can feel the heat radiating off his body and I feel guilty for wanting to take some of its warmth, even for a second. I wasn't lying when I said I didn't know. I still don't know what I want. But I do know that I'd rather sit in this confusion than spend a day doing errands for an assured future. Isaac takes another step.

"Can I do something?" And before I can say yes or no, Isaac wraps me in a hug. I feel my shoulders loosen, and I bury my face into the recesses of his arm, where it smells like clean laundry and cloves.

"I can't come in here again," I say, still holding on.

"I know."

"Not even to shop."

"I know."

"I'm sorry—I didn't mean to put anything on you."

"Don't be sorry." Isaac laughs, his chin resting on top of my head. "It was a slow day today."

Chapter Eleven

....

"They say that when you do the lipo, the fat goes to other places."
The MIL shifts her gray Lexus into drive, checking her reverse camera as she peels away from the curb in front of my house.

"Really?" I ask, hoping Marie doesn't sense the feigned interest in my voice.

"That's what they say." Marie raises an eyebrow matter-of-factly.

I take a big gulp of the Dunkin' Donuts iced coffee she was kind enough to bring me. I feel emotionally hungover from my conversation with Isaac last night. On top of that I feel guilty, knowing how wrong it was for me to have been there at all. I cringe thinking about what my MIL or Saul would say if they knew. It doesn't help my conscience that Marie picked me up early this morning to complete my wedding registry. As she waxes poetic about the pros and cons of preventative Botox, I play and replay last night in my mind, searching for some semblance of clarity in every word said and not said. Each and every time, my mind goes blank at that hug. That silly, unexpected embrace; I don't think I've ever needed and regretted something so much in my whole life. Including the box of Entenmann's Soft'ees I inhaled when I got home.

The close confines of the car don't help, and the MIL lowered whatever weather and traffic report she'd had on the radio before picking me up to an inaudible hum once I'd gotten in the car. My mother begged her to come inside for a cup of coffee, but the MIL insisted that we had no time.

There's so much of Saul in her, I think, as I study Marie's profile. She has symmetrical features, if a little exaggerated. Her nose appears to float above the rest of her face, like bread that had been left to rise for a minute too long. Its tip points up toward her eyes as if knowing they are the highlight of her face. Marie's eyes are hard to miss; two deep-set round emeralds, flanked by a set of lashes you could sew into a fan. "It was very rare in Syria to have green eyes," Marie reminds us often. *Isaac has green eyes.* "I got them from my grandmother, who was a famous beauty, by the way. Like her, I could pass for Ashkenazi if I wanted to, but who would want to?" She is always quick to add the last part. Marie's eyes are complemented by an auburn-tinted red mane that she maintains with bimonthly trips to the salon. Her skin isn't fair or olive, but defined less by tone and more by shallow wrinkles around her mouth and eyes. Tiny lines frame her mouth, like rays around a cartoon sun. When the MIL doesn't like something, she purses and puckers her lips, scrunching them in distaste, as if the air itself tasted sour.

Marie stops at a light. "One day you'll wake up, and your body will turn against you." She snaps her fingers, *"boom."* The MIL flicks her right blinker on. "But enough about that. Tell me, I hear Lucy's getting serious?" She peers over her left shoulder.

"I guess so." The last thing I want is to spend another minute talking about Lucy's love life. "He seems nice but we'll see." I don't want to come off rude or, worse, bitter.

"I'm just surprised. I wouldn't think your father would go for a boy like that. He doesn't seem his speed at all."

What the MIL means, of course, is that the Bakars move quickly, and in different circles. Dinners at the newest Manhattan restaurants. Travel expenses that could probably eat Saul's wholesale salary in one bite. David's mother certainly isn't baking her own knafeh or rolling her own yebra, I can tell you that much. As a matter of fact, she probably buys from my mother now, too.

The silence stretches its limbs out in the space between us. It is obvious that we are both thinking of what to say, how to best angle the conversation in our favor without offending the other.

"Lucy always did her own thing," I say. "Personally, that type is not for me."

The MIL smiles. "Well, you wouldn't be marrying my son if it was."

I turn to look out the window and see that the streets are just beginning to stir. Men unload wooden crates onto the sidewalk, unpacking colorful produce to line the stores with. The grocers pull up their gates and answer the phones, which had probably been ringing for at least an hour. I think about how sometimes it feels like this place is frozen in time, a time that only exists for us. It's a funny thing, predictability. To grow up knowing what was before you, the type of man you'd marry, the house you'd raise your kids in, the kind of life you'd live. How and when, I guess that was the only part up to you.

Some call it lucky. Sitto hates surprises, doesn't believe any good comes of them. Growing up in Aleppo, the only constant *was* change — cruel and sudden. So they came to the United States and built a fence around their lives here in Sheepshead Bay, Brooklyn, thankful for the fixed parameters of their neighborhood. The boundaries don't make them feel trapped; they make them feel safe.

"The younger generation, they're in trouble," the MIL says and sighs. "No values, no religion. They say some girls don't even go to the mikvah!" She frowns. "Look, I'm not saying don't be educated. Go to school. You want to work? *Fadal,* get a job two, maybe three days a week. Sell your macrobiotic vegan muffin with the hemp and the chia and the no flavor. But at the end of the day, know where you come from." She slaps the steering wheel with her left palm. "Have" *slap.* "Your" *slap.* "Priorities" *slap*. "Straight" *slap*. One of the MIL's nails is sacrificed for her conviction, but she pays it no attention.

"Saul went straight to his father's business. No college. He wanted to make money, *quick*. A good boy, but"—Marie looks over her left shoulder—"he doesn't have high aspirations. Just to afford to support his family. Family and G-D." She waves her hand. "Everything else is bull."

"Amen," I say, a little too eagerly. If the MIL sees right through me, she is gracious enough not to call me out. If there is one thing I've learned from spending time with Marie, and hearing Saul speak about her, it's that she chooses her words carefully. This isn't some benign morning talk about her son. The MIL is warning me. She wants to prepare me for the life I am about to live and, in doing so, protect her son. I can understand it. The MIL, after all, has three daughters of her own, all older than Saul. She married off all three without a hitch. But she knows, as every mother of daughters does, the way competition can seep between the bonds of sisters, even the strongest ones. She's no stranger to the constant comparing and the silent judgments; fuel for resentment and even distrust. She didn't mention Lucy because she's curious about her relationship. She brought up Lucy because she wants the differences between Saul and David in plain view where I can see them. Saul will give me a beautiful life, but it won't be a life like Lucy's. I should know this going in, and I do. The best part about Saul is knowing exactly what to expect from him. The worst part about Saul is knowing exactly what to expect from him.

"The first year will be hard." She flips down the driver's seat mirror and begins applying a deep brown shade of lipstick. I wait for her to say more, but she doesn't. *Hard, how?* I want to ask, even though I'm pretty sure I already know the answer. We spend our entire girlhoods under the watchful gaze of our fathers, anticipating the moment when we'll come to engulf somebody else's field of vision. Who will it be? What will he be like? We dress and we prep, hoping to meet him at every event. We plan our engagements and then our weddings. We rent our first apartments and taste real independence for the first time, and then—*what* exactly?

"Tough," the MIL emphasizes, as if recalling a memory from her past before allowing it to slip back into the recesses of her mind. And then, as if suddenly realizing where she is and who she is with, she smacks her lips together and clears her throat. "Let's go. She must be waiting." With that, Marie abruptly puts the car in park and turns the engine off.

The floor-to-ceiling windows of Wish You Well exhibit an aspirational display of home décor, a constant reminder to the women passing by that their coffee tables could always be better accessorized, their table settings more cheerful, and their foyers more welcoming. Suddenly, you need five separate diffusers, one in each room, and in varying scents and colors, because Eucalyptus Reed works well in a powder room but smells downright oppressive in the company of upholstery. Wish You Well has been open and servicing the community for nearly ten years, nestled between the bagel shop and my favorite Syrian bakery.

The boutique survives on an endless cycle of credit, its next meal dependent on the unequivocal guarantee that there would always be another wedding, birth, or housewarming to shop for. We show thanks with ceramic bowls, lacquered ashtrays, wooden serving pieces, or gift cards, with the assurance that the money will only be out of your pocket for so long, since you could expect to get the same in return when it's your due. I admire a Fornasetti candle, $275. In a normal world, Saul and I would never buy something like this. But when you invite five hundred people to your wedding, and at least half of them get you a gift card to this store, well, that Fornasetti candle doesn't seem like such a bad investment anymore. The irony is, of course, that the wealthier the couple, the more money they'll receive. It kind of follows the same twisted logic as designers gifting clothing and jewelry to celebrities, when in reality they're the class of people who *least* need free stuff. So Lucy will probably make out with more than I will, Nina with less than both of us (if she ever does get married, B'H), but we'll all be shopping at Wish You Well, the great democratizer of the Jewish community.

My mother says I'll probably get thousands in credit to stores like Wish You Well and various community women-turned-vendors' basements, where items like sterling silver salad tongs, sateen bedsheets, and hair extensions are sold, and that I shouldn't spend it all. Soon I'll have plenty of weddings to attend, and I'll use my existing credit to gift them credit, just like someone used theirs to bestow congratulations upon me, and so on and so forth, until money isn't really money at all, not backed by government-issued paper dollar bills or banks or even gold, but by happy occasions, and goodwill, and the assumption that those who give shall receive, and give again. But above all else, this system, like so many others, feeds on trust, in the institutions that keep us growing and thriving, but mainly existing, together.

"HiwelcometoWishYouWellhowcanIhelpyou?" A petite girl, whose age and address I know (though I can't remember her name because I'd never actually spoken to her before), briefly looks up from an iPad to greet us. She ropes her tongue around a giant green Starbucks straw as she speaks, sucking the remaining bits of her iced coffee from the bottom of the cup. Another girl, older, whom I only know by name, rearranges a mock display of a Shabbat dinner table. I take note as she repositions the kiddush cup behind the challah tray, to the left. The MIL lingers awkwardly behind me, taking great interest in a twelve-piece set of rainbow-colored Lucite napkin rings.

"Hi," I exclaim, louder than I'd expected to. "I'm here to register? My mother-in-law called Gloria to make an appointment? Marie? Maybe they know if Gloria's here?"

"Gloria doesn't come in until eleven." Jennifer—I remember her name is Jennifer—answers. She shakes the ice around by the lid of the cup.

"After she puts her kids on the van," Lisa confirms.

"What's your name?" Jennifer flips through a yellow legal pad on the counter. On it, I can make out the names of couples who are soon to be or recently married, the dates of their weddings scrawled beneath. I try not to look too taken aback by her question. Still, it stings to be asked your name and have your popularity be so openly questioned.

"Fortune Cohen," I say. "My fiancé is Saul—"

"Dweck," Jennifer says. "Got it."

"Have people been coming in for her, or . . ." Marie trails.

"We've had a few."

"Gift cards mainly?"

"I'd have to look it up, but since she hasn't registered for gifts yet, probably."

"It's late to register, no?"

"Usually the girls come in a month, two months before their showers. Did you have a shower?" Jennifer directs her gaze at me.

"She didn't want one," Marie says, falling heavily on the *want*, as if to say, *I tried, but what can you do?*

"Why not!" Lisa cries.

"Truth," Jennifer says, "you're smart. Why go through the hassle of exchanging all of those gifts before the wedding. Might as well take your time and wait. You're going to return everything for credit anyway, no?"

"But I feel like you get less gifts that way," Lisa says.

"That's what I think, too." The MIL nods.

"Like, I'm single, so people don't expect me to give wedding gifts. But if I'm invited to a shower, I always send a gift. Even if I don't go," Lisa says, rationalizing.

"To each his own," Jennifer says. "So, look around, see what you need first and then what you want. We have a checklist that a lot of girls like using also. But—this is his mother, right? So she can help you!" Jennifer chirps.

"Let us know if you need anything. We just got in *stunning* Hermès dishes. Perfect for your meat set." According to the laws of kashrut, I would need two separate dish sets—one for meat and one for dairy.

"I feel like she should do glass for her meat, no?" Lisa asks.

Jennifer contemplates. "Truth, they're light so you could do them for dairy, too. Or if you have enough credit, you can get them as a second meat set for when you have company over for the holidays or something."

"I will eat off these plates." The MIL smiles, running her fingers over the ceramic surface. I wait for her to point me in the right direction, but she just stands there. I wonder if she's ever been here before at all. The MIL's own plates are delicate, and traditional, and she takes great pride in them. Saul mentioned to me that she rarely used them, but she dusted them off when I first had dinner at his house. *They're not dishwasher safe,* he'd remarked. *Me? I'd never buy dishes that weren't dishwasher safe. But aboose my mother, she loves to do everything by hand.* The MIL is closer in age to Sitto than she is to my own mother, and comparing them helps me to better understand Marie. She usually seems so sure of herself. She does everything quickly and without hesitation. The cooking, the shopping, the decision-making. Though here she seems just as lost as I am.

"Then you'll need glasses, and maybe a set of scotch glasses for your husband. Does he drink scotch? We just got in this Baccarat set. Let me show you." Lisa motions for me to follow her.

"Oh, the Baccarat is *gorgeous,*" Jennifer says.

I try to use the dishes and glasses around me to imagine what married life with Saul would actually look like, that first year. I imagine him pouring scotch from that decanter into that glass, but that doesn't feel right. Wine, maybe wine is more believable? But no, I can't really visualize that, either. Are these things we'll actually use? As a couple in our young twenties? It all feels staged for some pretend life, as though the curtains can close at any moment.

"Gorgeous. Agreed." Lisa waves at us. "Come, I'll show you. You're gonna *love.*"

How's it goin? Saul texts me.

Great! I respond, thankful to do something with my hands other than fondle extremely breakable water pitchers.

Major bonding? lol

> We sang along to the radio the entire way here

funny

"Come and look at these serving bowls! They brought them out special," the MIL says.

I listen intently as Lisa and Jennifer, with encyclopedic knowledge, explain to me how the porcelain (hand-wash only) is lined with 24 karat gold (not microwaveable) and glossed with a metal finish (no acidic soaps). I admire these two girls, who know more than I'd ever know about this—plating and hammered silver and guest etiquette, fine—but at least they know a lot about *something*. What did I know? How to price "slightly imperfect" Hanes underwear and second-rate laundry detergent? I can tell how impressed the MIL is by them. She stands quietly, nodding in agreement at their every word, touching when told to. These are the types of girls, I think, that she'd like to see her son with. A woman who *elevated* him. Maybe that's what she really meant about Saul not being ambitious. She doesn't want me, a girl whose own mother cooks for a living, but who passes off store-bought knafeh as her own.

Sitto warned us that we'd need to know these kinds of things. *Pay attention,* she'd said, as my mother rolled yebra, hollowed out tomatoes and onions, made her own kibbe hamda balls. Nina, Lucy, and me. Sitto begged us to sit with her, to watch the way she prepared and served a meal, and even froze the leftovers for a later day. But Nina took no interest and Lucy was too busy being the baby. I, of course, said yes. Because that's what I do. I listened intently as Sitto explained the differences in oils for high-heat cooking. Where the cheapest kosher salt could be found by the bulk and why one should never buy pre-juiced lemons. I nodded along to the benefits of owning one good glass set of dishes as opposed to two separate ones for meat and milk. It's only natural, then, that I should begin doing more of the caretaking, too. Driving Sitto to her once-a-week nail appointments. Her bimonthly color. The occasional visit to the podiatrist or insulin check.

I clench my teeth as the MIL pretended to cut a steak with a fork and knife, admiring how the Sabre flatware glided so effortlessly across the plate. I nod along, continuing to add brushstrokes to a portrait I ultimately don't see myself wanting to be a part of. And yet, I set the table, not fully knowing whether I intend on sitting down to dinner.

Later, we pull up to my house.

"I'm so happy we did that," Marie exclaims, before putting the car in park. "Those girls were fantastic. And so *shatra*! Do you know them?"

"Me, too," I chirp, ignoring the MIL's question. I'd been successfully cajoled into two dish sets and coordinating table linens, which included things I'd never heard of but now, apparently, cannot live without. "Yeah, I think they're both a little older than me."

"So *shatra*." The MIL kisses the tips of her fingers. "And still single?" She shakes her head, "I don't believe it!"

As soon as Marie pulls away from my house, I text my mother to tell Sitto that we have to postpone our cooking lesson to later tonight. I begin walking toward the F train. Carmen isn't expecting me today, but I know she could use help cleaning and organizing the stockroom. Maybe I can convince Dad to finally go through that stack of bills on his desk. The truth is that I need to be anywhere but here. I put my head down and my earphones in, raising the volume on my phone until the chatter in my head is all but drowned out.

The F train lumbers into the station, slowly and reluctantly, as if its own mother urges it forward, two strong palms fixed upon its shoulders. My car is empty save for a Hispanic woman and her small daughter. I know it will fill up as we inch farther out of Brooklyn and into Manhattan. I grab the inner of two window seats near the subway doors. The train whizzes past Avenue I. Past Ditmas and Church Avenue and Fort Hamilton. My mind begins to wander as we creep toward the bridge that will take us across the river.

If Saul and I broke up, he'd be single for exactly one day before one of the many desperately single girls snatched him up. The train inches into Park Slope. Court Street and Seventh Avenue. Birkenstocks and maroon tops and unkempt hair. Saul's résumé is stellar. He idolizes his mother, respects his father. His ambitions will only grow so far as our family does; he doesn't aspire to be anything too great or powerful, as some men with wandering eyes and questionable morals do. He loves me, or at least he's convinced himself he does.

West Fourth Street. NYU hipsters and half-empty green juices. What would I do with all of the stuff? The dishes and the crystal cake stands. The leather gloves and quilted bag. The silver-framed baby photo of Saul that sits on my nightstand, a gift from the MIL designed to excite me over the genetic prospects of our future children. The wedding deposits. The apartment we were just about to start looking for. The ring.

Saul isn't my soulmate. I can't turn to any song on my iPod and fantasize about him. I don't melt when I kiss him. Our conversations don't dive into deep water, but they aren't baby pool, either. He does make me feel secure, or at least our relationship does. I like knowing that I'm in the same place as most of the girls I know and the others wish to be. My married friends always say that love grows and that having a child opens up an entirely new part of a person to love. You may not feel it right away, that spark. But the spark fizzles anyway, and when it does, you're left with just a man and his ability to make choices. Saul is clean shaven and solid. For the most part, I know what he's going to say before he says it. I could never realistically be with someone like Isaac, a man who wears slippers to work and is inclined toward resentment.

The train comes up for air and suddenly light floods the car. I pop open my phone and text Saul:

Order in and a movie tonight?

Within seconds, I receive his reply.

I pick the movie this time:)

I respond with a <3 and close my phone.

All of this time to think can't be good. I now understand why couples opt for shorter engagement periods: less time to ponder, to fight, to indulge every fleeting emotion. What I need to remember is that Saul is a good boy. *Adami*, as Sitto would say. He's dependable, and he actually likes being around my family. He showed that to me on day one, nearly a year ago today.

Grandpa Jack had already been in the ground six days by the time Saul came to pay respects at the behest of his grandmother, who played canasta with Sitto.

Grandpa Jack's health seemed to decline slowly, and then all at once. When he did die, we had no time to feel sorry for him or ourselves, which I guess was a good thing. My mother stood slumped over the kitchen island, the phone tucked between her ear and shoulder, her hands knuckle deep in a bowl of linguini and chicken juice. I knew that it was my father calling from the hospital to tell her that his father had died, because the conversation lasted less than fifteen seconds. This was uncommon, to say the least, for a woman who once spent ninety minutes maligning a piece of one-ply toilet paper.

"Use at your own risk!" she shouted over the house intercom.

My phone rang as soon as my mother set hers down and I knew that it was my father now calling me with the news, too, and it occurred to me that he might cry, which is something I've never seen my father do, and so I ignored the call so that my mother and I could cry in peace, together.

"And you *know* the shiva's going to *have* to be here," she sobbed, her tears falling heavily on my T-shirt. "Because G-D forbid any of *them* do anything." She cried harder. Mom straightened herself, rummaging through her oil-spotted Rolodex. "I'll have to call the caterer. And that stupid chair rental place. I have to assume we're going to get tons of people. And that waitress—what's her name? I heard she's doing all the shivas now. Get your aunt on the phone—she's probably booked by now! I'm going to need you and your sister to help out, okay? Where is Nina, by the way? I *need* my girls!" she wailed at the walls.

"Oh, and my carpets are *filthy*! *Filthy*! And I told your father, I told him, 'Morris, we gotta get the guy to clean the carpets, Morris.' But you know your father, leaves everything until the last minute and then the minute's gone! Oh, he was such a good man, Fortune. I thought about killing him every day for the last twenty-five years but your grandpa Jack was a good, good man. G-D knows Sitto's no Sunday morning picnic."

"Something good will come of this," Sitto whispered when we broke the news to her. They'd been married for nearly sixty-five years. "*Abal,*" she looked to Nina, myself, and Lucy, "G-D will send one of you a good *nassib* in his place." For six days, however, G-D seemed only intent on the taking.

We schlepped through the hours, a slow and steady chug of "my condolences" and cinnamon Altoids. My mother kept the grief contained to the living room, where she arranged eleven chair cushions on the floor for the mourners. For seven days, my father and his siblings would sit with their clothes torn, accepting condolences and fond memories from the dozens of people who would file in to pay their respects. We rose at six-thirty each morning. My mother and I prepped the coffee, helping the waitress out in the kitchen. Nina and Lucy were bound to the living room, where they straightened bridge chairs into perfect rows of ten and made sure that the mirrors were properly covered and the tissue boxes full.

Dozens of men filed in at eight A.M. for prayers and breakfast, the only two things a good Jew was ever on time for. I watched through the sliding doors as they gorged on the sesame bagels and sweet kaak, the skin on their forearms depressed by their tefillin. Their talk was so easy, fluid, the way they dusted the crumbs off their ties. Mornings seemed to be the best for my father, too. He spent his nights counting the hours until the rest of the world woke up with him. They talked business, sports, which houses were coming up and which were going down in the neighborhood. Dad floated through the mornings as if he were the host of some grand party, only to be deflated by the time ten o'clock rolled around and the last of the men went off to work. He'd retire to his room for a few hours, too exhausted to lay his body down.

The women came to pay their respects at eleven A.M. They came ready to work, spilling into the kitchen to help unpack and plate the contents of aluminum tins: mujadarah and spanach, cheese calzones and fried flounder. There was no rhyme or reason for the heaps of food, only that it anesthetized the grief.

"You see a surface, you cover it with a bowl of kaak!" my mother barked at no one in particular.

"Dry fruit everywhere!" Sitto proclaimed. "People look for the food"—she brought three fingers to her lips—"when they have nothing left to say."

I kept my distance from the den, where Sitto and the players sat around a petrified glass table. I counted "The Split-Tongue" and Barbara "screw-you-six-ways-'til-Sunday-for-a-better-game-of-canasta" among them. On the fourth day of the shiva, my mother sent me inside to deliver a tray of Turkish coffee.

"Honey, come. Come here," a handsome woman with weathered skin called out to me. Her accent was heavy, a mix of French and Arabic and South Brooklyn. Her voice was low and raspy, but she didn't have to raise it to be heard.

Sitto wrapped her hand around my waist as she pulled me farther into her circle of widows. She looked tired, more tired than I remember her ever looking. Her short hair was fried at the edges, and I knew her first order of business once the shiva ended would be a trip to Helen's for color. Her lips looked anemic in the absence of her brown lipstick, and her torn shirt carried the overbearing smell of perfume trying to moonlight as soap. I folded my body into hers.

"This is Sally and Morris's second, Fortune, named after"—Grandma lifted her chin with her free hand and smiled—"yours truly."

"Oooo." The women cooed in unity.

"Abal."

"Sabi andak."

"What a gawjoos girl," the woman who had summoned me said as she looked me up and down.

"I remember you when you were"—she paused and pinched her long fingers together—"dees tall. How old are you now, rohi?" she asked.

"She's twenty, Ruthie," Sitto answered. "Nina's the other one—the oldest, let me get—?"

"Lehh, how old is that one now?" a great-aunt asked.

"I'm not su—"

"She's twenty-five," I answered. The women looked down at their feet in silence. My grandmother looked at me, then up.

"Inshallah she will find someone this year," the woman—Ruthie—offered, breaking the silence.

"Inshallah." The women echoed, fortified by Ruthie's faith. Whoever this tiny woman was, the others looked up to her.

"Fortune, you know my grandson, Saul? He is very handsome." Ruthie purred.

"Lehh, he's too young for her, Ruthie," someone interrupted. "I have grandson, twenty-six year, good age for you. Has his own business already, making pencil cases!" She clapped her hands with glee.

"Lehhh," Sitto scoffed. "Nobody uses pencils anymore."

"What too young?" Ruthie challenged, whipping her opponent into place. "He is about her age, and very picky, our Saul." She wagged her finger at me. "But I think he will like you." Ruthie softened.

On the seventh and final day of the shiva, Saul Dweck came to pay his respects.

Chapter Twelve

....

"So, what are you thinking?" I spear a piece of sesame broccoli from Saul's to-go container and bite off its crown. The house is quiet and dark with Lucy and Nina both out.

"Is anybody home?" Saul asks, reading my mind. He smells clean, and his hair is still damp from the shower.

"I don't think so," I say. "I mean Sitto, but she's probably passed out in her room."

"Nice. It's rare we get to watch TV solo in the den," Saul says. He nudges me slightly and grabs the chicken and broccoli from the coffee table, forking a bite into his mouth. "So Lucy's out with that guy again."

"You mean David, her boyfriend? Yes."

"So do you like the guy? You never say."

"What's there to say? He seems nice. Lucy really likes him."

"Oh, come on, Fortune, there's no dirt? What are your parents saying?"

"You know my mother. She loves to play coy."

"Yeah, but I'm sure she's thrilled. Did they meet the future in-laws yet? I'm surprised David hasn't had the *talk* with your dad yet. Or has he and do you just not know?"

I know where Saul is going with this, and it isn't a game I want to play right now. "I mean, they're happy because Lucy's happy. That's all that matters. That's all I know." And it's the truth. If there have been any progressions, nobody has mentioned them to me. I'm sure they think they're protecting me by not having Lucy eclipse my spotlight.

"Oh, I'm sure Lucy's happy. Very happy." Saul rolls his eyes. "This is going to change the whole dynamic." He leans back and crosses his arms. "A guy like that."

"Relax," I say, smiling. "You're still the favorite."

"Oh, I'm sure they like me more as a *person*," Saul says seriously. "But you know, someone like David adds another element." He rubs his thumb and index finger together: *money.*

I try not to look taken aback. It is one thing for me to question my sister's relationship. It is another for Saul to do so. And what does he know about David that we don't? So he is well off. That doesn't make him a bad person. Was he insinuating something about Lucy? My mother? My whole family? My cheeks flush with embarrassment, then anger. If Saul is really as sure of himself as he pretends to be, he wouldn't feel the need to make these little snide comments.

Saul squeezes my thigh. "Anyway, you're right. Lucy looks happy and it seems like he treats her right. I just hope they wait until after the wedding to make any moves."

"We're getting married in two weeks," I say, annoyed. "Are you crazy?"

"Relax." Saul puts his palms on my shoulders. "I just don't want anyone taking the attention off you, that's all."

"I'm not worried about that." I grab the remote. "They just became official."

"I know how guys like him operate. And it's not like he needs time to save money or anything. Remember what a hard time your dad gave me? He practically asked for a last will and testament when I asked him to marry you."

"No, he didn't." He definitely did.

"He wanted to make sure I could support you. I don't blame him. I had to prove myself, it was good for me. Lit a little fire under my ass. I would want the same for my daughter," Saul says. "This guy . . . he doesn't have to do any of that."

"He still has to prove himself as a person."

"Yeah, but half the battle is won," Saul says, reclining. "And it's the more important half. That's all I'm saying. Sometimes guys with money don't have that fire. They don't need to. They have a cushion, don't need to work as hard."

"He's a doctor," I say.

"You don't think I would've loved to go to 'medical school'?" Saul makes air quotes. As if David went to a university for clowns.

I didn't.

"I had to go to work."

"Right," I say, not wanting to continue the conversation.

"I'm coming from a good place." Saul inches toward me, his face centimeters from my own.

"I know." I turn my face away slightly and he kisses me on the cheek. Then when I turn my face back toward him he kisses me fully on the lips. The lights in the den are bright, the door left slightly ajar to let out the smell of kosher Chinese food. Saul pushes his tongue against my teeth, wriggling it until I open my mouth. Eight months of kissing Saul, and I'm still not sure I am doing it right. He starts to grow more forceful in his movements and I abruptly pull away.

"Can you shut the lights?" I pull my half-zipped sweatshirt back up over my bare shoulder, suddenly ashamed of the cotton GAP triangle bra I have on underneath.

Saul gets up to shut the lights and the door.

"Better?" he asks, returning to the couch. He pulls me on top of him so that my legs straddle his waist. I feel the physical manifestation of his attraction toward me and it makes me want to jump and stay put at the same time. I freeze.

"I'm so attracted to you," Saul whispers in my ear. He hugs my body close to him as he kisses my neck.

I will my body to relax, to melt into the moment. But no matter how I try, my legs remain rigid, my shoulders fixed. Even though we'd never gone further than this, the anticipation that it might turn into something more sparks every nerve in my body. I've spent so many months pulling away from Saul that even I can't tell what I want anymore. My body has grown so accustomed to recoiling, sometimes I fear it won't open up when the time is right. Saul never pressures me. In fact, he seems to like that I am inexperienced, innocent. We both know without discussion that we are saving other things—*the thing*—for marriage. This is just a bit of fun; at least it is supposed to be fun. And maybe in the beginning it was. It felt nice to be desired, to be the cause of an actual, physiological change in another person. But as time went on, and the prospect of this person being the only person I'd ever experience things with became more and more real, my ability to truly lose myself in the moment dissipated. I'm in my head, constantly. It feels like I live in a forever state of panic.

Saul's motions grow quicker, more urgent. His hands are on my face, my neck, my chest. His hunger should be a turn-on for me, right? He's lost in the moment and I'm stuck in my head. All I can think is: *Is this it?*

Then: *What is wrong with me?*

I feel like a part of me has left my body and is floating above, watching Saul and this person I'm no longer familiar with. I sense the thought coming from a mile away and still, I can't avoid it. Like a gnat that keeps coming for my food, just as I'm about to eat, an image of Isaac flashes across my mind. *What if this was him?* The mere idea of it causes my body to relax, as if the message from my brain that this was wrong got lost in the mail.

"Are you okay?" Saul pulls back slightly, and it's only then that I realize I'd been shaking my head.

The slamming of the front door startles us both, and I quickly jump off Saul's lap. *Shit*, Saul says, adjusting his clothes and smoothing his hair.

The door to the den cracks open slightly and Nina pokes her head in.

"Oh, it's you," she says hurriedly. I think I can hear a man's voice behind her. I strain my eyes but it's too dark to see. Nina mutters a sorry and quickly closes the door. I hear her walk away, and I'm almost sure I hear giggles and a second set of footsteps. Saul doesn't seem to notice.

"Can you believe how soon we won't have to deal with that anymore? It'll finally be just us two." He reaches for the remote and flicks on the TV. The blue light of NY1 floods the room.

"It's hard to believe," I say.

The first truth I've spoken all day.

The light in Nina's room is on and her door is shut. I can hear her on the phone. Her voice sounds far away, as if she's having the conversation from underneath her covers. I consider knocking. Nina and I don't *talk*, not deeply anyway. But if there is one person who wouldn't judge me, or think I was insane, it's probably her. I reach my fist up toward the door and then decide against it. I'm glad I did, because moments later, Nina laughs. It's a coy, nervous laugh, followed by a simple "Shut up." She is definitely talking to a guy. And not just any guy, but someone she likes. I pivot next door to my own room, which is apparently empty now that Lucy is out with the crowned prince.

I'm the one who's getting married in two weeks, and yet I feel like the biggest loser in this house. How is that possible? Neither of my sisters had anything going on when Saul and I got engaged. Not that I wanted it to stay that way, of course not. But it is very apparent now that I'm not the only sister moving forward with her life. I already feel the attention slipping from Saul and me to Lucy and David. I'm not jealous, I swear, that's not it. It's just that seeing my sisters fall so naturally into new patterns—Nina with her job and potential mystery boy, Lucy's relationship being all anyone wants to talk about—makes my own journey feel forced in comparison. Or worse, boring. Like I'm just someone to deal with rather than obsess over.

The corners of Lucy's bedspread are tucked neatly beneath the mattress. Her knapsack, unopened, is on top of her bed. I begin to tidy up our vanity table, putting makeup brushes in the emptied mason jar where we keep them, color palettes and mascara in the single drawer. I start to rearrange the stack of books on the wall-hung shelf above the table when a photo album catches my eye. It has a glossy hard cover and computer-printed photos. There's a picture of Saul and me on the cover, beaming with joy, and beneath our faces in big block letters is written: SAUL AND FORTUNE'S PROPOSAL. I start to leaf through the album and immediately regret it.

Saul managed to catch me wholly unprepared. Had I the slightest idea about what he was planning, I would've gone to bed the night before in a cute nightgown, put some concealer beneath my eyes, a hint of highlighter on my cheekbones. But who the hell proposes at seven o'clock in the morning?

"Gotchya!" he said, when he saw my watermelon-colored retainer.

Now looking through the album, I think about how hard it is to believe that three months have already passed since the proposal. It feels like just yesterday that my mother shook me from my sleep and threw me down the flight of stairs and into the arms of the man I'd soon call "fiancé." She videoed the entire thing, too. So try as I might to forget the fact that my first inclination upon her waking me was to "stop, drop, and roll!" there is crystalline footage to remind me.

In the end, I wasn't *that* surprised to see Saul standing in the foyer. I was more confused as to why he chose to do it this way, hijacking my dreams at an ungodly hour, a fog of sleep trailing me as I descended the stairs, one foot in front of the other. Was he worried that in a state of full consciousness I might say no?

There's a close-up of me standing at the foot of the stairs, my pupils and mouth wide with surprise. Next to it, a wide shot of Mom and me. Her hands are clasped around mine as she leads me into the center of a heart fashioned out of rose petals. Saul is in the middle, cradling an acoustic guitar in his arms.

The guitar: Now that detail threw me for a loop. Is it horrible that my first thought was, *Please*, Hashem, *when can I tell the boy that he can't play a chord to save a foreskin's life?* My second, and more disturbing, thought, of course, had to do with the quality of my breath. Ninety-nine percent of the photos show my left hand covering my mouth, and so I look like I'm in a state of perpetual shock for the duration of the album. Really, I was just trying to shield my mouth, which was at least four Listerines shy of wife material.

"She's shocked!" my mother cried.

"And you said I wouldn't be able to surprise you." Saul smiled, taking my hand as he fell to one knee. The room began to spin, slowly at first, and then recklessly, like a globe off its axis. The bodies surrounding us became distorted and dismembered, a collective blur. For a moment, everything seemed to slow to a stop. The voices, the frequency of the whoops and whistles deepened, and deepened, until they hung suspended in midair. The chords on Saul's guitar grew sluggish, as if they'd been stripped of their wings and had nowhere to travel, trapped within the rubber walls of a jelly-filled balloon.

This must be a dream.

I was sure, sure that I had been dreaming. And then I heard it, a sound that, had I in fact been sleeping, would've rocketed me from the nadirs of a yearlong coma. With one hand gripped around the cordless phone, the other clutching a stomach full of aspartame, my mother wailed.

"*Moorrrriiiiiss!*" Her voice careened through the house, assaulting every square inch of marble personally. The notes from Saul's guitar hovered, the song on pause. "*Morris!* Get off the toilet! Your daughter's getting engaged!"

"Tell them to start without me!" my father yelled back from behind a closed door.

"So?" Saul looked up at me. "Will you?"

We both knew what my answer would be. How could it be anything else?

"Of course!"

"Diana. It's happening. He's doing it! Now! I gotta call Stephanie." My mother scrambled about like a chicken without a head, the cordless pressed against her ear.

"Yeah, Stephanie! He's on one knee as we speak! As we *speak*! Wait, hold on—hold on! I got a click."

"Bonnie, honey! She's shaking like a leaf! No, no she had no idea! Lisa's on the other line."

"Could you believe it, Lisa? It's finally happening *this very second—wait*, she said *what* about me?"

Sitto was injured at the time, and the pictures show her off to the side with the aunts and cousins, her knee resting on a Drive Medical dual pad walker.

Saul's family was positioned on the opposite end of the divided foyer. I immediately spotted the MIL, fortressed by her daughters Ruthie, Linda, and Sarah, who were in turn fortressed by their own small children—a Matryoshka doll of loyalty and blood and gel polish. I was surrounded by twenty cameras, every single one of them positioned to share a moment that should've been private. Me, in all of my morning glory, my smile about as natural as aerosol cheese, and Saul, looking like the deer who finally decided to embrace the headlights.

Of course, my mother looked picture-perfect. I hated her for her fresh color, her evenly concealed skin, for looking better than me in her airbrush yoga pants. Even Lucy and Nina had enough sense to dress for the occasion. And what was I wearing? An oversize T-shirt and magnified reading glasses I picked up while in the checkout line at CVS. Would Saul even be able to hear my reply through the spit retainer imprisoning my mouth? "She say yeah yet!?" my father shouted, barreling down the stairs in basketball shorts and a white T-shirt, *New York Post* in hand. At least him, I could count on.

Nina leaned lazily on the banister, looking bored. Lucy stood herself in front of me, extending her phone above our heads so that it angled for the perfect selfie.

"*Engaged!*" she screeched.

"*Abal* to all my girls." My mother smiled, roping us into a hug.

"Yes!" Sitto clapped a hand against her good knee. "*Abal* Lucy and Nina! And all of you, too!" She smiled, her eyes trailing the crowd of single women around her.

"My speech was top, no?" Saul's eyes met mine for the approval we both knew he didn't need, laughing as he slid the ring onto my finger.

"Oh my G-D," Tina cried. "It's *gorgeous!*" She grabbed my hand, tilting it left and right so that the light danced off the princess-cut diamond.

My hand was pulled in opposing directions, like a buoy taken by currents of Jewish women. Saul draped one arm around my shoulders. We smiled this way and that, left and right, up and down, pivoting every few seconds to accommodate the swell of flashes going off from various cameras.

"Kiss!" someone shouted.

"*Kiss!*"

"Did you forget about *me?*" The crowd parted. Marie made her way down the middle and toward us. "*Mabrook*, honey." The MIL took both of my hands in hers and leaned in. I kissed her cheek. "Go ahead, I'll hold them off while you get ready." As she pulled away from our embrace, the MIL called out to my mother, "Hair and makeup is already upstairs, waiting for you both! You're welcome."

I tried to open my mouth, to say yes, to say thank you, to say anything.

I just needed to brush my teeth first.

I close the album, reclining back onto the soft pillows of my bed. My eyes feel heavy and when I allow them to close, I see Isaac leaning against the wire shelving unit, his silhouette masked by the dusty glow of that single lightbulb. I don't allow myself to picture his face. Recall his expression. The excitement in his eyes as he looked at me. But there is one thing that is painfully obvious. One thing that I cannot deny: It felt good to be seen.

And thou shalt not approach unto a woman to uncover her na-
kedness, as long as she is impure by her uncleanness.

LEVITICUS 18:19

LESSON 3: BEHAVIOR DURING NIDDAH

The Torah says it plain and clear, ladies: "You shall not approach." Until you are made pure once again, you and your husband must separate physically. But what does this mean? Can he still kiss you? Embrace you? Greet you?

You may assume it's safe to sleep in the same bed. You'd be wrong. Let's dive deeper.

All kinds of work which a wife performs for her husband, a men-
struant also may perform for her husband, with the exception of
filling his cup, making ready his bed and washing his face, hands
and feet.

—RABBI ISAAC B. HANANIA, TALMUD: KETUBOT 61A.

These duties are all examples of *harchakot*: laws established by the rabbis in order to create distance between a husband and wife during the Niddah period. *Harchakot* quite literally act as a fence between the couple so that they aren't tempted to have sex during this time.

HARCHAKOT

No Physical Contact–*whatsoever*. A couple may not so much as pass an object to each other. Sit back as your husband retrieves his own salt!
(You may sit on the same couch so long as there is no chance of you falling into each other.)

Sleeping Arrangements–A couple must sleep on two separate mattresses with separate sheets and bedding. Furthermore, a wife should not make her husband's bed in his presence.

Appropriate Dress–It's forbidden for a wife to undress in front of her husband. A wife should opt for modest sleepwear during the Niddah period and keep covered the parts of her body she normally would around the house.
(Even during this time it's important for a wife to look beautiful for her husband and for him to enjoy her beauty.)

Sharing Meals–Dining alone together often creates a romantic setting. Therefore, a couple should place a *heker*–a reminder–on the dinner table. It should be an object (e.g., a snow globe or a glass figurine) to remind them that they are in Niddah.
(A couple must not share each other's food.)

During Illness–*Harchakot* should still be observed if one is ill. If one is severely ill, consult your rabbi.

LUCY

Chapter Thirteen

....

I'm too smitten to care that my parents *don't seem* to mind that my school grades are slipping because I have David, and he isn't going anywhere. I tell Mom as much, as we sit in traffic trying to get to the dressmaker. I flip the passenger seat mirror down and wipe last night's mascara from beneath my eyelids. I push all of my hair to the front, careful to cover the spot on my neck where David got carried away, and I smile remembering how I didn't stop him. On a typical Sunday morning, I'd be riding in the passenger seat of Giselle's car. Ever since she got her license at seventeen, she's picked me up for our routine run to the Starbucks drive-through, where there'd be a line of cars snaked around the parking lot. We knew we'd see Jeffrey and his friends there. Jeffrey and his friends were always there, loading up on black coffees and triple foam mocha cappuccinos, leaning with their backs against their cars, cigarettes looking less than natural in their hands. I looked forward to the meetups. I enjoyed seeing which poor freshman girl Jeffrey managed to wrangle into his passenger seat, knowing that it was me he really wanted. But that whole game seemed so irrelevant now, so *juvenile*. Giselle said she understood why I couldn't blow off today's appointment, but I knew that deep down, she didn't. Before David and I got serious, I was her meal ticket to boys, but it didn't take long for her to recognize that without me in the picture, she was one step closer to Jeffrey. I'm sure she called Sari instead and I'm sure Sari was thrilled.

"David says he's going to talk to Dad soon. He told me last night," I say, carefully studying my mother's profile for a reaction. The news was almost enough to make me forget that Jeffrey dumped me for prom, as Giselle said he would. And that Giselle dumped her date for Jeffrey, as everyone said *she* would. The move happened so swiftly, I almost threw my back out trying to catch it. When I told David, he said something like: *Only after she gets captured does the queen realize she's been playing chess all along.* Which I don't think I fully get, but it sounded smart enough to make me feel better. I won't waste another second thinking about it. My mother once told me that friends were just a means to an end. She was right. I have my sisters and that's all I really need.

"Did he really?" My mother gasps. She stops prematurely at a yellow light and the car behind us lets out a prolonged honk. My mother flips the bird in her rearview mirror and ducks when she realizes it's Mrs. Tawil. Not to worry, there will be warm smiles and pleasantries exchanged in the aisles of Spice tomorrow, like nothing ever happened.

"Are you surprised?" I tap my foot against the floor mat of the car.

"A little bit. I mean I'm not, but I am . . ."

"I thought you'd be thrilled."

"Of *course* I'm thrilled, honey. I mean I wish he would come around more, you two are always running off to here or there, the city and wherever else. But of course I'm thrilled. You know, it's just a lot with Fortune's wedding so soon. I'm not even done with her yet, and now I have to think about you, too."

"You say it like we're errands you have to check off a list. A little enthusiasm would be nice."

"You know what I mean, Lucy. It's not easy—marrying off two daughters. It's *work*. It's *hard*. But I'm not complaining! Don't get me wrong, these are good problems to have, thank G-D. Two weddings potentially so close to each other, G-D willing. It's a blessing. Just do me a favor, okay? Just promise me you won't mention any of this to Fortune. She'd never admit it, but you know how she is. I don't want her to think—"

"I'm not trying to steal her spotlight," I say defensively.

"I know you're not *trying* to." My mother flicks on her blinker and turns off Ocean Parkway and onto Kings Highway. "But just David being who he is, and you being who you are . . . there's going to be a lot of buzz around you guys. That's just the way it is. I can't stop people from comparing. People will always talk. I just don't want it to come between the two of you."

"Obviously." Although Fortune never lets on that she is anything less than content, she *is* human at the end of the day. She won't be able to help but notice what I get from David versus what she got from Saul, where and how we live, the volume of community chatter surrounding my wedding as compared to hers.

My mother pulls into the dressmaker's driveway, a narrow pathway set among a row of nearly identical two-family brick homes. There's a laundromat off the corner, and two older ladies sit out in front on foldable chairs, drinking coffee from paper cups and speaking in animated Arabic. One of them raises her voice as a truck's reverse sensors blare in the background. My mother turns off the car and when she opens the door, the smell of freshly baked pita bread wafts inside. She stays put. "I'm happy for you, Lucy. I am. Out of the three of you, you're definitely best equipped to handle that life."

I recoil a little bit. My mother says *that life* like it's a negative thing. "What do you mean, *that life*?"

"You know," she says hurriedly. "David's family is blessed. You won't have to worry about money. Your kids won't have to worry about money. But that kind of family comes with its own pressures. You'll have to keep up, but I'm not worried about you."

"Thank you, I think?" My eyes drift back to the two women having their coffee in front of the laundromat; foreigners, they look a little younger than Sitto. One of the women scowls as she takes a sip of coffee while her friend rambles on in their native tongue. They are completely unbothered by how passersby might perceive them. They are exactly where and with whom they need to be. For them, life is so simple, black and white even. When evil shows up on your doorstep and forces you to flee your home for a new one, life becomes so. Like Sitto, I'm sure they've spent their years in America only wanting to be comfortable. To eat and drink with friends and family, to worship and, yes, maybe make a little money along the way. A black Range Rover double-parks in front of the women and a young mother with a bouncy blowout pops out of the driver's seat. She still has paper pedicure flip-flops on her feet and cotton wedged between her red-painted toes. A sales associate from the children's boutique next door meets her halfway with a large yellow bag. They shout their "Thank yous!" and the young mother rushes back to her car where she revs her horsepower engine and speeds off to her next errand. I remember playing a volleyball game against an Ashkenaz yeshiva team from the Five Towns. After the game, one of the girls from the opposing team and I started talking. I asked her if I could borrow a dollar for the vending machines; I hadn't brought any cash. "Of course!" she said, reaching into her wallet. "And here, we thought all Syrians were rich," she said jokingly. I laughed it off, knowing that this was the perception we gave off. From the outside, the community appears like a Barbie Dreamhouse. Instead of pink Corvettes and swimming pools, we have Range Rovers and limestone. But as anyone living here knows, it's much more complicated than that. Because underneath the supposed Barbie Dreamhouse, there are lots of weeds that need trimming and pipes that need cleaning. There are roots that keep growing and growing until they blossom into beautiful trees, and others that languish under the pressure of all that soil. The community's success has no doubt surpassed the wildest dreams of those two women enjoying their coffee, but for the young mother running errands up a street that has been built specifically to cater to her every need, that dream has been her only reality. If you're among the lucky ones, you can turn a blind eye to all of the ugliness that comes with triumph. Maybe that's what my mother means.

"Your life won't be anything like mine and your father's, initially. That's for sure." She laughs.

"What do you mean?"

"I mean it was tough."

"Tough how?" I press on.

"Let's go. We're going to be late and you know how she gets." Mom unbuckles her seatbelt.

It occurs to me that I know next to nothing about how Mom and Dad met. I never thought to ask, since almost everyone I know has a love story that begins at a friend's wedding and ends at their own. But suddenly, I'm extremely curious.

"Tell me." I pinch my mother's hand intimately. Out of the three of us, Mom and I are definitely the closest. I was the baby she never expected to grow up. Which means that every display of maturity adds an ounce to my mother's already heavy heart. Sometimes, after a particularly heated exchange with Nina, she'll just hug me and whisper in my ear, *Thank you for being you.* Not that Fortune is hard, she's just, well, she's Fortune; as steady and unwavering as the days of the week, Fortune was always going to make my parents proud, doing what she was supposed to do. Growing up, she fell in with a good group of girls who baked challah on Fridays and attended rabbinical classes on Saturday after prayers. She strove for good grades but never possessed the sort of outsize ambition that would break my parents' bank. She wasn't too picky when it came to boys, never got caught having an underage drink, and dutifully told each of my mother's customers "Shabbat Shalom" as they swung by to pick up their orders. Fortune would have a good life, modeled by dozens and dozens of girls her age and above, one consumed with little risk. It's what works for her, and that's great. But I've never been much interested in following the example of others. I won't settle for boredom. I want to travel places and meet people and surround myself in the gorgeous textures that line the Bloomingdale's floor adjacent to Forty Carrots. And I want to do it with David by my side.

Mom loves hearing about my life. The stupid drama with friends and the excitement with David, she eats it up. Now it's time to let her indulge me.

"I want to hear how you and Dad met," I beg. "Please."

"Well, you know I didn't grow up so central. So *in* the community." My mother winces a little.

"Grandma didn't like it," I say, referring to my mother's mother, who died before I was born.

"I don't know if it was so much she didn't like it, as it was she feared it rejecting her. She was terrified of not being accepted."

"So she rejected it first." I nod, a classic strategy among high school girls with a crush.

"Right. And by the time I was a teenager, the community in Brooklyn had doubled, and then quadrupled, and expanded beyond Bensonhurst where it started, and onto Ocean Parkway. Then it moved to Midwood and deeper into Gravesend. We stayed on Bay Parkway. My mother always felt more of a kinship with the Irish and Italians; she'd grown up with them. That entire generation did. So did I, to some extent. But once the community got more affluent, things started to change. People started to go to the Jersey Shore in the summertime. Of course we didn't. I don't even think it was about the money or being able to afford it. To my mother, that was, like, the apex of the community. She wasn't going to go near it. Every Thursday I would wait for my best friend at the time, Rosie, to invite me to stay with her on the weekends. Sometimes she would and sometimes she wouldn't, but I would always have my bag packed just in case."

"Mom," I groan. "That is, like, very sad."

"I know. Pathetic, right? My mother used to say: 'Let them go and take all the traffic with them. Brooklyn is so nice when it's quiet.' But I hated the quiet. Brooklyn felt so lifeless in the summer, *so still.* Without the cars and the people in the streets and in the stores, you saw this place for what it really was. And let me tell you, it was *dirty* and *smelly* and *hot.* We pay crazy prices for homes to be *together,* not because the landscape is beautiful. Everybody knows that. But anyway, disapprove as my mother did, I think she was secretly thankful that at least one of her kids seemed to have a place in a community she never felt embraced by. So"—my mother takes a deep breath—"everybody knew that if you wanted to meet someone, you went to the Bradley boardwalk on the shore. You see, this is something that you kids don't have these days. And it's a shame, really. Because that's where you used to meet people. There was one spot. One. And if you were going to meet a boy, it was going to be there. We used to call it the 'mating gurney.' Can you imagine?

"So Rosie and I are on the boardwalk one Saturday night. This is the early eighties, mind you. I don't have to tell you what my hair and makeup looked like." I recall the pictures of my mother from that time, the ones she kept in an orange manilla envelope in the den. She was all fluffy hair, curled bangs, and blue eyeshadow. "Your father, he'd only been in the States for a year at that point. But the *boats* were always at least five years behind when it came to fashion trends. Of course your father didn't know it, and even if he did, he wouldn't care. He was as confident as John Wayne on a horse, I'm telling you. I still remember him and his pack of boys as they skipped toward us wearing wide-legged pants, each hem shorter than the next. Your dad was in the middle, and Rosie practically pushed me into him."

"This is actually cute," I interrupt my mother. "Continue."

"What can I tell you? Your father was charming. He had this blind confidence, even with the accent he tried to outrun. There was a mischief about him. We were both eighteen. I had plans to attend NYU in the fall and he had plans to open his own chain of retail stores. He was already on his way, working as the manager of his cousin's electronics shop on Fulton Street. He wanted to make enough money to support his parents. When he asked me out, I had to explain to him that he'd have to come to the door. He just laughed. I never thought he'd call my mother the next day."

"But he did?" I pressed on.

"Did you know that he loved new wave? On our first date, he took me to the Limelight. We drove into Manhattan in a Lincoln Town Car he borrowed from one of his buddies, the flickering lights of the Battery Tunnel a prelude to the night ahead. *Perfect hands for kibbeh.* This was the first thing Sitto would say to me after we finally met. In Halab, I would've gotten married quickly—my fingers were long and slender, perfect for making kibbeh. I never asked Sitto to teach me how to cook, but I had little else to do in those early days. Back then you had a specific duty to your mother-in-law. It's not like today, the girls get married and they run off to the city to live their own lives. No. We lived here, in Brooklyn, as newlyweds. Most people moved in with their in-laws right away. You're horrified, I know. It's hard to imagine, but that's what it was. I was expected to take care of Sitto, even while your grandfather was still alive. He went to work with your father and we stayed home. Cooking passed the time and made the silence more comfortable, so that's what we did. We minced onions and hollowed out vegetables; zucchini and carrots and onions, which we stuffed with allspice-coated rice and beef. We cut lemons and squeezed them dry into pots of sim-mering hamid and then used the flesh to rub our hands free of the smell of garlic. Everything had to be done by hand. 'You haven't tasted a cherry, until you've tasted a cherry from Halab,' Sitto used to say. You know how she is: Everything in America is shit. Everything in America is wonderful.

"We were cooking so much, it made sense to turn it into a business. Sitto didn't want me to do it at first. Neither did my mother, who *hated* the kitchen and nearly croaked when I told her I was dropping out of school to (in her words) 'get knocked up and sell chicken.' Part of me thought she was right; part of me couldn't disagree more. I was carving out a name for myself, even if she resented the circumstances under which it was built."

My mother pauses. Her eyes remain fixed on the windshield, and I can tell she's somewhere else. I worry that I've upset her in some way. I never knew my grandmother, and my mother rarely talks about her. But every year on the anniversary of her death, she quietly lights a single candle in her memory and it looks like her loneliness might swallow her whole. Sometimes I think we don't give my mother enough credit for how far she's come. This life wasn't a "given" for her, but she worked hard to make it so for us. Nina's ignorance of this crucial distinction is her blind spot. She looks at her life as a series of premeditated choices, made by everyone except her, when in reality, my mother, Sitto, and all of the women before them bore the brunt of difficult decisions so that we could have the easy ones. Nobody's setting you up for an arranged marriage. It's more like, *I know this man's father, mother, sister, brother, and he's probably most definitely our third cousin and can therefore ensure he won't cheat, rob, or hurt you.*

Anger is easier than vulnerability, and you can very rarely have both. Finally, my mother reaches for the door on her side.

"To be continued." She laughs, though we both know we'll leave this conversation in the car. "Let's go."

I push my door open and follow my mother up the stairs to the two-family home. She rings the bell and we both wait for an answer. Within seconds, the dressmaker, Clara, swings open the door. There are three young boys fighting in the background as their mother, Clara's daughter, zips around the living room in an ivory cotton robe, a gargantuan mug of coffee propped improbably in her hand. She shoos them toward the back of the house and we hear a loud crash, like something expensive breaking.

"G-D dammit," Clara mutters. Her accent sounds like my grandmother's. "I'm so sorry. Give me one minute," she says and disappears down the foyer. "*Fik!*" we hear her tell the boys.

Clara lives with her daughter and her three grandsons, who are all under the age of thirteen, and from the sound of it, they are reenacting an episode of *American Ninja Warrior.* They barrel toward my mother and me in sneakers and basketball shorts, snickering as Clara chases them toward the door with a weathered broom.

"*Alla ma'ak!*" Clara slams the door shut after them. Her daughter ascends the stairs. *Sorry,* she mouths.

Giselle once told me that she heard someone caught Clara's oldest grandson snooping in the basement, touching the bras and panties Clara sold on the side. But Clara has the best hands in the business, and alterations at Kleinfeld's or the Wedding Salon of Manhasset cost at least three times more.

We follow Clara as she slowly descends the narrow stairwell to the basement, three hundred square feet of yellowing carpet and a dressing room fashioned out of patterned bath curtains and some of the finest lingerie in the world. Velvet Jacques Levine slippers sell themselves atop black crates, next to worn cardboard boxes labeled PHOTO ALBUMS and SUKKAH DECORATIONS. A blank-faced mannequin dressed in a push-up corset and mesh underwear stands confidently in the center of the room. On every single one of the four walls, there is at least two *hamsas*. Some are framed with a prayer beneath; others are hanging from white hooks plastered to the walls.

"Come." Clara waves me toward a floor-to-ceiling mirror with a small platform in front of it. My mother begins to remove my gown for Fortune's wedding from its white garment bag.

"I'm last-minute, too, but even for me, the timing is tight." Clara takes the ivory beaded gown from my mother's hands. "Wow wow wow." She hangs the dress from the mirror in order to get a complete view. "How *gorjoos.*"

Clara invites me toward the makeshift dressing room. "It's fine," I say. "I'll just undress here." I shrug off my jean jacket and lift my white T-shirt over my head. Clara helps me pull my jeans from my feet. She looks close to my grandmother's age, except she is much more able. She wears blue jeans and a purple T-shirt with flowers on it.

"This one is not shy, heh?" Clara raises an eyebrow at my mother. "Not like your other daughter, the bride."

"Oh, they couldn't be more different." My mother begins to shimmy the dress over my head as Clara gently tugs it over my chest and curves. The beading makes the dress heavy, and I can feel the full weight of it hugging every inch of my body. Clara pinches some fabric from the straps on either side, lifting my chest with them. Without a word, she takes a pin from her mouth and slides it through the fabric.

"Does her chest look too . . ." My mother extends her hands in front of her own breasts. "Pronounced?"

Clara admires the dress in the mirror. "My opinion is I don't like to give an opinion. I got in trouble more than once for giving my two cents."

"Maybe we can add a piece of fabric just to cover up this part here slightly." My mother runs her finger along the deepest part of my cleavage.

"You said the dress just needed a hem. This is more than a hem."

"I know, I know, but we bought the dress last minute. I'll pay . . ."

Clara grunts as she gets onto her knees to examine the hem of the dress. "I can take some fabric from the bottom here," she says, her lips still pursed around a handful of pins. "Tell me, the bride, does she need pajama? I have beautiful bra and panty for the wedding night, too." She nods toward a standing rack of lingerie. "Beautiful white things for the wedding night, too."

"Why does it need to be white?" I ask. If it were my wedding night, I'd much rather opt for a color.

"White is nice." Clara grips my hand as she rises from the floor. "Pure."

"I think her mother-in-law might've gotten her something already. She asked me for her bra size."

"Her mother-in-law bought her wedding night lingerie? Is that a thing? That's so awkward." I couldn't imagine David's mother picking out my lingerie. How would she know what I liked? How it would fit me? I shake my head to get the image from my mind.

"It's not awkward, it's tradition," Clara said.

"At least Marie is somewhat modern. Imagine when I got married, Sitto picking out my wedding lingerie? I was surprised she didn't hand me a burka." Mom snorts.

"She probably went to Lisette," Clara surmises. "I know Marie, she buys from her. My price is much better but *hallas*, as long as she is happy. Do you have the shoes she will be wearing?" My mother helps slide the Stuart Weitzman nude pumps onto my feet as I lean on her shoulder.

"Lucy," Mom says, "you need a pedicure."

Clara crouches down once more and begins sliding pins into the hem of the dress. "And you?" she says. "Do you have boyfriend?

"You do." Clara looks up. "I can tell by the look on her face. So," she sings, "who is he?"

"David Bakar," I say as plainly as I can.

"Ahh." Clara nods. "Very nice. *Sabi andak.*"

"Thank you," I say.

"Let's cover this up more then." She pinches the opening of the dress so that it masks more of my cleavage. "You should have many *semechot*— happy occasions." She turns to my mother. "And many grandchildren."

My mother nods. "Amen."

Clara continues to work on the dress. "Tell me, how is your mother-in-law? I hear she is living with you."

"Thank G-D she's doing good. She's been living with us since my father-in-law passed."

"Good. Keep her with you. I see some daughters-in-law, even daughters, they don't want to live with the mothers. Sometimes they put them in homes or get them a live-in aid. You cannot do this. This is what kills them."

"That's terrible." My mother shakes her head, even though I know that hiring an aid here or there for Sitto is something I've heard her bring up to Dad more than once. An explosive argument usually follows.

My mother leafs through her Rolodex while Clara works. I check my phone—no messages. I wonder what Giselle is up to right now. I could always text her, but my pride is telling me not to. Why can't she text me? Why does there suddenly feel like there's a huge divide between her and me, between me and my entire friend group? I consider bringing it up to my mother, but I know what she'll say, that these girls are just jealous. That they've shown their true colors. Just a few weeks ago they were bloodthirsty for information on David and me, attacking me the moment I got into school. But they didn't waste time isolating me once it became clear that my relationship made me less of an attractive companion to the boys my age. I guess the girls follow the river of opportunity wherever it flows, and right now, that's certainly not with me. If David and I get married—*when* David and I get married, they'll want to be back in my good graces. They'll all want to be bridesmaids at my wedding, where all of David's single friends can see them looking their best. All I have to do is get through the rest of this school year— through prom and senior trip and senior ditch day, and whatever other asinine plans now seem below my maturity grade.

"Lucy!" my mother snaps, my eyes still glued to the blank screen of my phone. "We're done, honey. Are you okay?"

I hop off the platform and Clara unzips me. "Thank you, Clara!" I chirp.

"I'll have it ready for the final fitting next week," Clara says. "Don't lose weight in between then."

"Trust me, I won't." Then, I shoot a rapid-fire text to David.

> Dressmaker took shorter than I
> expected. Pick me up?

NINA

Chapter Fourteen

....

"Passover is *around the corner,* ladies. I don't care if you're here or in Miami, I promise you'll be constipated wherever you go. So Let's. Freaking. Work. Eight more counts!" Sandy, the exercise instructor, claps her hands to the beat of the music's thumping bass.

The studio is packed to the gills, and Fortune and I struggle to find space for our folded exercise mats and equipment. Close to eighty women ranging in age from Lucy's age to my mother's angle themselves for a spot in front of the fogging wall-to-wall mirror. This class is so popular that the entrance is sealed off by a red velvet rope until five minutes before class, when the crowd storms the studio, like thinness is up for grabs and not something you have to sweat to death for.

"Okay, everyone," Sandy gears up. "Light weights, two to three pounds, a booty band, and a mat. My pregnant girls, grab a ball. Let's go!" Like everyone else taking the class, she is impossibly tiny and flat chested. She has four children, but you wouldn't know it from her taut abs. Sandy spreads her toned legs into a split stance. The chatter in the room halts as she reaches her arms from side to side. We follow.

Lucy rushes over and takes her spot to the left of Fortune. "Hi," she mouths breathlessly. She's wearing an oversize black hoodie—probably David's—and spandex shorts that show off her round tush, even though the weather outside is brisk. I notice, not for the first time, the energy in the room shift as she enters it. For a moment, the eyes of the crowd drift from Sandy to Lucy, following her as she seamlessly jumps into the warm-up. The music's too loud for gossip, but if it weren't there'd be hushed whispers about my sister's relationship status. *Did you hear? It's a matter of time before they get engaged.* Never mind talking, the glances say it all; a mix of admiration and envy. And Lucy perfectly oblivious to it all, or a very good actress. Her eyes look tired and happy. When she raises her arms into a stretch, I smell David's cologne on her.

"Reach!" the instructor grunts.

Group fitness isn't really my thing, but I allowed my sisters to drag me to the cardio HIIT class, thinking it would be some sort of bonding experience. There are at least a dozen other things I'd rather be doing on a Sunday morning, but maybe I relented because Fortune's getting married so soon. I don't know, I'm going to miss her when she moves out.

"Jump!" Sandy's voice bleeds into her portable mic. She transitions into knee highs and then jump squats. Fortune and Lucy hit their hands with mechanical precision, their gazes fixed on themselves in the mirror even from as far back as the third row.

"Butt kicks in 5, 4, 3, 2—*go!*"

Panic grips my chest and I clasp my hands behind my back, squeezing my eyes shut as if I could force my sneakers toward my butt out of sheer will. The banana I inhaled on the way over sits squarely in the center of my diaphragm and I feel like I'm going to puke. I wonder if anyone would notice if I casually slipped out. Did Fortune have to place us in the G-D-damn center of the room? I count the number of bodies I'd have to weave through in order to reach the exit and decide that leaving would be too much effort. Fergie's voice gives way to Beyoncé's. I thrust my hips up and down for twenty counts.

Perhaps feeling the shake of my knees under the weight of my body, Sandy moves on to someone else's poor back. I feel the sweat congeal under my armpits, beneath my butt cheeks, and in between my thighs. I close my eyes and try to imagine that for the next forty-six minutes, I'm somewhere else. My mind immediately jumps to the night ahead.

The plan had unfolded naturally. In the organic sense, no witchcraft involved. There was going to be an Antlers concert at N6, the music hall in Williamsburg otherwise known as the bastion of hipsterdom and also everything that was wrong with it. Steven sent a link to the whole office. *Dad* immediately decried it as lame. Adam followed suit because that's what Adam does. Ethan said he was in because Ethan is always down for a good time and Yasmin quickly agreed. Steven emailed me privately to say that he'd already bought me a ticket, which I thought was sweet and then maybe a little weird? This would be my first time hanging out with anyone from the office on a weekend.

It's true that Steven and I have been spending a lot of time together since I started working at the Banana Stand, but up until now it had been in the context of work; to and from, maybe a casual bite afterward. Still, we've spent entire car rides without a moment of silence. Our conversations feel easy, effortless, and at the same time charged and exciting. I'm embarrassed to admit that I've never been this simpatico with anybody, let alone a boy. I find myself wondering if this is what it's like to be in a relationship, but I can't even imagine Saul and Fortune having the sort of rapport that Steven and I do. We talk music. Religion. Books. Even community gossip. It's funny, we discuss things going on here as much as we do anything else. Steven may be "one foot out" of Midwood, but his mother keeps him very clued in as to what goes on within its parameters. We both know he secretly enjoys it.

When we aren't together, we're texting. We recap our days. Make fun of Adam and Yasmin and Ethan. When I complained that my mother was both painfully aloof and controlling, he said he was a disappointment to his father, who constantly compared his salary with those of the boys he grew up with. The ones who followed more assured financial paths in wholesale, retail, or real estate. The closest we'd come to the *chance* of something more happening imploded after we nearly walked in on Fortune and Saul doing I shudder to think *what* in the den a few days ago. Steven had asked to use the bathroom while we lingered in his car outside of my house, listening to the new Dirty Projectors album. I stood outside the door listening to his urine stream as I mustered up the courage to ask him to stay for a movie. The house was dark and quiet, my parents were asleep upstairs, and I'd assumed, naïvely, that Fortune and Lucy were both out. We had settled on *Reservoir Dogs* and were walking into the den when we saw two bodies struggle to disentangle in the darkness of the room. "Looks like your sister beat us to it." Steven snickered as I walked him out. I still think about what might have happened if he'd stayed for that movie.

Tonight feels different. Steven offered to pick me up from my house, even though his apartment is a few blocks from the venue. We'd meet Yasmin and Ethan at the Mexican place across the street for drinks and tacos an hour before the show. If anyone hadn't suspected we were together before this, they definitely will now. I'm surprised nobody has said anything; they're not exactly a shy bunch. Still, Ethan continues to flirt with me, although everybody knows he and Yasmin are hooking up. It's sad how Yasmin allows him to openly flirt with other girls right in front of her face. I know they're "just having fun," but still, you can't tell me that doesn't suck. I don't care how *evolved* you are. She's in love with him and everyone knows it, including Ethan. Which makes him an asshole. Steven is kind of the opposite. He'll do anything to show me he cares about me except tell me he cares about me. It's kind of the running joke. When I first saw the venti black Americano sitting by my desk, I thought it was for someone else. I slid it over slightly toward Yasmin's stuff.

"That's for you, grumpy." Steven shrugged.

For days afterward, everyone teased us. They called me grumpy. They called Steven whipped. Until finally, he showed up with a traveler of French roast and enough Styrofoam cups for the whole team. Because that's the kind of guy Steven is. He was raised well.

"Grab your weights!" Sandy bellows, blasting me back to here and now.

Fuck this. I'd rather starve than have calories to burn. I collect my things and throw my phone in my bag.

"I'll wait for you guys outside," I mouth to Fortune and Lucy. There are still twenty-six minutes left of the class, but if I have to do one more burpee I'm going to drop-kick someone in the face. I text Fortune and Lucy to meet me at the juice spot a block away, hang my head low, and weave my way through the pulsating bodies.

"You couldn't order for us?" Lucy throws her bag down on the seat next to mine and rolls the front of her damp T-shirt into a stomach-grazing knot above her belly button. Her hair is slicked back into a sweaty bun and her cheeks are flushed. She frowns as she reads the ingredients on my green juice, which in actuality should just say: grass. "There isn't even an apple in here."

"That class was intense." I push the juice toward Fortune.

"You barely did it!" Lucy says. "If we had time I would have stayed for toning. Double. That's what everyone does."

"Everyone is nuts. I don't think I knew what a calorie was when I was your age."

"Well, you certainly do now."

"I'd rather spend my time doing other things than exercising for a hundred and eighty minutes," I say.

"You should have stayed. Facebook's not going anywhere." Lucy chuckles.

"Neither is your ass," I say, smacking Lucy's perfectly rotund behind. It bounces back in perfect harmony. Damn her youth and perfect genetic code.

"David likes it." She shrugs.

"Ew." I shudder. Although I admire Lucy's confidence, she's still my little sister. That being said, I would love to find the stork that dropped her off.

"Speaking of David . . . how's that going? I feel like he's been at the house a lot lately," Fortune says.

Lucy sighs as if she's been waiting for this question all morning. "He actually loves Dad. Isn't that weird?"

"That is weird." Fortune sucks the remnants of my juice through a straw.

"It's not weird at all, actually," I say. "That's all Dad ever wanted, to be loved. David's smart. I bet he knows that."

"Now it's just Mom he has to win over." Lucy rolls her eyes.

"Please. Mom was team David before he walked in the door," I say.

"I feel terrible for him. She started calling him every time her early-onset arthritis acts up and he's too nice to tell her he's busy."

"That's what years of rolling yebra will get you." I recall the cramping in my fingers every time they wrapped themselves against a grape leaf.

"It definitely wasn't this easy for Saul, that's for sure." Fortune shakes her cup, rattling the ice inside.

"I don't remember it being hard," I say. She seems off lately, but maybe it's just that she's stressed about the wedding being so soon. I tell myself I should remember to check in with her, but between work and Steven it's been hard to catch her for more than a minute in the kitchen, let alone actually by herself. And besides, she's probably fine—she *is* getting everything she wanted.

"Same," Lucy agrees. "But also, I guess there's nothing *not* to like about Saul."

"There's just nothing to *love,* either," I joke.

Fortune smacks my shoulder. "Can't wait to see what prince *you* bring home."

"Ahem." Lucy clears her throat. "S-T-E," she sings.

"Please. We're just friends."

Lucy leans in and lowers her voice. "I heard Mom yapping on the phone this morning—I think to Auntie Linda. She didn't want to appear *overly* excited." Lucy continues with her impression of Mom: " 'And she's with this boy, five days a week. He picks her up. He drops her off. Picks her up, drops her off. I know the mother, she's a very sweet, low-key woman. She used to be a Tawil I think—but I know nothing about the boy.' " Lucy's impression of Mom is spot on.

Fortune laughs. *"The boy."*

"I swear she'd marry me off to the busboy at the shawarma place if she could," I say. "You're so lucky you two don't have to deal with that."

Fortune pivots toward my sister. "Is there any talk? Like with David?" She is treading. Lightly, but treading.

"What do you mean?" Lucy plays innocent. "Nothing is happening anytime soon. You don't need to worry about that." I can always tell when my baby sister is lying.

"I'm not worried. I'm just curious because I've been hearing things. People talk, you know."

"Mom and Dad are basically planning the wedding." I want to cut straight through the BS.

"Nothing is happening until David talks to Dad," Lucy says. "When that's going to happen, I do not know." It sounds like the conversation has already happened, but Fortune doesn't appear to have caught on so I don't press.

"Dad knew Saul and I were getting married before I did."

"David's nothing like Saul," Lucy says, a bit too cheerfully.

"I'm just saying there's a process. I don't care *who* he is," Fortune snaps.

"Hate to break it to you, but David and Saul are typical AF," I say and roll my eyes. If Fortune isn't going to be honest, then I will. It's obvious that Lucy and David don't have to play by the same rules as Fortune and Saul did. David is a better catch, by everybody's extremely shallow standards, which means that Mom and Dad have done less to risk ruining their relationship, even at the expense of their self-respect, if you ask me. Which again, nobody ever does.

"David might be 'modern,' but his family is old school." Fortune appears bolstered by my defense. "His mother didn't make you break up, which means she approves of you and our family. Which means there's no way she's not pushing. Not to mention Mommy and Daddy—do you think they're going to let you date forever?"

"It's been four months . . ." Lucy laughs, as if people we know haven't gotten engaged after less.

"You'll be engaged by graduation in a few months. A big fat diamond as a present." I laugh. "Unless, of course, that's not what you want?"

"What do you mean?" Fortune asks, as if she's never considered this possibility, for herself or for Lucy.

"I mean, like you said, Lucy, you're in high school. I know you're into David and he's a great guy, blah blah. But what's the rush? Why not enjoy senior year with your friends, take the summer. If David really loves you, then he'll wait."

"I don't want this to come out the wrong way and I promise I don't mean to offend you, Nin, but until you've been there you can't understand. When you find the person you want to be with forever, you don't *want* to wait. You just spend every day, week, month in pure anticipation. So I may have found my person a little sooner than most of my friends but they'll catch up eventually. I'm not *rushing*, I just know what I want. Right, Fortune?" Lucy looks at Fortune for approval, but Fortune looks like she's seen a ghost.

"Right," she says hesitantly.

"Are you okay? You look like you just found out there was butter in your green juice."

"Ha, ha. Very funny. I'm fine," Fortune says, clearly not fine and leaving me to wonder what was said that might've upset her. If anything, I'm the one who should be upset. Of course, having Steven helps cushion Lucy's blow, however well-meaning.

"Anyway, have you tried on rings yet?" Fortune asks, her curiosity getting the better of her. "Do you know what shape you like?"

Lucy scrunches her nose. "Let me see yours." She extends her hand.

Fortune begins to slide off her engagement ring, a square cut with two baguettes on either end, and then stops. "I mean, yours will probably be bigger."

Lucy waves off the remark, even though we all knew it's true. "I told him in passing that I like an oval."

"Casual," I say. "In passing."

"A solitaire setting, clean. So the diamond is the thing that shines."

She slides Fortune's ring onto her finger and admires her hand. "What do you think? I'm not sure this is me."

"I had no say," Fortune mutters, suddenly seeming unsatisfied with the ring I watched her admire in the light for the past three months. "Saul's mom chose it."

"My fingers are long. They can carry a nice oval," Lucy says, unfazed.

The door to the café swings open and a group of girls bursts into the juice bar, the smell of the studio clinging to their damp clothes. They linger by the doorway as one of them bends over to tie her laces. Fortune, Lucy, and I remain tucked in a corner at our table, but I can hear them clearly.

"*Hazita*, she completely fell off the face of the earth," one of the girls says.

"Do you blame her? First, her younger sister gets engaged, fine. And now the younger *younger* one is, too. And to *him*? I'd hide, too."

"I heard their father had to take out a second mortgage on the house, *hazit*. For the weddings," a third whispers.

"And the mother already works like a dog."

The whispers dissolve into silence as the girls make their way into the store. I quickly drop my head. Having spent the past few weeks in a different part of Brooklyn, I forget how quickly my self-worth could plunge. I want to get up and scream, "Please, save your pity for someone who needs it." I shouldn't care what these girls think of me, and yet I do. I want them to know that I'm doing fine, better than ever, actually. Instead, I pretend as though I didn't hear. Lucy looks uneasy but holds her head high. Fortune mouths something to me from beneath the smoothie menu and I read her lips: *Is the mortgage stuff true?*

"Hi!" Lucy chirps to one of the girls, her grin too wide to be genuine.

"Oh my G-D, hi!" If the girl is taken off guard, she doesn't show it. "Were you just in class?" She gestures toward the door. "Oh my G-D, Fortune! Hi, I swear I didn't even see you."

"Can you tell?" Fortune circles her sweaty face with her finger. "Killed me."

"So . . ." The girl nudges Fortune's arm with her car key. "Next week, no? I'm psyched."

"Psyched," another one of the girls echoes.

"Thank you. Don't be late!" Fortune says so enthusiastically, I feel like I might vomit.

"I won't!" She spins around and heads toward the register. "Oh! Remind me if I forget, but I have a list of single girls' names, for under the chuppah. Text me later?" Then, as if registering my presence for the first time, she says to me, "B'H your turn will come soon!" I want to smack her.

Fortune tosses her empty cup in the nearby recycling bin. She has that weird look again. "One hundred percent I will pray for them."

Lucy tugs at Fortune's sleeve and rolls her eyes. "Let's get out of here." She stands up and unravels the knot in her shirt.

"I'll drive," I say, and we rush out onto the sidewalk.

Chapter Fifteen

....

"Where are you going?"

Fuck. Fuckity fuck.

I don't dare turn around. Instead, I rifle through my bag for the keys I know aren't there. "Nowhere." I mutter, my back still toward my mother.

"Do you always go nowhere in those jeans and that top with those shoes and your hair blown out?"

To make matters worse, a horn blares in front of the house. I know immediately that it's Steven, notifying me that he's here.

Don't honk! I text him hurriedly. I need 2 minutes.

My mother flicks on the lights in the foyer and I turn around to face her. If she notices my makeup, she's at least kind enough not to mention it.

"I have a thing. For work." I say it as nonchalantly as I can. "A concert."

"Is that your friend?" My mother cranes her neck to see over my shoulder. I move an inch to the left. She rises to her tippy-toes. "What's his name again?" She damn well knows his name.

"Steven is giving me a ride. Yes."

"Well, tell him to come in then," my mother says coyly as I shake my head. "Why not?"

We both know why not. The smell of MSG-glazed chicken wafts out of the kitchen and through the halls. I could practically hear the frustration coming from my father's chopsticks as he tries and fails to dip a soggy piece of teriyaki broccoli into more teriyaki. Saul and David listen intently as Dad tries to explain to them why he only pays his bills in cash. In a few minutes, he'll pull a wad of cash from his sock and tell the boys that a man's shoe is the only truly safe space to store his money. The house is dark save for the iridescent glow cast over the kitchen table where they sit with Lucy and Fortune, eating Chinese takeout. One big, happy family.

"Because why should he have to come in? Mom. Stop. *Please*," I beg.

No problem. Steven replies.

"I want to meet the boy you've been working with all this time. Put a face to the name. Don't make it a big deal." She takes a step forward toward the door, indicating that she has no intention of backing down.

"But you're making it a big deal! I never saw any of Lucy's guy friends come into the house before picking her up!"

My mother nods, *uh-huh*. "I know his mother, they're good people! I'm sure he won't mind."

"Three seconds ago you didn't know his name."

"Nina, please. Don't be dramatic. This boy is less likely to drink and drive after he's forced to look me in the eyes. It's my face he'll see before he does anything idiotic."

"Are you serious?"

My mother pulls her robe tightly across her chest and reties the belt. "As a heart attack. Let him come in or you're not going." She crosses her arms over her stomach.

"You're insane." My mother smiles, welcoming the accusation. "I'm going." I fidget with the door handle, not brazen enough to open it completely.

"Morris!" my mother shouts. "Mooooooorriiiis."

"Sh!" I slam shut what little of the door I had opened. "I really hate you!"

"You'll thank me one day." My mother turns around. "We're in the kitchen. I promise not to embarrass your *friend.*"

Oh my God, I text Steven.

> My mother is actually fucking psycho, as you know.
>
> She's making you come in.
>
> I'm so sorry
>
> I will repay you
>
> OMG I hate her

Before I can bombard Steven with another message, I see the lights of his car turn off. Steven steps out of his car and makes his way toward my front door. I crack it open and meet him on the front porch, closing the door slightly behind me.

"I'm so embarrassed." I look down at my feet. Steven's wearing his beat-up checkered Vans.

"Nina." Steven cocks his head to look me in the eye. "It's not a big deal. Relax." He smiles. "It's just . . . I thought you were different."

"Shut up!" I punch him in the arm.

Steven pretends to be in actual pain and rubs the spot where my fist made contact. His hair is growing back in, and I catch a brief glimpse of how he looked in high school. Younger, but also more innocent. "I have a mother. And sisters, and I'm part of *this*. Remember?"

"I'm just warning you. It's the entire Brady bunch. Sisters' fiancé and boyfriend and my grandma and dad."

"So basically, it's a Sunday night." Steven smiles and I notice, for the first time, that he has a tiny snaggletooth on the left side. "Hi." He ropes me in for a hug and I smell the familiar scent of his deodorant, laid on a little extra tonight.

"Yeah, but didn't you choose to get away from all this? Ugh. Hi." I groan, hugging him back.

"You look pretty." Steven takes me in with his eyes.

"Stop." I look back at the floor.

"If your mom is going to treat this like a date, I may as well act like a good one. No?" Steven smirks.

"You can take the boy out of the community, but you can't take the community out of the boy." I laugh.

"Touché," Steven says. "Let's go. Your mom is going to want to feed me eighty-five different things and jot down my family tree. If we don't want to miss the opener, we have to move fast."

Inside, the kitchen is eerily quiet, which means they know we are coming. I say a silent prayer, clear my throat, and move toward the dinette. I'm halfway down the hall when Sitto appears, as if out of nowhere.

"Hi!" Steven appears surprised and does an awkward half curtsy slash bow, which is so fucking hilarious that a disgusting hawking sound escapes from my throat instead of laughter. Sitto shoots me a dirty look.

"Hiya, *rohi*," she says to Steven. "And who are you?" I can see Sitto sizing him up, her swollen fingers wrapped around the top of her walking stick. A tiny smile dances on the edge of her lips, which are painted a deep shade of purple. Sitto always has lipstick on and her hair is always perfectly coiffed, even when there isn't a chance of her leaving the house.

"Steven," Steven says, as if suddenly remembering who and where he is. "Steven Shami." Steven walks toward Sitto and gently kisses her on either cheek.

"I think my grandmother said she knows you. My mother's mother—Panina. Panina Tawil?" If Steven's confession surprises Sitto, she doesn't show it. But I can't help thinking, *When did Steven discuss me with his grandmother?*

"Of course!" Sitto purrs. She leans her walking stick against the wall and takes Steven's face between her hands. "I know your grandmother since I am a small girl in Syria. She left before me but *sure* I know her." *Left.* As if she got up and walked out of a restaurant after paying the check. Sitto seems genuinely pleased, and I breathe a small sigh of relief. Still, I'm anxious to get this whole thing over with and get out of here. We're one introduction away from Steven realizing how bizarre this entire thing is. As much as I hate to admit it, our relationship up until now has been predicated on a mutual disdain for some of the community's more "ancient" ideas and customs. Steven wouldn't have vouched for me at Banana Stand if he thought I was a typical Syrian girl, and I've been subconsciously trying to live up to that version of myself ever since. Partly because it's genuinely who I am but also, if I'm being honest, because I worry it's the only version of me that Steven is interested in. It's easy for misfits to band together; the question is whether our connection could withstand conceding to the very thing we agreed to dislike. I've never allowed myself to imagine Steven within the context of my family. The possibility of it ruining what we have—*whatever* that is—was too much to bear.

"And your grandfather, G-D bless, was a good man. I was sad to hear when Panina joined the club."

"Club?" Steven asks.

"Of dead husbands," Sitto says matter-of-factly.

"Ah." Steven smiles and nods his head. "Right."

"Not such a club anymore." Sitto lets go of Steven's face. "Clubs are supposed to be exclusive, no?" She smiles wickedly.

"Unfortunately." Steven shrugs.

"Come." Sitto turns slowly back toward the kitchen before reaching into her apron pocket. "Candy?" she says, offering a plastic-wrapped sesame log to Steven.

"I love these." Steven seems genuinely delighted and takes the candy.

"Good boy." Sitto nods and walks toward the kitchen, beckoning us after her. "And don't let these boys intimidate you. Them two like to hear the sound of their own voices."

Steven and I linger behind Sitto for a moment and he squeezes my hand. "Why didn't you tell me your grandma was a fucking boss?" he whispers.

"My grandma is a fucking boss," I say. And I follow her into the kitchen.

To my surprise, it's just my dad and mom sitting at the table.

"Where'd everyone go?" I ask.

My mother begins stacking empty food containers and scraping bits off of plates into a large sauce-stained brown bag.

"Saul and Fortune went to test out mattresses. They left that to the last minute if you ask me. And Lucy and David went for a drive." She waves her hand and says, "Somewhere."

Part of me feels disappointed and wishes my sisters could be here to witness Steven's presence after pitying my loneliness for so many years. Steven approaches my father first and he stands up to shake his hand.

"Steven Shami. Nice to meet you."

I refrain from looking at my mother but can see from the corner of my eye that she's smiling and it's pissing me off. Even though Steven seems to genuinely not mind, it was so *her* to manufacture this scenario. Steven isn't even my date! Not officially, anyway.

But she is collecting extra duck sauce packets like a woman who has won at life. I half expect her to crack open one of those fortune cookies she's holding and bestow a prophecy upon us. She's secured the future of her daughters and now she can kick back and relax. That's what she's thinking. It's glaringly obvious. And embarrassing!

My father takes a seat and kicks out the chair next to him, motioning for Steven to do the same. "Thank you for setting Nina up with the job. We've been loving the peace and quiet in the house." He laughs and cracks open a fortune cookie with his teeth.

"Hilarious, Dad." I turn to Steven. "Okay, I think we can go now. We're going to be late." I tug the sleeve of his jacket, an army green windbreaker I don't recognize.

"Oh, she's great," Steven says, earnestly. "Everyone at the office loves her."

My mother raises one eyebrow.

Steven sits down on the allocated chair. "She's crazy organized and super professional."

"Is she?" My mother doesn't even bother hiding her skepticism.

"Is that so hard to believe?" I shoot back.

"Maybe bring some of that organization here," she says. "We'd love to see it!"

"Define professional." My father tosses the entire second half of the cookie into his mouth. "At a rock concert."

"Label." I correct him.

"Same thing." He waves his hand.

"Right." Steven strokes his chin and laughs. His restraint calms me down, and I hold back from defending myself.

"*Hallas,* leave her alone," Sitto says.

"I'm just teasing," my father says. "And your father is in wholesale, no?"

"Accessories, yeah."

"JHP Holdings?" my father asks, even though he clearly already knows the answer.

"That's the one." Steven rises to stand somewhat awkwardly beside me and shifts his weight between his feet.

My father nods. "I'd buy from him if I thought he could cut me a good deal."

"I'll see what I can do."

"Na," my father says unconvincingly. "I know your grandfather well. I traveled east with him when the girls were little. He would show up to the factories with bags of pita bread—the Chinese loved him."

"That's him. I heard the stories."

"Oh, but they're all true. Whatever you heard."

"I hope not." Steven smiles. I tug at his sleeve again and he pulls his arm back slightly.

"If it doesn't work out with the music, you have a nice business to fall back on."

I let out an audible groan. "Thanks for the life lesson, Dad."

"It's fine," Steven says. "I'm used to it."

"It's hard for Nina to understand that when we came to this country, we actually had to work. There was no such thing as following your *passion.* We followed the money, that's it."

"Are we doing this right now?" I begin to back away and this time I grab Steven's arm hard enough that he stumbles back.

"*Fik.*" Sitto slaps my father on the back. "Leave them alone. I remember you having your fun, too."

"It was work, work, work." My father slaps the table three times for emphasis. "Well, I would ask you where you work, but I already know.

What you do, I know I won't understand. So I'll leave you alone now."
My father squeezes Steven's shoulder warmly.

"I appreciate that," Steven says, waiting for me to cue him.

"Okay! Can we go?" I turn to my mother. *"Mother?"*

"Be safe," she says. "Have fun. Put the alarm on when you get home."

"Fantastic," I say. "Thanks."

"The star of riches is shining on you." My father reads the slip of
paper from the fortune cookie. *"Kisa amak.* I think this one was meant
for Lucy." He laughs heartily at his own joke.

"Morris!" My mother gasps while Steven and I burst out laughing in
unison.

"He's not wrong," I say.

"Ugly," my mother says, shooing us out. "Ugly to talk that way. *Kish.*
Go!"

"Bye bye!" I sing.

"Good night!" Steven calls over his shoulder. "It was nice meeting you."

"Alla ma'ak," Sitto shouts in return.

"Shut up. You can quit the act now," I say as we open the door and
the cool air hits my face. "You did good."

"I wasn't acting," Steven says.

I squash my instinct to challenge Steven once more and let his last
words linger for a bit. He is saying all the right things. He is sending all
of the right signals. My rational mind is telling me it's my move, but as
Steven leads me to his car, the fear of being rejected continues to hold
me back.

When I suggest we just listen to the Antlers, Steven tells me that it's
bad luck to listen to an artist's music before seeing them perform live. I
think that's stupid, but I don't disagree out loud. I look out my window, at the other cars inching up Ocean Parkway, and I notice an old
coffee cup of mine still in the door's lower side pocket. This is the first
time in a long time, maybe ever, that I've felt comfortable enough to
leave garbage in another person's car (at least one I'm not related to).

Steven and I sit in silence as he floats between lanes and the bass of an older Modest Mouse tune thumps in the background.

"You know you're better off staying in one lane," I say, "even if it's not moving. All of the other cars will eventually switch out, and then your lane will be the quickest."

"An interesting theory," Steven says, switching lanes again. "But patience isn't a virtue of mine."

Could've fooled me! I want to say.

The other cars begin to peel away as we make our way up the road; turning onto O or L or Avenue I until, finally, we pass Ditmas, and then Church, and speed up onto the Prospect Expressway and out of Midwood. Just as we venture beyond the community's invisible parameters, my mind wanders to Ethan, as if a switch has been activated in my brain. Ethan, who has been on a flirting campaign for weeks even though he is hooking up with my edgier, more available coworker. Ethan, who insinuates on the daily that he'd ditch Yasmin for me. If there's one thing I've learned since joining the Banana Stand, it's that men play by the same rules no matter where they're from. I wasn't intentionally teasing Ethan; I was raised to guard myself and some habits are difficult to shake. Ethan accuses me of playing hard to get when, in actuality, the prospect of him, while intriguing, is mainly terrifying. It was easy to want someone like him while I was still on the inside, when the possibility itself seemed disproportionately out of reach. Now that all I have to do is take it, I'm not so sure it's what I want. And then, of course, there's Steven, the hundred-and-fifty-pound elephant in the room. What's the point in my grand exodus if I'm just going to end up with somebody my own mother could've set me up with? She and my father are probably doing the hora in the kitchen at this very moment, marveling over how I could've met my *nassib* this way! I have no doubt my mother is taking credit, recalling how she stuck her neck out for me and convinced my father to allow me to take the job in the first place. Sitto will probably tell both of them to shut up, that it's *Hashem* who deserves the credit, for He works in mysterious ways. And just like that, the rebellion I had staked my entire identity on would have been squashed. I could follow my heart and allow myself to be pulled toward Steven, but then who would I be? And then there's the question I can barely bring myself to ask: Would he even like that person?

I doubt Steven was thinking any of this when he swapped his Marxist beanie for a kippah upon meeting my parents. How *naturally* he slipped back into character; bravo, really. Sure, next to David and Saul he is *different* and *not mainstream.* He's practically an atheist by the community's standards, which is one of the worst things a person can be after liberal. But he shook my father's hand as if he'd been courting girls for years. Not to mention the kiss on the cheek and the invocation of his grandmother, for G-D's sake.

I look over at Steven, who is absentmindedly mouthing the words to "Milk" by Kings of Leon. When the song kicks up he taps his fingers against the steering wheel. It takes everything I have not to punch him in the arm. I want to know what he's thinking. And if he isn't thinking anything, I want to know that, too. Can't we just pick up where we left off? How about at my door when you told me I looked pretty before roping me in with a hug?

"They're just too good." Steven bobs his head to the music. "Too. Fucking. Good."

I lower the window and lean my head out of it, allowing the breeze to kick up my hair. I repeat the mantra I used to say to myself every time my mother asked me for anything. *One breath in, one breath out.* I need to get out of the car. I need to know what Steven's thinking so I can tell myself I thought it first. And then I need to figure out what it is that I want.

Several empty shot glasses are already scattered across the tattooed table by the time we get into the restaurant. The bowl of guacamole looks like it could use refilling, too, and I catch Yasmin scraping its edges with a ragged tortilla chip before she sees us and stops.

"Yo!" Steven bumbles over to the table. "Where's Ethan?" he asks before I can.

"Bathroom." Yasmin sounds annoyed as she points to a graffitied brown door on the far side of the restaurant. It's clear she doesn't like me, and I am done trying to win her over. That ship has long sailed. A waiter walks over and swaps out the empty bowl of guacamole for a new one and throws down a woven basket of oily tortilla chips.

"Sunday nights are all you can eat," Yasmin says, to no one in particular.

"Cool." Steven pulls out a chair for me and I take a seat. "Drink?" he asks me. "I'm gonna head to the bar. It's probably quicker that way."

"Sure," I say. And Steven makes his way toward the bar at the back of the restaurant.

"Cute that he doesn't even ask you what you want," Yasmin says, in a way that indicates she actually doesn't think this is cute at all. She flips her hair, thick, curly, and not at all frizzy, over to one side of her head. Even though I hate to admit it, Yasmin is ridiculously pretty. I don't know why she spends her energy disliking me when there is actually no competition between us. She taps her fingernails on the table, trying to catch the beat of the LCD Soundsystem song that blares from the restaurant's speakers. She glances at the bathroom door before quickly looking away. "You think Ethan's holding out on us?" she says.

"What do you mean?" I ask.

"I mean, no guy takes that long to pee, if you know what I mean. Should we go find out?" Yasmin smirks. She is clearly testing me, calling me out on my bullshit. She wants me to know that she sees right through my façade. I'm not cool, or different, and I'm definitely not down to try whatever drug Ethan is most definitely doing in the bathroom. She stands up and pulls her black miniskirt down, but it's still dangerously short. She's wearing sheer black tights with strategic rips in them and black combat boots. "You down?" She knows exactly who I am.

Fuck it. I'm about to follow her when I see Steven headed our way, two tequila sodas in hand.

"Um." I stop and take my drink from him.

"Right." Yasmin laughs. "That's what I thought." And she hurries off to the bathroom. Steven looks confused and I try as best I can to explain that Ethan is probably doing drugs in the bathroom and Yasmin is going to join him and you can, too, if you want because I'm cool. I'm cool.

"Should we?" I ask Steven, and even though I want him to say no, it still surprises me when he does.

"Come on." He laughs and takes a seat, taking a long sip from his drink.

"What do you mean?" My face goes flush. I squeeze a wedge of lime into my drink and allow the alcohol and acidity to burn my throat until my drink is 75 percent finished. Strong.

"You don't do that shit," Steven says, more seriously now.

I want to laugh with him, to tell him that I'm not even sure what shit, exactly, they're doing. But he probably knows, has probably done whatever they're doing before. And I want to be cool. So instead I say, "You don't know me." I finish the remainder of my drink and fish in my bag for a twenty-dollar bill. I hand it to Steven. "For my drink."

"Stop," he says, pushing the money back toward me. "It's on me."

"Didn't we already establish that this wasn't a date? Don't let meeting my family put you under any kind of pressure." I slide the money back to him. "I can pay for my own drink. You can go if you want." I nod toward the bathroom door where Yasmin has disappeared inside. "Go. I'm not judging."

"I have no interest in that," he says. "Did I do something?"

"You did nothing." I feel emboldened by the alcohol. "Absolutely nothing."

"Why are you being like this?"

"Like what?"

"I'm not into drugs. I never have been, despite what you may have heard. And neither are you."

Aha. I raise my eyebrows in amusement, because this is what I was getting at. "I'm sorry. I didn't know my mother would be in attendance tonight."

"Come on." Steven smiles, but I'm not biting. "I think I know you well enough to—"

"*Aha! Bingo.* What do you actually know about me? Who I was in high school? Oh, because I'm a girl from the community I must act or be a certain way?"

Steven pulls back. He looks confused, and maybe a little hurt. He runs his fingers through his short hair. "Wow. You're just trying to ruin this now."

"Ruin what?" I laugh sarcastically. "What exactly is this? Because I have no idea." I wave my finger between us. My head is swimming. I haven't eaten since that G-D-forsaken green juice this morning and I'm feeling the full effects of the tequila. I toss an oily tortilla chip into my mouth. Steven opens his mouth to say something but whatever it is, it's interrupted by Ethan and Yasmin, who barrel toward the table like a freight train.

"*Hey, gang!*" Ethan shouts, hitting Steven across the back. He looks like an oversize camp counselor in his board shorts and black hoodie. You have to be fucking beautiful to pull an outfit like this off, and Ethan is. Yasmin ropes her fingers through the loop in his waistband where a belt should be.

"We're back." She looks directly at me.

"How long you been here?" Ethan tries to gauge whether I know if he's high or not.

"I'm gonna get another drink," I say, ignoring him. I make my way toward the bar. I can feel their eyes on me. I order two chilled shots and toss them back before throwing my money on the countertop and steadying myself against it. If I was going to self-sabotage, I may as well do it right.

FORTUNE

Chapter Sixteen

············

hen we were little, Mom bought us an ant farm to keep the dirt out of our nails. It soon became my responsibility. Nina insisted the ants should be free and Lucy quickly lost interest. But I loved watching them, studying their movements, however repetitive they might've been. You see, to the ants who have never known life outside of the acrylic barrier, the farm felt massive. Grandiose, even. The ants collectively paved each route, pummeling their tiny bodies through the sand until a viable path was formed. And they did this countless times. A path to get to the water. A path to get to the food; tiny pieces of bread and fruit that I slid in through a trapdoor at the bottom. The ants were strong, but they were also intelligent. They were efficient, and hardworking, and in their quest for survival, they seized on the predictability of their small but comfortable lives. Insulated and with no imminent threat to their existence, my ants thrived and multiplied. Until one night a stray cat jumped up on the ledge outside where I kept them and blew the whole thing to bits. Sometimes I still wonder how my little friends did on the outside, if they managed to escape at all.

If there were a welcome sign upon entering the community, it would be: BROOKLYN! IT'S SO CONVENIENT!

Followed by: EVERYTHING WE NEED IS HERE.

There's the traffic. And the incessant honking. The honking! Has it always been this bad? People fight and curse each other's mothers from behind the safety of their steering wheels, and then smile politely in the street. *Hi, honey, how are you? And your mother, still in Florida?* We're all in a rush to get to the store. Shabbat waits for no one. Every single one of us is a priority customer with the receipts to show for it. The trucks load and unload day and night, feeding a community whose belly never seems to fill. We paved the routes and we follow them. North, south, east, west. All roads lead to somewhere, all roads lead to nowhere.

After the weekend, the garbage piles up on the sidewalk. Piles and piles of black Hefty bags that reek of lamb juice and potato scraps, cooked oil and soiled napkins. Yesterday's meal is already a frozen memory, wrapped and stored for a busy day or an unexpected death. Time to start planning the next. All of your kids are coming, and the grandkids, the in-laws, your mother. Break out the cookbooks, spring open the Rolodex, arrange the pots. Set the table and hire extra help. Let's make a menu. *Do you want to hear my menu?* I just can't make another menu. Complain incessantly about the menu.

The work, it's too much. What I'd give to be a man and go into the office! To leave my work at the register, leave someone else to deal with the mess and the cleanup, the grocery bill. But stop? Never! There's no crueler punishment for a mother than an empty table. Asses in chairs are the currency in which our mothers deal. The only thing worse than having to cook for thirty people is not having thirty people to cook for. And so we write lists. And then we shop so we can cross off the list. And when the meal is over we feel a dip in our adrenaline and sometimes, even, our serotonin. Some women sink into a despair after the High Holidays. The comedown can leave you feeling empty, rattled. It's true that all you did was complain for weeks leading up to and during the meals—but much like the grandchildren you begged for, it's a beautiful chaos and it reminds you of what it is to be alive.

When Passover is behind us, the street corners will light up with gossip. This one went here, that one went there.

I heard the weather in Florida was terrible. Terrible. I heard the single scene at the Tel Aviv Hilton was a disaster, no boys for the girls. They say the food on the Cancun trip was inedible. Dog food. What's the difference where I am? I'm a slave to the kitchen either way, whether it's sixty degrees or eighty-five. It's not a vacation. I'd rather be home. I'm happy at home! Really! With my duct-taped cabinets and Dixie plates, overpaying for shmura matzo. Everything is here, it's so convenient. I even saw containers of salt water on the shelves in Kosher Palace! And at $3.99. The nerve! You know I had to buy just one, though. If my husband won't take me away, he can spring on the iodized water. Who can be bothered to kosher the dishes? Next year I'll buy a separate set of everything, just for Passover. I can't even think about next year. My sights are set on Shavuot. It's early this year. No meat for seven days; what should I make? Better start filling my freezer. Stuffed shells and fried fish, cusa jibben and, of course, the sambusaks. The little ones love the sambusaks. I'll be picking sesame seeds out of my couch through August. Don't wait until the last minute. Blink and Rosh Hashanah will be here! A honey-dipped apple smack in the face.

There are also the familiar faces. The neighbors you've had forever. A chat on every street corner. The leaves that shed and grow with the passing seasons, wiping clean the sins of the preceding year. There's forgiveness and bloodlines and a way of life that may seem inexplicable to others but makes total sense to those who practice.

I always wondered how the ants distinguished one another. To me they all looked the same, but I was sure they had some kind of system to tell one another apart. You could see by the way they moved that, beneath the supposed homogeneity of their days, there was complexity— a system that relied on one thousand things going right, each and every day. All it took was one stray cat to upend it.

A soft knock at my door startles me to attention.

"Forch? Do you need help?" my mother asks, reminding me of what

I came upstairs to do. I'm supposed to be packing up my room. Or my closet, at the very least.

"I'm good!" I say, glancing down at my watch.

"How's it coming?" my mother asks, and I can tell she wants to come in.

"I'm almost done."

"Okay, just don't forget about your appointments tomorrow. Rosie did me a favor squeezing you in, and there's a lot to do before you dip."

"I know," I say, even though I completely forgot. I'll be doing my first *tevilah* in the mikvah the day after tomorrow, and I have to be ready. That meant waxing, everything. A clean manicure, pedicure, no polish. The MIL would meet us at the mikvah at eight A.M.

"Okay." Mom's shadow lingers beneath the door. "Let me know if you need help. I'm just dropping Sitto off at her card game."

"This late?" I glance at my watch. It's eight o'clock.

"I'm not arguing." My mother sighs.

How does one pack up their room for a married life? I'll start with my alarm clock, even though I only ever use my phone. That ancient picture of Grandma Nina, sitting cross-legged on the edge of her bed (Bensonhurst, 1952). The Harry Potter series. Maybe one day I'll read them. The card my mother wrote to me on my sixteenth birthday: HAPPY SWEET 16! WE ARE SO PROUD OF THE YOUNG LADY YOU HAVE BECOME.

I just need to focus on the essentials. Jeans. Blue jeans. Black jeans. Skinny jeans. Jeans that graze my ankles. Jeans that flare at my ankles. Those were a mistake. I stack them on top of one another. Blouses I never had a use for; maybe I will now. Socks folded like tennis balls. Bras and underwear still wrapped in tissue paper recently purchased for the woman I'll soon be. I throw them into an open suitcase.

"Don't try and do it all in one day," my mother warned me. "You'll go crazy."

I'll go crazy if I don't.

A weathered Champion sweatshirt of my mother's. The one she disguises herself in to sneak out to the mikvah at night. It's a good disguise. But maybe it's time she finds a new one. My high school yearbook. A yellow Post-it note jokingly left for me by my father—"Employee of the Month."

Our parents would be only a fifty-minute drive away from our new apartment on Fifty-second and Second Avenue. Saul signed the one-year lease and surprised me with it. We'd discussed how it was more financially prudent to take a cheaper apartment in Brooklyn, but his father agreed to help us with rent. The one-bedroom was close to the FDR. Forty, not in rush hour. A quick zip up through the tunnel, as my mother frequently reminds me. Saul's mother has apparently told him that he can bring his laundry home, when we come back for Shabbat. My mother has said that she'll meet me in the city whenever to browse the sale racks at Bloomingdale's and get frozen yogurt with strawberries and carob chips at Forty Carrots. A phone call away. We'll live in the city for a year, and then it's back to Brooklyn. In the meantime I'll have a husband and my own Costco card. I'll need to separate our whites from our colors and drive into Brooklyn for "errand days."

I want my own life. I want the mess and the chaos of it. I want to make hard decisions and I want to question them afterward. I want to need my mother and I want her to not be at my disposal. I want to miss her call, by accident, because I was *busy,* and I want her to wonder what I might be doing. I want the envy of my sisters. I want them to listen to me, in disbelief, as I tell them that marriage is not all it's cracked up to be. And I want to be lying, even as I say the words.

How do you pack for a married life when it feels like much of the same?

My greatest fear is nothing changing. My greatest fear is being unprepared for change. In times like this my mother would tell me: It's only temporary. The first day of school. The zap of a hair removal laser. Trips to the hospital room where Grandpa took his last breaths. Unpleasant experiences all come to an end, eventually. Or you could just pinch yourself hard in the arm until they do. Physical pain makes it difficult to focus on anything else.

I begin folding sweaters. I line them up in a row. A snow globe of the Twin Towers catches my eye—a reminder that tragedy can turn yesterday's junk into something valuable. A stack of twenty-dollar coupons to Bed Bath and Beyond. A stack of Sitto's recipe cards. A stack of Polaroids all taken one day during senior year, when something so stupid had the ability to turn your whole day around.

Would Saul and I stay up late like Lucy and I sometimes did? Rooting around in each other's things? Desperate for clues into what the other person's life—independent of each other—was like? Will Saul always be curious about me? Will he still want to *know* me, even after he's had me? Will he like the person he sees? Will it matter?

It isn't temporary. It never has been.

A pack of bobby pins. A small tin box full of free samples from Sephora. A rich face cream, a Dead Sea scrub, bought from a freestanding booth in a Fort Lauderdale mall. What kind of woman do I want Saul to see when he opens our medicine cabinet?

How do you pack for a married life?

Why couldn't I accept her help? My mother, the task *queen*. With her lists. And her Rolodex. And her encyclopedic knowledge of domestic life. And her friends, and their stories—*lessons*. You should *listen*. One day it might come in handy. One day you'll see. But I have been listening. And listening. And now it feels like I've packed all the wrong things.

"The city is a petri dish of bacteria, Fortune," my mother told me. "Everyone's infected, so it's best to stick to your own." The homeless and the students and the Communists with the under shaves. The crooks and the party drug rapists and, most dangerous of them all, the anti-Semites. The anti-Semites are everywhere, lurking in the shadows cast by the tall buildings, steaming your soy milk at Starbucks, running your government, and writing you a ticket at the expired meter. There they'll be, gunning for your freedom *and* your wallet.

A sample of our wedding invitation: I pack it with the intention of getting it framed. A picture frame with a photo of Saul and me inside, taken at our engagement. I move on to the vanity I share with my sister.

This wedding is so obviously for my parents and *their* friends. Of the three hundred invitations we delivered, only one hundred were for Saul and my friends—and my mother's *still* complaining that she couldn't invite the whole block, her colorist, and whoever else she crosses paths with on a Monday!

"I'm mortified, Fortune. Mor-ti-*fied*. I used to buy challah from Susie every week! Every week! Remember?"

But that was five years ago, Ma! According to her logic, I should invite Blanch Pinhas! Afterall, she *did* loan me a bobby pin in fifth grade!

"So that's it. It's over. It's Zomick's challah from here on out and don't expect your father to pay the bill when you crack a tooth!" she shouted, wiping a bead of sweat from her brow.

"And Robbie and Paula Cohen, how am I going to look at them? Paula subs in at our canasta game on occasion. That's over!" She looked to Lucy and Nina, whose heads were bowed in concentration as they stuffed invitations like dutiful elves.

"You know I'm not one to exclude. It's just not the kind of person I am. I know some girls who go tit for tat, and frankly, it's disgusting."

Nods all around.

Envelope > Tissue > Invitation > Seal > Stamp > Pass! > Envelope > Tissue . . .

Liquid blush. Mascara, brow gel. A makeup brush. Makeup brush cleaner. A nearly empty tube of under-eye concealer. Panty liners. I stuff a box into the side zipper of my suitcase.

I heard somewhere that not everybody bleeds their first time. Something tells me that I will. Nothing sets the mood like a little vaginal hemorrhaging! Never mind the fact that I'll probably be *terrible*. For the most part, Saul tiptoes around the subject, as if it's his job to protect my innocence rather than break it. His timidness around the subject stands in contrast to Isaac's blunt characterization of me the other night. My bedroom window is positioned on the side of our house, and from it I can see Spice. The lights are on. The lights are always on. So long as there's an eight P.M. need for coriander, Spice will be open to fulfill it. And even though I swore I wouldn't, I wonder about Isaac and if he's thinking about me, if he, too, is replaying every single line from that conversation. I come to the conclusion that he's not. He probably forgot that conversation as soon as it ended. I wouldn't be able to zip my suitcase if it were any other way.

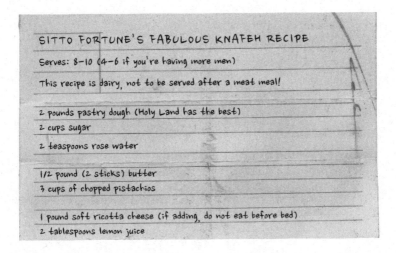

SITTO FORTUNE'S FABULOUS KNAFEH RECIPE

Serves: 8–10 (4–6 if you're having more men)

This recipe is dairy, not to be served after a meat meal!

2 pounds pastry dough (Holy Land has the best)
2 cups sugar
2 teaspoons rose water

1/2 pound (2 sticks) butter
3 cups of chopped pistachios

1 pound soft ricotta cheese (if adding, do not eat before bed)
2 tablespoons lemon juice

I fold the recipe card and stuff it into my wallet, for safekeeping.

NINA

Chapter Seventeen

....

I don't remember handing over my ID at the door, but there's a stamp on my hand that reads NO REENTRY and my ticket stub is torn. The line of people waiting to get into the show reaches up the block and snakes around the corner, and I think that if I have to wait on it, I might not make it inside. Luckily, Ethan knows the guy at the door. He made sure to mention this at least four times at the restaurant: "I know the guy at the door." This, I remember. Inside is dark and smells of loose beer and stale butter. We make our way past the merch table, where Ethan salutes the tattooed young boy who mans it. I stop to look at a heathered gray T-shirt and feel something catch against the rip in my jeans' knee. When I move back, a loose metal part sticking out of the table pulls the thread and I'm left with a gaping hole in my jeans. I tear at the loose threads and toss them on the floor, reassured that at least I look like I belong.

Steven is already making his way downstairs, and for the first time since we started working together, he doesn't wait up or even look back at me. I watch as the staircase swallows him whole and the thumping bass from the opening band increases in intensity. My mouth feels like it's both drowning in saliva and dangerously dry. I know I'm going to throw up tonight, it's just a matter of when. I consider heading to the bathroom before the show to stick my finger down my throat, but as I'm about to, Ethan grabs my hand and pulls me toward the stairs. He leads me through a sea of people—most of them girls who are dressed exactly like me, in torn Levi shorts and black stockings and combat boots, but with cooler haircuts. I follow his lead and manage to smile as he high-fives the various people we see along the way. It seems like he knows everybody. He doesn't know how drunk I am because if he did, he wouldn't have abandoned my hand midway, allowing me to wobble down unassisted. I stumble over the last two steps and make it to the bottom where the room smells like a bunch of people who haven't done laundry since they moved out of their mom's house. I fight the urge to gag and clutch the railing to steady myself, following Ethan into the lounge, where everything looks like it's been dipped in blue. The room is crowded, and we have to weave through throngs of people before we make it to the center. I scan the perimeter for the nearest bathroom but I don't find it. I look for Steven but I don't see him, either. Yasmin saw some people she knew in the line outside and I haven't seen her since.

I swallow deeply and try to concentrate on what's in front of me, even though my brain feels like it's suspended in jelly.

"Beer?" Ethan shouts above the loud music. He has that grin on his face, the same one he had on the day I met him—like a child that's up to no good. Can't he see that I need water and a bagel? I squint, trying to make Steven out in the crowd, but it's useless. It's almost like every boy here is in an army green utility jacket and has a grown-out buzz cut.

"Sure," I manage to say. At least a beer might fill my stomach. There's a layer of people crowding the bar but Ethan stretches his six-foot frame and waves the bartender down, signaling for two beers on tap. When he hands me mine, a third of it splashes out of the plastic up and onto the floor and I pretend to care. We cheers and I take a sip. Ethan downs half of his cup and licks the foam from the stubble on his upper lip.

"Lookin' for someone?" he shouts. The music is getting louder. I can feel the feet against the ceiling closing in over our heads. "Your eyes are all over the place, girl." Ethan smiles. "Either you're twisted, or you're looking for someone."

"The former," I say. "And the latter."

"All right." Ethan laughs.

"I'm drunk."

"Come on." He takes my hand and leads me, again, toward the staircase. "Opener's wrapping up. Let's get a good spot before the show starts."

I look around, again, one last time. I spill out the remainder of my beer in a nearby trash can while Ethan's back is turned, and then I run to catch up with him. The venue is small and crowded, standing room only. There are already at least three hundred people crowding the stage. I'm thankful to stand in the back, by the exit, but Ethan begins politely shoving to get to the front, signaling that he's meeting someone. People are annoyed but they comply. I consider texting Steven to ask where he is but decide against it. I'm too embarrassed. The mere recollection of our conversation is enough to make me hurl.

"Come on!" Ethan motions me forward. "Steven's texted that they're up front."

Okay. I inhale. A hand holding up a phone shoots out from the crowd, at least fifty feet in front of us. I recognize the stack of beaded rainbow bracelets. Steven told me his niece had made them for him, and I thought that was sweet. I look down and focus on my feet, because looking up only reminds me of how suffocated I feel, how many people I'd need to bypass in order to make it out of here. I inhale and exhale. I count to thirty-five before bumping into a pair of beat-up Vans, and I'm sure I've never felt so relieved to see a pair of feet, and maybe, just maybe, that's what love is. I look up to find Steven looking down on me, his face a jigsaw puzzle of concern. I hold his gaze. *Get me out of here,* I telepath, but Steven's expression turns blank and he turns his attention to the stage, where the lead guitarist has just plugged into the amp. The speaker lets out a loud shriek and the crowd erupts in applause as the rest of the band takes the stage. It feels like the entire audience greets them with a collective inhale of pot, and smoke congeals in the air above my head. The keyboard, the drums, everything starts up and the crowd begins to sway around me. The lights at center stage flash red, blue, and white in tandem with the music, which is quick and erratic. I close my eyes to block out the color. Steven takes a step back so that he's side by side with Ethan, both of them behind me. I don't have to turn around to know that they're sharing a joint. When Ethan offers me a hit, I don't say no. But when Steven doesn't interfere as I'd expected him to, I'm forced to take it. I inhale from the soggy end of the rolled paper and hold the smoke in my lungs until it burns so much I let out a loud, barking cough. I cough some more to get the trapped smoke out of my lungs and blink away tears. I search the floor frantically for a water bottle and take a sip from the only thing I can find, Ethan's beer from earlier.

"Someone's rusty!" Ethan leans over and yells into my ear, taking the joint from my fingertips.

Just when I thought I couldn't get dizzier, the room turns over on its side. There are too many instruments being played at once, the lights can't keep up with the music, and I can't keep up with them. The lead singer is so close to his mic I think he's going to eat it. I tilt my nose up to the ceiling and suck in through my nostrils just to confirm they're still attached to my face, but it's almost like there is no air left in the room. I feel my heart pick up its pace, trying to match the rhythm of the beat onstage.

This is it, I think. *This is how I'm going to die.*

I start to panic, my eyes darting from left to right, desperate to map out an easy escape. I'm three seconds from bolting when I feel a hand around my waist. I'm relieved when the voice that matches it is steady.

"Let's go," Steven says. I follow him.

We make it halfway up the block in silence before I stop to steady myself against a metal scaffolding pole. And there, I proceed to projectile vomit all over the sidewalk, all over my combat boots. It feels so good that I don't even care that Steven's standing right behind me, holding my hair back. I really let it rip.

When I'm done, I let out a small whimper.

"Are you . . . done?" Steven says, still holding my hair in one hand.

"Water," I manage. I pull away from him, too ashamed to look him in the eye. My boots are covered in upchucked guacamole, tequila, and today's juice. I lean down and start to untie them. I kick them off to the side and feel the cool sidewalk beneath my stockinged feet. "Let's go."

Steven looks down at my boots. "You're not gonna—" I begin to walk up the block. "Nope. Nope, she's leaving the boots." He hurries to catch up and grabs my hand. "Slow down. There's a bagel place on the corner."

I look down at my feet the entire walk, careful not to step on anything sharp. I'm too parched to speak. The bagel shop stands on the corner like some emblazoned mirage in the Mojave Desert. Steven holds the door for me and I beeline for the fridge, where I down a bottle of water. I feel myself coming down from the alcohol, but paranoia from the pot still grips my chest. I excuse myself to the bathroom and swish water in my mouth before spitting into the sink. I do this three or four times and wipe away the mascara that's run past my undereye and down my check. I look like hell. I fish in my pockets for some lip gloss and find a piece of gum.

When I come out, Steven is sitting on a stool by the window. I slide into the one next to him, thankful that we don't have to face each other.

"Hi," I say, looking down.

"This is for you." Steven slides a cafeteria tray toward me. There's a plain bagel cut in half, topped with tuna, lettuce, and tomato.

"I appreciate the effort at whole wheat," I say sarcastically.

"I thought you might like that," he says.

"You know deli tuna is like, not real tuna, right?" I pick a piece of toasted bread off and eat it.

"You know you went into that nasty bathroom barefoot, right?"

"Touché." I smile.

"Now eat." Steven nods toward my half and takes a bite out of his. His eyes are lazy and pink but he concentrates on his sandwich like it's a math problem he can solve. He breaks eye contact with it only to look out the window in front of us. I watch his jaw as he chews and swallows, his shoulders slumped forward slightly, his foot still tapping in tandem with the beat we left behind. I reach over and take his green army jacket from the tabletop in front of us and swing it over my shoulders because I just want to be closer to him.

"Cold?" Steven swallows his last bite and takes a swig of soda. Then he looks at me. I mean he really looks at me. Despite the vomit, and the pettiness, and the shit with Ethan, and my mom. He looks at me simultaneously as if I'm some foreign object and the most familiar thing he's ever encountered. He sees me.

Before I can stop myself, I take his face in my hands and pull it toward mine. I'm shaking but not cold. I know exactly what I want. And so, under the punishing light of the bagel place on the corner, I kiss him.

LUCY

Chapter Eighteen

....

It's 5:31 A.M. and the sun has barely risen, still suspended over the horizon as if it can't decide if it wants to go back to sleep or not—and we are very, very late. David's right hand is over mine and he maneuvers the steering wheel of his car with his left, with ease and the tiniest bit of arrogance, the same way he seems to do everything. I wonder what it must have been like to never hear your parents bicker over the credit card bill. For your mother to be the woman others struggle to keep up with. To never have to compromise, on anything. It's a wonder to me that David didn't turn out to be a total asshole. Of course I'd never tell him that his salary won't cover half of our lifestyle. We both know that his family money is the cushion that allows him to drive his Range Rover Sport.

David speeds through a traffic light that's just turned red.

"Slow down!" I squeeze his hand. We've been out all night. We went to his apartment after dinner and now my mother will be waking up soon. I texted Fortune to cover for me last night but she was already asleep. Luckily Nina was still up, and when my mother called out from her room late last night after hearing the door open, Nina yelled back that she and I had both gotten home at the same time. Now all I have to do is sneak into my house before she or Sitto wakes up.

David stops a block short of my house, on a street with an apartment building where no Jews live and there's little risk of being seen.

"So." He sighs, a smile creeping across his face. There's already a small shadow of stubble forming across his cheeks. His eyes look heavy and tired. And still, I think he's the most handsome man I've ever seen. He squeezes my hand gently and I lace my fingers through his, raising his hand to my lips and kissing it. Being with him makes me bold. I have a sense of power I'm now sure I never want to live without. In just an hour and a half, Giselle and I will have to start walking to the train to catch first minyan at school. But I don't care. Prom, finals, graduation, senior trip. They're just steps on the path to getting what I already have.

"Last night was . . ."

"Fun." I smile, completing David's sentence.

I think back to the night. David made us bowls of cereal because the sushi hadn't filled us. We sat across from each other laughing over corn-flakes and after every few bites David would lean his entire body over the table and kiss me, saying that he couldn't help it. It wasn't long before we abandoned the cereal and made our way to the couch. I still haven't seen David's bedroom. It feels like some invisible boundary we can't cross. I think we both know that being in bed together would make not going all the way impossible. Not like the couch makes us innocent. Less than five minutes later and my shirt was on the floor, my legs wrapped around David's waist. I moved up and down slowly, in a rhythm that felt right, feeling David's pace quicken or slow depending on where I put my hand, as my lips grazed his ear. I pulled him closer as he whispered to me that he loves me. And to the surprise of us both, I told him I was ready. At first he pretended not to know what I meant. But when I pulled my face from his and showed him I was serious, he said, "I can't. Trust me I want to, but I can't. There will be a time for that, but it's not now."

I don't know what I would've done if David had complied. My suggestion was more of a test, an attempt at getting a promise out of him. Everyone says he'll propose soon, but I'm not even sure if he's spoken to my dad yet, and without that we can't really finalize a date for the wedding. Plus, I want to hear it from him.

David unfastens his seatbelt and faces me. The sun has fully made its way up the horizon and its rays stretch over the car, light flooding the windows. The birds are singing their songs and I feel like G-D-damn Snow White, without all of the innocent bullshit.

"So you're leaving school early, you said?" David asks. He always looks a little uncomfortable when acknowledging that I'm still in high school.

"Yup. Fortune's going to dip in the mikvah for the first time today, so we're all going: me, Nina, my mother, her future mother-in-law."

"Nice." David digs his hand in his pocket and produces a small blue velvet box. My heart drops into my stomach. I open and close my eyes, just to make sure the exhaustion isn't causing illusions.

"What—" I manage to say.

"Before you say anything"—David cuts me off—"I want you to know that this isn't the moment. The moment *will* come; there will be flowers and a violinist and all of our closest friends and family. But this isn't it—I'm not going to open the box right now, but I just wanted you to know, while it's just the two of us, in this moment, which is so perfect—"

"Are you going to be this nervous when the time comes?" I laugh.

"Definitely not." David smiles and stammers on. "I want you to know that you have me, that I'm ready to make that promise to you and that it's only a matter of time. I've had this ring for two weeks but after last night, I just couldn't hold it in anymore. I'd propose to you right now if my mother wouldn't murder me."

"We don't want that." My cheeks hurt from smiling. "I love you," I say. David buries the box back in his pocket. "Tease." I stick out my lower lip.

"I love you." David leans forward and kisses me. I kiss him back and breathe him in. I'm hit with the prospect of losing him and I squeeze my eyes shut to make the thought go away. It's almost six, and I really should go. I take off my seatbelt and look into David's eyes. There is so much desire for me in them, I seriously consider blowing off school and telling him to just drive. But he can wait, apparently. We have our whole lives for that.

David offers to back up the block to my house but I decline, not wanting to risk anyone seeing me. I blow him a kiss after closing the door and skip home.

The son of the guy who owns Spice is outside the store, raising the metal gate that covers its windows and doors. I wave to him quickly and wonder why nobody is talking about how hot he is. I make a mental note to mention him to one of my friends and disappear inside the house.

LESSON 4: MIKVAH IMMERSION

After counting her seven clean days, a woman will immerse in the mikvah, the ritual bathhouse. Only afterward is she no longer considered a Niddah, and may resume relations with her husband. The purpose of the mikvah is to "beautify and cleanse." Therefore, a woman must make careful preparations in order to ensure that the purifying waters reach every part of her body.

Before immersion:

- Hatzizot (foreign objects) such as jewelry, contact lenses, and Band-Aids must be removed. Dissolvable stitches are okay.

- Wash the entire body with soap and warm water, checking every inch from head to toe.

- Clean ears, nose, and navel thoroughly with a Q-tip.

- Remove all makeup and polish from toes and fingernails. Clean under nail beds.

- Brush and floss teeth. Clean braces and remove dentures if applicable.

- Any hair that is usually removed should be removed. It is Sephardic custom to remove all pubic hair, but this is not mandatory.

- Examine your breasts.

- Use the toilet if needed.

- A woman should not knead dough, eat red meat, or cook with staining vegetables before immersion.

Once all of the preparations have been completed, a woman may immerse.

FORTUNE

Chapter Nineteen

··········

It's funny how you can spend your whole life not knowing what goes on in the modest stucco building a mere two hundred yards from your house. I never much noticed the mikvah, or that it was dedicated in David Bakar's late grandfather's honor and was therefore certainly donated by his parents. I can't recall ever having seen anybody walk in or out, probably because most of the foot traffic happens at sundown and not eleven A.M. on a Monday, which is now. The streets are awash in food wrappers and idle gossip, complaints over the price increase at Glatt Mart and the inevitability of lingering matzo constipation. Women pound their "errand" wedges into the pavement, their long locks whipping behind them like laundry left to hang in a breeze. They look way too beautiful, I conclude, especially for an avenue of Brooklyn whose defining characteristic is its particular brand of smell—meat water.

It's not like I expect Brooklyn to take a moment of silence now that it's time for me to dip. But it definitely doesn't help that the mikvah sits sandwiched between Toe Curling Shawarma and Beautiful Cleaners. The small building is the same shade as salmon sashimi and is the only pop of color in a sea of scuffed brick and pigeon shit–stained awnings.

"Let's go!" My mother hurries in front of me, Lucy and Nina by her side. Sitto hangs back with Marie, who has offered to help her walk.

"Coming!" I pick up my pace and rush in behind Nina. Once the door closes, all of the noise from the street is blocked out and a quiet calm settles in.

My mother doesn't even have so much as a buffed cuticle inside before she starts to sob. "I'm sorry," she mutters, mainly to Marie. "This is very emotional for me."

Her slight shoulders shake violently in an attempt to muffle her cries. She breathes like a woman in labor. It occurs to me that I haven't seen her cry since the fall of the Kibbeh Saniyeh in '06. It was six P.M. on erev Rosh Hashanah, and the time had finally come to remove the five-hours-in-the-making Kibbeh Saniyeh from the oven, when the Pyrex slipped from her tenuous grasp, collapsing in a heap of glass shards and minced meat all over the kitchen floor. I saw the whole episode in slow motion, and it was one of the more terrifying experiences of my teenage life. The ground looked like a bloodbath. Down went the Kibbeh Saniyeh, and down went my mother.

"My knees! They gave out!" she hollered, scrambling to piece back together what was clearly unsalvageable.

"My kibbeh! My knees! My kibbeh! My knees!" she wailed, bulgur coursing through her desperate fingers. I did the only thing I could think of doing. I crouched down behind her, rubbing my mother's heaving back as her tears soaked the now oversalted dish.

"Kapparah," I whispered, over and over again. The Kibbeh Saniyah had died to atone for our sins. Better its desecration than ours.

"Kapparah," she concurred, rising from the floor.

She hasn't attempted the recipe since, and any mention of it sends her into an unshakable stupor.

The check-in area of the mikvah is small and neat, with white marble floors and modern sconces that look straight out of a Crate & Barrel catalog. It smells like our living room after one of my mother's canasta games—a delicate mix of potpourri, coffee, and *lashon hara*. My mother holds her tears long enough to acknowledge the woman who has been sitting patiently behind the small white lacquer desk at the entrance. Atop it sits a phone, tissue box, laptop, and a small silver bowl of lebes, white Jordan almonds coated in layers of candy. I've heard that it's customary to throw them at the bride after she dips. The woman, whose hair is covered, lifts her eyes from the computer screen in front of her and, with a tilt of her head, asks my mother if it's all right to begin. She smiles sweetly and scans our faces before landing on mine "First *tevilah?*" she asks.

"Yes." My mother clears her throat, answering for me. "Fortune Cohen. She's getting married the day after tomorrow so this will be her first dip, yes."

"How exciting!" The woman clasps her hands together. "And you brought a small crowd. Better that way, some girls get overwhelmed with all of their friends being there the first time."

A small crowd? My mother alone would've been a small crowd. This is a party. Not to mention that I don't feel close enough to any of my friends to bring them here.

"Am I right to assume you've taken your bridal courses?" the woman continues.

"Yes. Sandy Beda taught me," I say.

"Ah! Sandy. I love her. Well then, you're in good hands."

"Are we going to have to *watch* her?" Nina asks. She looks a little worse for wear today. But I'm in no mood to get my head bitten off.

"Of course not—I'm sure you remember your first time!" The woman chuckles naïvely. She stands up and smooths her skirt.

"Actually, I don't," Nina says, her voice audibly irritated.

The woman places her hand on Nina's shoulder. "Everything in due time, but it's good you are here. It is a big *zechut* to participate in a first *tevilah*. Especially for single women. The gates of heaven open when a woman dips and *Hashem* is available to her, listening." She turns to me. "Before you dip, your sisters are welcome to dip a toe in the mikvah. The waters are very holy before a bride submerges. It'll be good luck for them."

"This one doesn't need luck," my mother says, squeezing Lucy.

"Oh my G-D," I mutter.

"*Humdullah*, let's go." Sitto breaks the ice. "It's getting late and my knees hurt from the walk."

"Yes, okay! Fortune, you're going to follow me through this door." The woman points to one of two doors. "Your family will go through the other. They both lead you to the pool. Just ring me when you're done washing and we can get started. Oh!" She scurries off and picks up an iPod connected to a speaker. She shuffles for a moment before settling on spa music. Pleased with her selection, she places the iPod down.

We stand awkwardly for a few seconds before my MIL breaks the silence by presenting me with a woven basket the size of a small Shetland pony. I stare at it blankly before Lucy nudges me in the ribs and I take the mikvah basket. I've heard about these things, but they've always remained more or less a mystery to me. I equated them to the two survival items granted to each contestant on those wilderness shows. Like, *here's a machete and a pot, although they won't be of much help to you!*

"Open it!" the MIL says excitedly.

My mother, sisters, Sitto, and MIL crowd around me as I explore the contents of the basket, removing the gifts that would usher me into womanhood one by one. I unfold monogrammed hand towels, my new initials imprinted on them in lavender and pink. I unwrap a large terry cloth bathrobe and slippers of the same fabric. Alibaba bath pearls spill out of their cylindrical Lucite containers. There's a Mason Pearson brush and Vanilla Soufflé body cream nestled beside a Diptyque candle. I unveil a large waffle cosmetic bag (monogrammed, of course) and open it to find Q-tips, cotton balls, polish remover, a small compact mirror, and a pack of kosher *bedikah* cloths, for checking to make sure I'm clean. There is under-eye cream and bobby pins and a small variety pack of cotton underwear.

"This is so nice." I look into Marie's eyes, and I mean it. For the first time since I've met her, Marie appears genuinely moved. It's as if she, like me, is finally making peace with the fact that this is happening. Her only son is about to be married. This is the culmination of all of her planning. Every phone call with her sister deliberating if she liked this dress or that. Every conversation with a salesperson that started with: "I'm buying a gift for my future daughter-in-law. She's simple, nothing with too much *gazz*." Every argument she had with her husband over whether to invite *that* couple or not. And the earlier moments, too. Making sure Saul was bathed every night, his stomach full, homework completed. Every sleepless night spent worrying about his happiness and security. It's all been for this moment, and it's me to whom she passes the baton. I feel an immeasurable amount of guilt for having deceived this woman, Saul's mother. If she knew about even an eighth of the doubt I had, she'd pry this silk pillowcase right out of my cold dead hands. And she wouldn't be wrong! The mere *idea* of her finding out about my conversations with Isaac was enough to churn my stomach. I have real nerve accepting these gifts, and yet I do. Again, I take one step closer to a reality I still don't know if I want. And yet, a voice that I don't recognize as my own thanks Marie once more.

"For nothing." Marie waves her hand and leans in closely. "You don't need to use it all today. They have everything here already—maybe it's better to save this stuff and have it fresh for your new apartment."

The attendant claps her hands together for what feels like the fifth time and says, "I don't mean to rush you, but we do have another appointment right after yours. Usually we don't slot, but for first timers we like to keep it intimate. We understand that some girls may be initially uncomfortable with having walk-ins while they're here. So, should we get to it?" She places her hand on the small of my back and leads me to the door. I wave awkwardly to my mother and to Marie, and I follow the attendant through a door and into a spa-like bathroom.

"Oh, excuse me!" my mother shouts. "Is it okay if my other daughters dip a toe while Fortune changes?" I hear her tell Lucy that she should go, too; there is a special prayer she can say to conceive a baby boy, G-D willing, in the future. I don't think any such prayer exists for a girl.

"Of course," the attendant responds.

I can hear my mother and Nina bickering as I disappear behind one of the doors.

"Nice family," the attendant says as she leads me into the white marble bathroom. It's set up like a spa, with three glass shower doors and small lockers for your belongings. There is a large double sink with soap, moisturizer, and rows of Lucite jars holding everything from Q-tips to rubber bands to cotton balls.

"They are," I agree, lingering awkwardly by the shower.

The attendant leans down and pulls two white towels from the shelf beneath the sink. She hangs them on the rod outside one of the showers and takes my hands in hers, inspecting my fingernails. "Good," she says, as she notes I don't have polish on. "Just the ring has to come off." She winks. She gestures down at my feet.

"My toes are clean, too," I say.

"Fantastic. So take your shower, do your checks. We have everything here for you to clean with. Make sure to be thorough, between your fingers, behind your ears. Take your time. There is shampoo and conditioner in the shower, although I know some girls like to bring their own. If you wear contact lenses, you're going to have to take them out. We have disposable shavers, too, if you'd like." She rattles off her spiel like she's done it a hundred times before, *today*.

"I'm okay."

"Great." She claps her hands once more. "When you're finished washing, just pick up that phone right there and dial 1. I'll come get you." She motions to a white landline sitting atop a small table.

"Sounds good."

"Okay, then—good luck!" She exits through the same door we came in.

I take a deep breath and stand in front of the mirror for a moment before I begin to undress. I feel exposed even though I'm the only one in here, which probably doesn't bode well considering what I'm about to do. I remove my socks, my jeans, my T-shirt and bra. Every part of me is smooth, having been waxed and plucked and lasered in the weeks and months leading up to this day. I've always looked younger than my age, but now with all of the weight I've lost, my body does, too. My breasts look like two kids-menu pancakes, and when I push my long hair to the front, it covers them entirely. I take two Q-tips and a washcloth into the shower and raise the temperature of the water until it burns my back. I begin to scrub. I rub every single part of my body. I scrub my feet and in between my toes, the backs of my legs, under my arms. I reach behind my ears and between my inner thighs. I massage shampoo into my hair and scratch my fingernails across my scalp until it feels clean and raw. I dig wax out of my ears and blow my nose until my ears pop from the pressure. But no matter what I do, I can't seem to get clean enough. No matter what I do, I don't feel ready.

The water turns from hot to lukewarm, signaling to me that it's time to come out. I wrap my hair in a towel and unravel the robe my MIL bought me, cloaking my shivering body inside it. I pick up the phone and dial the number 1. "Ready." Another step closer.

"What's the boy's name? Where's the wedding? And are you honeymooning right after or waiting a bit?" The attendant is talking as she leads me into the chamber, but I'm just nodding along. Inside, the lights are dim, a two-hundred-gallon water-filled square the size of a hotel Jacuzzi dug into the center of the room.

"Why don't you disrobe and get in. Then I'll call in your family."

"Oh," I say, my face turning red. "Just my mother, please."

The attendant raises her eyebrows and disappears, returning with my mother just as I enter the tepid pool.

"Are you okay?" my mother asks, a look of concern on her face. It's only then that I realize I'm crying.

"Just overwhelmed," I manage.

"And she totally understands, your MIL," my mother says. "She was surprised you let her come here in the first place."

"Oh, good." I haven't even thought about her.

"Are we ready?" The attendant steps forward. "Do you know your family mikvah custom?"

"She'll dip seven times," my mother says. "Wait—let me get a mental snapshot."

Mrs. Beda's voice fills my head as I bend my knees and sway slightly in the warm water. *Try to have purpose, with each dunk,* she'd said. I unclench my toes and fingers and close my eyes. I relax my jaw and shoulders and try to imagine that the water is actually purifying me, just as the booklet says. I begin to say the blessing out loud as my mother looks on, her hands over her mouth.

"Baruch Atah . . ."

I bend my knees fully and submerge, allowing the full weight of the water to close in over my head. Underneath, without the gaze of my mother, or the attendant, or my sisters, without the distraction of familiar surroundings and the pressures that push and pull at you like an everchanging current, I have clarity. It is still and silent and I can feel my lungs fill deeply, even though I'm completely deprived of oxygen.

Here, in this small tub of rainwater and sea glass tile, I feel free.

I know what I have to do.

I straighten my legs and spring up from the water, feeling the damp air hit my face.

"Kosher!" the attendant shouts—and then I do it again six more times. When I do finally emerge from the waters, my naked body full of goosebumps, I feel the way I should: clear. I look back down at the pool and imagine all of my doubts and fears, real and imagined, swirling inside it. "This is where I leave you," I whisper. I know what I have to do.

NINA

Chapter Twenty

....

When Fortune steps out of the mikvah, a crisp white waffle robe cinched around her small waist, we pelt her with lebes. I take a little too much joy in this ridiculous custom, I'll admit. My mother runs to hug her, tears streaming down her face.

"Leh leh leh leh leh!" Sitto howls with joy, clapping her hands from a comfortable armchair in the corner of the room where we'd been waiting. A joyous remix of the Hebrew poem "Lecha Dodi" booms from the iHome speaker in the corner. It's set to an Arabic melody I recognize from the countless weddings I've been to. Marie sways her hips to the seductive beat as my mother rocks Fortune in her arms.

"Does she look okay to you?" Lucy leans over and whispers.

"Who, Mom? Isn't she always this dramatic?"

"No, Fortune." Lucy continues to throw almonds, intermittingly popping one in her mouth. My mother pulls away from Fortune for a moment and I catch a glimpse of her face. She looks terrified, and pale.

"Maybe she's just nervous about having sex. It's all very real now." Lucy shrugs.

"Come on." I pull my sister toward Fortune. "Let's get in there." Lucy and I envelop Fortune in a three-way hug. With my arms wrapped around her, I can feel her body shiver. I run my hands up and down her arms to try to warm her up.

"You're scaring me. How cold *was* the pool?" Lucy squeezes Fortune.

"Not cold at all!" the attendant hollers from the side. "It's a warm eighty degrees at all times." I crane my neck to catch a view of the clock in the corner. It's already half past eleven and I should be getting to work. My mother agreed to loan me her car since I missed my ride with Steven to be here. "Forch, are you okay?"

"You look like you've seen a ghost," Lucy says. In the background, I can hear Marie tell my mother that there is nothing in the world like sisters.

"I'm good, you guys." Fortune gives us a reassuring smile. "I will be good. I promise."

I squint my eyes at her in an attempt to read her face, giving her one last chance to tell me. But Fortune doesn't bite. Her color still hasn't returned, but she gives me an assured smile. "Go." She squeezes my hand tenderly. "I know you have to."

"Okay." I pull back. "Okay. I love you, okay? And *mabrook*! Really, I'm happy I got to be here." I say my goodbyes to my mother and Marie. I run to give Sitto a kiss on the cheek but she stops me. "Take your shoe off," she demands.

"What?"

"I said take your shoe off. You are not leaving before you dip a toe," she says sternly.

"What? Oh G-D."

"Yes!" The attendant claps. "Yes, yes! We have five minutes before our next dip. Please, the waters are holy—it'll only take a minute, honey."

"Go." Sitto bangs her walking stick into the ground as if she's about to split the sea.

"Fine." I grunt, ripping off my boot and sock. I limp submissively toward the door that separates us from the mikvah. Lucy follows me. "What are you doing here?"

"What?" she says defensively. "There's no ring on my finger."

"Yet," I say.

"Yet."

I drive a little faster than I'm supposed to. I can feel my adrenaline coursing through my feet, my legs, my hands; my entire body feels like it's buzzing with nervous excitement. My lips are chapped from kissing and I hug Steven's green utility jacket a little closer to my body, the one I had wrapped around my shoulders last night.

Text me when you're here. We both know how much you suck at parking. Steven texts.

> 5 minutes . . . make an excuse
> when you leave.

Steven and I left the concert last night and never went back. Ethan called Steven a few times before he made up some excuse about his stomach and some bad queso eaten at the restaurant before the show. The truth was that after I kissed Steven and he kissed me back, we kind of never stopped. Until the employee behind the bagel counter politely asked us to leave, and we of course obliged. Neither of us said anything as we walked back to his car. We didn't have to. The energy between us, the same one that had been quietly simmering since we reconnected, had been unleashed. That I had been the one to set it free was a surprise to us both.

"So . . . what does this mean?" Steven said as we both settled into his car. Despite having his tongue in my mouth for twenty minutes, Steven still seemed unsure of where we stood. He was just as insecure, just as scared as I was. *Every pot has a lid*, Sitto is fond of saying.

"Isn't there some workplace code against office romance?" I teased. My hair was messy and hanging loose from its topknot. Steven brushed a strand from my eye and twirled it around his finger. "Screw the code," he said. His eyes looked red and tired, but he kept them on me.

"On a scale from one to ten, how happy is your mother going to be?"

"On a scale from one to ten how happy is *your* mother going to be!" Steven pushed me playfully. Then he leaned over the small partition that separated us and kissed me again.

Here. I text Steven. By some miracle I find a spot directly in front. When I see him come out of the office entrance, I get out of the car and walk around to the passenger door. Steven fumbles awkwardly toward me. He looks like the high school boy I grew up with dressed in men's clothes: black jeans, a white T-shirt, and a black boxy chore jacket that hangs loose over his slender shoulders. "Enjoying my jacket?" he says as I lean my back against the car and he steps closer.

"Very much so." I hug it tight against my body.

"I'm glad. All good with your parents last night? Did they notice anything?"

"You mean that my clothes smelled like weed and vomit? Thankfully, no. I stuck everything in the washing machine the minute you dropped me off. Lucy got in after me but I was already in my bed. I'm still so embarrassed. I can't believe you had to see me like that."

"Yeah . . . I mean vomiting on the first date . . . not your best look." Steven grins.

"Shut up." I punch his arm. "And it wasn't a date, remember?"

"Oh yes, it was." Steven steps closer. "And you're my girlfriend now."

"Your what?" I try to mask my excitement, but it feels like every muscle in my face is twitching toward possibility. "I'm your girlfriend." This time, I don't question him.

"Now tell me how much you're dreading walking in there right now." He nods toward the office. The bar where I had my office inauguration is dark and, in the harsh light of day, looks sad and sleepy. That night feels like ages ago. How is it possible that so much has changed in a few short months? It's funny, you can go years where it seems like nothing changes at all. *I've* gone years where nothing has changed, nothing except my age.

The wind rustles a few leaves on the floor and blows an empty blue cup from the curb into the street, where a guy with large headphones picks it up and tosses it into the trash can on the corner. The cup nearly misses and scares the crap out of a small black French bulldog, who is taking his morning pee on a fire hydrant, causing his leash to get tangled around it. His owner, a young woman with a nose piercing and bleached hair, bends down to untwist it and is nearly knocked over by a cyclist, a middle-aged man with an insulated bag of delivery food balancing perilously on his front handlebars. He curses her out and speeds away, but not before turning around to get a glimpse of her ass as she bends down once more. A young couple stops to help her. The man is cradling a tiny infant in a BabyBjörn against his chest. He pushes his wire frame glasses up and says in solidarity: "Something must be done about these cyclists." All around us, people from all over the country mill about this specific block in Bushwick, each with their own individual reasons as to why they've decided to make this their home, their community. There is no one consensus that brought them here, no collective code to live by.

I take Steven's hand and squeeze it. "Let's go." He wraps his arm around my shoulder and together we walk inside. It's us, and then it's them. This time, that doesn't feel like such a bad thing.

FORTUNE

Chapter Twenty-one

....

Nobody ever tells you how lonely having a big family can be—how isolating it feels, like being lost at sea; a dozen buoys floating around you, visible but out of reach. I hate it when the house gets this quiet. When bodies return to their beds and the only sound coming from the kitchen is the rhythmic hum of the refrigerator. Darkness turns everything into a still life. Dad always gets home after sundown, and the first thing he does is make sure all the lights are switched off. The sound of his heavy feet dragging across the marble floor can't be mistaken for anyone else's. My father has the type of walk you can hear, one that betrays not just the physical weight of his frame but the emotional one, too. My mother sighs to be noticed, a deep, inexhaustible sigh, the power of a thousand cavernous yogi breaths, and my dad, he just walks. He shuffles throughout the house, flipping every light in his path, inviting nightfall into the house. Sometimes he leaves Post-it notes on the walls: SHUT LIGHT! This drives Mom crazy. So sometimes, she'll shut the lights in the kitchen while he's still eating, just to prove a point.

"Sorry!" she'll say. "It's a habit!" And Dad will laugh, and you can almost see a glimmer of something, not exactly love, but a warm acceptance of each other that could've once been mistaken for it.

I descend the stairs to the foyer slowly, nearly tripping over the pair of sneakers I left strewn across the landing, and I imagine my mother's karmic glee had she been here to witness my potential fall. *I'm always telling everyone to take their shoes up!* I can hear her say. How many times has she told herself she wouldn't let the stray shoes by the staircase bother her? How many times has she walked by an orphaned boot, its sole caked with Brooklyn's grime, and harnessed all the self-control she could muster not to emerge the aggrieved victim in a house full of undeserving, unappreciative, filthy "hotel guests." How many times has she descended the staircase, expecting, even wanting to nose-dive over an UGG slipper, a busted nose a small price to pay for being right. How many times has the disappointment of a clear landing surprised her?

Ahhh, she'd sigh. My mother, the perpetual sigher. Her sigh is specific. It's not a sigh of relief, nor is it a sigh of exhaustion. My mother's sigh is a call for attention; nearly undetectable to the untrained ear, it's a cry for help. My mother sighs at Shabbat dinners, when, as the last to arrive to the table, she sees that her husband and kids have all started eating without her. She sighs upon waking up, another day filled with frying in vegetable oil stretched before her. She sighs every time she enters an empty kitchen. She sighs every time my father comes home from work and she sighs when he doesn't. She sighs when the doorbell rings and she sighs when nobody answers it. She sighs as she carries her own shoes up the stairs because the parenting coach interviewed by Hoda Kotb says mothers must begin with leading by example. She sighs as an act of solidarity with herself.

There's no way around the living room, which has turned into a living memorial of what could have been. My mother has tried as best she can, but the white boxes from Wish You Well remain in plain view. Silver cake knives and wooden fruit bowls taunt me from inside their plastic bubble wrap. *Return me! Return me!* That morning with Marie seems like a distant dream, but as much as I don't want to, I know at some point I'll have to face the music and bring these gifts back. There are so many gifts. We invited, well, I don't actually know how many people to the wedding, but many of the guests sent presents before the day arrived. A stack of gift cards I kept neatly tucked inside an envelope have surely been voided from their respective stores. But there are ceramic platters, and glass candy bowls, black cooking roasters and Dutch ovens, there are dish towels and candlesticks, water pitchers and wine decanters, bookends and Baccarat butterflies. I have everything I need except for the life where this stuff belongs.

It smells like dinner in Tupperware. Lucy is out with David again, living a dream I definitely crushed for myself. Dad is still at work and Sitto has long retired to her room, where she'll watch the Game Show Network until pinwheels dance on the insides of her eyelids. As for Nina, it's clear who she's with. She left the house without a word, and nobody had the guts to question her. It's obvious she and Steven are together now. We all tiptoe around the subject, too scared to say something that will set her off. It's funny, a month ago, I was the only sister with a ring on her finger, and now I'm the only one alone.

I'm surprised to find my mother in the kitchen, lining aluminum trays with four-by-four squares of puff pastry dough. I slide into the kitchen stool beside her and reach for the box of disposable latex gloves on the island. My mother works the contents of a large glass bowl, a sweet blend of finely chopped meat, sautéed onion, and tamarind paste.

"Wash your hands first, honey." She scoops a small handful of meat into her palm, rolling it into a circle the size of a golf ball before flattening it onto the surface of a wonton.

I have a choice, I think, as I scrub my hands clean beneath warm water. I could go back upstairs. I could shut the door to my bedroom and open a book. I could disappear into the fictional lives of its characters. Or, I could help my mother complete her orders, and we could bake lahmajin in silence before she musters up the courage to ask me why I did what I did and I get angry because why does it take me breaking off my engagement at the eleventh hour for someone around here to ask me how I'm feeling.

Then again, there's always the possibility that she'll say nothing. I wash my hands, rubbing the small indent on my left index finger where a ring used to be.

My mother hands me a wooden spoon. "You can be generous; the meat shrinks in the oven."

"Who are these for?" I ask. My mother and I have never been good at small talk, the way she and Lucy are. And we don't fight like she and Nina do, either. Both exchanges require a special skill I do not possess. I tend to move around words like a soldier on enemy ground, both clumsily and as though my life depended on it. Inside my own head, the words come together so clearly. It's making them make sense to others that's always been my problem. I know that now.

"These are for the shul." My mother completes one tray and moves on to the next one. "Your father is always saying that the men come out of minyan on Saturdays starving." The kitchen countertop looks like a study in organized chaos. At least a dozen Post-it notes are stuck across it. They say things like:

MAISY'S ORDER (DELIVERY)

SHUL

PANKO FRIED CHICKEN GOURMETTES

JALAPEÑO SPICED AREYES?

"That's nice of you," I say. Really, I'm wondering if my mother is taking on charity work to re-up her goodwill in the community. Your family stock certainly takes a hit when your daughter blindsides her fiancé two days before the wedding. I'm sure my mother is concerned about her business, too. My father is always saying that in this community, your name is really all you have, and it kills me to think hers might suffer because of what I did. I had zero intention of tarnishing our name. I just feared that staying quiet would be catastrophically worse.

"It's nothing for me." My mother rises to put a completed tray into

the oven. She's wearing the blush pink embroidered robe she had customized for the wedding day. MOTHER OF THE BRIDE is printed in white
cursive in the space between her shoulder blades.

"You're wearing the robe?" I ask, surprised.

"Why not?" My mother hides her face, turning her attention to the
numbers on the oven. "It's a good robe, 100 percent silk. I needed a good
robe." She runs her fingers over the lapel, as if considering, for the first
time, the possibility that the robe might not in fact be 100 percent silk.

Nina told me that the most surprising thing about the wedding being
called off was that I had been the one to do it. I'm not sure what to make
of that. She told me she was proud of me. She used words like "agency"
and phrases like "your truth." She promised me that my life would be
better off for it, even as I sized up her life, struggling to determine its
comparative value, computing how many years it'd be before I wound
up like her, by no choice of my own at all.

It's not what I wanted to hear, but I know I needed to hear *something.* My mother has barely said a word about it in the past month. I
wonder if she blames me. I wonder if she blames herself. It would be
easier if there'd been wrongdoing: a gambling issue, suggestion of a
prenup, a business deal between families gone awry. Anything would be
easier than admitting the truth: that I didn't love Saul. That I'd stayed
in a relationship for over a year and accepted a proposal and planned a
wedding all because that's *our way.* Breaking off the engagement felt
like the first real choice I've ever made. I've been too easy, compliant, a
blank canvas for others to throw their identities at—and I don't want to
be that anymore. Saul used to tell me that I was easy to love. I don't
want to be easy to love; I want it to be hard to love me and I want someone to do it anyway, because not to would be too unbearable.

My mother scans the contents of our fridge, her eyes in search of everything and nothing all at once. She toys with a ketchup bottle, cooking
wine, a mason jar stuffed with preserved lemons and crushed garlic. Tomorrow there'd be a row of mason jars just like it, full of pickled cabbage,

cauliflower, and peppers. My mother always turned to food in times of distress (the cooking, not eating of it). We've had many freezers filled by tragedy, with six-braided challah, fried kibbe, Pyrex after Pyrex of jibben: spinach and squash and artichoke encased in egg and cheese. Some of it she sold, but most of it stayed in our freezer for months, growing tough and hard with frostbite until my mother dumped it, *haram*, the work that'd gone into making it thawing like ice in a sink.

"How long did you know?" My mother's eyes remain fixed on the contents of the fridge.

"Know what?" I deflect.

I knew that she needed to understand, to have a look at the larger picture and see where she might've missed a piece of the puzzle. Maybe she could fix it for Lucy, or even Nina. But implicit in her question is blame, and I'm not going to incriminate myself.

"I mean, did you ever talk to anyone? About anything? G-D knows you never mentioned anything to me. And your friends, they seemed shocked, too. I just don't understand, I just don't understand how you could let it get this far, the wedding two days away, deposits made, flowers on tables! Your father had a speech prepared for the ceremony, did you know that? Your father . . ." My mother shakes her head. "He killed himself for this wedding—it was his pleasure, of course. You know we only wanted you to be happy. But if you *knew* . . ." My mother closes the fridge door, untying and retying the belt on her robe before approaching the table to sit back down. "I'm sorry," she says. "I know that this is just as upsetting for you. But you seemed happy with Saul. Were you not happy?"

"It's not—"

"You certainly didn't give off the impression that you were miserable. I know you wouldn't have been miserable." My mother says it more like a question, begging to understand. "Saul would've given you a good life. He's a decent boy. He comes from a good family. Sure they're a little old-fashioned. Marie—she's a tough woman. But they're good people, Fortune. You know I would never let you get into something I didn't think would be good for you. *Ever.*"

"*There.* That's what I'm talking about, Mom. It's not all about what's 'good' for me. And what you think is 'good' for me may not be what I want!"

"You know what I mean, Fortune. I wanted you to be happy. That's all I'm saying."

"And what is happiness to you, Mom? It's not something you can buy at Spice, you know. There's *more* to it." I inhale and concentrate on folding the wonton in front of me. I dip a brush into egg wash and paint the dough, folding up all four corners and pinching them into a triangle shape. The mention of the store where Isaac works brings him back into the forefront of my mind, where I'd worked so hard to keep him out. If he's heard about me breaking things off, he hasn't said anything. And I'm sure he's heard. Everyone has.

"I'm sorry." My mother shakes her head and peels off a piece of dough from its plastic sheet. "I don't even know who you are right now."

"Maybe that's the problem."

My mother lets out one of her deep, suffering sighs. "Let me tell you something, Fortune." She pauses, considering her words. "As someone who's been married for almost thirty years, I know a thing or two about happiness. I know what it is to make a life."

"But that's just it! I don't *want* your life!" My tone surprises even me, but it's too late to turn back. "Has that ever occurred to you?"

"And what's so bad about my life?" My mother looks at me quizzically. She has no idea. "I have a good marriage—fine, it's not a *fairy tale,* but what is? I'll tell you, the love you think you want is saved for the pages and the screen. It isn't *real.* This"—my mother opens her arms to the house around us—"this is love. This house. Our family. We've built something, your father and I. Together, we raised three daughters. We *own* this house and up until recently, we did so without a mortgage. Tell me, where did I go wrong exactly?"

"You didn't go wrong. I just don't want *this* life." I whisper the last part.

"What do you mean?" My mother looks genuinely confused.

"*This.*" I point to the window that overlooks the street we live on. "I want more."

"What *more* is there?"

"I don't—I don't know." I stutter. "But I want to find out. I want that opportunity!"

"Are you saying—outside of the community?"

"It's not about the community!"

"I knew it was a mistake to have you go work with your father in the city," she mutters. "I tried explaining this to Nina. But *news flash,* there isn't much more than this." My mother draws a square box in the air with her fingers. "People out there spend their whole lives trying to achieve what you've been given so easily: a strong sense of home, community, tradition. And not just that, but a feeling of *safety.* One day you *will* be a mother, and when that happens, you'll thank your lucky stars that you know the names of every child your kid goes to school with and their parents, what kind of boys are taking your daughter out. It's so easy to write off familiarity as a curse when you're young. You think I don't know what it's like? Don't you forget, I didn't grow up in this." My mother stabs a defrosted wonton with her fingernail. "I *had* a mother who turned her nose up at this life because she was terrified it would reject her. I had a mother who preferred I go out there, in search of the elusive 'more.' And I'd take this over that any day because in the end, my mother died with few enemies but even fewer friends. By day two of the shiva, everyone she'd ever known had already come to pay their respects, every story had already been told. She died looking out the window."

I knew little about how my mother grew up. My grandmother had died before I was born. I knew that my mother's parents were born here in America. I knew that my mother spent her childhood in closer contact with her Italian neighbors in Bensonhurst than she did with the Syrian Jewish families who had only recently put down real roots in Brooklyn. I knew that as much as she complained about Sitto and her antiquated ways, she had been a kind of surrogate mother to my own. She taught her everything she knows about keeping a home, a kind of sensei in the art of *our way.*

We sit in silence as I help my mother complete her next culinary feat, the filling and folding of spinach and cheese emwats. I slip into a meditative state, repeating each step methodically. Flatten, fill, fold. Flatten, fill, fold. When I've completed twelve, I dip a brush into a new bowl of egg wash and brush each one. Then I shake a jar of sesame seeds over the batch.

"It's not your fault." I clear my throat. My mother pauses, her thumbs pressed into the dough.

"Of course it is." She sighs. "A mother should know, should have a clue about what's in her child's heart. I could honestly say now, looking back, I should've known. How could I have been so wrong? It's not just the wedding—we'll all get over that. What, so it's gossip until something juicer inevitably takes its place. No—it's that I had no idea. My daughters don't talk to me. And maybe that's because I don't say the right things, or I don't listen, *really* listen. But it's not for lack of trying, I promise you that." My mother's eyes are wet and round, her pupils clouded like an overcast moon.

"Stop it, Mom. We know you're there for us."

"My mother never opened up to me," she says, allowing a fat teardrop to fall onto the tray beneath her. "Vulnerability was seen as a sign of weakness, mindless chatter got you in trouble, and friends were just people better positioned to use your secrets against you. But when I met your father, when I really immersed myself in the community, I was shocked. I couldn't believe the way people spoke to one another, so openly. It takes getting used to. Everybody knowing your business. But Sitto, for all of her grievances, she took me in as one of her own, almost immediately. She criticized my cooking, my parenting, my relationship with G-D, the way she did her own flesh and blood!" My mother laughs, a loud, phlegm-ridden laugh. "But there was a sense of family. *Suffeh,* as they say. A culture of tradition, a shared history, there was always food on the table, and Sitto would call people in off the street to come and eat it. If a man's business is suffering, there are ten men ready to step in and help. A young girl cannot afford a wedding dress? Money is raised within minutes. The dead, *hazit,* are not yet dead, before the food for their shiva begins to arrive!"

"That is true," I agree.

"But my mother, I think part of her resented the way I'd thrown myself into my life as a married woman and a mother, how I embraced a community she avoided. I missed her, but it was easier to be Sitto's daughter. Trust me when I tell you, resentment, it's a useless emotion. Like locusts, it plagues you, eats away at you, multiplies infinitesimally, and it won't stop until a relationship is beyond repair. Of course, resentment is saved for the things and people we need the most." My mother looks down now, her eyes trained on the potato she's been peeling to within an inch of its life. "I don't want that for my daughters."

"You don't have that."

"If we can't be honest with each other . . ."

"You want to know the truth?" I say.

"Please."

"Do you want to know what my first thought was—my initial reaction, to hearing about that girl who got too drunk at the wedding?" I pause, half shaking with my admission. "I was jealous."

"Jealous?"

"I mean I'd never want the whole community talking about me, although, look at me now. But part of me envied this girl because she had the opportunity to make the mistake. And once she did, the gates opened for her. She was sent to Israel—"

"Some would call that punishment, exile . . ."

"I'd call that freedom."

"I don't think I understand, Fortune." My mother shakes her head.

"Saul was my first boyfriend. He was my first kiss. The first person to tell me he loved me. I went from all of those firsts into an engagement, all within a span of a year. I know it was meant to feel like a reward—the natural conclusion for having done everything right. But it didn't. All this time, I've just been aching for the chance to make a mistake."

"There's no glory in suffering, Fortune."

"I don't think we view suffering the same way, Mom."

My mother spreads her fingers on her lap and sighs. Her freckles stand out in the warm glow of the kitchen light, a constellation of brown marks, a shade darker than her skin, spread loosely across her face and over the bridge of her nose. When she went out, my mother did her best to hide her freckles under a light layer of foundation. She thought they aged her, cursed her days spent without protection in the sun. I couldn't disagree more. Her freckles give her youth, and when she smiles, they dance around her face, rising and falling with the swell of her dimpled cheeks.

"You know," she says, "we had dinner with David's parents. Before all of this."

"I know."

"Lucy isn't like you." My mother searches my face, begging me to understand. "She wants this. She wants David."

"I know that." I try to hide my hurt. Does my mother think I'm selfish enough to sabotage my sister's engagement because my own didn't work out?

"Whether or not his parents get cold feet now, that's another story."

"They won't."

"I hope you know I want to do right by you," my mother says, taking my hand. "I want to do right by all of you."

"I'll lie low," I tell my mother what she wants to hear but can't say. "Until this blows over, I'll disappear."

LUCY

Chapter Twenty-two

....

Word must have gotten out that David and I chose a wedding date because suddenly, every girl in the senior class wants to be my little bitch. David's parents offered to pay for the wedding and, to everyone's surprise, Dad exchanged pride for money and said yes. Instead of your typical Thursday night wedding in the ballroom of Lev Aharon, David and I will be getting married at The Plaza—on a Sunday. Everybody and their mother wants to be a bridesmaid. I'd be flattered if it weren't so transparent; there's been so much ass-kissing, my butt cheeks have lipstick marks on them. I'd go so far as to say that my engagement has single-handedly repaired the blemish of Fortune's broken one—or distracted everyone from it, at the very least. It's been two months since Fortune blew up her life, but the memory of her engagement—or really, the sudden lack thereof—hangs over all of us. I wonder how it'll feel for her to have to walk down the aisle as my maid of honor after envisioning herself as the bride for so long.

My mother can't help but compare our two experiences, as if talking about it incessantly might help her understand where exactly it all went wrong. When David proposed to me a month later, in Central Park on Memorial Day weekend, my mother brought up Fortune's ring. "Oh, you can tell David *really* knows you, Lucy. He picked out the ring himself and nailed your style! I'm pretty sure Marie chose Fortune's ring. I don't think Saul had *anything* to do with it." When it came time to begin shopping for David's swanee, my father never once complained about having to spend the money. What's a Hermès belt when you can ensure your daughter will be well taken care of for life? A worthwhile investment, that's what it is. Plus, my parents don't have the finances of the wedding to worry about. And whereas my mother's guest list for Fortune and Saul's wedding seemed to unravel like a Torah scroll, she kept this one short and sweet, plucking off names one by one, as if great-aunts and old friends were merely hairs that needed to be tweezed from a raw chicken. She blamed it on the room at The Plaza being small, but we all knew she wielded her newfound power like a cop with a ticket book. A limited crowd in Brooklyn was a pity; Brooklyn had a boisterous open-door approach to celebration. A limited crowd in Manhattan, on the other hand, was exclusive and added to the party's appeal. We've all seen my mother's orders multiply recently. Do people really think that buying a dozen kibbe might score them an invite?

I'd be lying if I said I hadn't been worried Fortune's actions would spook David's parents. As if Fortune's flightiness might signal a mutation in our collective genetic code. Even now, my friends try to keep the rumors from me, but I'd have to stick my head in the sand not to hear them. The first one to break the surface is that Fortune is a lesbian. The rumor mill is always quick to set the gay card in motion, as if an actual biological aversion is the only possible reason a girl might turn down a chance at matrimony. The rumor stays above water for about a week, until somebody with enough clout decides that she doesn't have it in her. The second piece of gossip, of course, has to do with money. And this is the one I wish had been kept from me: that my parents, in their own silent, passive-aggressive way, urged her to do it. Why? Because they want her with someone more like David. Somebody who wouldn't just keep her comfortable but would elevate her status and, by association, my parents' status. Obviously, anyone who knows my mother or my father knows that this is the furthest thing from the truth. Are my parents enjoying the added benefits of their daughter being engaged to someone like David? Sure. The extra attention in line at the supermarket is nice. A bump in orders here and there. But as my father—who has seen an uptick in the number of charity invitations that slide through his mailbox—likes to say, "Do they think David's paying my bills, too?" He even stopped going to shul on Saturdays after being called upon for an aliyah three weeks in a row. It's a big honor to be called to the Torah, but it doesn't come without the price of a donation and my father was just about done shelling out. "My relationship with G-D used to be the only one that didn't cost me!"

I suspect that rumor had been planted by the other side. Marie and my mother are perfectly friendly on occasions when they see each other, but we all know that a woman with a bruised ego would do just about anything for her son. Marie is not about to see Saul's prospects dim and they haven't. I hear he's already dating someone new, and the best part? She's a friend of Fortune's. She was supposed to march in the wedding. For G-D's sake. It's like Sitto says: "Eat or be eaten." Men used to be hunters. Now they just sit back with their forks and knives waiting for the meal to come to them. Even scandal can't mar their prospects. It's like Giselle said, "All a guy here has to do is take a shower."

Speaking of men and showers, David is almost done with his. I hear the water shut off and the slam of the glass door against the rubber barrier. I've been in his apartment enough times to recognize his rhythms and routines, even when he isn't standing in front of me. I smooth my hair and sit up straight, with my back against his headboard. I check my teeth and skin in the reflection of my phone.

"Oh, hello." David emerges from the bathroom with a towel wrapped around his waist. The hair on his chest is still wet and looks darker than usual.

"Hello to you." I pat the spot on the bed next to me and David plops down, the weight of his frame sinking the mattress, making me roll toward him slightly. He's always been slim, but David's been spending more time at the gym in preparation for our wedding and the small pocket of belly fat has solidified into muscle. If David's trying, then that means I better try to up my game, too. I don't want him to think I take him for granted. I don't want to feel like the lucky one in this relationship. He props up onto one elbow and cradles the side of his head in one hand.

It occurs to me that Fortune and Saul were way too complacent with each other. They only knew each other for a year and yet they acted like an old married couple. The *chase* dissolved into a slow and steady crawl to the finish line and then what? The most exciting thing to come out of their relationship was when Fortune pulled the plug. I look at David, freshly showered, looking up at me, and think how at the end of the day, men just need to feel needed. It doesn't make me weak or pea-brained to admit it. Men are a very simple equation that most women want to overcomplicate. It's addition, girls, not calculus. When a newborn cries, we give them the breast, not Veal Milanese. Well, men aren't much different. What more do they want than to be stroked and pacified and told, over and over again, that they are the entire world of the woman who cradles them?

"So, what are you thinking for today?" he asks.

"Aren't you sick of me yet?"

"Only a little." David laughs. We were out all last night. Dinner and drinks with David's friends, then back to his apartment. David drove me back to Brooklyn at four A.M. I slept for six hours, showered, and took the cab David called for me back to his place. My parents said nothing about any of it. It's amazing what a 6-carat stone on your finger could do. My phone pings and I grab it from the bedside table.

"Who's that?" David asks.

"Giselle—asking if I'm sure I want the bridesmaids in ivory. She keeps complaining that it washes her out. I've had it up to here with her."

"Yeah. Your friends are . . . interesting."

"You hate them. You can say it."

"Of course I don't hate them." David gets into bed next to me. "They're just petty, as they should be at eighteen."

"Am I petty?" I say it jokingly, but part of me wants a serious answer.

"You're years beyond those girls." David pulls me closer to him and takes my phone out of my hand, tossing it to the other side of the bed. "Come on, it's *Sunday*. And I know how much you love a plan."

"Not true," I say, even though it is true. "I can do this all day." I spread my body across his bedspread. I've learned that these heaven-sent threads are sateen from the brand Matouk. I've learned a lot of things since dating David. About Diptyque candles and Jo Malone soaps. Orchid plants and bath linens not purchased at Marshalls. Luxuries that he's grown so accustomed to, he isn't even aware that people live without them. The best part about David is that he's not a snob about it. It's not like he *needs* his sweaters to be 100 percent cashmere; it's simply that anything less might cause his virgin skin to erupt in hives. "Plus a bagel."

"Plus a bagel," David says half mockingly. His body hovers directly over mine and his hands are pressed into the bed on either side of my face. I wrap my hands around his neck and pull him toward me. When he kisses me, I feel my entire body melt into a pool of desire. I help him wriggle me out of my shirt and jeans. My lips don't leave his and my hands are in his hair, on his neck. I feel much older than eighteen when I'm with him and at the same time, I feel exactly eighteen. I've kissed boys my age before, a peck here or there, mainly after discovering alcohol in my junior year. Those kisses felt awkward and hasty and left nothing to be desired. It isn't like that with David. Everything with him feels like a gateway drug. David moans as he runs his hands up my leg, my stomach and boobs, leaving a trail of goosebumps. I reach for the towel around his waist. A loose tuck and a high cotton count, that's all that stands between us. I pull it apart, simultaneously pushing David off of me and reversing our positions, so that my legs straddle his torso. I don't look down. His face is flush, and it's obvious he doesn't want to stop.

"Three more months," he says, more to himself than to me. "Get past the summer, and then I can have all of you."

"But think of how much better our honeymoon will be if we start now—if we got the learning curve out of the way." David's married friends were always saying how much better their sex lives had gotten over the years. They depicted the first months of marriage as a series of awkward stumbling blocks, sexually. I want to get that part over with as quickly as possible.

"I don't have anything," David says, referring to protection. I made the choice not to go on birth control because David is nearly thirty and itching to be a dad. We want to get pregnant as soon as possible after the wedding.

"I'm not ovulating." I started my Kallah classes with Sandy Beda, the same woman who taught Fortune. Plus, the lessons from our Halacha classes are still fresh in my mind. I know that women typically ovulate two weeks after a period, and I'm three weeks past mine.

"Are you sure?" David is breathless. "I kind of wanted the first time to be more special for you."

I pull back slightly and hope David doesn't notice. It's an unspoken but understood fact that David has been with people before me. How many, I don't care or want to know. I tell myself that it doesn't matter. Whatever experiences or relationships he's had before me are insignificant now.

"This is all I want." I lean forward and kiss David fully. "I swear."

"I hope I don't embarrass myself." David jokes.

"Like I'd know the difference?"

"Is this you trying to make me feel better? It's been a minute, but I'm pretty confident."

"Is this *you* trying to make me feel better?" David's arrogance in this moment only makes me want him more.

"Listen." David gently pushes me off of him and sits up, urging me to do the same. "This is as much about you as it is about me. It's important that we communicate, you know, that we—"

"David." I pull him toward me. "Will you just shut up and kiss me?"

This time, when David assumes his position over me, I feel the weight of him. I wriggle my exposed body under the comforter and throw it over David's back. Sunlight is streaming into his apartment and the drum of Sunday Soho foot traffic kicks up outside. David doesn't try anything right away, even though everything about my body language screams open invitation. He inches his hands slowly and confidently up my thigh, leaving a trail of goosebumps in his wake. With his hands between my legs, I inch closer.

"Is this okay?" he asks breathlessly.

"Hmhm." I don't want him to stop. He scoots down and kisses my belly button, moving downward with every peck.

"What about this?" He doesn't wait for me to respond. I tussle with his hair and my body shakes with desire. I pull him up abruptly.

"Do you not like it?" he asks.

"No." My entire body feels warm. "No—I loved it. I'm just, I'm ready."

"Are you sure?"

"Yes. I just . . ." I shift my weight and prop my body slightly up. I still don't look down. It's not that I haven't seen it before, but I'm scared I might chicken out if I have to face that thing head-on right now.

"Better?" I can tell David is eager to continue but trying his hardest to be patient. That he wants to please me makes me want him even more, which doesn't seem possible.

I take a deep breath and close my eyes. I heard some girls don't even bleed their first time. It'd be a sin to ruin these sheets. I contemplate asking David whether we should grab a towel but before I know it, he's moving inside me. If you've ever felt pain and pleasure at the same time, with such great intensity, you'll realize that they are basically mirror sensations. You can't have one without the other. I pull him closer and try to move in tandem, even though at moments it makes it hurt more.

"I love you so much," David whispers in my ear. When we kiss, and his whole body shudders, he finally feels like mine.

NINA

Chapter Twenty-three

....

"Hand me the breadbasket, *rohi.*" Sitto looks uncomfortable in the plush red velvet chair. She has one hand on her walking stick, and with the other she takes the basket that Steven dutifully hands her. "You know you are my new favorite," she says devilishly. We are sitting in the bridal room at The Plaza Hotel where moments ago, Lucy and David presumably shared their first plate of food as husband and wife before entering the ballroom for their first dance to Céline Dion's "Because You Loved Me." My baby sister is as basic as they come, but she looked brilliant in a Monique Lhuillier ball gown, her full brown locks styled into smooth round waves. She wore a silver crown atop her head, and around her neck she wore the diamond tennis necklace David's parents had bought her as a gift. When she walked down the aisle, a bouquet of white orchids spilling from her hands, all five hundred seated guests went quiet. It wasn't my style, but she looked breathtakingly beautiful.

"Are we ever going to get her out of here?" Steven whispers to me and takes a sip of whiskey. He looks virtually unrecognizable in his navy blue slim lapel tuxedo. He wears the gray kippah David's parents had made special for the wedding, and every few minutes he straightens his bow tie. He insisted on coming in here to change out of the Cole Haan dress shoes he'd borrowed from his father, pointing out the blisters on his ankles where the leather had dug in. Now, he wears Converse. A pair of black high-tops I pray to G-D my mother will be too high on perfume kisses to notice. Steven and I may have squandered our individual rebellions for each other, but remnants of the fight still remain. I won't fight him on the shoes.

"She's tired, *hazita.*" I clink my drink against Steven's and catch a glimpse of myself in one of the gold-flecked double mirrors. The entire bridal party wore ivory, with the exception of Fortune and me. We got to choose. Naturally, I chose black; the slinky slip dress scored at a Naeem Khan sample sale has a low back and is adorned with gold floral embellishments. I wear my hair up in a tight bun and my collarbones shimmer with the gold powder the makeup artist insisted on applying.

"In my day, the girls fattened up when they were in love." Sitto takes note of me. "*Ekel.*" She offers a sesame breadstick. "If you're going to drink, you better eat. Take something before I bust out of this dress." She shuffles in her seat and, indeed, Sitto's dress looks like it might pop at any moment. It's a modest frock, a deep purple the color of eggplants. Sitto hasn't been up for shopping lately, so picking her dress fell to my mother. An impossible errand. She did well—the dress is covered in delicate beading and shiny black pearls the size of pupils. Sitto's makeup was applied carefully: Too much foundation and the creases in her face would look more obvious, not less, and her dyed hair had been sprayed, coiffed, and teased to mask the spots where it is thinning.

"That ceremony was fit for a queen. I have never seen so many white orchids, *mushalla.* Even if every guest takes home a bunch, they'll still have enough to fill a house. Inshallah they donate the rest to the shuls, *haram* for them to go to waste. And did you see the way David looks at your sister? *Aboose hiyati.* True love." I can hear the music getting louder on the other side of the heavy oak door. I feel nice and loose from the alcohol and eager to get on the dance floor. As maids of honor, Fortune and I have an unspoken duty to be hype women for Lucy all night. I have no doubt they're wondering where I am.

For as far back as I can remember, every wedding reception has started the same. After the ceremony, the guests flood the ballroom where the dancing and eating take place. The food is buffet, always buffet. Syrians are far too energetic, late, and unreliable for a seated dinner. Not to mention finicky over food; you will never find two guests who agree over an appetizer, let alone an entire course. There's usually about thirty minutes of drinking and mingling before the bride and groom enter the room as husband and wife, usually to rowdy applause and an announcement by the DJ. They have their first dance. Sometimes, it's followed by the father-daughter or mother-son dance. After those formalities are out of the way, it's time for the main event: the party, and it begins with a tribute to our elders, otherwise known as the *nobeh*. For about six or seven songs, fifteen to twenty minutes, the DJ will harken back to Egypt, to Lebanon, to Damascus. I can hear the familiar ascent of the ebullient violin, the merging of the traditional oud with the modern synthesizer. Nancy Ajram's voice spills over the speakers with longing and joy. Nobody from my generation speaks Arabic. We mangle the words into a false translation but nevertheless, when "Ah W Noss" is played—and it is played often—we sing along to our manufactured chorus: *Boosy, Boosy, Boosy!*

"Let's go, Sitto, this is for you!" Steven and I help Sitto out of her chair and lead her out of the bridal room and into the hall.

"Mabrook."

"Thank you."

"Mabrook, Mrs. Cohen."

"Abal!"

"Mabrook! Beautiful."

"Sabi andak. Thank you."

"Mabrook!"

"Abal, inshallah by you next."

We move slowly past the throng of well-wishers and into the ballroom of The Plaza, which is dressed exquisitely in white florals and candlelight. The guests are dressed to the nines, and they make a path for us to enter the middle of the crowded dance floor. Sitto can barely walk on her own, but she will dance.

"There you are!" Lucy is radiant, and sweaty. Olga, the bridal attendant, dabs Lucy's forehead with a white napkin and lifts a straw from a glass of ice water into her mouth. Lucy beckons us toward her. Steven passes Sitto's arm to my mother and heads toward the other side of the dance floor, where David and the men dance separately before the music transitions to English and the two sides converge. "See you," I mouth to him. "Save me," his eyes seem to say. Steven isn't exactly the *mosh pit of men* type but he goes anyway, to spectate as much as to show he's there. My mother grabs my hand, I grab Fortune's, and she grabs Lucy's as we form a circle around Sitto. She sways her hips seductively to the beat and raises her arms in the air, twisting her hands as if she is screwing in a lightbulb. *Boosy, Boosy, Boosy!* The guests around us close in, clapping as we rotate around Sitto, and she moves to the music of her youth, now Farid al-Atrash, a deep and unmistakable yearning for home, set to a faster tempo courtesy of the DJ.

Leh leh leh leh! Some of the elder women in the crowd howl with joy as David's mother and grandmother make their way inside the circle. Lucy takes the hands of her new family and together they dance.

"*Aboose,* Sitto," Fortune leans in and shouts into my ear. She looks at ease, maybe for the first time in months, but still, I can see the vulnerability behind her eyes. While I don't think there is a single part of her that regrets what she's done, it'll take some time before she's completely comfortable being on her own. Sitto and David's grandmother hold hands now, mouthing the words in their native tongue like they're sharing secrets. I wonder if they had envisioned this when they fled Syria. I wonder if they had even allowed themselves to dream this big, this wild. I imagine that when you are forced to leave with nothing, hoping for anything other than survival feels like excess. How did we get here? Thirty years ago my grandmother and father were refugees, and today they're complaining that the lamb chops at the glatt kosher catered wedding in the ballroom of The Plaza Hotel are well done. If we don't ask these questions, if we don't stop to think, we run the risk of losing everything.

Lucy pulls me into a dizzying dance. All around me, there are faces. My mother's, Sitto's, Lucy's, and Fortune's. First cousins, second cousins, Giselle, Sari, and some friends whose names I can't remember. At least two dozen girls waiting for their turn and wondering if it'll be with one of the boys across the dance floor. Each of them having painstakingly chosen their dress, styled their hair, and had their face made up, probably under the watchful eye of their own versions of a mother in a robe. I'm pulled into an extended circle as Lucy and my mother take center stage, hugging and dancing and looking to see who will be next to punctuate the center. From the corner of my eye, I see Olga carefully leading Sitto off the dance floor and toward a round table, where some of the great-aunts are seated. While the music ends for some, for others it's just the beginning. Round and round we go, dancing for others in the hope that when it's our turn, they'll be there to dance with us.

I pull my hand from Fortune's sweaty grasp. "I'm gonna get a refill!" I shout over the music. I weave my way off the dance floor like a quarterback holding the winning touchdown. When people acknowledge me, they don't have that pitiful look I'd grown so accustomed to. Sitto is already knife-deep in a piece of lamb when I reach her. The floral centerpiece from the table sits on the empty chair next to her. She hadn't even waited for the party to end. G-D, I love this woman. Whoops and hollers ricochet from the dance floor as the music transitions to a David Guetta hit, and the two sexes converge.

"When I was your age, I could've danced all night." She stretches her flesh-colored stockinged leg in front of her. "When I was your age, I *did* dance all night. Where is that *adami* boyfriend of yours? He's a lost puppy without you."

"So you've noticed that, too?" I laugh.

"What did I always tell you?" Sitto forks a sweet potato. "Every pot . . ."

"Has a lid," I finish. "Yeah, you were right." Sitto and I both pivot slightly to watch the ensuing rave on the dance floor. My mother and father dance together surrounded by a bunch of their friends. Even Carmen is here, possibly having more fun than anybody. I nearly miss Fortune slip away from the dance floor, the kid who owns Spice following closely behind. I track them as they head toward the bar together. My mother had felt guilty and invited him and his parents at the last minute. I guess I'm glad they did. Fortune certainly seems to be.

"You know." Sitto leans in. "Your grandfather had a saying when we moved to this country. He would say: *It's* Halab *against the world.* Of course, you could have coffee with the Italians. You could do business with the Chinese. You could shop in the Mexicans' store, and you can speak the same tongue as the Arab. But at the end of the day, a Syrian Jew only has a Syrian Jew. We have to stick together." She balls her hand into a strong fist. "Tell me, where else can you find this?" She spreads her arms in front of her. The room is buzzing with chatter. Some are no doubt talking about the wedding, maybe a few have even found cause to complain. *Are you invited to this one next week? Do you have the bris tomorrow morning? You heard, so-and-so's daughter got engaged?* There are five stages of plant life cycle. Sometimes I think that for Syrian Jews there are maybe three: Birth, Marriage, Death. It's the prolonged commentary in between each one that makes us seem eternal.

"Don't roll your eyes," Sitto says. "What more could you ask for? Listen, now that you have found someone, maybe you'll hear me. People outside the community, they want you to believe that this is a trap. Especially the women—they are always running these days. Running, running from the home. To the city, to the Bergdorf's, to exercise. 'The kitchen is suffocating.' Who really believes this? Tell me. Tell me *how* you can think this is true. The kitchen is the center of the home; it is the sun around which all of the other planets orbit. Take away the kitchen and you have no home, just brick and cement. Without it, you have no tradition. You don't have this, The Plaza," she says disparagingly. "Yes, it is wonderful to be here. It is beautiful, *mushalla*, of course it is. But what comes *after* tonight, what comes next—that, Nina, is the real beauty." She presses her palms into the table. "The *suffeh*, the presence of tradition in the home. *That* is where the seeds are planted, watered, and grown. Religion gives you fear, but tradition gives you a sense of home. Don't think"—Sitto shakes her head—"a mother's job is the hardest in the world. It's one thing to instill a love of home in your children, it's another to make sure they go out and build homes of their own. And close by. Of course, you must stay close. Uh-huh." Sitto nods toward the dance floor, seeming satisfied with herself. When I look in that direction, I see Steven, his eyes scanning the room like lines on a heart rate monitor. "Lost puppy." Sitto squeezes my knee tenderly. "*Humdullah.* Go get him before he wets himself *yanni.*"

"Sitto!"

"Go." She shoos me off the chair. "You are young. Go enjoy yourselves. I wouldn't be sitting with you if my knees still worked. Believe me that." I do as I'm told, straightening my dress and lifting its straps as I get up. When Steven's and my eyes lock, I make my way toward him.

LUCY

Chapter Twenty-four

....

Just because I'm married doesn't mean I've stopped trying. I keep my body tight. I do dance cardio in a sauna suit four times a week. I combine boxing and Pilates on Fridays and get lymphatic massages on Sundays by a Brazilian lady who comes to my house and leaves me bruised. I eat Scandinavian crackers that look and taste like the shit they produce. I grow out my nails and get Russian gel manicures, keeping the tips polished and smooth. I laser everything: my arms, pits, upper lip, sideburns, legs, big toes, stomach line, lower back, bikini, butt hole. I get biweekly blowouts on top of biannual keratin treatments on top of quarterly highlights, and sometimes I buy lingerie just because. I light amber-scented candles all over the house and spray our sheets with a gardenia fragrance, and, when David gets home, I greet him with a smile and a kiss. This is the one piece of rabbinical advice I am determined to follow. "What kind of person do you want to be for your spouse?" he'd said to us in a private meeting right before we signed the ketubah. "You have to *be* that person when you open the door. You have to be that person every time you greet each other. No matter the day you might've had."

The attraction between us is simple. I seem to have none of the humility my sisters harbor over their bodies. Nina keeps hers frail and draped in oversize clothing, the definition of her bones peeking through cotton T-shirts and rips in her jeans. Fortune's weight fluctuates, a physical reflection of whatever she has going on inside that head of hers. We had all been taught the inherent value of being thin, and we all know genetics aren't in our favor. My father's side is plagued by obesity otherwise neutralized by towering height. On the other hand, my mother comes from a family of women whom you'd have to stretch to five feet, with legs that accrued cellulite no matter how deep or frequent the squat.

David texts to say that the taxi he sent for me will be outside in ten minutes. We have dinner reservations in the city at eight. Where, I'm not sure. I make a mental note: Another thing to love about David, he is always surprising me. In the month since we've been married, there've been more gifts and flowers than I can count. He even picked up the check on my girls' night last week. Unbeknownst to me, he'd called the restaurant in advance and put down his credit card. I was initially embarrassed by the gesture, but when confronted he simply said, "Your friends are single, and I can afford it. Why should they have to shell out?" How could I explain to him that these dinners with my friends are some of the only instances in which I actually feel my age—my older husband footing the bill only deepens the obvious divide in our lifestyles.

In high school, we'd openly daydream about the guys we'd end up with. The only horizon we could see beyond yeshiva was marriage, the true marker of independence and the only way out of our parents' homes. The shotgun was fired, the race had begun, and I was the first horse out of the gate, sprinting toward the finish line, while they idled by the stables, waiting for a jockey to choose them. But I've seen some of my friends change. They don't seem to be as focused on marriage as they were in high school. Giselle even went so far as to tell me that marriage did not indicate independence, not at all. "All marriage affords a woman, really, is a transferal of her dependence from one home to another." She's on some CUNY bullshit but still, Sitto was right when she said ideas were changing in our community for my generation; I was just too shortsighted to see it.

I know the arrangement is more a matter of convenience than anything else, but driving into Manhattan, to meet him where he works, feels like stepping into something foreign. The city does not belong to me, nor I to her. Manhattan seems to tolerate my presence for only so long until it's time to spit me back over the bridge. As if I can't keep up. David says everyone here is a Midwestern transplant. I, on the other hand, have tons of hustle and probably too much energy. I feel more at home in Brooklyn anyway, and I'm glad we decided to get a place here, near my mother, instead of in the city.

ETA? David texts me.

Pulling up in two.

I check my reflection in the driver's rearview mirror, wiping a smidge of mascara from beneath my eye. The taxi driver's eyes meet mine in the mirror.

"Where are you from?" He narrows his eyes.

"From here." I notice my body beginning to shift uncomfortably in the seat, readying myself as the restaurant comes into view, a quaint Southern Italian spot in the West Village. A recommendation, no doubt, from one of David's colleagues.

"No, I mean where are you *from.*" The driver turns around in his seat to get a better look at my face.

"I was born here, in Brooklyn," I clarify.

"Your parents?" He remains unconvinced. I scan the dashboard for his Taxi ID card. His accented English sounds uniquely similar to Sitto's, deep but more buoyant, Egyptian, maybe.

"Syrian," I offer, my hand gripped around the door's handle. "My parents are Syrian."

"Jewish? That's where all the Syrian Jewish people live, where I picked you up from." He's not asking.

Another text from David: They won't seat me without you.

"I'm not sure," I mumble and thank the driver, trying to appear nonchalant as I hobble toward the restaurant's doors.

The maître d' leads me through the restaurant and out its back doors, into a wide garden patio. The atmosphere glistens with countless tea lights. They hang overhead and are strung through the branches of tall trees. Tables are set closely to one another, and waiters wearing white jackets over sailor-striped shirts glide between them, carrying trays of half-empty glasses. We continue toward the back, past a pair of picnic tables where a particularly lively group of women in matching Peter Pan collars and culottes laugh over drinks. The maître d' takes a sharp left, guiding me toward a quiet table offset by two towering mandarin trees. "Enjoy your dinner," she smiles as she pulls a chair out for me to sit.

"You look great." David stands up to greet me. He's wearing a navy sport jacket, perfect for the crisp fall weather outside. On nights like these, David takes harried showers in the hospital's changing room; the dark blue jeans and white button-down that hang in his locker are the source of many punch lines from his colleagues.

"I'm glad they let you sit." I smile.

David kisses me on the cheek. I feel the eyes of the Peter Pan collars on my back and I lean into David. I'm definitely inclined toward paranoia, especially when it comes to women who don't know me, women who aren't familiar with the world we come from. I'm used to the suspicious eyes of outsiders. I know the questions that form in their brains when David introduces me as his wife. I imagine the snide things they might say behind my back. David is only thirty, but he's eleven years older than I am. It doesn't help matters that his height and demeanor display a maturity that leaves much for me to catch up to. In Brooklyn, I feel powerful beyond my nineteen years, a master of my domain. I take to my role as a wife naturally; I have dinner on the table most nights, I keep the soap dispensers in the bathrooms full. Sitto has started coming over on Fridays. We braid challah and hollow out squash, carrots, onions, and peppers, stuffing them with heshu and wrapping them for freezer storage. I keep three glass bowls on my entry console table filled with kaak, sesame candy, and chocolate-covered almonds. With the help of my mother-in-law's housekeeper, who shows up on my doorstep once a week, I keep David's scrubs ready and our sheets clean. But out in public, I feel my age, a creeping reminder that I should either be out making mistakes or with my nose in a textbook, not out to dinner with a husband. Twice on our honeymoon, a lady staying at the same hotel pulled me aside to ask if I "wanted to tell her anything."

The few times I hung out with David's colleagues, I left feeling nauseated. David and I grew up in the same place, but he is capable of leaving it behind. In conversation, he easily swaps community slang for a rhetoric I like to call "Manhattan asshole," while I rely on words whose meanings dissipate beyond the parameters of our enclave. At home, I'm confident. I'm convinced it's what drew David to me, despite, or perhaps because of, my age. But at times I wonder if he'd be more compatible with someone like Nina, someone who'd challenge him and whose knowledge of politics might impress his friends on the outside. When I tell him this much, he dismisses it as nonsense. *I want you,* he says, and I choose to believe him. But then watching him and Nina or Steven argue around the dinner table, I can't help but think he wants more or, worse, that he resolved to not need it from me.

"How was your day?" He takes my hand over the table and threads his fingers through mine. His yellow gold wedding band dances in the light overhead.

"Busy. I started prepping so I'm not swamped for the dinner tomorrow night. What about you? How was work?" I scan the to-do list in my head while David discloses some expletives about his chief resident. My kibbe peas are cooked and in the fridge. Potatoes are diced in squares and soaking in a large bowl of iced water. Chicken has been shredded and is marinating in a mix of its own juices, tomato paste, oil, garlic, and cinnamon, my mother's recipe. My yebra has been stuffed and rolled; all that's left is to cook it. My table is set and so is my alarm. If I get up by seven tomorrow, all of my food should be done by three, giving me enough time to relax and take a shower before my family arrives for their first Shabbat dinner by David and me. There's a slight added pressure because Steven is coming, too. Nina sprung it on me last minute, but I should've guessed. They've eaten basically every meal together since getting hot and heavy over the summer.

"Anyway, I don't want to talk about work." David laughs, rubbing his index finger and thumb into his forehead.

"My dad really wants you to go to shul with him tomorrow before Shabbat," I say.

"Really? He didn't ask." David looks peeved.

"He's not going to say anything to you, but I know he does. He says it in his own way. 'Steven is coming . . .' You know."

"Steven practically works from home, when he does work. You're going to compare me to Steven now?"

"I'm not comparing you. I'm just telling you what my dad says without saying it."

"I don't have the luxury of leaving my 'office' at three P.M." David flags down the server. "I'll take a Tito's *up*, with three olives. Lucy? Tequila?"

I still get momentary lapses of panic every time I order a drink, even though I barely ever get carded. And if I did, Fortune's old ID never fails.

"Casamigos Blanco, ice and lime on the side, please." It helps not to flinch; it helps that I have the tolerance and palate of a Marriott casino regular. It's just, I know the drink won't taste the same, being that I'm a month late on my period. At first I chalked my missed period up to the air travel done on our honeymoon, but we've been back for a few weeks now and it still hasn't come.

David, sensing my frustration or nerves, relents. "I'll go with your dad, all right? You just have to understand that when I am able to go to shul Fridays, my dad likes me to go with him."

"Right." To be honest, I don't give a shit either way.

"How are the lovebirds anyway? Still together?"

"Don't be a dick."

"I'm serious!"

"They're very much still together. And I'll probably need an engagement dress soon. And you need a suit."

"I have plenty of suits."

"Something new, for my *sister*!"

"Do you remember what Steven wore to our wedding?"

"That's not fair. They were just starting out. We invited him last minute!"

"Converse."

"Whatever. He's different. That's Nina's type."

"To a black-tie wedding at The Plaza." David snorts.

"You sound like a snob."

"Shit, I know."

"Anyway, you don't really care, so stop pretending."

"And *haj* with this 'different.' What's so different about him? He likes shitty music and wears Converse to weddings? Trust me, there's nothing different about being a liberal, I see plenty of them at work." David scoffs.

"Libertarian, I think he said."

"Oh G-D."

"He's your future brother-in-law. You can't hate him."

"I don't hate him. I just think your sister could've done better."

"He's her first boyfriend." David has a protectiveness over Nina that irks me to no end.

"Exactly my point."

"Whatever. Where's the menu? I'm starving." I'm very much done with this conversation.

"The waiter comes with a blackboard when we're ready."

"Is that like an environmental thing?"

"It's more the vibe of the place."

Sometimes, David has the worst way of making me feel inferior, or dumb, or like I just don't *get it*.

Our server returns with our drinks.

"It's not like there were guys knocking down Nina's door." I take a generous sip of mine.

"Enough about them. I know it upsets you. She's your sister and you love her." David raises his glass. "Cheers to us. I love you, Luce."

I tip my half-empty glass toward his.

We've definitely gotten closer since she got together with Steven. Nina actually *asks* for my advice. Like, she'll literally call me and solicit my opinion on something, which never happened before. It's fun to have someone to bitch with, about in-laws, commitments, Mom. Also, for someone who proclaimed our entire lives "not to care," Nina cares a whole fucking lot. About her eventual wedding, and the venue, and who's invited, what we're wearing, her bouquet, her headpiece, the DJ, the fourteen varieties of salad offered by the buffet, her first dance song, the flavor of her cake (as if she'd eat it anyway), the timing of her hair, makeup, birth control. I could go on but I'm honestly boring myself.

"I'm late." I swirl the lime wedge around in my now-empty glass, but David's attention is elsewhere. I consider dropping the topic entirely. It's clear David didn't hear me. We're not *on* tonight, and it's pissing me off.

"Sorry, what'd you say you wanted?" David searches for the blackboard in question. "The branzino?"

"I didn't." The hum of the restaurant grows louder as more people filter in and take their seats. Like most other spots David chooses, the clientele at this one is moneyed, young, and hip. There isn't a designer logo in sight, but every twentysomething looks like they've been dressed in thousands of dollars' worth of leather and vintage jewelry. I much prefer to eat Uptown, where you could flaunt your wealth openly. But David is selective in how he chooses to show his wealth. Everything about his appearance is understated, as if that somehow makes up for his considerably lavish lifestyle. He's always quick to remind me of how he traded in his Porsche for a Jeep Wrangler last year, after nearly hitting a pedestrian while turning onto our block. "Nobody needs that much speed," he proclaimed.

On his days off, he wears black Birkenstocks, which he replaces once a year, only because his mother insists. She still takes him shopping once a season, spoiling him with a new coat, boots, and a trove of cashmere sweaters each time September rolls around. David is one of those men who could wear a poncho and look good. He has a nice, clean face. Dark eyes, darker eyelashes, and when he smiles, his otherwise taut cheeks swell to produce two deep dimples. I smile, imagining that the result of my delayed period might inherit those dimples. His intelligence, charm, his precocious nature.

"I'm late," I say again, louder this time.

"What do you mean?" David's listening now.

"A month." There'd been a pit in my stomach for days. But now, with the facts cemented in real time and spoken aloud, I feel it shrink. David looks at me; his eyes are processing, as if I'd just asked him to solve for pi.

"A mon—but how?" he stammers. "Did you take a test?"

"Don't worry." I shake my head. "I did the math and it's close enough to the wedding that people will assume it's a honeymoon baby. If it's anything . . ."

"I didn't even think about that. Did you take a test?" David waits for an answer. I have none for why I've waited this long to take a test or to tell him. "Should you really be drinking?" he asks, gently taking my glass.

"Nothing's confirmed," I say, a little defensively. "I didn't take a test."

"A whole month . . ." David repeats. "Well, we have to know." He puts his palms against the table and pushes his chair back. "There's a Duane Reade on the corner." He stands up and tosses a few twenties on the table. "Excuse me." He taps a busboy, nearly causing him to drop the dirty dish tower propped precariously in his hand. "I'm so sorry. There's been an emergency."

"Are you serious?"

He is. I grab my bag from the table and follow his lead.

"Are we coming back?"

David is already on the move, weaving his way through tightly packed tables like a quarterback with the winning touchdown. I run after him, hoping to catch wind of how he feels. This is a good thing, right?

The last time I peed in the employee restroom of a Duane Reade while someone waited outside was at my bachelorette party. It's a night I cringe to remember, and I can still recall seeing Nina and Fortune out of the corner of my eye, watching the shenanigans from a comfortable distance, close enough to judge but not partake. David had rented us the sprawling suite in a new hotel on Bowery whose name I cannot for the life of me remember. Nobody between us had a credit card to put the room under so David offered to reserve, and ultimately pay for, our two-night stay on the Lower East Side. Plus, most of my friends had lied and told their parents they were going on some post–grad school seminar trip that weekend, not a raucous bachelorette party that ultimately culminated in two separate visits to the hospital, for alcohol poisoning and a bad high, respectively.

Fifteen seconds pass.

"Let me in. I'm too nervous." David turns the handle and I unlock the door, letting him inside.

"How long again?" He reaches for the box.

"Two minutes."

Sari, whose older brother Marcus frequented the Meatpacking District six out of seven nights a week, had gotten us into The Box, a burlesque nightclub downtown where you could exclusively watch performers eat each other's shit in the company of other privileged New Yorkers with limited gag reflex and heavy wallets. Giselle thought it would be a good idea if we all dressed in matching Hervé Léger bandage dresses of varying colors (her mom owned five she could swipe from her closet, Freda had her own, as did Rachel, so we were all covered). Mine was an eggplant color. Fortune lent me the YSL Tribute pumps Mom bought her for her engagement, which was nice. It goes without saying that Nina wore her Cheap Monday black jeans, which probably cut our chances of getting into the club by half but didn't sabotage us entirely.

"Time?" David taps his foot nervously.

"Thirty seconds." I peek over at the test, which lays screen side up. David leans against the edge of the sink, his elbows between his knees. He can't see the second pink line starting to form, its color deepening like a fresh wound.

We decided to stay in and order takeout on the second and last night of my bachelorette. I opened the door, fully expecting to see a bellboy holding a box of hot pizza. Instead, there was a cop, and for a millisecond I believed he was an actual cop, and I panicked, because three out of ten of us were seventeen and we were practically housing a liquor store along with a batch of brownies made with 100 percent raw cocoa and weed-infused avocado oil.

"Are you the bride?" he asked.

"Yes." I stood in my false bravado, ready to take the fall for my friends, whose parents believed them to be in some tristate Westin, dancing *rikudim* in a same-sex circle and not here. In hindsight, it should've been a giveaway that the "cop," with his Ricky's-bought uniform, knew that there was a bride at all, but I hadn't put two and two together. Imagine my surprise, then, when a chorus of hollers swelled behind me, my friends hooting and clapping as the so-called lawman proceeded to unbutton his shirt and gyrate his hips, a vintage stereo perched dangerously on his shoulder. Imagine *his* surprise, to find he'd been summoned to a bachelorette party of recent high school graduates. G-D bless his professionalism, he did his job for the ten minutes we allowed him to stay. (There was a bridge chair and acrobatics involved. We got squeamish.)

"Two lines, two! What does that mean?" I emerge from the memory to find David, towering over me, his fingers clutching the test in midair.

"Should we take another one?" I say reflexively.

"That's positive. That's a positive, right? What the fuck am I talking about? I'm a fucking doctor. This isn't rocket science, Lucy!" David is on his knees now. His face is bright and big in front of me. He cups my cheeks in his hands.

"Luce," he whispers.

"Oh my G-D."

"We're going to have a baby," he says, confirming what a part of me had already known. I touch my hands to my stomach and feel it change and grow beneath them, even if it is too early. We're going to have a baby.

Nineteen, the same age my mother was when she had Nina. Had she been scared, excited? How did my father take the news? Had he even been there when she found out? Did she, like me, experience a tidal wave of fear, anxiety, and a love so big for something that did not yet exist? Something tells me she took the news like she takes everything else, plainly at first. *This is what's done,* I imagine her telling herself. But the impact of milestones always hits us eventually. Sometimes, not for years and until we've gotten a minute to rest with our eyes closed, our lives playing before us like a film reel. Those images reverberate, an endless credit loop to accompany us.

David is already on the phone, scrolling through my contact list to find the number of the gynecologist I'd seen exactly one time.

"When was the date of your last period?" he asked, sliding the phone from his ear.

"I don't know. I'd have to check my app."

"Ballpark?"

"Nine-ish weeks ago I guess, sometime around there."

"First week of last month." David spoke excitedly into the phone. He hit the speaker button as the nurse on call rattled off a list of dates we might be able to come in.

"That would put you around eight weeks," she said. "We usually see patients around that mark, when a heartbeat is detectable. We can get you in after the weekend. Wednesday at two-thirty work?"

"Yes." David punches the appointment into my calendar while I consider how the fuck I am supposed to sit with this news for six days before seeing a doctor. What if I lose the baby before then and don't know? Should we share the news, and with whom? How was I meant to behave, now that it's been confirmed I'm growing a human?

David, sensing my panic, hangs up the phone and wraps me in his arms.

David is good. He's dependable, strong, smart, financially secure. He'll be such a good father. But right now, for the first time in our relationship, I don't want David.

I want my mother. Or maybe, I just want to be mothered. The reality that I'll soon have to be that person for someone else fills me with a doubt so inexhaustible, I fear it will swallow me whole if I let it. Because deep within me, in the caverns of my bones, in the place where something pure and miraculous is taking form, I'm still somebody else's baby.

Chapter Twenty-five

············

My eyes are open long before my alarm signals it's time for me to get up. I turn over and reach for David, but his side of the bed is empty. He's already left for work. Our house, two blocks in either direction from both of our parents, is dark and still. The house belonged to David's older brother before his family grew and it was passed down to us. It's a nice house. A three-bedroom, 2.5-bathroom house with a basement and its own laundry room. It's modest in comparison to the house he grew up in, which is a plus—an opportunity to grow, a nice-size springboard for our lives and his ambition. Part of what drew me to David was his drive to earn on his own, independent of his family. Part of what annoyed me about David was his reluctance to admit that we'd have very little, let alone this house, if it weren't for his parents' help.

We spent two months fixing up the home before moving in. With the help of a handyman who worked for David's father, we coated the walls in a layer of fresh white paint. We ripped up the carpet on the first and second floors and installed hardwood, staining it a silver-gray shade of oak. David's mother helped select area rugs for the den and bed-rooms, all versions of the same beige bouclé wool. She had window treatments put in every room. "They're what tie a space together," she said. I didn't tell her that my parents still had paper shades in their house. David picked out our bed frame and sofa from a CB2 outlet he dragged me to in New Jersey. The sofa, a velvet blend in royal blue, was deep and large enough to accommodate at least eight people comfort-ably. Our bed frame is white tufted leather and looks and feels like marshmallows. I spread my body over the sateen sheet, Matouk, pur-chased from Bloomingdale's with some of the registry gift credit we received.

The doctor said I am allowed one cup of coffee per day, and I intend on claiming it. When I pass the small dining room off the kitchen downstairs, I count the chairs around our table, a wedding gift from my parents.

The set belonged to Sitto, originally. I'd sat around the table many times as a little girl, devouring her legendary Shabbat food and wiping my oily fingers on the cardboard that lined its undercarriage. The din-ing table has a butternut wood veneer and two extendable leaves, for company. It still has its original sheen and, thanks to a little polishing, looks brand-new in the space.

Eight chairs. Exactly enough to accommodate our family for dinner.

Sitto

Mom & Dad

Nina & Steven

Me & David

Fortune

I lay out a table setting for each person as the percolator bubbles. A place mat, dinner plate, salad plate, cutlery, water glass, wineglass, kip-pot where the men will sit. I roll the monogrammed napkins I received as a shower gift from a great-aunt into tight cigars and slide them into silver napkin rings (swanee gift). I text Nina to tell her I'm not going to make it to the Piloxing class we usually take together on Fridays. Nina, in preparation for her engagement, has turned into a walking BowFlex commercial. Where her skin once sagged around bones, she now has muscle. Her body looks amazing, athletic even. She and David frequently share nutrition tips and recipes: Pancakes made with only a banana, one egg, and raw oats. Ghee mixed into their morning coffees to fill them for hours. The physiological benefits of intermittent fasting. Whatever. If you ask me, Nina has just taken one disorder and swapped it for another.

You suck, she replies.

Eat shit, I created life, I think.

I take out the challah that Sitto and I baked together last week and set it on the counter to defrost. I ignite three burners on the stove, placing a pot of olive oil to simmer over each. When the oil is nice and hot, I divide a large Ziploc bag of precut onions among them, stirring each with a wooden spoon. I crack a window and let the cool morning air waft into the kitchen. Outside, a mother pushes her infant in a large bassinet stroller as she speaks hurriedly into her phone. The pharmacy on the corner pulls up its gates. A man wearing a bloodstained butcher's uniform hoses down the sidewalk in front of his shop as his employee (son, maybe) pushes a broom across the dirty sidewalk water.

My mother approaches her own kitchen strategically and efficiently, armed with menus and ingredient lists she keeps in a palm-sized notebook safely tucked into the same kitchen drawer as the Saran wrap. Her recipes are oil stained and written in barely legible chicken scratch on index cards she keeps neatly stacked in an old Louboutin shoebox in the cabinet above the oven.

"She's always rushing," Sitto would say. Sitto likes to linger in the kitchen all day, and Shabbat dinners mean a full forty-eight hours, at least, spent toiling over a hot stove. If you don't resolve to love it, you become a slave to it. And Sitto has resolved to love it; how the hours fly by, her only meal coming from a sample taste taken here or there. The sound of Arabic news, or soap operas, coming from the television next door. The playful competition that comes from sharing recipes with your sisters and friends. (She puts tomato sauce in her hamid, *ya haram.* This one makes white spaghetti instead of red.) My mother, whose own mother never cooked Shabbat dinner, let alone for forty-eight hours, resolved to do it all and in an eighth of the time. She boasted frequently of her ability to prepare a robust Shabbat meal in two hours (between seven and nine A.M., with the right help). She loves to imitate my father's face when, in their first year of marriage, he came downstairs ready for work only to find my mother sitting idly in front of ABC 7, stacks of warm tins sprawled out on the kitchen counter.

My current home has none of the chaos of the one I grew up in; the arguing, the mess, the sound of the intercom bleeding through the walls, and my mother's intermittent sighs. Those *sighs*. As much as I hate to admit it, there are many things I miss about living with my parents and sisters, but the sound of Mother's deeply disappointed exhalation definitely isn't one of them. There are so many things I'd like to do differently. To begin, David and I don't argue about money. Or rather, he doesn't tell me how to spend his. And in return, I show my gratitude by making sure the house he comes home to each evening is in perfect shape. My mother may have taken to her role as a Syrian homemaker, but part of me suspects she secretly resents it. You can see it in the kitchen spills, her infrequent trips to the grocery ("I'm busy, too"), and her refusal to fulfill requests when she does go ("My bill was too high, blame your father"). But I am living differently than my mother, and as much as I hate to admit it, part of me feels determined to surpass her. Isn't that what she wants?

As soon as the onions turn translucent, I go to work. As I approach my first conquest, a plastic shrink-wrapped pound of chopped meat to brown for tadbilah, I'm hit with a wave of nausea so intense it brings me to my knees. I sink to the floor, my eyes shut. The onions are burning. The thought of handling pink slime makes me gag, and gag, until a well of vomit rises within me, stopping at the base of my throat where it remains just long enough to taste it, before spilling onto the floor. After I'm done, I feel no relief, the smell of burnt onions threatening a second groundswell. I prop myself up and reach for my phone.

Can you come over? Important, I text my mother.

She responded immediately: Y?

G-D she's annoying.

Just come.

Okay. W/ Nina though.

Fine.

"Why are you sitting on the porch?" My mother folds her arms against her chest as she ascends the stairs. "It's chilly." Fortune and Nina follow behind her.

Nina speaks animatedly into her phone: "Personally I love the green on you, but it's your choice." She turns her back toward us, as if she is about to disclose nuclear codes.

"Is she aware that she's literally turned into everything she always claimed to hate," I whisper to my mother and Fortune. The nausea has subsided slightly, thanks to the one less challah roll I now had for dinner.

"Leave her alone." My mother smirks. "She's happy."

"She's much more pleasant to be around," Fortune adds.

"She needed this." My mother agrees. "Some girls do."

"Who is she even talking to?"

"Who do you think?" Mom rolls her eyes. "Steven's mother. All day on the phone talking about this and that. You guys would kill me, the number of questions this woman asks."

"It doesn't look like Nina minds."

My relationship with my own mother-in-law is far less entwined, an arrangement that seems to suit us both. I've heard (from Nina and Fortune) that this is not always the case. Nina and Steven's mother spend an unholy amount of time together. When they're not together, lunching, planning, shopping, they're on the phone, laughing about this or that. Nina doesn't have many friends, but I still find it strange. I'd much rather absorb my mother-in-law's wisdom from a distance, noting the way she runs her home like a high-profile crisis management consultant. Not a throw pillow out of place, her table set like a still-life painting. The kitchen always immaculate and smelling of Palmolive soap and ammonia, even at one P.M. on a Friday! I know that having grown up in that home—whether he'd like to admit it or not—David has certain expectations of me, and I am determined to meet them. Sometimes I can see the hurt on my mother's face, as I ponder whether my MIL would do this or that, my mother's own imagined shortcomings laid bare.

We all crane our necks to look at Nina, who is pantomiming wildly as she laughs into her phone: "You do *not* look like a frog!" she screeches. "You are the mother of the groom, and the fit is *Drop. Dead. Legit.* You can't see me, Ma, but I'm actually dropping dead."

"*Ma.*" I raise my eyebrows. "That was quick. Okay."

"We're going in!" my mother announces, leaving Nina to do her dropping dead.

"Your onions burned," my mother notes when we get inside. She stirs the contents of the pot. "What time do you want us tonight, by the way?"

"I don't know. Seven? I just need an extra bridge chair. I'm short one," I mutter, realizing I'd forgotten to account for Steven. It would take some time for me to get used to the idea of Nina being engaged.

"No you don't. Fortune's not coming." My mother looks at Fortune. "*Right?*"

"What? Why not?"

"I'm coming," Fortune insists. "Ma, stop."

"There's a Shabbat dinner in the shul for singles," my mother says. "Very elegant. They're saying a lot of nice boys will be there and I want Fortune to go."

"That's so embarrassing." Fortune opens my pantry, grabbing a king-size bag of honey pretzels.

"Those will bloat you," my mother says.

"I'm not going." Fortune ignores her, sucking the salt off one.

"Lucy." My mother widens her eyes at me.

"Don't look at me. I have nothing to do with this."

"There's no shame, honey." My mother softens her approach. "Tons of girls will be there."

"Exactly." Fortune discards the slimy pretzel for a new one. "Tons of girls who didn't break off their engagement at the last second."

My mother throws her head back. "This again?"

"Yes, this again."

"So what, you're going to sit in your room for the rest of your life because it didn't work out with one boy—which, by the way, *thank G-D.* I mean talk about someone who wasn't for you. The girl he's with doesn't hold a candle to you."

"Sharon? You loved her growing up."

My mother ignores her and walks toward the small kitchen window above the sink. "Lucy, you have coffee? My head's on fire."

"Yeah." I nearly forgot about the percolated pot, the smell of which is enough to make me retch.

"You perked a whole pot? For who?" My mother pours herself a cup. "Splenda?"

"In that blue jar." I point to the kitchen table. "Anyway, Forch, you should go. You could always run here if it sucks. I'm down the block from the shul," I suggest.

"I'd just rather not put myself in that position." Fortune throws the bag of pretzels on the counter.

"Oh, *please.*" My mother sighs.

"Mom. I mean this in the nicest way possible—but I need you to back off. I am going to be fine. I am *fine,*" Fortune says. "You just need to let me live."

"Let you live?"

"Yes."

"Okay. She needs to live," my mother says to Nina and me, throwing up her hands.

"Thank you," Fortune sounds weary.

"You just let me know when you want me to step in—"

"Thank you," Fortune says again. "I know where you live."

"But if you do change your mind, I'm sure I have something you can borrow." I stir a Splenda into a mug of coffee and hand it to Nina.

"I'm sure there will be other things." Fortune shrugs, never one to decline a peek into my closet. "I'll take a look."

"Where's your meat tenderizer?" My mother rummages through my drawers. "Let me put this on simmer and we can all go up."

There's a fat chance that Fortune will find anything in there that fits her, but we're all too delighted by her willingness to mention that part. Plus, Fortune seems to be trying to pull herself back together. Whereas Saul seems to have cleaned himself up, propped up by the influx of attention he received from a clawing pack of single girls, Fortune seems to have embarked on a month of magical eating. On her small frame, the twenty or so pounds gained weigh heavily. She recently started wearing makeup, blowing out her hair, on the advice of Sitto, who couldn't bear to watch her namesake float around the house in leggings and an oversize Hershey Park sweatshirt. Fortune rifles through the racks of dresses in my closet before coming upon a two-tone crêpe midi dress I'd worn to graduation.

"That's cute," my mother remarks. The dress, which I'd purchased with David one Sunday in the city, is black and cream colored and has a turtleneck and long sleeves. But the thigh-high slit betrayed an entire leg when you walked. The slim fabric gathers in the midsection in a dramatic knot. It is sophisticated and sexy, and just what I'd needed to give me some extra armor when seeing the rest of my graduating class, who I miss, just a little.

"Take it. I won't be wearing it anytime soon." I look at my mother and try with half of everything I have to hold back my smirk. She raises her eyebrows. Nina squints her eyes at me. Fortune holds the dress up against her body. I allow the silence to drag on. Nina looks at my mother and then back at me. My mother takes the dress from Fortune, gathering a bunch of the no-stretch fabric in her hands and pulling it apart to test its elasticity before looking at me again. Her eyes burn one thousand holes into my forehead.

"She's pregnant." Nina's eyes narrow.

"She's not." My mother tiptoes, careful not to upset the rare confession.

"Are you?" Nina pushes forward.

"I think so."

"You *think* so?" My mother beams.

"Oh my G-D!" Nina clasps her hands against her mouth. I could tell she's doing the math but she's kind enough not to do it out loud.

My mother runs toward me, enveloping me in a hug. "You better not be joking." She pulls away from me, her face turning serious.

"I swear."

"Oh my G-D!" My mother hugs me again. "I'm going to have a granddaughter." Her palms press tightly into my back.

"Or a grandson," I manage.

"We don't do boys," Nina says definitively.

My mother squeezes her eyes shut. "Healthy baby. *Sabi andak.* We could use a boy around here."

"*Mabrook,*" Fortune says, placing the dress back on the rack. "I can't believe my baby sister is going to have a baby. That's amazing, Lucy."

"But how—when?" my mother says, catching on. "Must have been night one! How far along are you?"

"Maybe if I'm quick, I'll catch the grade. Imagine, two cousins so close in age?" Nina says.

"Let's get a ring on you first." My mother rolls her eyes lovingly.

"Did you see the doctor yet?" she says panically, the initial shock wearing off. Now, there'd be questions. "Does David know?"

"Were you trying? Oh my G-D," Nina realizes, suddenly. "Lucy is going to get so fat." She claps her hands with glee.

"Honey, you're right behind me. Your body won't know what hit it once you start feeding it."

"Shut up," Nina says, knowing I'm right.

"I hope Steven likes you thick," I say.

"Enough." My mother shakes her head. "I gained the most with Nina." My mother shrugs. "You always gain the most with your first."

"How much?"

"Fifty-three pounds."

"See? Whatever. We're all going to get fat anyway. Daddy's genes," I say.

"I'm surprised, though," Nina says, and sits cross-legged on the floor. "Can David have kids this quick, with his job and all?"

"What?" There is no point in trying to hide my annoyance. She may have a college degree and a subscription to *The New Yorker* (which she never reads, by the way), but I'm David's wife. What does she know about when David wanted to start a family?

"He always talks about completing his residency first, that's all I'm saying." Nina continues, "It's not like he needs the money. Why wait?"

"It's not about that." I huff, noticing the panic I feel every time the potential for David's unhappiness is brought to light.

"Does he know?" Fortune asks.

"Of course. You had to see his face when the test said positive. He cried." A small fib, but what the hell.

"No, I'm sure he's thrilled," Nina says, still clearly unconvinced.

"He's going to take off for the first appointment, he's so excited."

"I don't think your father made it to one of my appointments with you. Fortune, do you need me to zip that?" Fortune is crouched just on the other side of the closet door, angling her arm and neck in order to zip the back of a new dress.

"I can't imagine Steven missing an appointment." Nina flips her hair to one side.

"Forget it, Steven is going to be the diaper genie," my mother says.

"Like one of those dads who wears their kid on their body with that carrier thing," Fortune adds.

"Oh G-D." My mother helps Fortune with her zipper. "The men are so different now."

"True," I say. "Back then, they all had jobs. At least Steven's always home, though. I'm sure he'll be a big help if you do get pregnant."

Nina glares at me, the implications of my comment threatening to unravel all of the gains we'd made in our relationship recently. I consider, for a moment, apologizing, but my sisters and I are no good at sentimentality. Anyway, she started this with the insinuation that she somehow knows David better than I do. Nina can afford to be knocked down a peg or two. All of this wedding stuff is getting to her head. Her thick, impermeable head. Sometimes I think I liked her better when she was miserable. It doesn't help her case that almost overnight, she and my mother turned into Lorelai and Rory Gilmore, partaking in all of the shopping and planning and gossiping. It's the ones you least suspect, I guess.

"Crap." My mother sniffs the air in my 150-square-foot closet I'd had converted from a small bedroom. "Something's burning."

"I'll go check the oven," Fortune says.

By the time Nina, Mom, and I get downstairs, Fortune is already gone, a yellow Post-it note tacked to my fridge with AUNTIE:)! HAD TO RUN. The dress hangs forgotten and lifeless over a club chair by the door, leaving us all to wonder where she is going, what new life she is running toward. But then I also think of Nina and what it is about this life that pits us against each other the way that it does.

FORTUNE

Chapter Twenty-six

....

Working at Baby Boom was Dad's idea, which hurt. As if I hadn't felt useless enough. His suggestion that I leave Mr. Cheap for a more appropriate job hadn't felt like a suggestion at all. And what qualified as "more appropriate" anyway? Was it working at some hipster establishment like Nina? Certainly not. Although against all odds, her job *did* lead her to a fiancé. But that wasn't what my parents had in mind for me. Their hope was that I'd find a job in the community, preferably in a place where I could rehabilitate my tarnished reputation as the girl who practically abandoned Saul Dweck at the altar. The layette department at Baby Boom, the community's number one destination for infant, baby, and toddler clothing, was a natural fit. Lucy got me the job. And I resented her for it in more ways than one. She had invited my mother, her mother-in-law, and me along to choose her layette, her unborn baby's future wardrobe. Because, like most people, Lucy and David decided to keep the baby's sex a surprise, she had to choose two layettes, one for a boy and one for a girl. For two hours we deliberated on cotton onesies and whether the future prince or princess would grow too quickly out of a size 0–3 month footie pajama, how many burp cloths were too many, and whether a sleep sack was necessary at all. By the end of it, Lucy had two small mountains of clothing in front of her, one predominantly pink, the other blue, and some gray and beige neutrals in the middle. The store was so crowded that Linda, the twenty-year vet of the layette department, kept on having to run up front to assist customers at the register.

"You guys really need to hire more help," Lucy said finally.

"Ya think?" Linda had a heavy Brooklyn accent and her bubblegum pink lipstick needed reapplying.

"Fortune's available," Lucy shrugged, nudging me in the lower back.

"I am?"

"Oh, that would be *fantastic.*" My mother clapped her hands.

"You're hired." Linda folded a pair of oatmeal-colored leggings. "But don't be afraid to speak up. Our customer likes having an opinion she can argue with."

On my first day, I approached the register at nine A.M. to find Linda ringing up a cotton nightgown with tiny red cherries on it.

"So they got you, too." She didn't look up, but I recognized her. My new coworker was the young girl who had gotten too drunk at that wedding, the one they found half-clothed in the pews the following morning. I'd heard she got sent to seminary in Jerusalem and then to an aunt in Boca. I guess the next step on her apology tour was behind the register of Baby Boom, with me.

"I'm Fortune," I said, although we needed no introduction.

"Val," she said, and nodded toward a pile of rumpled-up pajamas. "Those need folding. You can shelve them when you're done."

Val has a way of ordering me around that doesn't feel denigrative or mean. She is matter-of-fact and honest, two qualities that make her indispensable to Baby Boom. I have to admit we make a good team. Val as the lieutenant and me as her trusted foot soldier. Val has this impressive control about her, and it is difficult to imagine her losing that, no matter how young she'd been or how many drinks she'd had. It makes more sense that she would have developed the armor afterward.

My newfound friendship with Val is perhaps the only positive thing to come out of my job at Baby Boom. The pay is terrible and it's cruel punishment, having to help girls you went to high school with, cousins younger than you, choose layettes for their newborns and back-to-school clothes for their first, second, and third children. Every day, dozens of expectant girls walk in, their bellies as round and hard as seedless watermelons.

"And you have to treat each one like *they* are the most important. Especially the first-time moms," Linda advised me on my first day.

I'm getting the hang of it. The platitudes. The guessing games. High and wide, must be a girl! Girls steal your beauty, and you look too pretty, it's definitely a boy! Recently, Val and I started taking bets. First to ten correct gender predictions wins—so far, she's up by one.

Even though Val is younger than I am, she started to take me under her wing socially. Val gets a lot of attention from boys in the community who think she puts out, even though I know for a fact that she doesn't. Most of them don't even recall the scandal that might have given them this notion. And yet this stain on her reputation clings to her, like the smell of onions on your hands. On Monday nights, we go to the hookah bar where the Israelis from the other side of Nostrand hang out. Most of them don't know me and I don't know them, which feels nice.

The hookah bar feels like the kind of place Isaac might frequent. Monday after Monday I wonder if I'll run into him, and what I might say if I do. It stung when he didn't reach out after I called off the engagement, and there is no way he didn't hear about it. I'd told him as much when he approached me at Lucy's wedding. "Your mom invited my whole family," Isaac had said sheepishly. "She didn't have to do that." Still, we never spoke about that night in Spice. It seemed we were both happy to leave that memory where it belonged, hidden in the dim light of the stockroom. We'd danced for a bit and shared a drink, but I couldn't help but notice how Isaac looked at me differently now, like an object of pity, not desire.

"Looking for someone?" Val asked one night.

"Is it obvious?" I squinted my eyes against the thick haze of hookah smoke that clouded the air.

"You look like you're scanning the horizon for warships." Val laughed. So I told her about Isaac. I told her about that night in the stockroom. It felt good to talk about it, to hear the way the scene played out out loud as opposed to in my head.

"You know it's not about Isaac, specifically," Val said when I was done.

"What do you mean?" I asked.

"I mean he was a stand-in. It could've been anybody. You were just desperate to put something between you and Saul because you knew he wasn't right for you. You knew you couldn't go through with it."

For days afterward I thought about what Val said. It felt nice to have someone be honest with me for a change. I may not have a fiancé like Nina or a soon-to-come baby like Lucy, but for the first time in my life, I had a friend.

LUCY

Chapter Twenty-seven

············

In my recurring nightmare, I leave my baby behind on an airplane. The realization that I've forgotten something very important to me comes slowly, and not until I see my eggplant-colored carry-on slide onto the baggage claim conveyor belt. The first thing I do is clutch my stomach, and I'm surprised when I feel its flatness, my abs tight and tucked into jeans that don't have an elastic waistband.

I've already had the baby.

I run.

And I run.

The airport is a maze of lines secured by barrier ropes and TSA agents who all share the same exhausted expression. I pass all of them. At some point, I lose my shoes. As I'm running, past magazine stands and vending machines stocked with yogurt parfaits, I scan the faces of my fellow travelers. I look for David even though I know I won't find him because he's busy taking notes on someone else's life. When I finally reach the gate, my mouth doesn't work. I tap my pockets for my boarding pass before seeing it on the floor, sprinkled across the stained blue carpet in tiny paper shreds.

My baby! I yell through lips that are sealed shut. My eyes grow large. I look insane, I'm sure, but I don't care. I just need this flight attendant to let me back on the fucking airplane.

"I'm sorry, miss," she says plainly. "You'll have to wait for all passengers to disembark before we can let you back on the plane." She pushes her chair back from behind the desk and stands up, revealing a swollen belly the size of a beach ball. I point to my stomach in a show of solidarity before realizing that it is empty. *My baby!* I'm screaming with my eyes. I'm pointing at the airplane. I'm opening an overhead compartment using my two hands and thin air. I'm clawing at my empty stomach with such force, my shirt tears and my nails, long and manicured, puncture my skin. All the while, she just stares at me, a mix of boredom and pity etched across her progesterone-laden face.

And then I feel it, as if it's been there all along, a kick in my lower abdomen so subtle, I think it's been imagined. I press two fingers into the spot where I felt the jolt. I press harder, and something inside responds. My stomach feels solid and stretched, and when I look down I see a belly so grown it juts out past my feet.

I always wake up sweating. The mini fridge David recently bought whirrs in the corner. My mouth feels stiff and dry from all the breathing it's doing for my nose, and I need water. In a hurry to cement myself in reality, I fling my body up and over the side of my bed. The rush of blood to my head urges me to slow down and so I sit for a moment more, my belly pressed against the top of my bare thighs, and I breathe. It was just a dream. I feel another kick, harder this time, and when I look down, I see the outline of a limb taking shape beneath my skin. Beneath my veiny skin, a fully formed body moves deliberately, like a handlebar slowly being turned. I reach for my phone and do the same thing I've done every morning since my first doctor's appointment. I open the app, the one that tells me how big my baby is in fruit.

Winter melon!

AT 38 WEEKS, BABY CAN COME AT ANY MOMENT—TRIPLE- AND THEN
QUADRUPLE-CHECK THAT HOSPITAL BAG!

I screenshot a photo and send it to David. To my surprise, he answers right away:

Mmm my favorite. How'd you sleep?

Horrible.

Oy. Pillow again? That thing looks like the Pillsbury torture boy.

No, just isolation, I think, before shutting my phone. I reach for the
box of tissues on my bedside table and forcefully blow my nose. I'm not
at all alarmed when the mucus comes out dry and bloody. I've gotten
used to breathing through my mouth and cannot imagine the day when
my nose will once again be operable. I pad over to the window to see
that yes, the weatherman is right. Heavy rains are already starting to
pool on the sidewalks and streets. The pharmacy and butcher, usually
open by now, have their gates pulled down and secured shut. I turn on
the TV and allow the warm glow of ABC 7 to wash over the dusky
room. I turn up the volume so I can listen as I wash up.

"April showers," one of the anchors says way too jovially.

"You can say that again!" his co-anchor responds. "What our buddies
over in California would do for some of this right now, huh, Jan?"

"That's right, Pat, that's right."

My hospital bag sits patiently in the corner, where it's been for six
weeks. I packed it so long ago I can't even remember what's inside. I
allow the shower to fill with steam before stepping in, careful not to
catch a glimpse of myself in the fogging mirror. I'd originally objected
to the rain shower, prioritizing pressure over a calming effect. It was one
of the few "arguments" David and I had while renovating. As in most
cases, he turned out to be right. The baby agrees and begins to kick
rhythmically—hiccups, maybe—as the hot water cascades over the
hump of my belly. I breathe a sigh of relief knowing that bb (as we call
him or her) is well inside. Its movements, once frequent and urgent,
have slowed but become more distinctive. Every time it moves inside, it

feels like a slightly rusty knob is churning in my stomach, and I can see the outline of its frame readjusting beneath my skin, stretched so thin.

Against the orders of my mother, mother-in-law, and, most important, Sitto, I'd purchased a single pack of Pampers, wipes, and ointment and stashed them in the closet of the soon-to-be nursery. My crib and changer—a matching set in a neutral ash wood—are being held at the baby store a few blocks away. The owner, a family friend, assured me that both were just a phone call away from being delivered and assembled. The nursery is bare, save for a gray rope area rug, a rocker, and a standing bookshelf that resembles a tree, three items closer, I suppose, to inviting in the *hamsa,* or evil eye. I fought against the idea initially, of keeping the baby's room bare until it's born. The notion that planning for your baby's healthy arrival might in some way jinx its luck is, to me, entirely irrational. But the custom is so widely practiced that to do anything else seems equally as nuts. Baby showers, gender reveals—joyous markers of pregnancy to others, but to us, they are merely public displays at tempting fate. Planning ahead brings a higher possibility of inviting bad luck into your home. So why take the chance?

I did convince David to install the car seat, appealing to his logic over superstition.

The rest of my baby needs are listed on a piece of paper and in stock at the pharmacy on my corner, ready to be ordered with a phone call right after the baby releases its first cry, and not a moment before.

The Pampers were purchased before Sitto's health worsened. And I could feel their presence in my home burning a hole of guilt deep within me. Her deterioration only further proved her point, of not counting your chickens before they hatch. She was always warning against the perils of growing too comfortable in your life, too accustomed to good fortune—her namesake. "G-D can take it away in a second," she said, snapping. And so He seemed to. A week after we celebrated her seventy-third birthday, Sitto was rushed to the hospital with a fever and the weight of the world on her chest. She remained in good spirits at first. And it comforted us all to see that she was still bossing the hospital staff around, still bartering with my mother to sneak her a slice of knafeh the next time she visited, organizing games of canasta from the bed in which she lay paralyzed with advanced pneumonia.

I saw the lines in my father's face deepen as she grew complacent; too tired to spit on the hospital food, too hopeless to request (demand!) a bedside manicure. In the nearly twenty years since I've been on this earth, I can't recall my grandmother's nails having ever been without her signature periwinkle polish—a color I've never felt matched her spirit.

"The house just feels so quiet, it's weird," my mother said to me on the phone last night. "With Sitto in the hospital and Nina moving out . . . it's just me, Daddy, and Fortune."

"You finally got your peace and quiet," I said wryly, trying to lighten the mood.

"I mean you know more than anyone I had my things with her, but it was nice having her around. Even if she didn't know when to s-h-u-t-u-p."

I wasn't sure if my mother was talking about Sitto or Nina, or both, or if it mattered either way. "The house is too big for us three," she continued.

"I'm happy to leave a crying infant at your door whenever you need some noise."

"I will raise that baby," my mother said. "She's like a mother to me." Her voice grew heavy on the other line.

"I know," I said.

There's a brilliant skylight in our shower. Sometimes, the pigeons mistake it for a toilet and I pray for rain, wishing for that clear, unobstructed view of the sky. Today, fat droplets fall cleanly on its surface, wiping all of the muck away. I watch the rain like that for a while, until I can no longer feel the water on my skin.

It's noticeable, then, when I feel a rush of liquid, unlike the rain shower's cascade, spill between my thighs and onto the penny-tiled shower floor. And although I've made countless false-alarm phone calls to my doctor in the past couple of weeks, I'm certain, with every fiber of my being, that this gush of water breaks from deep inside me—that this baby is coming.

When the delivery doctor tells you, "It's time," you will be shocked, even after you've labored for eleven hours and asked seven different nurses, twenty different times, if you are any closer to ten centimeters. My mother grips my left knee. David holds my right knee and my hand at the same time, sprawled across the hospital bed like a human goalpost as he tries his best to be my husband and not my doctor. Nina, Fortune, and my mother-in-law stand on the opposite side of the hospital-room curtain in anticipation. My father is on the other side of the city, sitting by Sitto's bedside, unsure of what he should be waiting for.

I push like I am saving two lives instead of one. Even when the doctor tells me to slow down, to wait until I feel the peak of the contraction, I don't. I push. I push from a place I've never felt before, as if I've discovered a hidden region of my body and unleashed the pressure valve on its potential. I hold my breath to within an inch of my life with each thrust, expelling the terrible thoughts that crop up in my brain every time I'm given a moment of pause. We all know what it means when my father doesn't respond to any of our messages in over an hour. Nevertheless, I keep pushing, my ear tuned to the ups and downs of the heart rate monitor to my left.

When the doctor announces, "Crowning!" I hear Sitto's pulse slow.

"Last one, give me a big one!" The nurses rush to my side. A baby scale is wheeled into the room.

I push, desperate for life, as I imagine Sitto taking a final, shallow breath.

"Dad? Do you want to catch the baby?" the doctor asks.

"He will not—" I say. "Look, ahhh." I give a final push, and if I'm going to die, it's going to be this one that kills me. And then, relief. Our collective breath hangs in the balance as all of the adrenaline in the room comes to a frozen pause.

Finally: "It's a girl!" The doctor beams, holding my squealing daughter in the palm of his hand, her face red and wrinkled, like a disgruntled old lady.

"A girl," my mother says, crying. "Look at her hair!" She laughs through tears.

"We're going to hold off on the cord clamping for a few minutes, Doc," David says as he lowers himself beside me.

A nurse cleans her off slightly and places her in my arms. Her hair, thick and brown, covers her tiny head like a mushroom cap. She stops her squealing and nuzzles her head in my breasts. David strokes her shoulder blade, his complexion blotchy and tear stricken, as I touch my cheek to hers.

How do you explain the feeling when your child turns to you for the first time, her tiny pink lips open and ready to accept whatever you have to give?

Sandra. Following in tradition, our baby girl will be named after my mother-in-law.

"She's ours." David tickles our daughter's ears. She's curled up cozily in my chest, hungry for the thick yellow substance that stained many of my white T-shirts during my third trimester. I can look at her nose for hours, just her nose, tiny and round as a button. I take inventory of her body as she is taken for testing, all six pounds and four ounces of her. When the afterbirth is finished and I get her back, I note her two ears, her collarbone, the birthmark beneath her left nipple. A cherry. Sitto warned me of them, a symptom of my not indulging in whatever food I was craving. (At the time, pecan pie.)

"She's beautiful," I say and look up, expecting my mother to agree, but she is gone. Nina slides the dividing curtain slightly open and peeks her head through.

"Is it okay if we come in?" she asks gently.

"Of course," David replies, running to embrace his mother. Fortune and Nina approach my bedside. They walk quietly, like mice on a kitchen floor.

"Should your mother-in-law hold her first?" Nina whispers.

"Where's Mom?" Part of me already knows the answer.

"She's on the phone with Dad." Fortune hands me a cup of ice chips. "Lucy, she's so beautiful." She smiles through tears.

"Is it—" I find myself unable to finish my thought. Fortune begins to cry. Nina embraces her, her free hand squeezing the knee my mother had her hand on only minutes before.

"Sitto would've loved to meet her. A great-grandchild," Nina cries, kissing the top of Fortune's head. "She waited. Dad said she waited." Nina lets out a sad, wet cough.

"She would've wanted us to be happy. And look what we got in return." Fortune kneels down to study the baby's profile.

"Sandra Fortune," I say. "After Sitto, too. That will be her name."

"I love it," Nina says. "But don't say her name yet, not until after David names her in shul." With that, Fortune and Nina back away from the baby, allowing my mother-in-law to enter the fold.

"Can I?" she squeals. "You did amazing, oh my G-D."

"Of course, Grandma." I smile, handing the baby to her.

As soon as Sandra leaves my arms, I'm hit with the realization that through all of the chaos, I hadn't made any arrangements.

"David! The list!"

"Already called," David says. He gets down on his knees and plants a long kiss on my sweaty forehead. I allow myself to forget how terrified I feel, just for one second, knowing we're about to do this thing together.

"The crib and changer are already being assembled in the nursery," Nina adds.

"I picked up your layette and dropped it off at your house when Mom called to say you were in labor. Your neighbor offered to wash everything for you. She said she has a key." Fortune smiles and it's the first time in a long time that I see a real smile there.

"And Mom will bring the baby's going-home outfit either today or tomorrow, whenever you're ready to leave," Nina says.

"Gail and Linda stocked your freezer," my mother-in-law chimes in, referring to my sisters-in-law. "You're set with meals for the week, including Shabbat." Her eyes remain glued on the baby as she gently rocks her back and forth. "Do you want to feed her?"

"Thank you, wow," I say, only half managing because I know I'll just sob if I try to say more.

"I had the candy store deliver nuts, dried fruits, pretty cookies, to your house. *Mazza*, obviously." My mother swings through the curtain, as if she'd been here all along. "But with everything—you know, there may not be a chance for visitors this week." Her voice trails off.

"Better to keep people away from the baby," my mother-in-law says as she hands me Sandra while my mother washes her hands in the sink. I bring the baby to my breast, where she roots around for a moment before enveloping my nipple with her tiny mouth. Just like that.

"Congratulations, Grandma!" My mother embraces my mother-in-law.

"Ma, I'm going to go see if I could pull some strings for a private room," David says. "Come with?"

A silence falls over the room after David and his mother leave. Neither I nor Nina, Fortune nor my mother, knows where to begin or whether we should start at all.

Nevertheless, it feels like a familiar place to be, this intersection between grief and celebration. How many times have we been at this crossroad together over this past year?

"Let me see her." My mother floats toward me. As she gets closer, I can see that her mascara has collected in a wet pool beneath her eyes.

"Thank G-D," she says, laughing. "She's got my nose."

"Imagine her with Daddy's schnoz." Nina inhales deeply. "*Hazita.*"

"It's cute as a button." My mother breathes a sigh of relief. "That's some of my Ashkenaz bloodline in her."

"She looked like Sitto when she came out," I say. "Her face was all mad and squishy." I scrunch up my nose and pout my lips, doing my best impersonation of Sitto (and the baby).

"Lehhhh," Nina spits, imitating Sitto perfectly.

"That's the face she makes when she tastes my cooking."

"That's the face she made when she tasted *anyone's* cooking but her own," Fortune corrects our mom, allowing us to process Sitto in the past tense.

"I'm going to miss that face," I say.

"You can always look at this one," Nina says, pointing to my daughter.

"Sandra Fortune." I say it again and again.

"You're going to torture your mommy, I can't wait." My mother coos, scooping the baby up. "Wait until Grandpa sees you."

"Another girl to break his heart," Nina says.

"Shh. She's not going to break anyone's heart." Fortune coos as she takes the baby from my mother. "Auntie loves you. I love you *so much.*"

"I need to make arrangements for the shiva," my mother says suddenly, her voice catching.

"Where will we sit?" Nina asks.

"Our house," my mother says. "Where else?"

"I'll call the caterer," Nina offers.

"I can handle the bridge chairs," Fortune says. "The tissues, mints, all of that stuff."

"I'm going to miss the funeral," I say as it dawns on me. I hug Sandra closer to me, hoping the feel of her body will help ease the pain in mine.

"It's okay, honey," my mother says and strokes my sweat-streaked hair. "Hopefully you'll make the *Arayat* next week."

"Three meals a day?" Nina asks, sliding the phone from her ear. *The caterer,* she mouths.

"I guess," my mother says. "We should make hair appointments, for later today. Who's going to speak at the funeral? Your father, I'm sure."

"The rabbi," Nina adds.

"I'd like to write something," Fortune says quietly. "For someone to read, obviously. Maybe one of the uncles."

"That would be nice." My mother puts her hand on Fortune's shoulder.

"We'll help," I say and nod toward Nina.

My mother sighs. "Your father's not going to be easy to deal with. I'm going to need all of you to chip in."

"We literally all just said we'll help," Nina says.

"I'm just saying, I know how you girls get *busy.*"

"I just had a baby," I say dryly.

"Not you." My mother flicks her wrist.

"What, us?" Nina points at herself and Fortune.

"Yes, you two."

"Don't worry about us."

"I'm just saying."

"Why do you have to just say?"

"You know what? Forget it."

"Guys!" Fortune yells. "Can we not right now? I mean really. *Haje.*"

And with that, we all agree.

Haje.

Acknowledgments

....

Zook, could you believe I'm writing my book acknowledgments? When you broke the glass 'til death do us part, neither of us imagined there'd be a big juicy novel thrown into the marital mix. Thank you for sticking through it with me. For your support. Your brain. Your one-line zingers (of which I used many). For joining me on those late-night walks when all you really wanted to do was pop in a Manischewitz Passover cake and watch *The Great British Bake Off*. I love you. If you would've told newly married, twenty-one-year-old me that I'd push out three babies and a novel in the next decade, I wouldn't have believed you.

But there are people who always seemed to believe in me:

My fourth grade English teacher, Mrs. Fish, whose words encouraged me long after I left her classroom. Alana Newhouse, whose mentorship guided me through some of the most confusing times of my young adult life and whose own writing has become invaluable to me. Noa Shapiro for recognizing a glimmer of something in the earliest pages and for your work in shaping them. Andrea Walker for putting me at ease during a tough transition. The New School MFA Creative Writing program, where the seeds for this book were planted and watered. My Grad Girls writers' group for your friendship and feedback when this book was nothing more than a diary entry. My best friends, *lifers,* this book would've been completed at *minimum* two years earlier if it weren't for our group chat. Thank you for all the welcome distractions.

My agent, Jamie Carr—I truly cannot imagine doing this with anyone else. Thank you for your patience, your warmth, and your assuredness. Each time I hear you talk about this novel I think to myself, *Wait, I wrote that?*

To my editors, Monica Rae Brown and Sara Birmingham, for picking up where others left off and making me feel totally okay about it. And to the entire Random House team for championing *Sisters of Fortune* into existence.

This novel is a work of fiction. These characters, this family, and these situations have been entirely crafted from my imagination. That being said, I'd be nowhere without my own sisters, Rosalind and Raquel. I'd say I wish we spent less of our childhood fighting over clothes, but then I'd probably have no material. And my brother, Maurice, how are you so sane? I wouldn't trade those twenty years of incredibly heated Shabbat dinners for one second of peace. I love you guys. (I still can't believe our parents managed to marry us all off.)

Which brings me to Mom and Dad—thank you. Mom, for feeding us, clothing us, and keeping us together around your dining room table. You complain constantly, but you never, ever stop. And for the record, you were right. Rolling yebra is a b*tch, and I should've paid more attention. Dad, I inherited my love of books from you, and I most certainly wouldn't have written one without your unwavering encouragement. Thank you for being my number one reader. For always picking up the phone. I'll never be as funny as you, but only one of us got a book deal, so . . .

And to my second mom and dad, my in-laws, who have never been anything but kind and supportive, you show us nothing but the good parts. Thank you.

My grandma Esther, the physical embodiment of *suffeh*, I'm so grateful I get to share a name with you. Thank you for fielding all my calls about recipes, timelines, and the occasional cuss in Arabic. I'll never get tired of cooking with you.

To my grandparents who passed, who fled Egypt and Syria and overcame great hardship so that I could write while drinking matcha lattes in trendy cafés, thank you.

And finally, to the Syrian Jewish community who raised me, nurtured me, and kept me feeling safe and full—thank you. Our children are the luckiest to be raised in your warm embrace.

Glossary

....

Abal by you (*idiom*)
Arabic phrase spoken by community members of all ages, used to wish good fortune upon the receiver.

FREDA: I heard about your daughter's engagement, *mabrook*!
SARAH: *Abal* by you!

aboose (*adjective*)
"Adorable! The absolute cutest. "

FREDA: Did you see the baby yet?
SARAH: I did, *aboose*. He looks just like his mother.

adami (*adjective*)
Wholesome; modest; a real catch of a man.

SARAH: He's so *adami*. I couldn't be happier.
FREDA: Of course, what more could a mother want for her daughter?

B'H (*adjective*)
Shorthand for "*B'ezret Hashem*"—with God's help.

FREDA: I'll see you tomorrow at two for mahjong?
SARAH: B'H.

fadal (*verb*)
Arabic expression meaning "Please! Go ahead."

FREDA: My Shabbat dinner plans just fell through.
SARAH: *Fadal*! Be by me at seven.

haje (*exclamation*)
"Enough!"

JACK: I'll take another kibbe.
RUTH: *Haje*! Dinner's soon!

hallas (*exclamation*)
"Enough!"

JACK: Says there's an accident by the tunnel.
DAVID: *Hallas*, we better go.

hazit/hazita (*adjective*)
Used to express pity on someone; an adjective used to describe a pathetic person but, like, not in a mean way.

SARAH: She went and got a French manicure and everything; he never proposed.

FREDA: *Hazita,* that's terrible.

haram (*adjective*)
Forbidden and/or a shame.

SARAH: My girls decided to go vegetarian. My whole dinner went in the garbage.

FREDA: *Ya haram.*

kisa amak (*verb*)
"Kiss my ass!"

GRANDDAUGHTER: Why can't I go to Cancun with my friends? All of the girls travel alone now!

SITTO: *Kisa amak!* You'll travel with your husband.

mabrook (*noun*)
"Congratulations."

FREDA: I'm pregnant!

SARAH: *Mabrook!*

nassib (*noun*)
A husband; a bona fide Syrian prince charming.

LINDA: I don't want to go to the wedding tonight. I have nothing to wear.

LINDA'S MOM: You're going. Your future *nassib* could be there!

nobeh (*noun*)
Traditional Middle Eastern dance party where men and woman raucously mimic screwing lightbulbs in the air to Arabic music.

Auntie Pauline threw a *nobeh* for Sitto's eightieth. Sitto was so moved by the music, she sprang out of her wheelchair to dance.

rohi (*noun*)
Term of endearment usually expressed by a parental figure to a child; honey; love; sweetie.

DAUGHTER: Do you want kaak with your coffee?

DAD: Thank you, *rohi.*

Sabi andak (*verb*)
Arabic phrase spoken by community members of all ages, said to bless a person with a baby boy.

SARAH: Shabbat shalom, Sitto!

SITTO: *Sabi andak.*

Sitto (*noun*)
Grandmother.

SARAH: I'm going to my friend's house.

MOM: It's Friday; we're visiting Sitto.

swanee (*noun*)
Gathering between a bride and groom's families in which they exchange both lavish and traditionally Jewish gifts with each other.

I really wish my daughter's best friend had kept her swanee limited to just family. There was an Hermès Kelly on display, not to mention all of the Christofle; what kind of unrealistic expectations does that set for the girls?

SY (*adjective*)
Shorthand for "Syrian," usually in reference to a community member.

BOY #1: Did you see that girl? Tall with blond hair and blue eyes.

BOY #2: SY?

BOY #1: Doesn't look it.

teil (*adjective*)
To act trivially or superficially; petty; stupid.

LINDA: I'm not going. A verbal invite is not an invite!

LINDA'S MOM: Don't be so *teil,* I play canasta with her mother!

ABOUT THE AUTHOR

ESTHER CHEHEBAR holds an MFA from the New School and has had her work featured in *Glamour* and *Man Repeller*. She is a frequent contributor to *Tablet* magazine, where she covers Sephardic tradition and community. Chehebar's first book, *I Share My Name*, is an illustrated children's book explaining the Sephardic tradition of naming children after their grandparents. Esther Chehebar lives in New York with her husband, their three children, their Ori-Pei named Jude, and a couple of fish. This is her debut novel.

Instagram: @estherlevychehebar